Growing up in a family of murder mystery ~~~~~~ son learned early to look for means, motive and opportunity.

After studying English Literature – with a sideline in crime fiction – at Lancaster University, she set about teaching herself to write her own stories, while also experiencing enough of the world to have things to write about.

Two careers, a lot of airmiles, one husband, two children, three houses and forty-five published books for children and adults later, lockdown finally gave her the means, motive and opportunity to create her own murder mystery – with the aid of her scientist husband's knowledge of poisons. *The Three Dahlias* is the result.

THE
THREE
DAHLIAS

KATY WATSON

CONSTABLE

CONSTABLE

First published in Great Britain in 2022 by Constable
This paperback edition published in 2023 by Constable

5 7 9 10 8 6 4

Copyright © Katy Watson, 2022
Excerpt from *A Very Lively Murder* © Katy Watson, 2023
Illustrations by Liane Payne

The moral right of the author has been asserted.

A CIP catalogue record for this book
is available from the British Library.

ISBN: 978-1-40871-643-4

Typeset by Hewer Text UK Ltd, Edinburgh
Printed and bound in Great Britain by Clays Ltd, Elcograf S.p.A.

Papers used by Constable are from well-managed forests and other responsible sources.

Constable
An imprint of
Little, Brown Book Group
Carmelite House
50 Victoria Embankment
London EC4Y 0DZ

An Hachette UK Company
www.hachette.co.uk

www.littlebrown.co.uk

To my Doctor Watson, with love

The Aldermere House Convention

Celebrating the life and work
of the Princess of Poisoning
Lettice Davenport

and her Lady Detective
Dahlia Lively

Saturday 28th August – Monday 30th August

Convention Guests:
Rosalind King, actress (Dahlia Lively, 1980–1985)
Caro Hooper, actress (Dahlia Lively, 2003–2015)
Posy Starling, actress (Dahlia Lively, *The
Lady Detective,* soon to begin filming)
Kit Lewis, actor (Detective Inspector
John Swain, *The Lady Detective*)
Libby McKinley, writer (*The Lady Detective*)
Anton Martinez, director (*The Lady Detective*)

VIP Delegates:
Heather and Harry Wilson
Ashok Gupta
Felicity Hill

Convention Organisers:
Marcus Fisher
Clementine Jones

**The family of Lettice Davenport, and
custodians of Aldermere House**
Hugh Davenport,
nephew of Lettice Davenport, and his wife,
Isobel Davenport
along with their granddaughter
Juliette Davenport

Welcome you all to a weekend of mystery and murder!

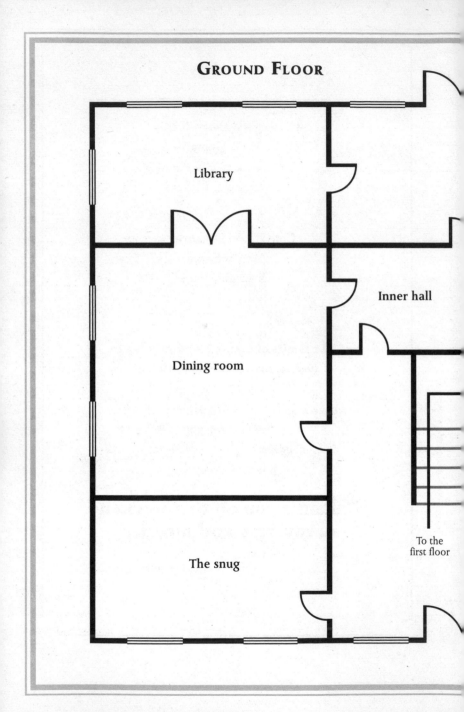

GROUND FLOOR

Library

Dining room

Inner hall

The snug

To the
first floor

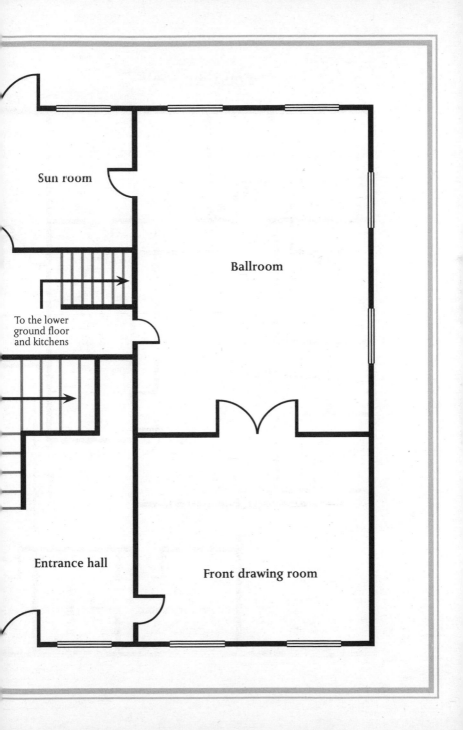

Sun room

Ballroom

To the lower
ground floor
and kitchens

Entrance hall

Front drawing room

FIRST FLOOR

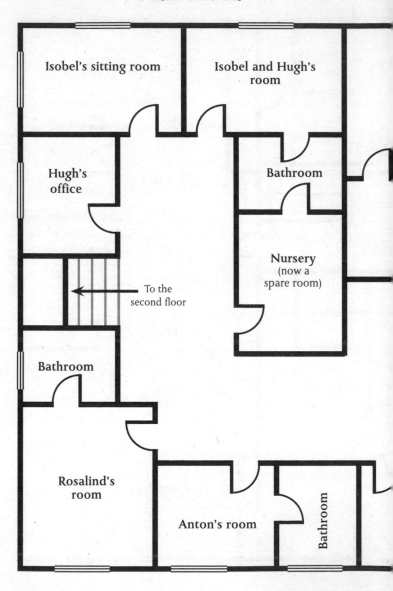

Isobel's sitting room

Isobel and Hugh's room

Hugh's office

Bathroom

To the second floor

Nursery (now a spare room)

Bathroom

Rosalind's room

Anton's room

Bathroom

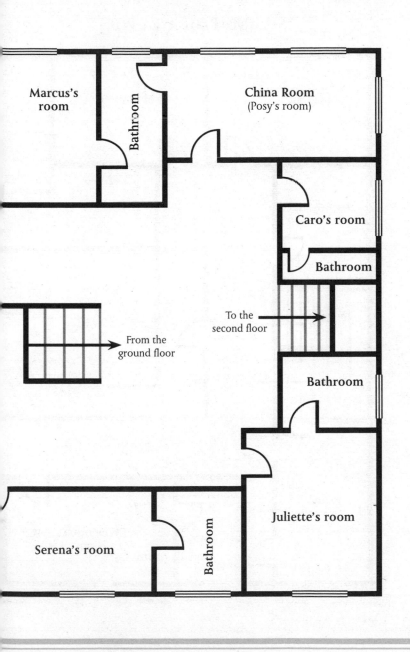

SECOND FLOOR (ATTIC)

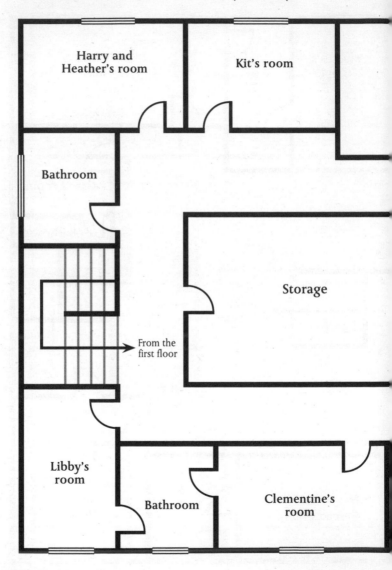

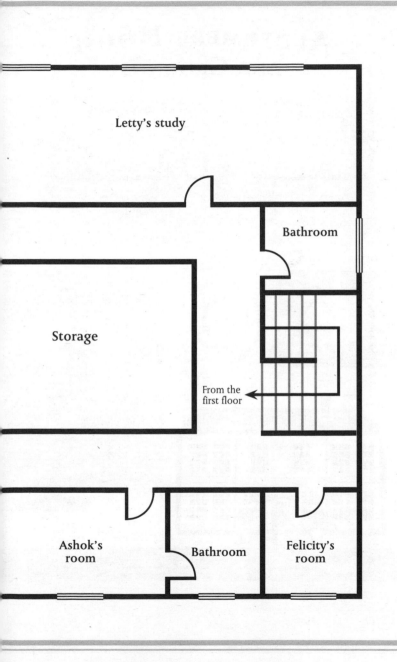

ALDERMERE HOUSE
AND GROUNDS

South Lawn

Grand marquee

Formal gardens

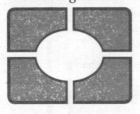

Murder
Spiral

West Lawn and
convention stalls

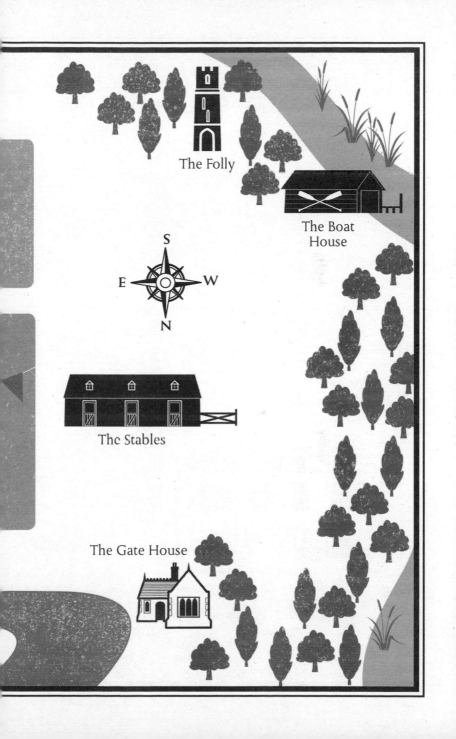

Friday 27th August
Rosalind

Chapter One

'Home can be a sanctuary or a prison, a haven or a horror,' Dahlia
said, sipping thoughtfully on her White Lady cocktail. *'It all depends
on who you have to share it with.'*

Dahlia Lively *in* **A Lady's Place**
By Lettice Davenport, 1934

The last of the late August sunshine slid away behind the alder trees
by the river as Rosalind watched, Amaretto in hand, leaning against
the windowsill to take the weight off her aching knee. Outside, crick-
ets chirped in the darkness, and a cooler breeze swept in from the
east. Her eyes felt droopy; the drive from London had taken it out of
her in a way it never used to.

Aldermere House wasn't ready for sleep yet, even if she was.
Beyond the miniature box hedges, fading lavender and – of course –
bright dahlia flowers of the formal gardens, the South Lawn already
hosted a giant, white marquee that shone in the fading light.
Tomorrow, there'd be stalls and people and activity everywhere.

Even now, the house was busier than Rosalind was used to. But
then, she hadn't been back for a while. How long had it been since
she'd been to stay with Isobel and Hugh? She shook her head. Too
long to remember.

So why did she remember her *first* visit, almost forty years ago, like
it was yesterday? She could still feel the thrumming excitement in her

chest as Hugh's Rolls Royce Silver Spirit had pulled into the driveway of his family estate, knowing that she was going to meet not just his parents, but his famous Aunt Letty, too.

Everything had felt so new, then. They'd only just begun filming *The Lady Detective,* and playing Dahlia Lively, the detective of the title, still seemed more like a dream than reality. Meeting Hugh on the set, there as the family representative to see that his aunt's books were treated faithfully, was another piece of the fairy tale. Falling in love with him? Inevitable.

Especially after he'd brought her to Aldermere.

Because for Rosalind, Aldermere had been more than some old English manor house. It was a place of stories, and mystery, and possibility, and she'd experienced the strangest sense that a secret world had been opened up for her, and she had to hurry in before the door shut behind her.

She'd visited Aldermere House on countless occasions in the decades that followed, but it hadn't given her that feeling in a long, long time.

Behind her, Isobel bustled around the library, her powder-blue dress and matching cardigan almost glowing in the sunlight from the window, her pale pink lipstick still perfect as she pursed her lips, considering the glass jug in her hands, before placing it on a high-up shelf. Rosalind watched as she locked the drinks cabinet, and pocketed the small silver key.

'Worried about the hoi polloi getting in?' Rosalind joked. Isobel had embraced the Lady of the Manor role, the moment she'd gone from being Rosalind's flatmate and friend to being Hugh's wife. And now she'd had decades to perfect it.

Isobel rolled her eyes and groaned good-naturedly. 'When we started talking about this whole convention thing, it was only in the grounds. But then suddenly Marcus – that's the organiser, have you met him yet? He's around here somewhere.' Rosalind shook her head, and Isobel continued. 'Anyhow, suddenly he was selling VIP tickets for people to *stay* here, and I was organising dinners and fork lunch buffets and all sorts. Honestly, I don't know why Hugh agreed to it in the first place. He hates this sort of thing!'

'Probably because he knows he can hide out in his study while you deal with all the Lettice Davenport fans descending on the place.'

'True.' Isobel sighed, but managed a smile all the same. Isobel was always smiling. While Rosalind had one of those faces that made people ask why she was scowling at them, Isobel's lips seemed to naturally fall into a delighted smile without her thinking about it. 'Still, at least it has been a good excuse to get you here for a visit, at last! Juliette's been asking for ages when you'd be coming again.'

'Juliette likes to grill me for backstage gossip about famous people,' Rosalind said with a flap of her hand. Otherwise, being all of eighteen – no, nineteen now, wasn't it? – Rosalind was sure that Isobel's granddaughter had more important things to do than hang out with her grandma's friends.

'The perils of being a "national treasure", I suppose.' Isobel flashed her a teasing smile, as she quoted that damn magazine article from last month back at her. For a moment it could have been forty years ago, with them in their trailer on the set of *The Lady Detective*, Rosalind dressed in her best Dahlia Lively wide-legged trousers, tailored shirt and ropes of pearls, and Isobel decked out as her trusty maid and sidekick, Bess.

The film that had made them friends. That had introduced them both to Hugh. That had set up Rosalind's career – and Isobel's marriage.

But it wasn't the early eighties any longer – or even the 1930s, whatever the set-up at Aldermere seemed to suggest. They were firmly in the twenty-first century now, and her life and Isobel's had split onto their own paths a long time ago.

'And anyway, I'd rather Juliette be gossiping with you than on the phone to that awful boyfriend of hers.' Isobel shuddered. '*Not* the right sort, I'm afraid.'

'Do you think he had something to do with her leaving university?' Rosalind asked.

'Probably. She says she left because it wasn't going to teach her anything useful, and she'd rather be back here at Aldermere working in the family business. She's been on at Hugh for months to let her do more work on Letty's estate – compiling her old notebooks, that sort of thing. There's a publisher who's interested, but the notes are so scattered . . . Anyway, I rather suspect that's just the excuse, and she's back here for that boy, even though she *claims* they're not really together. But what can I do? She thinks she's too adult to listen to her grandmother, and her mother—'

The silence after Isobel broke off hung in the air.

'How is Serena?' A delicate subject, always. But Rosalind was one of the few who could get away with addressing it. Not just as Serena's godmother, but as the friend who had seen Isobel through the morning sickness on set, had helped her hide the growing bump as filming drew to a close, and the flatmate who'd helped with the middle of the night feeds and a cot and all the other baby stuff in the too small two-bed they shared, before Hugh and Isobel met and fell in love, marrying when Serena was two.

Isobel's heavy sigh said more than her answer could. 'She's in the right place, at least.'

Rehab again then, Rosalind assumed. Maybe this time it would stick.

'You and Hugh have done all you can for her.' Rosalind wasn't sure that was true, but it felt like the sort of thing a friend would say. 'You've got her help. Now she just needs to accept it.'

Isobel's wobbly smile was grateful. She moved away to brush a few specks of dust from the nearest bronze bust, and Rosalind knew the discussion was over. Casting around for a new subject, she took in the room anew. She'd spent so many hours in the library and adjoining Sun Room at Aldermere – the favourite place for after-dinner drinks – that her memory filled in her surroundings more than her eyes.

But now she really looked, she could see the changes. The painting by a middling-famous impressionist that Hugh's father had always been so proud of had been replaced by the local landscape that used to hang in Hugh's study. The leather wingback chairs looked tired and worn, the rug almost threadbare.

Had Isobel moved the better things to where they couldn't be damaged by the guests? Except Rosalind was sure that rug was the same one she'd been walking on since her first visit. The chairs, too, were familiar old friends.

Rehab, Rosalind knew from the experiences of friends, wasn't cheap.

'Why *did* Hugh agree to hold this thing here at Aldermere? He normally dismisses all those sorts of events requests from the fans, doesn't he?' Rosalind had seen him rip up requests to visit the house at the breakfast table, dropping the shredded paper beside the shred-less marmalade. But if they needed the money . . .

'Oh, goodness only knows. Marcus was more persuasive than most, I suppose. He's head of the Lettice Davenport fan club, you know? Of course you do. Anyway, we've worked with him on a few bits and pieces before. Nothing like this weekend, though. And then there's the new film – Hugh is discussing letting them *film* here, if you can believe it.' Frowning, Isobel surveyed the room with its priceless heirlooms and well-stocked cocktail cabinet. 'Maybe we'll keep everyone except those staying at the house out of here altogether. We can do coffee in the front drawing room. It's next to the ballroom for lunch, anyway, so that will be easier for everyone. I can lock this room during the day. Yes, that would be better.'

The front drawing room was also furnished with the pieces of Hugh's family furniture that Isobel had never been entirely complimentary about, if Rosalind remembered correctly.

'Still, Marcus is *thrilled* to have all three of you here for this weekend,' Isobel went on. 'Three Dahlias at the same convention! Last-minute ticket sales went through the roof when that was announced, I believe.'

'Heaven knows why,' Rosalind grumbled, glancing out of the window at the giant marquee, squatting on the South Lawn. 'I haven't played Dahlia in thirty-five years, and even the TV series has been off air for the last three or four. The new movie hasn't even started filming. Besides, you'd think fans would be coming to see the place where Letty wrote her books, not us.'

Isobel gave her a fond smile. 'They are, I'm sure. But to so many fans you – and Caro Hooper, and whoever this new girl is, too – you're Dahlia Lively, brought to life. *Of course* they want to see you. And all three of you together? That's a real coup for Marcus.'

'I suppose.' Rosalind didn't much like the reminder that she wasn't the *only* Dahlia, to be frank. For so long, she'd been the only one to grace the screen and give those perfectly crafted putdowns, to raise that solitary eyebrow at a murderer and have them crumble into a confession.

She always tried to be honest with herself, though, even when others weren't. She knew she was the old guard, now. There were newer, younger actresses ready to take her place.

But they'd never take her crown. She would forever be the *first*

Dahlia Lively on the silver screen, and that counted for something. The only actress Lettice Davenport had lived to see play her greatest creation. And Letty had loved her in the role.

'Now, what next?' Isobel placed her hands on her still slender hips and surveyed the room, one low-heeled shoe tapping against the wooden floor where the worn rug didn't cover it. The frown line between her perfectly arched eyebrows deepened. 'This weekend *has* to go perfectly.'

Her tone gave Rosalind pause. She seemed . . . stressed. She'd never seen Isobel stressed before. Even as a single mother in the early eighties she'd been an oasis of calm.

'Isobel?' she said, softly. 'Is everything okay? I mean, is it just the convention tomorrow that has you . . . a little worked up?' She couldn't ask about money outright, of course. Isobel would be horrified at the implication and clam up completely. Still, if she needed to talk . . .

Isobel's shoulders stiffened even more.

'It's nothing. Well, not nothing. But nothing we need to talk about.' Her words were clipped, almost as if she were talking to a stranger, rather than her oldest friend.

'Are you sure?' Rosalind stepped closer, awkwardly placing a hand on her friend's shoulder. They weren't the touchy-feely types, never had been. But she'd never seen Isobel like this, either. Not when she found out she was pregnant, not when Serena's father ran off at the news. Not even when Hugh broke his engagement to Rosalind to marry Isobel instead. Never. 'You know you can talk to me about anything.' That was the advantage of a long history together. Context and understanding.

Isobel hiccupped a laugh that was almost a sob. 'You'll say I deserve it.'

'I wouldn't.' Rosalind admitted to herself that there was a chance she might *think* it, under the right circumstances. But she wouldn't say it. Their friendship had only survived as long as it had by both of them *not* saying the things they were thinking, when it mattered.

'I think . . . no, I'm sure.' Isobel checked over her shoulder at the library door, then met Rosalind's gaze, her blue eyes wide and wet, and Rosalind felt time slowing, never quite enough to halt what was coming next. 'Hugh is having an affair.'

Rosalind's heart stopped beating, the sound of the mantel clock replacing its steady thump with its own sluggish tick. None of the clocks in this house were ever right, Rosalind remembered, as if that mattered at all. Time wasn't important in a house stuck forever in the golden age of crime.

Her senses caught up with her in a whoosh, carrying her heartbeat along with it.

'I'm sure you're wrong,' she said, shaking her head as if to rid it of the very idea. 'Besides, aren't we too old for all that nonsense now?'

Isobel snorted. 'You and I might be, but you know it's always different for men.'

Everything was, in Rosalind's experience. But especially this.

'Hugh loves you. He *chose* you.' Rosalind swallowed the pain in the words. Isobel was her friend and it was almost forty years ago, now. 'You have the perfect life here together. Why would he cheat?'

Isobel didn't answer immediately, and before Rosalind could press her, there was a knock on the library door.

'Mrs Davenport?' A pretty twenty-something in jeans and a t-shirt appeared in the doorway, her hair tied back in a simple ponytail. She had a clipboard in her hands, and a harried look about her. Rosalind recognised her as the convention assistant Marcus had sent to sweet-talk her into taking part in the event, way back in the spring.

'Yes, Clementine?' Isobel turned, her smile back in place, even if her eyes were still sad. 'What is it?'

'So sorry to disturb you, but the catering staff would like to run through the menus for tomorrow's dinner with you, if you have the time? There have been a few last-minute changes, I believe, and there are some questions about the wine pairings, particularly.' Her soft, Scottish accent was apologetic, but insistent.

Isobel sighed, her smile never wavering. 'Of course. I'll come now. Sorry, Rosalind, I won't be long. Perhaps you could go and bother Hugh in his study? If it's wine pairings they want to talk about, he'll be far more use than me.'

'Of course.' Rosalind watched her friend walk away with the younger woman before she followed her out, through the doors that led to the dining room.

Aldermere felt less welcoming alone. Despite all the activity she knew was going on outside, and down in the lower ground-floor kitchens, as she moved through the empty dining room – its table already set for sixteen – she felt alone in the house. A ghost, trapped in her own history.

She remembered so many days here.

That first dinner, when Hugh had introduced her to his family as the woman he intended to marry. Or the day, less than a year later, when they'd ended their relationship down by the folly, and she'd still had to sit down at this damn mahogany table for dinner afterwards.

Was he really having an affair with someone else? Rosalind wasn't sure she wanted to know.

Through the dining-room door, she passed into the grand entrance hall, with its sweeping staircase and imposing family portraits. The golden dinner gong, set in a recess beside the door, trembled a little as she let the door fall closed, and she reached out to steady it.

Beneath it, on the telephone table, was an envelope addressed to Hugh. She picked it up, to take to him in his study.

The light was poor, the wall lamps more for atmosphere than practicality, and in the semi-darkness she could almost imagine that she saw Lettice Davenport herself – not as the mischievous elderly aunt she'd met in the eighties, but as a young woman – descending that curved staircase. A man's white shirt tucked into her skirt, short bobbed hair and that ever-present grey felt hat she wore in photos. The epitome of the 1930s woman who made her own rules.

Or was that Dahlia Lively, not Lettice? Rosalind had asked her once, if Dahlia did all the things that Letty herself wasn't allowed to. Letty had grinned, and replied, 'Perhaps. Or perhaps the things I got up to were too scandalous even for Dahlia.'

Rosalind hoped that was true. Everyone needed a *touch* of scandal in their lives, didn't they?

At the foot of the stairs stood a dollhouse replica of Aldermere House, and Rosalind lingered to examine it. It was like looking into a miniature world. The rooms flowed from one to another just as they did in the real house, and Rosalind picked out Letty's attic room study, her own assigned guest room looking out over the front driveway, even the tiny gong beside the dining room with its table set with minuscule knives and forks. And there, beside the replica staircase, was another dollhouse, with ever smaller rooms and features.

'Lettice was a very visual writer, you know.'

Rosalind started at the unexpected, unfamiliar voice. 'She used this dollhouse to plot out her murder mysteries – who was where when the murder was committed, and with whom. That sort of thing. Every book she ever wrote started here, with this model.'

Trying to calm her breathing, Rosalind straightened again, but didn't turn away from the dollhouse.

'Apart from all the ones that *weren't* set in stately homes,' she said. Really, was there anything more annoying than a man assuming they knew more than you? 'She used maps for those. Letty told me herself, many years ago. The dollhouse was up in her study then, of course.'

She turned, at last, and found herself glaring at a large, florid man wearing a sports jacket over a stained white shirt, who appeared to have come from the front drawing room. His face turned a little pucer as he recognised her.

'Ah, of course. The celebrated Dahlia Lively herself, Rosalind King. So glad you were able to join us this weekend. Of course, you're an old friend of the family, aren't you? You must come here all the time.' With an amiable smile, he made his way over to stand beside her in front of the model.

'Sometimes,' Rosalind said, shortly.

Her tone didn't put him off, or slow the wide, knowing smirk that spread across his face. 'It's an honour to meet you.' He held out a hand and, reluctantly, Rosalind shook it – only to have him bring it to his lips for a kiss instead. She held back a shudder, and snatched it back.

She wouldn't have done, back in the day. But times had changed. And besides, there had to be *some* advantages to growing older. Caring less about offending other people was one of them.

'I'm Marcus. The organiser of this whole carnival!' He spread his arms wide as if Aldermere itself was in his domain, his control. 'We have actually met before, although I don't imagine you remember. I played one of the teenage members of the criminal gang in the third Dahlia Lively movie with you!'

He gave her a hopeful look, for all his words about not expecting her to remember. Which she didn't. 'Did you really? Imagine that.'

'Long time ago now. Anyway, I look forward to getting to know you better this weekend. I have a feeling it's going to be the sort of event that goes down in Dahlia Lively history.'

'For the right reasons, I hope.' After forty-plus years in the entertainment industry, Rosalind liked to think she'd developed a good sense for people. And Marcus vibrated with the sort of energy she went out of her way to avoid. He'd made a good choice sending Clementine to persuade her to attend, she decided, as he headed for the stairs. If he'd come himself, she was certain she'd have said no, however much she was needed.

Mostly certain, anyway. Aldermere had a strange way of drawing her back in, even when she intended to stay away.

'Of course, of course.' Marcus chuckled to himself as he thumped up the stairs, one heavy footstep after another, his plump hand grasping the bannister. 'I'm sure Lettice herself would approve of everything I have planned.'

Rosalind wasn't sure that was altogether reassuring.

As Marcus's footsteps faded, she glanced around to ensure that she really was alone, and unobserved, this time. Her knees cracked as she bent in front of the dollhouse again – daily yoga could only do so much – and looked inside.

There, lying on the dining table, was a miniature figure – one she was almost certain hadn't been there before. A frown creased her forehead as she reached in to pick it up. It looked like one of Letty's dolls from the study, the ones she'd used to plot out her mysteries. But Rosalind had never noticed this one on any of her previous visits.

Waxy pale skin. Closed eyes.

And a tiny bottle marked *Poison* clutched in its hand.

Saturday 28th August
Posy

Chapter Two

Posy Starling grabbed hold of the rail beside the luggage rack as the train lurched out of Kings Cross station, its wheels squealing against the tracks as if it resented having to leave London at all.

She knew how it felt.

London had been her safety net ever since she left LA – and her parents – behind. Now, she was headed out into the wilds of the English countryside, with no idea what to expect.

She'd officially been cast as the latest Dahlia Lively for less than twenty-four hours, and she was already out of her depth.

Posy held back as the others stashed their weekend bags and took their seats. Anton, their director, took the longest, which didn't surprise her since he had a massive suitcase with him. She'd only met him a few times, but he'd been wearing basically the same thing at every one of her auditions – scuffed-up jeans and an open-collared shirt. She'd got the impression that he was too busy thinking about more important things to care what he looked like.

But as she watched him try to heft the huge case onto the rack, she took in the well-tailored, dark grey trousers he was wearing today, and wondered if she might have been wrong.

'I've got it.' Kit Lewis, her new co-star, reached back and took the handle of the suitcase from Anton, swinging it up onto the rack with surprising ease for someone of his slender build. He didn't make a big deal of it, though, which Posy liked. He grinned at Anton, then went back to stashing his own stuff and finding his seat.

There'd been a lot of articles written about Kit's casting – the usual 'political correctness gone mad' brigade, pointing out that since every other iteration of Detective Inspector Johnnie Swain in print and on screen had been white, this one should be too. But watching Kit take his seat opposite Libby, their scriptwriter, Posy thought he had just the right feel about him. Policemen were supposed to be helpful and make you feel secure. She didn't know Kit well – outside the chemistry read they'd done together, they'd hardly met – but she already sensed he'd be able to pull that off well.

Ahead of her, Anton opened the battered leather satchel that was slung over his shoulder and flicked through the contents to retrieve his mobile phone. Posy watched him idly, the thick stack of paper filling the bag catching her attention. Could that be the new script?

She looked away as Anton's head jerked up and the flap of the satchel fell closed. Wouldn't be good to be caught spying on the boss. Posy shoved her old duffle bag on the rack beside Anton's case.

'So, is everybody ready for our weekend of murder and mayhem?' Anton rubbed his hands together, a wicked gleam in his dark eyes, as he took his seat beside Libby. The elderly couple in the seats across the aisle shot them a concerned look. Obviously they hadn't watched Kit in the Sunday-night period drama he was starring in currently. Or maybe they didn't recognise him in street clothes. Out of costume, actors always looked different. Since moving to London, Posy could count on her fingers the number of times she'd been recognised.

Maybe that was a sign of how long it had been since she'd had a role that mattered.

But actually, now Kit had taken off his jacket – even in August, London was cold in the early morning – Posy could see he'd dressed up for the occasion. Brown cords, braces and a shirt, unlike the ratty jeans and tee he'd worn when she'd auditioned opposite him.

'Born ready,' he said, shooting Anton a grin. 'Can't beat a bit of mayhem on a bank holiday, can you?'

Posy took the seat beside him. 'Depends on the kind of mayhem, I guess.'

'Spoilsport,' Kit teased, tilting his head closer to hers, and Posy couldn't help but smile. 'How about you, Libby?'

'You know me, Kit. I'm all about the murder, not the mayhem.' Libby's voice was as dry as the straw hat she held in her lap.

'That's true.' Kit leant across the gap between the seats, his arms resting on his knees. 'And does that mean you've finished writing all our murder and mayhem for us? Only it's getting kinda close to our shooting dates and all . . .'

Anton reached out to cuff Kit's shoulder with the novel in his hand – *not* a Lettice Davenport, Posy noticed. 'Have faith, man! Don't you know, this woman here has saved more movie scripts than you've had overpriced pints in London pubs.'

'Yeah, she's a script doctor extraordinaire, I know.' Kit gave Libby an apologetic smile. 'It's just . . . you know. There's still a lot of talk about . . .'

'The curse.' Anton groaned, and tipped his head back against the headrest with a despairing eye roll. 'Kit, how many projects have we worked on together?'

'Three.'

'And how many of them have people said were cursed?'

'Just this one, actually.' Posy hid a smile at the mischievous grin on Kit's face as he spoke. 'And you have to admit, they're not exactly lacking evidence.'

The supposed curse was something Posy only knew about from internet rumours, googled on the way to and from her audition, but there were plenty of those to choose from. Starting with the reason that Posy had been brought on board as Dahlia Lively in the first place. If it hadn't been for a traffic accident that put the original actress in hospital – and plaster and physiotherapy for months to come – Posy's agent would never have got the call about the audition.

Then there was the investor who pulled out after a fraud investigation was launched into them, the fire at the stately home they'd originally planned to film at . . .

And then there was the script.

The first script, as Posy understood it, had caused a row between the production team and the Davenport family. The team loved it, the family thought it was 'a travesty of everything Lettice Davenport stood for', according to one report.

To make things worse, it had then been leaked by someone connected with the film – accounts varied on who – and released on the internet. Where hardcore Dahlia Lively fans and newcomers alike had panned it so completely that the original head writer had quit the business and disappeared indefinitely into the wilderness on some retreat – *after* being summarily fired.

That was when Anton had brought Libby on board to fix it. Or, Posy guessed, rewrite it from scratch.

She'd never heard of Libby McKinley before, despite all her years in the industry, but when she googled her last night, after Anton told her about the weekend and who'd be attending with her, it became clear that was because she hadn't been paying attention. Libby might not make a big deal about it, or seek the spotlight or the media interviews, but she'd worked as a script doctor on scripts for seven out of ten of the biggest movies that had come out in the last decade. She was usually uncredited, but the internet knew everything.

'Look, if everything goes well this weekend, we'll have the script approved *and* be able to film at Aldermere House itself. Home of Lettice Davenport, people.' Anton looked between them, apparently searching their faces for an appropriate level of excitement. Posy smiled and nodded in return, and saw the others do the same. 'There's no curse here! We are on the up. Okay?'

'Right, boss,' Kit said, still looking unconvinced, while Posy nodded again.

She needed this film. Cursed or not. But she'd really rather it wasn't, when it came down to it.

'Of course we are,' Libby added. 'The script is done, Kit. It's with Hugh Davenport right now. That's why I'm here – to iron out any last issues with the family so we can start filming. Don't worry so much. I've done this before, you know.'

'Yeah, I know.' Kit looked more reassured by Libby's words than Anton's.

At least that cleared up one mystery for Posy. It had been a while since she'd done an event like this, for sure, but even so, she knew they would normally be travelling with a publicist. Given all the negative press swirling around the movie, she'd found it even stranger when she arrived at the station to discover it was just the four of them facing the hordes of rabid fans alone.

She'd tried to ask Anton about it, but he'd shrugged and said that there were only four rooms available at Aldermere House for them, and Libby had wanted to come. And since he wasn't about to leave his two stars at home, there wasn't room for a publicist.

It hadn't rung true, at the time. But if he needed Libby there to get the script approved, well, that made sense. And Anton had told her that the presence of *a* new Dahlia Lively had been confirmed for the convention weeks before she was actually cast in the role. She hoped nobody would be too disappointed when they found out it was her.

Posy glanced at Libby again. She must be about the same age as Anton, late thirties Posy guessed, and despite her quiet, reserved demeanour, was obviously capable of holding her own in front of directors, actors and Davenport family members alike. Even if she looked like she was heading to a WI afternoon tea in her floral tea dress and cardigan.

Wait.

Dread mounting inside her, Posy looked from Libby, to Kit, to Anton and back again.

Anton's dark grey trousers and sports jacket could have been him making an effort. Same for Kit's slightly baggy brown cords and braces. But put together with Libby's village fete chic? Posy stared at her denim-clad knees, and felt the weight of her pale suede moto jacket on her shoulders as she imagined the write-ups on the fashion blogs.

'Posy Starling made another sartorial error over the August bank holiday weekend, almost as awful as the dress she wore to the 2014 Oscars ceremony (her movie, you'll recall, did not win, which was just as well as she'd never have made it up the stairs in those glass shoes. Or possibly it was something else impairing her balance . . .)'

'Did I miss a costume memo?' she asked, bluntly.

Anton gave her a faintly patronising smile. 'Not at all. But yes, the Aldermere convention will be, well, period themed, so we all dressed accordingly.'

She would have dressed accordingly, if anyone had bothered to warn her. Anton had barely told her more than the name of the place they were going when he called last night to formally offer her the role and invite her. '*Aldermere House, home of Lettice Davenport herself! Nothing to stress about, it's a bit of a photo op for the fans, really,*' he'd told her.

'Don't worry,' he said again now, still smiling in spite of the scowl she knew had settled onto her face. 'I did bring a few things along for you, in case you wanted to join in the spirit of things a little more.'

'That would be . . . good,' she said, watching doubtfully as he jumped up and headed for the luggage rack. Why had he assumed she *wouldn't* want to join in?

Okay, she could probably guess why. Even if she hoped that she – and the world – had moved past all that when she left LA, Posy knew it wasn't really the case. When people looked at her, they didn't see a twenty-nine-year-old actress who was serious about her career. Some of them saw the know-nothing child star, or the awkward young teen who couldn't quite grow into her looks.

But that was if she was lucky. Most of the time, if you said the name Posy Starling, people only got one mental image – and it wasn't from any of her films.

When they thought of Posy Starling, people instantly saw that intrusive, hideous photo of her unconscious on the sidewalk outside the Magpie Club in LA, waiting for the ambulance and the paramedics that would save her life. They saw her vomit-slicked hair and grey skin, the tiny snakeskin dress pushed too far up her thighs. Her bare shoulders, caught mid-shudder as the drugs wreaked havoc in her body.

It didn't matter that it was over five years ago now. That she'd been through rehab and come out the other side. That she'd changed continents, changed her life, changed *everything*.

She couldn't change how the world saw her.

Until now. This film was her chance to show everyone another side to her. The grown-up, professional side.

She wished she'd had more time to prepare.

Posy watched Anton bob and weave with the movement of the train as he rifled through the contents of his suitcase. He emerged holding a floral tea dress, not unlike Libby's in style, but with pastel, watercolour flowers where Libby's were crisp-edged browns and reds.

'What do you think?' He gave the dress a little shake, so she could fully appreciate its awfulness. Beside her, Kit raised his eyebrows, then turned to look out of the window.

'It's not very . . . me, is it?' That was about as much diplomacy as Posy could manage at this time in the morning.

'Well, you're not supposed to *be* you this weekend, Posy. That's what acting is all about.' Anton took his seat, placing the dress on her lap, along with a pair of vintage-style shoes in her size to match. 'This weekend you're Dahlia Lively, the Lady Detective.'

She looked at the dress again. It didn't look particularly Dahlia-like either, in Posy's opinion. But then, what did she know? She'd picked up the first book in the series to read but she still hadn't had the chance to start it. All she had to go on was re-runs of the old TV series with Caro Hooper, that she used to watch at her gran's on a Sunday afternoon.

That Dahlia had been all men's clothes, cigarette holders and sass. Not floral tea dresses.

'Posy . . . listen.' Anton leaned forward, his elbows resting on his knees, his voice soft so they all had to lean in to listen. Kit drew his attention from the window, and even Libby looked up from her phone. 'I know you're new to the project, that you haven't had a lot of time to sit with the role yet. But if there's one thing I want you to

24

know before we go into this weekend, it's this. This film is going to be seminal. Important.'

Up close, Posy could see the crow's feet forming around his eyes on his tanned face, and the lines that started by his nose and disappeared into the dark thatch of his beard. She mentally revised her estimate of his age up by a few years. Early forties, she decided, for sure. The media always described Anton Martinez as a young and up-and-coming director, but she supposed he'd been up-and-coming for a while now. Shouldn't he have, well, up-and-come already?

Posy twisted the fabric of the tea dress between her fingers, and stayed silent.

'We're doing something *new* with the Lettice Davenport novels,' Anton went on. 'We're bringing them into the twenty-first century! It's not just the non-traditional casting, or the filming techniques – or even Libby's new script. It's the *feel* of the whole thing. And the fans won't get that until they can see the finished product.'

'Which they won't have done this weekend.' Kit folded his arms behind his head and sat back, one ankle resting on his knee. 'So I guess we'll have to rely on natural charm and wit. Good job you brought me along.'

Anton rolled his eyes. 'What you need to do, all of you, is stop worrying about the script, or talk about curses, or what other people think, and trust the process.'

Kit's mouth curved into a wry half-smile. 'Ah, but that's the actor's bane, isn't it? We're only ever worth what other people think of us.'

'Dahlia Lively never cared what other people thought,' Libby said, her tone thoughtful. 'She cared about the truth.'

Which effectively put an end to that conversation.

Posy leapt to her feet, then reached out to grab the rail as the train took a corner, the world suddenly unstable beneath her feet. 'I'd better go and get changed into this.'

Wriggling out of jeans and into a dress in the filthy, tiny train toilet wasn't an experience she'd recommend to others. And somehow, the dress itself looked worse on her body than off. The mirror was grimy, so she fished her phone out of her jeans pocket and took a top-down selfie, studying it in the poor light.

Damon would love me in this dress.

The thought flickered through her head before she could stop it. She tried not to think of Damon these days. Still, when he turned up and started occupying her headspace, she did what her therapist had told her to do, and examined whether the things he was saying or doing in there were true.

Damon wouldn't love her because, as far as she'd been able to ascertain, Damon was incapable of love. He *would* approve of the dress, though, because it was exactly what he'd always hoped she'd wear. Feminine, soft, malleable.

All the things that Posy wasn't.

And neither was Dahlia Lively, by all accounts.

At least that was something they had in common.

With a sigh, Posy unlocked the door and headed out into the carriage.

'What do you think?' She struck a pose. 'Will I do?'

Kit winced. Libby looked like she thought Dahlia's creator was probably rolling in her grave somewhere.

'Perfectly Dahlia!' Anton grinned. 'The fans are going to love you.'

Chapter Three

'*Hazelwood Manor has been my sanctuary all these years.*' Dahlia
stared up at the house, her eyes very wide. '*My haven. And now . . .*'
Now, nothing felt safe any longer.

Dahlia Lively *in* Death Comes to Hazelwood
***By* Lettice Davenport, 1944**

Aldermere House rose up against the blue of a perfect English
summer morning, its Georgian brick frontage solid and imposing, its
many windows watching. Sitting high in the back seat of the vintage
car that had collected them from the station, Posy watched the puffy
white clouds pass across the August sky as they rattled along the gravelled driveway.

She could almost believe they'd travelled back in time, to a world
that had long disappeared. Did people still live in stately homes like
this, even in the twenty-first century?

Well, if they had Lettice Davenport's royalties to pay for it, it
seemed they did.

'There it is, ladies and gentlemen,' Anton said, holding onto his
seat in front of her as the thin wheels and inadequate suspension
attempted another bump in the road. 'Aldermere House itself. Home
of the Queen of Crime.'

'That was Agatha Christie.' It was the first time Libby had spoken
in hours. 'Lettice Davenport was the Princess of Poison.'

'Of course, of course.' Anton waved away her correction, talking with his hands as usual, now the path was smoother.

'This was where she really lived.' Kit sounded faintly awed at the prospect of visiting Aldermere. 'You know, I read every single one of her mysteries when I was younger, and I think I must have read them all again since my agent told me about my audition.'

Anton twisted back from the front seat to point at him. 'And that's the kind of dedication that's going to make *our* film better than any of those that came before it.'

The new Dahlia Lively reboot hadn't been on Posy's radar before her agent had called, sounding as bemused as Posy felt at the news, to say that she'd been asked to audition for the role. She fingered the outline of the books she carried in her bag. *The Lady Detective,* the first Dahlia Lively novel Lettice had ever written, and *Princess of Poison,* a posthumous biography of the author herself.

The books would tell her the heart of the character, but it was this convention that would show her what the fans *expected* her to be. And that was what mattered. If the uber-fans hated it, they'd be so vocal on the subject that no one else would bother to watch it.

The potential reviews scrolled through her mind unbidden, as they pulled up the driveway. '*Posy Starling as Dahlia Lively is the most unlikely casting choice – and, to nobody's surprise, an abject failure.*'

In her head, her film critic was always Sol Hutchins, the acerbic writer who'd written the book – literally – on her rise to stardom and subsequent fall. He'd had a ringside seat of course, as her dad's best friend. These days, she thought she remembered Uncle Sol's voice more clearly than her father's, even though she hadn't seen either of them since the day she left LA.

The car jolted to a stop a distance from the house. Peering around Anton, Posy saw it was because the wide, gravelled driveway itself was packed. She waited for the driver to open the door, then swung her legs out, knees together to allow for the hideous tea dress, and stepped down from the running board.

The gravel crunched under her feet as they moved towards the house, taking in the circus before them. Aldermere House, it seemed, was merely a backdrop to the real event – a cacophony of activity and noise that spanned the large expanse of grass to the right of the house, beyond the ornate fountain in the centre of the driveway.

Lines of people snaked and swerved between flags laid out over the lawn, with more arriving as she watched, jumping from the back of a red double-decker bus, or piling out of more open-top cars. Further into the gardens, and leading around to the back of the house, bunting and lights hung between the trees, and stalls were set up selling jam and cakes and cups of tea. The scene had the feeling of a village fete, the sort Posy vaguely remembered from her childhood in England, before the family moved to LA for her career.

She didn't belong here anymore. But here she was anyway.

Beside her, Libby stumbled to a stop.

'Okay?' Posy asked, reaching to steady her.

'Yeah.' Libby stared at the scene before them. 'Sorry. Just . . . that fountain. It wasn't on the plan of the grounds or the photos I looked at. I'll need to rework a couple of scenes at the front of the house to accommodate it if we're filming here. Shame to miss it out.' She shook off Posy's hand, and carried on towards the front of the house, leaving Posy staring after her.

Maybe Libby was as nervous about this weekend as the rest of them after all. If the family didn't approve her script, this could all be over before it started. That was a lot of pressure for one woman.

'Posy!' Anton called over his shoulder, and she hurried to catch them up.

'Don't forget to turn off your phones before you check them in at the door,' said a young woman in an olive-green skirt suit, with perfect victory rolls in her pale auburn hair and a clipboard in her hand, as she led a smaller group of people towards the main entrance of Aldermere House. 'This is an *immersive* experience, after all – and Dahlia Lively never had the advantage of mobile technology!'

'We have to turn in our phones?' Kit asked, horrified at the idea. Posy silently felt the same, but knew better than to show it.

'Like the lady said, it's immersive!' Anton waved at the woman in the olive suit. 'Hey, Clementine! Where's the boss?'

Clementine looked over and smiled widely at Anton. She ushered the small gang of attendees – two women and two men, all in immaculate period costumes – in the direction of the entrance. Then she hurried towards Posy and the others, scribbling something on her clipboard as she walked, her slender hips sashaying in her pencil skirt.

'You made it.' Clementine leaned in to kiss Anton on both cheeks. 'I thought you film types were always fashionably late.'

'Couldn't wait to get started,' Anton replied. 'Now, let me introduce you to everyone.'

Clementine laughed. 'I think I can identify at least two of them on my own.' Turning to Kit, she held out a hand, her blue eyes sparkling. 'Kit Lewis, right? I watched you in that BBC drama you did recently. You must be our new Johnnie Swain.'

'Glad somebody was watching,' Kit joked, with his usual warm smile. 'And yes – Dahlia's loyal and loving detective inspector, that's me.'

'And Posy Starling. Our new Dahlia herself.' Clementine turned her wide eyes on her, and Posy responded automatically with her 'meeting the fans' smile. 'I couldn't believe it when I read Anton's email this morning! I grew up watching you on telly, and at the cinema. I think I watched every film you ever made. It's so great to see you, well— it's lovely to have you here, this weekend, I mean.'

Posy ignored the obvious slip. She knew what Clementine meant – everyone there did. It was good to see her working again, after everything. A career as a child star, it turned out, was no guarantee of acting work as an adult. Especially when your reputation entered every audition before you.

'It's great to be here.' Posy looked up again at the looming house, and tried to put some enthusiasm into her words.

Clementine peered at her clipboard. 'Now, I don't know how much Anton has told you about this weekend . . .'

'Not much,' Posy admitted, with a smile. 'It was all rather last minute – for me, anyway.'

'I wanted to retain the element of surprise.' Anton waggled his heavy, dark eyebrows as if it were all a wonderful joke.

Maybe it was. Maybe casting her as Dahlia was a prank Anton was playing.

No. Posy straightened her shoulders, tossing her hair back. She'd earned this role, she'd be *brilliant* in this role, and this was her weekend to prove it.

'Posy Starling as Dahlia Lively tries her best, but' – oh, shut up, Uncle Sol.

The film critic in her head silenced, Posy concentrated on Clementine's explanation of the weekend ahead.

'So, this weekend is an immersive back-to-the-thirties experience for fans of golden age murder mysteries in general – and Lettice Davenport in particular, of course. It's a chance for fans to revisit the world of Dahlia Lively herself. Happier times, when the only thing anybody had to worry about was murder.' Clementine's eyes sparkled as Kit laughed at her joke. 'That's why there are no modern cars allowed on site – everyone has been driven in from the station like you were, in period vehicles.'

'And no mobile phones allowed? Really?' Kit asked, obviously hoping he might be an exception.

'That's just for the people staying at Aldermere House itself,' Clementine explained. 'That's you four, and then what we're calling the VIP delegates.'

Before Kit could try to flirt for phone privileges, a man dressed in full black tie came bustling through the crowd carrying a loaded silver tray on one hand, his remaining hair slicked back from his round, red face.

'Ah, here's Marcus,' Clementine said, beckoning him over.

'Is he the butler here?' Kit asked. 'Because I could definitely use a glass of whatever he's got on that tray.'

'He's the boss, this weekend at least,' Anton corrected. 'But I second the drink request.'

'Marcus is the head of the Lettice Davenport fan club,' Clementine said. 'And the organiser of this convention, which makes him *my* boss, at least. But he likes to play the butler at events like these, sometimes.'

'He's a Dahlia Lively stalwart – you know, he even ran last year's convention a few weeks after his heart bypass op,' Anton added. '*That's* dedication.'

'Anton! You made it.' Marcus lowered his tray from above his shoulder to allow them to take a glass. The others reached for the bucks fizz, while Posy held back. 'And you brought your stars with you. Excellent!'

'Marcus, this is Kit Lewis and Posy Starling – our Johnnie and Dahlia.' Anton indicated them each in turn, before turning to Libby. 'And this is our own Lettice Davenport, our script doctor Libby McKinley.'

'*Delighted* to meet you all!' Marcus boomed. 'I used to be something of an actor myself, you know. In fact, I am the *only* actor to have appeared in both the original films *and* the TV series with Caro Hooper. You know, Anton, a cameo in the new movie would complete the hat-trick . . .'

Anton's smile seemed a little forced. 'Let's see how we get on this weekend, first, shall we?'

'Of course, of course.' Marcus clapped a hand on Anton's shoulder. 'Still, it would be something to talk up in the media – something other than this damnable curse anyway! So unfortunate, that script getting out that way.'

Anton's mouth had settled into a tight line, and Kit spoke up instead, his smile firmly in place. 'Ah, but without it we wouldn't have the lovely Libby on board, and that would be a travesty!' Somehow he'd managed to get himself between Marcus and Anton without seeming to move at all. Impressive. 'Now, what I want to know is who these VIP delegates are. I mean, I was pretty sure that *we* were the VIPs. I'm starting to feel offended over here, Marcus.' The spark in his eyes made it clear that he was joking, and Marcus laughed.

'Oh, you four are our most important guests, of course.' Marcus still sounded faintly obsequious, all the same. 'The VIP delegates are the few, specially selected attendees, who've paid a little extra—'

'A *lot* extra,' Clementine murmured next to Posy.

'For some added benefits this weekend. Like the chance to actually stay at Aldermere House, with all of you!' Marcus finished.

Anton and Kit looked about as excited at this prospect as Posy felt.

'They also get early access to their chosen events, photo ops with all the speakers, and to attend all the luncheons and dinners,' Clementine explained. 'Day delegates are only allowed in the grounds, unless they've booked a ticket for one of the meals, or one of the indoor events, like the house tours. The family insisted.'

'How on earth do you keep track of where everyone is, or should be?' Posy supposed that having their home overrun by Lettice Davenport fans couldn't be a lot of fun for the family. But it probably paid well. Maybe the Dahlia Lively royalties weren't as good as they used to be.

Clementine held up her slender wrist and let the sleeve of her light linen jacket fall away to show a garishly coloured wristband circling it. 'Everyone here has one. We have different colours for day delegates, plus special ones for the VIPs and for speakers, guests and the family. In fact, you might as well all put yours on now.'

Detaching a strip of bands from her clipboard, she handed one to each of them, and watched as they put them on securely. Posy stared at hers, silver against her pale skin. Somehow, it felt like handcuffs.

'Our Clementine takes *very* good care of everyone.' Marcus leaned close to his young assistant. Clementine didn't look entirely comfortable with her boss's proximity, but also not sure enough of her place, or job, to step away. Posy knew that feeling. Something about the man reminded her of her Uncle Sol, but perhaps that was his florid complexion.

'Just doing my job,' Clementine said, softly.

'Ah! Now, here's another of our very important guests to greet you. How fortunate!' Marcus balanced his tray on the bonnet of the nearest vintage car, and waved a hand at a tall, elegant woman with white hair, who stood on the steps to the front door of Aldermere House.

She didn't smile, or wave in return, but started walking towards them. Which was when Posy realised who it was.

Rosalind King.

Chapter Four

'A script is just words on a page. It's how people interpret them, how they act, that makes all the difference. And in this case, it seems that someone chose to take the action off stage – and to the mortuary.'

Dahlia Lively *in* All The World's A Stage
***By* Lettice Davenport, 1938**

'Rosalind, my darling! How wonderful that you're here!' Anton kissed Rosalind's cheeks with a lot of enthusiasm, given that she was old enough to be his mother. Maybe age didn't matter when the woman in question was Rosalind King.

Anton had worked long and hard to secure her for a part in the film, Posy knew. A way to link the new versions with the originals, and draw in traditional fans who might have otherwise been reluctant. Looking at Rosalind, Posy could see why.

Her white hair was stylishly cropped, pinned back in a way that had hints of vintage style, without looking like a costume. Similarly, her wide linen trousers and white shirt were timeless, her make-up classic. She looked as if she could dress this way every day, while still fitting seamlessly into the vibe of the convention.

Uncle Sol was back with a vengeance. *'Rosalind King spends her too brief scenes in the movie looking as if she can't quite believe her agent got her to agree to the part. Neither could I.'*

Anton gestured towards Posy. 'Let me introduce you to the newest addition to your Dahlia club, Posy Starling.'

'It's a pleasure to meet you,' Posy said, her voice sounding strangely rusty.

Rosalind ran her gaze from Posy's messy blonde bob, down to the hideous tea dress, then back up again.

'I'd hardly call it a club, Anton,' she said, dismissing Posy. 'There's only two of us, after all.' Her gaze flickered back to Posy for a second. 'Well, three soon, I suppose.'

'And here's the other member now!' Marcus clapped his hands with delight. 'How wonderful, to have all three Dahlias here at our little convention. The fans are going to love it!'

They turned to watch as a vintage motorcycle and sidecar came careening across the gravelled driveway, sweeping to a stop beside them. Swinging her leg over the cycle, the rider pulled off her helmet, revealing a brightly coloured headscarf, with blood-red lipstick to match.

Another face Posy knew instantly, if only from the screen. Caro Hooper – the actress synonymous with Dahlia Lively in a way even Rosalind King couldn't manage. Rosalind had only played the Lady Detective in three films; Caro had played her for thirteen years of TV adaptations, covering every one of Lettice Davenport's full-length Dahlia books.

In fact, Posy wasn't sure Caro had ever played anybody else. She *was* Dahlia.

'One wonders that director Anton Martinez didn't manage to shoe-horn Caro Hooper in there somewhere, too. Or perhaps he could have asked her to reprise her role as Dahlia instead of Miss Starling. It could only have improved matters.'

'Oh, isn't this marvellous?' Caro unpinned the scarf from her hair, shaking out the curls beneath. With her tweed jacket, plain shirt and navy sailor trousers, she looked exactly the way she did on screen, playing Dahlia. 'All us Dahlia lovers together. Marcus! Always a delight.' She grabbed his upper arms and placed a firm kiss to his cheek. 'And Rosalind, of course.'

No kiss there, Posy noticed.

Marcus took on responsibility for the introductions, and Caro had a comment for everyone.

'Ah, our illustrious director,' she said to Anton. 'You know, three Dahlias in one film would really be something. Just a thought.'

Posy hid an annoyed grimace. Of course she'd want in on this too. With both Rosalind *and* Caro in the movie, it was possible that nobody would notice Posy was the star at all.

Caro flashed Anton a cheeky smile and moved on, as Marcus introduced Kit as 'the new Johnnie'. Posy had seen enough of the old TV shows on rainy Sunday afternoons to know that Johnnie – Detective Inspector John Swain – was Dahlia's on-again, off-again lover in the stories.

Caro patted Kit's cheek and said, 'A good, strong jaw – that's excellent. Johnnie needs to be the sort that you can rely on, in and out of the bedroom, don't you think, Rosalind?' Lowering her voice to a stage whisper, she added, 'And she should know. She married hers!'

'You weren't tempted by yours, Ms Hooper?' Kit teased.

Caro's eyes widened, horrified. 'Oh, please, call me Caro. Ms Hooper sounds like my mother. And *my* Johnnie was already married, so no dice there. But his wife was divine.'

How old was Caro, Posy wondered? She'd played Dahlia for over a decade, but she still looked to be no more than about forty. Which meant she could have been younger than Posy when she got the part – and now it was all she was ever known for.

Well, not quite all. Off screen, Caro was notorious for one of the messiest divorces in British TV history. Posy had still been living in the US, dealing with the consequences of her fall from grace, so she'd missed most of it, but she did remember reading something about Caro setting fire to her ex-husband's tie. While he was still wearing it.

She'd gone on to marry a woman, Posy remembered vaguely, although she didn't talk about it much. There'd been one article she'd read, where Caro had told the interviewer 'I don't know about you, kiddo, but I fall in love with the person, not the parts.'

Caro had a smile and a handshake for Libby, telling her she couldn't wait to see what she did with the script. And then she turned to Posy.

'And you must be the latest Dahlia.' Her scrutiny wasn't quite as obviously scathing as Rosalind's, but Posy was left with a general sense of disapproval. 'Well, times change, I suppose. But you're join- ing an illustrious tradition here, you realise.' She didn't add, 'You'd better live up to it,' but Posy could see the words hanging in the air like bunting.

'Now, where can I park Susie?' Caro patted the motorcycle at her side like it was a pet.

'Stables will be best,' said Marcus. 'We've moved the horses out to display all the other vintage vehicles for the visitors to gawp at, and you know the fans will want to get a look at Susie. Come on, I'll show you where to put her.'

Clementine took over, ushering the rest of them in the right direc- tion, ready to show them to their rooms, talking the whole time. But Posy wasn't listening.

Instead, her attention flickered between Caro and Rosalind, each heading in different directions, but both seeming to her further down the path she was already standing on. Both showing her what the future could bring, as a member of the Dahlia Club.

'Posy?' Clementine called from the stairs to the front door. The others had disappeared inside.

She shook her head. 'Coming.'

This wasn't her future. It was her competition. Here, at Aldermere House, she had to convince the crowds of fans – and Uncle Sol in her head – that she was a more worthy Dahlia than Rosalind King and Caro Hooper, all while they were standing right beside her.

Back straight, Posy hurried towards the door. She was ready for the challenge.

The grand style of the entrance hall of Aldermere House, with its gilt-framed family portraits and red brocade curtains, didn't lend itself to the efficient-looking reception desk that had been set up inside the doors. It was little more than a folding trestle table, loaded with ticket envelopes, leaflets for the activities planned for the weekend, and a small display of Dahlia Lively books. No sign of a computer, or any other tech beside a vintage-looking radio.

There were plenty of volunteers wearing the official convention waistcoats, though, and as Posy watched, Clementine deftly paired each of the group up with their own volunteer – but not before confiscating their phones.

'You'll get them back on Monday,' she promised.

'What if there's some sort of emergency?' Kit asked, refusing to relinquish his latest model iPhone in a hurry.

Clementine raised an eyebrow. 'Social media emergency or real-world emergency?'

'Either.' Kit's gaze slid away, and Clementine gave him a knowing smile.

'In a real-world emergency, you come and find me,' she said. 'I've still got contact with the outside world if we need it – as has Marcus, and the Davenport family. It's only the delegates who are paying for the immersive experience of having their tech taken away. And you guys, of course.'

She didn't answer the question of what would happen in a social media emergency.

As Anton, Libby and Kit were led away by the volunteers to be shown to their bedrooms for the weekend, Posy couldn't help but question it.

'I'd have thought the convention would *want* social media coverage of this event.'

Clementine, leaning over the reception desk as she fiddled with the papers on her clipboard, sighed. 'The convention, yes. The family, no.'

'So it's still the family of Lettice Davenport that live here?' Posy asked.

'Yeah. Her nephew, Hugh, his wife Isobel, and their granddaughter.' She straightened, clutching her clipboard to her chest, the metal clip clinking against the heavy, old-fashioned locket around her neck. 'They requested no photos inside the house itself, so Marcus came up with the whole "immersive experience" excuse. The day delegates outside can take as many photos as they like, though, so hopefully we'll get some traffic through from them.'

'I'm sure you will. It looks brilliant out there.'

Clementine beamed. 'It does, doesn't it? Now, come on, let's get you to your room.'

Posy followed Clementine as she moved towards the stairs, and the oversized dollhouse that dominated the hallway. The house was incongruous, a childish thing in such a refined, traditional hall, and Posy stared at it until she realised: it was a replica of Aldermere House itself.

Clementine must have seen her frowning at it because she said, 'Yes, it's the real, original one. Isn't it incredible to have it here, where we can all enjoy it?'

'Oh, absolutely,' Posy replied, despite having no idea what she was talking about. Rosalind would know; Caro would know. Every other person at Aldermere that weekend would probably know. No way was Posy admitting that she didn't.

She looked more closely at the dollhouse, hoping for an explanatory plaque or something. 'Wait, is that a dead body in it?'

There, up in the attic space of the dollhouse, was a small figure with a knife firmly stabbed through where its heart should be.

Laughing, Clementine sat the figure up more prominently. 'I think Marcus put that there. He has a pretty warped sense of humour, sometimes.'

'I guess it is a murder mystery convention,' Posy said, doubtfully.

'And that will be me, later this morning,' Clementine replied. 'Well, not in the attic with the dagger, but in the stables with the silk scarf, I think.'

Posy blinked in confusion, and Clementine handed her a copy of the leaflet with the day's schedule on it. 'The convention murder mystery,' she explained cheerfully. 'I'm the victim. Might be my only chance to sit or lie down today, so I'm taking it!'

An older couple appeared on the stairs, dressed in matching tweed jackets. Two of the VIP delegates, Posy recognised.

'Clementine, dear, do you have a moment?' the woman asked. 'It's about the . . . facilities nearest our room.'

'Of course.' Clementine's smile looked a little forced. 'Excuse me, Posy.'

While Clementine dealt with the couple's plumbing problems, Posy bent down to get another look at the creepy dollhouse. She was so engrossed checking for more dead bodies that she didn't hear the man behind her approaching until he spoke.

'Amazing, isn't it?'

Posy jerked upright as she spun around to find a tall, tanned man standing behind her, his hands in the pockets of his slacks. He could have been anywhere between his mid-fifties and his seventies, Posy thought, with his greying hair smartly styled, and the lines around his eyes adding warmth to his smile. He reminded her, more than anything, of some of the older actors she'd met in Hollywood. The ones still playing romantic leads against twenty-something girls, even after they were old enough to be their grandfathers.

'Sorry, I didn't mean to startle you.' He held out a hand. 'Hugh Davenport. Welcome to Aldermere.'

'This is your house. I mean, you're Lettice Davenport's nephew.' Belatedly, she reached out to shake his hand. 'Um, thank you for having me.'

His laugh was as friendly as his smile. 'You're very welcome. Although she was technically my first cousin once removed – my father's cousin.' He gestured towards the family tree. 'But I always called her Auntie. You were admiring her doll house. Do you know the story?'

A glance towards the stairs confirmed that Clementine was still busy with the other guests. 'I'd love to hear your version of it.'

'Not half as much as I enjoy telling it, I'm sure.' Hugh leaned a hip against the table. 'The dollhouse was a gift to Aunt Letty from my grandfather, when she was a girl. She stayed here often during the summer holidays and such, and since Grandma and Granddad had only boys, he wanted her to have something of her own to play with.'

'That was kind,' Posy murmured.

'Mmm. Anyway, she grew up and it got forgotten and dusty, until she came to stay again one summer when she was in her twenties, I think. She was already published by then, and she was working on a stately home murder mystery. One night at dinner, she complained that the draughty window in her room meant her notes kept blowing off her desk, and she couldn't keep track of who was where when. My father dug out the old dollhouse, and cleaned it up for her to use.'

'She must have loved that.'

Hugh laughed. 'Actually, I believe she said that she'd have rather he fix the window in her room. But she *did* use the dollhouse to work out the plots for every other mystery she wrote that was set in a grand old house like this one.'

Posy looked down at the dollhouse, then reached in to retrieve the tiny, murdered doll. 'Using these?'

'That's right.' He took the doll from her, holding it between two fingers. 'This should be up in the study. I'll return it. And it looks like you have places to be, too,' he added, looking over her shoulder. 'Hullo, Clementine. Everything going smoothly so far?'

'Perfectly, thank you, Mr Davenport.' Clementine's voice was soft. 'Posy, if you're ready?'

'Right. Yeah, let's go.'

Clementine moved past the dollhouse, and up the sweeping staircase with its deep forest-green carpet, studded with gold emblems. Her fingers wrapped around the heavy wooden bannister, Posy started to follow, but paused to stare down at the hall, and the roof of the replica Aldermere, and Hugh Davenport crouched in front of the dollhouse, still holding the little stabbed figurine.

Posy had never starred in a period drama before, but maybe this was what it would feel like. Like she was living in two times at once, walking from the modern day into Lettice Davenport's world, and back again.

With any film you had the movie world and the real world, the lines between them never as clearly drawn as it would seem from the finished product. There were always crew members ducking out of sight, wires and equipment to avoid tripping over, constant reminders that the life she was living for the cameras was a fake.

But here, this weekend, there were no cameras. No phones, no modern tech.

Just her; a twenty-first-century girl in a world she didn't quite understand.

'Posy Starling as Dahlia Lively appears like someone who has accidentally time travelled back to the 1930s and isn't quite sure what she's doing there.' Posy scowled at the critic in her head, and hurried to catch up with Clementine.

At the top of the stairs, a landing opened up in both directions, with another staircase straight ahead leading to the floor above. Clementine turned left, and led her to a room at the corner of the house.

'We've put you in the China Room, if that's okay?' Clementine said, as if the name should mean something to Posy. 'It has a lovely view towards the river, over the alder trees. Plus, of course, it's the room that Lettice wrote into her second Dahlia Lively mystery, *Never Underestimate a Lady.'*

Posy smiled, and mentally added book two to her reading list. 'That's perfect, thank you.'

She almost retracted the statement when Clementine opened the door, though. Inside, the walls were covered in the sort of blue and white patterns that Posy's English grandmother had displayed in her china cabinet. On tea cups they were fairly inoffensive. Surrounding her on all four walls, the chintzy patterns felt almost claustrophobic.

She might not have read *Never Underestimate a Lady* yet, but already she could see why this room would make someone want to commit murder.

Posy dropped her bag onto the faded blue and white bedspread and turned to look out of the window. Outside, the gardens of Aldermere House seemed to stretch for miles. Formal gardens, outbuildings that Posy assumed were the stables, then meadow and woodland, a stone structure she couldn't even begin to guess the purpose of, then trees and finally the river.

'The bathroom is just through that door there.' Posy turned to see where Clementine was pointing. 'It's a Jack and Jill bathroom with the bedroom on the other side, so make sure you lock both doors when you're in there! There's a lock on your side of this door, too, if you want to lock that at night.'

'Who's sleeping in the other bedroom?'

Clementine checked her clipboard. 'Um, Marcus, actually.'

Posy tried not to shudder. 'I'll definitely lock the door.'

'Good plan.'

'So, uh, what do I do now?' Posy asked, a hopefully endearingly clueless smile on her lips. 'I mean, do I have a schedule? I'll be honest, Anton kind of dropped this on me last night, and I'm not really sure what I'm supposed to be doing.'

Indicating the leaflet still clutched in Posy's hand, Clementine smiled reassuringly. 'It's all on there, don't worry. There's the murder mystery after lunch, then you have a film panel in the main events tent before dinner. Until then, you can just settle in. Or there's the house tour before lunch, if you'd like to see more of Aldermere?'

If the China Room was representative, Posy would be happy to skip it. But this was where Lettice Davenport had lived, written and died. So it had to be the next best thing to reading her way through the biography in her bag.

'House tour sounds good.'

'Great!' Clementine grinned, backing away towards the door. 'In that case, we're meeting by the dollhouse in twenty minutes. See you there!'

'Wait!' Posy called, and Clementine paused, eyebrows raised. 'Are you *sure* I can't get my phone back? If I promise, promise, promise not to post any photos of the house?'

She didn't care about *posting* to social media. She just needed to be sure that no one was posting about her. Especially since the news had broken about her playing Dahlia Lively. If anyone was going to post any dirt they'd dug up on her, now would definitely be the time.

Not that there should be any dirt. She hoped.

Checking over her shoulder, Clementine shot her a secret smile. 'I'll see what I can do. Come find me this afternoon, okay?'

Relief seeped through Posy's shoulders and spine. 'Thanks, Clementine.'

Clementine shut the door behind her and Posy set about unpacking her bag and freshening up. Wash bag in the bathroom, pyjamas under the pillow, outfits hung by day in the wardrobe. Just as she'd been doing in hotel rooms across the UK and America since she was tall enough to reach the hanging rail.

It felt good to be doing it again. Good to be *working* again.

With the last of her clothes stowed away, Posy washed up, then fixed her make-up in the bathroom mirror – making sure the second door was locked first. The taps were stiff, and groaned when she tried to turn them. The shower, over the ancient bathtub, looked like it might have been installed when indoor plumbing first became a thing.

In the bedroom, the sunlight streaming through the windows showed up the faded patches on the peeling wallpaper, and the carpet underfoot was worn almost back to the underlay. Posy figured her guess had been right; those royalties weren't rolling in right now. Hopefully that meant that Hugh would agree to Libby's script whatever he thought of it, just to get the cash.

'Everybody wins,' she murmured to herself, as she headed for the door. She hoped she'd be able to find her way around without getting lost. Maybe the house tour came with a map . . .

The envelope on the floor stopped her in her tracks. It must have been pushed under her door while she was in the bathroom. She frowned as she picked it up.

Probably it was more convention info from Clementine, or perhaps a note from Anton. But neither of those explained the way her heartbeat kicked up as she opened it. Or the dryness in her mouth as she reached inside to pull out . . .

Photos. Of her.

For a moment, she could almost believe that it was those classic paparazzi shots that covered every website that ever mentioned her – a much younger Posy Starling passed out on the sidewalk outside the Magpie Club.

But they weren't. These were photos of her, now – or at least, not as long ago as she'd like. The photo-stamped date in the corner showed they were only a couple of weeks old. But even without that, she'd have known exactly when and where they were taken.

Outside a London flat, owned by her ex-boyfriend, Damon, on the one night she wished most of all she could forget. The night she risked everything – her sobriety, her slowly rebuilt reputation, her heart – and went to him when he called and told her he missed her. And here was the proof. Photographic evidence of her, so out of it she was practically unconscious, slumped against the railings of Damon's flat after he kicked her out of bed and told her it was just a one-off.

She'd thought she could pretend it never happened. She'd gone to meetings, she'd stayed away from temptation, she'd tried to forget.

But somebody wasn't going to let her.

The photos, slippery and glossy, slid out of her grasp and onto the carpet, leaving her with a single sheet of paper. A page from a script, with *The Lady Detective – 25th August* printed at the top.

And on the back of the text was scrawled the words:

Meet me at the folly at 3PM.

Chapter Five

How did they find out?

Posy yanked the door open, scanning the landing, but there was no sign of whoever had pushed the note under her door. She stared at it again, reality sinking in. There had been a photographer on the street that night and they'd recognised her. She should be grateful the pictures hadn't appeared on the internet yet.

Except the fact they hadn't meant that someone had been saving them for something.

Blackmail.

The thought of the word made her shiver. Her public embarrassments were more than enough to fill the proverbial book, but they were also old news. She'd been on her best behaviour since leaving LA for London two years ago.

Apart from that one night.

Before yesterday, it wouldn't have mattered. The world would roll their collective eyes and be satisfied that they were right. Leopards didn't change their spots and all that.

But now she was Dahlia Lively. The high-profile lead of an apparently cursed film. And if someone told *Anton* . . . He'd taken a chance on her, giving her this part. Her agent had made that clear. She couldn't give him any reason to regret that. Or to think that she might add to the curse that seemed to be on his film, rather than help fix it.

Getting auditions had been hard enough with her history. She needed this film, so she had to be squeaky clean. Which meant finding who wrote this note, where they got the photos and what they wanted for them.

Of course, first of all she had to figure out where the damn folly was. Maybe the house tour would come with a map of the grounds, too. Then all she had to do was pretend that everything was normal, until she straightened all this out. Even if she had no idea how.

Act, Posy. You're supposed to be good at that.

A crowd had already gathered around the dollhouse, waiting for the tour of Aldermere House. Posy watched them from the staircase, picking out the people she recognised before turning to those she didn't, wondering if one of them had slipped that envelope under her door.

Caro stood with her back to the replica house, chatting to the couple who had approached Clementine earlier. Both in matching tweed jackets, far too heavy for the warm August day, they each had a jewel-laden miniature magnifying glass hanging from their button hole. *Uber-fans,* Posy mentally catalogued. And clearly, they were already in Caro's camp – as was the young Indian guy in the incongruously festive jumper, who hovered on the edge of their conversation.

She found Rosalind apart from the group, standing in the doorway to the next room. Marcus, meanwhile, was nowhere to be seen – neither were Anton or Kit. But Libby stood near the dollhouse, beside a woman with bright blue hair and tattoos down both arms. She'd *definitely* been with the VIP delegates; blue hair wasn't a common Golden Era affectation, even in perfect victory rolls like hers was. Her thirties-style skirt suit, red lipstick and seamed stockings meant that, even with the hair, she looked more like she belonged here than Posy did.

Posy's attention focused back on Libby as a thought occurred. Libby would know who had advance copies of the script – before the stars, even. She'd also have one herself. Libby could have sent the note . . . and if she hadn't she could help her narrow down who could have.

Posy was about to make her way down to talk to Libby, when a sudden rush of air alerted her that she wasn't alone on the staircase. As she turned to see who was there, a young woman with long, strawberry blonde hair and dressed in what was definitely *not* period costume, crashed into Posy's shoulder on her way past.

'Sorry!' the girl sang back, waving a wristband-less arm in apology, but not stopping. Posy guessed she had to be one of the family. Hadn't Clementine mentioned a granddaughter?

Just then, Clementine appeared from the room behind Rosalind, a smiling older woman in a perfectly tailored skirt suit and pearls beside her.

The girl from the stairs approached her, only to be rebuffed with a look, and a few words that Posy couldn't hear. They were easy enough to lipread, however, even though the woman's smile stayed firmly in place. *Not now.* Yep, that looked like a grandmother and granddaughter relationship to her.

'Are we all here?' Clementine asked, her gaze flickering from the assembled crowd and her ever-present clipboard. 'Great. Then I'll hand over to you, Isobel.'

The older woman smiled patiently as the chatter died down and people turned to face her. 'Welcome, everyone, to Aldermere Hall. I'm Isobel Davenport, the wife of Hugh Davenport, the nephew of the author Lettice Davenport. And in case you're finding all that a little confusing—' A tinkling laugh, echoed by the small group. '—we're going to start our tour at the family tree on the wall over there.'

Posy turned dutifully, along with everyone else, to take in the elegantly inked scroll-style hanging that had pride of place beside the doorway to the drawing room beyond. It was hard to make out all the details further up, but she managed to pick out Lettice's name, as well as her nephew's, right at the bottom of the scroll.

'The family tree was originally created over two hundred years ago,' Isobel said, as they admired it. 'It has been added to with each new generation of the Davenports, of whom Lettice is only one of what has long been a highly illustrious English family—'

'What about the dollhouse?' the blue-haired woman broke in, clearly not interested in any Davenports who weren't writers of crime fiction. 'Can you tell us more about that? It's the actual one that Lettice used, right? The one that she wrote into *A Very Lively Christmas*?'

'That's right!' Caro said. 'When we filmed that story we had a replica made, but it wasn't nearly as nice as this.' She stroked the roof, possessively. 'Just as well though. One of the cameramen crashed through it on the last day of filming. Smashed the thing to smithereens.'

Everyone laughed at that. Everyone except their tour guide.

'I believe she did, yes,' Isobel said, answering the blue-haired woman's question as if Caro had never spoken at all. 'Until her death, the dollhouse sat in her study – yes, we'll see that later in the tour – and she used it to map out her stately home mysteries, using little figures to represent different characters, and where they were at the time of the murder.'

'Letty told me once that all her country house murders were set at Aldermere, really.' Rosalind moved closer to run an idle hand along the top of the model. 'Even the ones that seemed to be set somewhere else, abroad or what have you. She always began with the set-up of Aldermere and worked things out from there.' The casual way she spoke of the late novelist caught Posy by surprise.

'Yes, well.' There was a hint of annoyance creeping into Isobel's voice now. 'These days we keep it here in the entrance hall for visitors to enjoy. Now, let's move on to Lettice's study.'

Together, they traipsed up the stairs after Isobel. Posy fell into step beside Isobel's granddaughter as they climbed to the first floor.

'You're Posy Starling, right? Clementine told me you're the latest Dahlia actress. I'm Juliette Davenport.' She was perky, in a way Posy vaguely remembered being once. She was almost impressed that Juliette seemed to have hung on to that sort of enthusiasm for life all through her teens.

Posy forced a smile. 'Nice to meet you, Juliette.'

'So, tell me.' She leant in a little closer. 'Kit Lewis. Single?'

'I'm honestly not sure!' Posy laughed. 'But I'll tell him you asked.'

'I've got a bet going with a friend that I can get a selfie with him this weekend,' Juliette admitted.

'Oh, well that we can definitely do. He loves a camera.' The day of their chemistry read, she'd seen him take selfies with at least two of the assistants.

Juliette beamed. 'That would be great! Thanks.'

'No problem,' Posy said. 'So, is that why you're taking a tour of your own house? Looking for Kit?'

'Not much else to do around here while this circus is going on, you know? And I promised Grandma I'd show my face.' Juliette scowled at her grandmother's back. 'She was probably hoping I'd be wearing something like that, though.' She waved a hand vaguely at Posy's tea dress.

'Trust me, this was not my choice, either.'

They shared a smile as, at the top of the stairs, Isobel began lecturing them on the history of the house again.

'You're in the China Room, right?' Juliette said. 'Let me know if you need migraine tablets. Grandma has a whole stash of them upstairs.'

'Two nights with that wallpaper and I might,' Posy admitted. 'What on earth was anybody thinking, decorating it like that?'

Juliette shrugged. 'It's been like that for*ever*. And after Letty put it in her book, they couldn't change it, I guess.'

'This place is so *weird*.'

'Try living here.'

Isobel led them along the landing, past Posy's room, and up the second staircase to the next floor. Here, the ceilings were lower, slanting inwards as the roof pitched, almost an attic space rather than another floor.

'Of course this would have been the servants' quarters, originally,' Isobel said, as if having a house large enough to require servants was perfectly normal.

Posy had lived in a house that large, once. Maybe her parents still did, although they'd probably had to sell it to pay off the debts. She didn't want to know.

'Does the house have any, like, secret passages and stuff?' she asked Juliette instead, thinking again about how that note had appeared under her door.

'Why?' Juliette looked surprised at the question. 'Aren't the endless staring portraits, murderous dollhouse and spooky attic rooms enough for you?'

Posy laughed. 'It just seemed the sort of thing a house like this might have.'

'Yeah, I can see that. If you're hoping for a quick escape route from your fans, there are a million places you can hide at Aldermere, but I've never found any secret passageways, despite all the summers I spent searching when I was a kid.'

The attics meandered along to a door at the back of the house, which opened onto a large room that had to be several servants' bedrooms knocked together. Books lined the walls on all sides, even up to the windows that slanted in with the eaves. In the centre of the room sat a heavy, battered desk – complete with old-fashioned typewriter and a stack of papers set beside it, like a typed manuscript.

The VIP fans gasped as one it seemed, amazed to be in the actual room where genius had occurred. Rosalind lingered in the doorway, apparently reluctant to enter the room. By contrast, Caro was running her fingers across the books on the shelves, murmuring to herself as she touched the covers.

The shelves weren't only home to books. Each also held trinkets and keepsakes, all free from dust and decay. Someone looked after this room very well.

'This is the study where Lettice wrote almost all of her seventy-nine books and short stories,' Isobel said, as they all gazed around the space where the magic happened. 'On the shelves are first editions of most of her books, as well as some important memorabilia connected to her career.' It sounded like she was reciting a script. Posy supposed she must have given this tour plenty of times in the past.

According to the back cover of the biography in her bag, Lettice Davenport had died in 1990, two years before Posy had even been born, and she'd been writing almost to the very end. Which, given that she was a golden age crime author back in the thirties, meant she'd been working well past the usual retirement age.

Rosalind glided across the room to take a seat in the chair behind the desk, swivelling it round to face the window instead of Isobel and the group. From where she stood, though, Posy could see the look of relief that flickered across her face as she sat. There had been an awful lot of steps up to the attic, and Rosalind was getting on a bit . . .

Actors and writers. Both professions where you only retired when no one wanted you anymore.

What was the last thing she'd seen Rosalind King in, anyway?

She was being catty, now. Rosalind could only be sixty or so. But still . . .

Posy tuned back in to whatever Isobel was talking about – something to do with the inspiration for Lettice's first book, she thought. But she couldn't keep her attention from straying back to Rosalind, and to Caro.

The other two Dahlias. An exclusive club, sure, but one Posy knew she needed to earn membership to. Watching them, studying them, would help.

It was how she'd always approached developing a character – watching people. Her most famous role – as the teenage princess, Marissa, in three increasingly dreadful movies – had been based on a woman she'd watched at a cafe in Paris, sipping coffee, chatting with her friends.

Now, she tucked away in her memory how Caro chattered in low tones to the woman with the blue hair, ignoring Isobel, obviously secure in the knowledge that her stories were more interesting. The way that Rosalind rested one hand on the windowsill, staring out towards the gardens at the rear of the house. Posy angled her own hand and placed it on the nearest shelf, her neck twisted to look half over her shoulder.

She smiled, as she realised she wasn't the only one mirroring Rosalind. Juliette had drifted away from her to stand at the next window along from the actress, also resting one hand on the sill as she looked out of the window. Posy wondered what was so fascinating out there.

'Hugh and I have tried to keep this study as it would have been when Lettice was writing here, although I have to admit that some-times I think Hugh sneaks up here to work – or for a bit of peace and quiet.' Isobel gave a small laugh. 'But we've also displayed some of Lettice's most meaningful keepsakes and memorabilia on the shelves for visitors to enjoy. Like the Diamond Dagger lifetime achievement award she was presented with, just before her death. And, of course, the jeweller's loupe that the studio gave her – studded with genuine rubies and diamonds – when filming concluded on the last of the original Dahlia Lively films.'

'Before that, it was yours, wasn't it, Rosalind?' Caro said. 'Must have hurt like hell to give *that* back.'

Rosalind didn't respond, and Caro joined the VIP fans as they moved closer to study the loupe as Isobel lifted it from its glass case. Posy followed, frowning. What the hell was a loupe, anyway?

'It's just like ours, isn't it, Harry?' The woman in the tweed jacket nudged her husband, and they both held up their mini magnifying glasses.

'Except ours aren't rubies and diamonds.' Harry picked up the real thing for a closer look.

'They definitely look the part, though,' Caro said, studying them both. 'When *I* was Dahlia, I had this really plasticky one that didn't look authentic at all.'

'Lower budgets on TV than film, I suppose,' Rosalind said, proving she was paying *some* attention to the tour. 'Besides, weren't there an awful lot of thefts from the sets on that show?'

'Extras taking souvenirs,' Caro said. 'Bound to happen on a show as popular as mine.'

'There must be a lot of valuable stuff in this study,' the guy in the Christmas jumper commented, as he looked around. 'Bet your insurance premiums are through the roof on this place.'

'Yes, it must be a nice little nest egg, all this stuff,' Harry added, exchanging a look with his wife Posy couldn't read.

All the money talk made her wonder. People mentioned money when they either wanted people to think they had it, or when they needed it, in Posy's experience. If one of the fans here needed money, how far would they go to get it?

She supposed she'd know if one of them met her at the folly at three o'clock.

'But of course we'd never sell it,' Isobel said, shutting down the discussion. 'The items in this room are my husband's family legacy, and that is what matters most.'

'Of course, of course,' Harry said, placatingly.

'It's a privilege to see them,' his wife added.

Mollified, Isobel continued. 'Now, on this shelf we have some of the figures she used in the dollhouse downstairs.'

The figures were creepy, Posy decided, moving away to study the other shelves. There were yellowing books on poisons and anatomy, what looked like the knot from a noose, a small bottle with a poison sticker on the front, and even a line of bullets in front of a shelf of hardboiled detective fiction.

'Oh! Is this The Hat?' Caro asked. Posy glanced up to see the second Dahlia perching a grey cloche hat on her head at a rakish angle, and posing with her lips pursed into a kiss, before laughing. 'Lettice wore this hat in every one of her author photos, didn't she?' Caro passed the hat on to the woman in tweed to try, who duly passed it around the rest of the group while Isobel tried desperately to get it back where it belonged on top of the bookcase.

Posy continued her own inspection of the room. 'There was also a full shelf of Lettice's own books. Checking to ensure that no one was watching her, Posy pulled out the second book on the shelf, *Never Underestimate A Lady,* the one that Clementine had said featured the China Room. She flicked through, but couldn't immediately find a reference – although the back cover showed a picture of the author, wearing the same hat Caro was handing around so carelessly.

When Isobel began to usher everyone out of the room again, Posy slipped the book into her bag to study when she was alone. She'd nip back later and return it.

Posy hurried to catch up to the others, and realised that she wasn't the only one lagging behind. Rosalind still stood by the window, staring out at the gardens.

'Are you coming, Rosalind?' Isobel asked from the doorway.

Rosalind blinked, shaking her head slightly. 'Of course.'

Curious, Posy glanced out of the window as she followed Rosalind out, and saw a smaller, secluded garden, away from the fete-like atmosphere of the front lawns. Flowers and greenery were planted in a circular pattern, with a bench at the centre, where two people sat.

She recognised Clementine by her olive suit and the mustard silk scarf around her neck – funny, she hadn't realised the organiser hadn't joined them on the tour. It took her a moment longer to realise that the older man sitting with her was Hugh Davenport.

She couldn't see his face, but from the way he stared at his hands, his head bowed and salt and pepper hair silvering in the sunlight, she guessed that whatever they were discussing was serious.

She wondered if Rosalind knew what it was.

Chapter Six

Dahlia smiled at him, as she signed another autograph for one of the girls dressed in a flattering facsimile of her own appearance. 'Oh, Johnnie. Don't be jealous, now. I don't suppose policemen really get 'fans', do they?'

Dahlia Lively *in* Fame and Misfortune

***By* Lettice Davenport, 1967**

Lunch was being served in the ballroom which, Isobel told them airily as she deposited them at the bottom of the stairs, was through the drawing room. The group dispersed, mostly in the same direction, but Posy held back and watched them go, still wondering if one of them was her blackmailer.

It was the photos that had her on edge. The idea that someone had been watching her when she was at her most vulnerable. Capturing that moment to share with, potentially, the world.

The idea that they could still be watching her, right now, without her knowledge.

It made her blood run cold.

Posy stopped by the reception desk at the front door hoping to see Clementine – and maybe her phone – but there was no sign of either. Instead, she picked up a copy of the map of Aldermere House and Grounds and studied it.

There, at the far edge of the paper, beside the wavy blue lines that seemed to represent a river, and the childishly drawn trees beside it, was a circle marked *Folly.* So that was where her blackmailer wanted to meet her.

Posy shoved the map in her bag and headed into lunch.

The ballroom was packed. Posy assumed the diners were speakers and guests at the convention, or people who'd bought tickets to eat with them. Marcus didn't seem shy about selling access to the house, or the stars he'd invited, even if he hadn't cleared that with them first. Which creeped Posy out a bit, especially after seeing those photos.

In one corner, at a prettily laid circular table, Caro held court with some of the VIP fans from the tour that morning. From the laughter and table banging going on, Posy assumed she was telling more tales of her time as Dahlia Lively.

Rosalind sat at a smaller table, with Isobel and Juliette, who Posy noticed was texting on her phone under the table. She couldn't see Anton or Kit anywhere, but then she spotted Libby on the far side of the room. The writer was holding a cup of coffee close to her chest as she stood by the large picture window, looking out over the lawns and stalls at the side of Aldermere House. Skipping the queue at the serving stations for now, Posy grabbed a cup of coffee and headed over to join her, mentally rehearsing her questions as she went. She *liked* Libby, she didn't want her to be a blackmailer. But if she was, Posy intended to find out.

'How's it going?' Posy asked, leaning against the windowsill beside her.

Libby blinked, apparently surprised by her appearance, then gave her a tentative smile. 'Oh, okay. It's . . . weird being here, is all.'

'Yeah.' Posy surveyed the room around them. Even beyond all the people in 1930s and '40s dress – not forgetting the guy in slacks and a Christmas jumper – she felt like she had slipped through time.

Posy lowered her voice. 'I'll be honest, this place gives me the creeps. That dollhouse in the hallway . . .' She shuddered, making Libby chuckle.

'I don't mind it so much. But then, I've been spending the last few months writing about murders and such somewhere like this, so maybe I've just got used to it.'

'Of course you have.' Posy cast around for an innocuous way into the questions she *really* wanted to ask. 'But you're a latecomer to the project, like me, right? Had you worked with Anton before? Is that why he brought you in?'

Libby shook her head. 'No, but my agent had, a few times. And she knows I'm a huge Lettice Davenport fan, so when Anton contacted her looking for a script doctor I guess I was the obvious choice.'

Seemed like everyone involved was a lifelong Dahlia fan, except Posy. 'What do you love most about her books?'

Head tilted, Libby considered the question. 'I guess they've always been part of my life – my gran gave me one to read when I was about eleven, and I never looked back. Where I grew up, we were kind of in the middle of nowhere, so books and movies were my escape. My way to see the world. I suppose they still are.' She gave Posy a small, embarrassed smile. 'Anyway. Being here at Aldermere, where Lettice wrote so many of her books, is incredible to me. I felt like I knew the place before I even stepped foot inside.'

Hadn't she mentioned something about maps of Aldermere, when they'd arrived. 'You must know it pretty well from all your research, too. Doesn't it have a folly somewhere?'

'Uh, yes, I think so. I'm not quite sure where. Down by the river, maybe?' Libby scrunched up her face as if trying to remember. 'It's not a feature in the script, so I didn't really spend much time on it.'

The confusion could be an act, but Posy didn't think so. She ploughed on with her second question.

'You said on the train that the script is done. Do you think we'll all have the final version soon?'

Libby shrugged. 'Anton forwarded it on to the "important stake-holders" a few days ago.' Anton's words, Posy guessed, from the way Libby put air quotes around the phrase. 'I'm not sure who he counts as important, though.'

'Not the lead actress, apparently.' But Libby, Anton or one of his 'stakeholders' had ripped a page from the script and used it as a black-mail note. A way of telling her that she had to pay attention, that the person who had her photos had the ear of her director, too.

Maybe Libby was too obvious a suspect. If she'd wanted to black-mail Posy, using the script pages was about as obvious as signing the damn note. No, Posy didn't think Libby was behind this. Which meant she had to talk to Anton next, and find out who else had the script – or if he was behind it himself. Why a director would try to blackmail his lead actress was beyond her, but she wasn't ruling anything out yet.

Where was Anton, anyway? And Kit for that matter? She hadn't seen them since this morning. If she had to take part in this conven-tion, why didn't they?

Libby was peering over Posy's shoulder again, but when Posy looked she couldn't see anything behind her except the window, and the guy in the Christmas jumper telling cracker jokes at the dessert table.

'I'm sure you'll get it soon,' Libby said, but she sounded distracted. Draining her coffee cup, she placed it too close to the edge of the windowsill, and it clattered to the ground, splashing the dregs of her coffee over her skirt. 'Oh, damn it!

Aware that people were turning to look at them, Posy dropped to her knees at Libby's side, thrusting a napkin from the nearest table towards her. Together, they mopped up the few drops that had hit the carpet, and righted the coffee cup beside the saucer that had shattered into several pieces as the cup landed on it, before Isobel came bustling over.

'Are you okay? Where are the catering staff?' One hand on her hip, Isobel wafted some paper towels towards them, but didn't get down and help. '*This* is why Hugh told Marcus we didn't want the daytime events inside the house.'

'It's fine,' Posy told her, straightening up. 'I think Libby got the worst of it.'

'Oh, you poor dear. Did it scald you? I have some cream some-where . . .' Isobel fussed over Libby with a concerned smile.

One of the catering staff, dressed as a 1930s domestic maid, hurried across the room to them, and Isobel handed her a wodge of coffee-stained paper towels. 'Ah, there you are! Can you finish clear-ing this up, please?'

'Of course, ma'am.' The maid knew her part well, it seemed. 'I'm sorry I wasn't here. I was just fixing a camomile and ginger tea for Mr Fisher.'

That made Isobel tut good-naturedly. 'Of course. Marcus and his tea. Do you know,' she said, leaning towards Posy as she murmured the words, 'the first time he came here for a meeting about the convention, he couldn't believe I didn't still keep his particular favourite tea in the kitchens. He actually sent his assistant . . . you know, Clementine? He sent her out to the nearest shop, five miles away, to buy some. Honestly! I did feel for the poor girl. You'd think he'd carry it with him, if he's that particular, wouldn't you?'

'Do you need more coffee, miss?' the maid asked, and Posy shook her head.

'It wasn't mine. It was—' She turned to indicate Libby, but she was gone. 'Libby's. I guess she must have gone to get changed.'

'Ah, Isobel!' Marcus approached them, sipping from a white china cup just like all the others. 'Good to see you still have my special tea in. Have to drink it quickly now though. Almost time for the murder mystery!'

'That sounds like fun,' Posy said. Actually, it sounded kind of excruciating. Hundreds of wannabe detectives racing around the grounds trying to solve a contrived murder before everyone else. 'I'm looking forward to watching it.'

'Oh, you'll be doing more than watching, my dear!' With an extreme jollity Posy felt was unfounded, Marcus grinned and leaned in close enough for her to smell the gingery tea on his breath. 'You'll be taking part. We've all got our parts to play in the murder mystery!'

'Really?' Posy asked, weakly. 'What, exactly, am I going to need to do?'

Tapping the side of his nose, Marcus grinned again, showing yellowing teeth in his red face. 'Just you wait! All will be revealed . . .'

'I can't wait,' Posy lied. 'Um, I meant to ask you. Do you know where Clementine is? I needed to speak with her about . . . something.' She finished, lamely, realising that it probably wasn't a good idea to mention wanting her phone back in front of Marcus and Isobel. But Clementine had said to find her 'this afternoon' and it was now, officially, after noon, and Posy's fingers were starting to twitch.

'Oh, I imagine she's over at the stables already.' Marcus reached into his jacket pocket and pulled out a slimline pill organiser, popping open the correct section and tipping two tablets into his palm. He tossed them into his mouth and swallowed them with a mouthful of his tea.

'The stables?' Posy asked. Maybe she could find her there . . .

'Yes! She'll be getting ready for her big part as the victim in our murder mystery by now.'

Or not. Posy's shoulders sank. 'I suppose I'll catch her after that, then.'

Across the way, she spotted Anton and Kit entering the ballroom. 'Sorry, I just need to . . .' She smiled apologetically, and left Marcus to Isobel.

Anton and Kit had joined the shorter of the two lunch queues, so Posy slid in behind them and said a breezy hello before she noticed the unusually sour look on Kit's face and the tightness around Anton's eyes.

'You guys missed a great house tour,' she said, mostly to fill the awkward silence that bubbled around them. She wanted to ask where they'd been, but the vibe from them both didn't encourage questions. Had they been arguing? 'We got to see Lettice's study and her memorabilia and everything.'

'That sounds fun.' Something of Kit's smile returned as he spoke, and there was a daring glint in his eye. 'Maybe I'll have to sneak up there later and take a look for myself. See if I can find anything that screams "Detective Inspector Johnnie Swain" at me. Get inspired, you know?'

'We're not looking for antiques for this film,' Anton snapped. 'We're looking forward. You won't find a Johnnie who looked like you anywhere in this house.'

Before Posy could think of anything to fill the stunned silence that followed, the VIP fans descended. Three of them, anyway – Harry and his wife, plus the blue-haired woman. The guy in the Christmas jumper was still waiting for his dessert, by the look of things.

Caro seemed to have disappeared and, in her absence, the uber-fans had decided to latch onto the next most famous option. Since

Rosalind was still deep in conversation with Juliette, that left Posy and Kit.

Anton, probably wisely, decided to slope off towards another table with his plate.

'Hello, there!' Harry said, juggling his coffee cup and cake plate into one hand, so he could shake Posy and Kit's hands with the other. 'We met this morning, didn't we? I'm Harry, and this is my wife Heather. And of course, we've seen *you* on the telly, young man, so no introductions needed there.'

'We're big fans,' Heather interrupted, and Kit preened, just a little. 'Of Lettice, I mean. Well, obviously, or we wouldn't be here!'

Posy hid a smile as Kit deflated. 'Hopefully by the end of this weekend we'll have won you over too,' he said.

'We had a Dahlia Lively themed wedding, you know,' Harry said, ignoring Kit's comment. 'Heather's idea, of course, but I loved it!'

'Each of the tables was named after one of her books. I made these individual centrepieces for each one, including the murder weapon.' Heather smiled proudly, as Harry nodded.

'It was Dahlia who brought us together, you see,' he explained. 'We met at a special library event where Lettice came to speak—'

'It was a couple of years before she died,' Heather put in.

'And that was it! We knew we were meant to be.' Harry beamed at his wife. 'Thirty years we've been married, and this weekend is our anniversary present to each other.'

'We'd normally be at our friends' beach house in Florida for the summer,' Heather confided, with the air of someone who was trying not to brag. 'Since Harry was able to retire so early. But we couldn't miss a chance to visit Aldermere.'

'But enough about us,' Harry said. 'Have you met our Fliss yet?'

'Felicity Hill.' The blue-haired woman gave Posy an assessing look as she held out her hand, not unlike the one Rosalind had given her on her arrival. She appeared to be only five or six years older than Posy, but she still had that same condescending look down pat. 'I'm the secretary of the Lettice Davenport fan club.'

'You work with Marcus?' Kit asked.

Felicity shook her head. 'As little as possible, really. Marcus is all about the big events, the occasions, that sort of thing. But he leaves the paperwork – well, web work, mostly – to me. I maintain the group's website, send the email newsletters, keep the blog up to date with the latest news, manage all the social media. All the stuff that actually matters to the majority of our members.'

'Strange to think of all that modern technology being used to celebrate a novelist whose whole ethos is set in the 1930s,' Posy said. That sounded safe enough. Knowledgeable enough.

'No stranger than using all those cameras and technology to film a movie,' Felicity pointed out.

Posy winced. 'True.'

'What do you all think about it?' Kit asked. 'The new film I mean.'

'Well, it's always good to encourage a new generation of fans.' Heather sounded doubtful, even as she said it. 'All this talk of a curse, though . . .'

Felicity rolled her eyes. 'That's just nonsense, Heather. Or maybe a promotional strategy . . .?' She gave Kit and Posy a questioning look, which they ignored.

'No smoke without fire, that's what I always say.' Harry folded his arms across his chest. 'Was the same when I was in business. Had to look out for the faintest whiff of smoke. You mark my words, if that director of yours doesn't get a handle on things soon, it'll all be over before it starts. The fans won't stand for it, even if the family will.'

Quite what insider knowledge Harry thought he had to make such a pronouncement, Posy had no idea. But then, in her experience, men of Harry's type rarely needed any knowledge to believe they were experts on a subject.

Heather, sensing they were losing their audience, dragged the conversation back to the weekend at hand. 'Harry and I have been coming to these conventions right from the start, haven't we, love?'

'Of course! Marcus was in touch with us as soon as he had the idea to hold them. We're somewhat famous in Dahlia circles you see. A bit like him, really,' Harry said.

'We collect the memorabilia, have all the autographs – we must get both of yours.' Heather pulled a small, black notebook and pen from her bag and handed it to Kit, pointing at the next blank page for him to sign.

'And we never miss a convention. This is the first year Marcus has managed to get it held here at Aldermere, though.' Harry's gaze roamed covetously around the ballroom, as if he were mentally tagging all the items of Lettice's home's inventory he'd like to take away with him for his collection.

Kit handed Posy the notebook, and she flipped to the next page to sign her name. After a moment's hesitation, she printed DAHLIA LIVELY, underneath before handing it back to Heather.

'No way we were missing the chance to be here, where she wrote all her wonderful stories!' Heather added. 'Did you know, so many of her mysteries were set in houses just like Aldermere, some people started to get suspicious. And when Lettice's maid went missing, towards the end of the war, there were all sorts of rumours. Some locals wanted them to drain the mere itself to look for her body!'

'As if the authorities didn't have enough to be going on with, what with the war effort and everything,' Harry huffed. Posy suspected he was one of those men who talked about the war years as if he'd been there himself, when he couldn't possibly have been born until after it was all over.

'So what happened?' she asked Heather, curious. There seemed to be mysteries everywhere at Aldermere.

'Oh, the maid sent a letter from Scotland, a few months later, saying she'd met a man and run away to get married. People were still talking, though, until she came back for a visit and the whole thing blew over.'

'She wasn't missing at all?'

'Apparently not.' The younger guy in the Christmas jumper rolled his eyes as he joined them at the anti-climactical ending to the story, and stepped forward to offer Posy his hand. His smile was friendly, and he looked to be younger than her – the only person in the room besides Juliette who was – and Posy almost relaxed. Until he said, 'I'm Ashok, by the way. Ashok Gupta. Although obviously today I'm here as–' He inched backwards to point to his jumper with both hands, waiting for Posy to guess.

Posy's eyes widened, and she glanced over at Kit for help. Kit shrugged, unhelpfully.

'Um, a Christmas special episode?' Posy guessed.

Ashok sighed. 'Anyone?'

'You're Detective Inspector Johnnie Swain going undercover in *A Very Lively Christmas,* when he hands out the gifts to the children at the end,' Felicity answered promptly.

The Christmas jumper was more of a vintage design, now that Posy looked at it properly. If she'd read the books, she'd have known that.

Too late now.

'So, Posy,' Heather said kindly, in an obvious rescue attempt. 'Tell us, which is *your* favourite Dahlia mystery?'

'Oh, um–'

'Oh, Heather, leave the girl alone,' Harry said. 'She might not even be a fan. Yet.'

'No, no, no,' Ashok put in. 'She must be, because Anton promised – remember? In that interview he gave when it was announced that he'd be making the new movies. Last year? He said that "as an uber-fan himself, he couldn't imagine casting or working with people who didn't love Lettice Davenport's novels as much as he did."' He sounded like he was quoting from the article, which was a bit terrifying, Posy decided.

'And I do,' she lied. 'I mean, who didn't watch Caro as Dahlia on Sunday afternoons with their grandparents, right?' The best way to sell a lie was with a bit of truth. She *had* watched them – or at least, she'd been in the room while they were happening.

'But you have read the books as well, right?' Felicity asked. 'I mean, the shows were good, I suppose. But the books . . . they're when the characters really come to life. Dahlia, she practically jumps off the page!'

'Of course!' Oh, it was all lies now. 'It was a while ago, though, so my memory of the details isn't always exact. But I'm rereading them right now – just starting, uh, *Never Underestimate a Lady*, again. Since I'm staying in the China Room while we're here at Aldermere.'

That distracted them for a few seconds, as they all cooed over the creepy descriptions of the room in the book – and merrily spoiled the ending for her. Not that she cared. But she'd definitely be checking the pattern on the walls for any discrepancies before bed.

'So which is your favourite?' Ashok asked. 'Of all the Dahlia Lively mysteries, I mean.'

'I don't think I could pick one,' Posy hedged.

'Oh, but everyone has a secret favourite,' Heather said. 'It's like children! We all say we don't, but . . .'

Everyone laughed at that.

'I think my favourite has to be *The Lady Detective*,' Kit decided, as the laughter quietened. 'That moment when Dahlia walks in and throws Johnnie's investigation up in the air. It's perfect.'

'Right!' Felicity said, beaming at him. 'I love that moment. When she flings open the door and says . . .' She waited a beat, for them to chorus along with her.

'That's because only an idiot would think *this* was a suicide,' the others chanted. 'You're not an idiot, are you, detective inspector? Only I can't *abide* idiots.'

They all laughed, and Posy smiled too, hopelessly lost and hoping against hope that no one would notice.

Of course, they did.

She saw the looks between them, the nods, the sly glances, and she knew. She was being judged and found wanting. Again.

'Who's singing my refrain?' Caro wafted back into the room, all red lipstick and knowing eyes, and descended on the group. 'I did so *love* saying that line. In fact, when we were filming it, I'd purposely stand in the wrong place, or block the camera or something, just so I could say it again!'

Posy was almost certain she'd done nothing of the sort – not on the first episode of a new series with a new director, when she'd had no proven track record or reason for them not to fire her. She wouldn't have risked it.

But it fitted the mythos Caro had built around the character. *Dahlia* would have done that, perhaps, so in Caro's narrative, so had she. The two had become so intertwined over the years, Posy wasn't sure the actress knew the difference anymore.

With Caro standing firmly in her spotlight, no one seemed very interested in Posy anymore. She was about to slink off towards the stairs, when the sound of a silver fork against glass rang through the ballroom. Everyone fell silent to look at Marcus, standing on a straining chair at the front of the room.

'Ladies and gentlemen, Dahlia Lively fans all. I'm afraid I must announce that a murder has been committed.'

Chapter Seven

'What fun!' Dahlia clapped her hands together with glee, ignoring Johnnie's disapproving stare. 'A game of murder! My favourite!'

Dahlia Lively *in* A Rather Lively Murder
***By* Lettice Davenport, 1932**

'Not a *real* murder, of course,' Marcus announced from his perch atop the antique-looking chair, to relieved laughter. 'But a game of murder, much like in *A Rather Lively Murder*. The object of today's exercise is to solve the murder *and* apprehend the murderer before the clock on the stable yard outside chimes five this afternoon – which gives you three hours to do your best.'

A murmur of excitement went up amongst the assembled company. The chair wobbling a little beneath him as he gesticulated, Marcus continued to explain.

'Like all good murder mysteries, ours will start with the discovery of a body, in this case in the stables.'

'Ah, of course. Just like in *The Devil and the Deep Blue Sea*,' Caro explained to all the people who were now looking at her, not Marcus. 'That's the one where Dahlia acquires her motorcycle – with sidecar, of course.'

'Did I hear that you have the original from the show now?' Ashok asked eagerly. 'I would *love* to ride on that!'

Marcus cleared his throat, and most of the room turned towards him, although Posy could see Caro and Ashok still whispering like kids at the back of the class. Or, like kids did on TV shows, anyway. Educated alone in trailers on film sets, Posy had never actually seen a classroom past primary school.

'So, at precisely two p.m., I will fire this starting pistol—' He pulled a tiny gun from his jacket and waved it around dramatically. 'And you will all rush to the stables. Along with the body, there will be four clues for you to follow up, by talking to our suspects, who will be scattered around the grounds. Each suspect you talk to will help you narrow your list of possibilities – or send you chasing after further clues, just like the Lady Detective herself! But remember, you won't be the only investigators seeking the truth this afternoon – or hoping to win the prize of free tickets to next year's convention. Out there in the gardens, another group are being instructed by a volunteer right now. As VIP delegates and early-bird bookers, you'll have a fifteen-minute head start over them, but that is all.'

The clock over the fireplace chimed, and Marcus raised his starting pistol.

'If everyone is ready . . .' He fired, the sound of the shot rattling the chandelier and the windows.

Before Posy could blink, it seemed the room had emptied out. She made to follow, but Marcus stopped her.

'Not you. Or you three,' he added, motioning to Caro, Rosalind and Kit. 'You four are suspects!'

'Suspects?' Rosalind sounded insulted at the suggestion. 'I think not.'

Anton laughed at that. Even though Marcus hadn't singled him out for taking part, it seemed he wasn't desperate to rush and find the culprit, either. 'Ah, you're going to have to acclimatise to not being the fabled Lady Detective again, Rosalind. There's a new Dahlia in town.'

Rosalind's expression soured. Beside her, Caro didn't look any happier at the reminder.

They were going to have to get used to it. Posy wasn't going anywhere, blackmail or no blackmail.

She turned to Marcus and asked, 'What do you need us to do?'

'Just a little bit of acting,' he replied, airily. A flurry of creamy envelopes appeared from his inside jacket pocket – his butler's outfit appeared to be designed around hiding items about his person – and he fanned them out towards them. 'Inside are your instructions – which area of the grounds to loiter in, what to say when detectives approach you, and where to direct them next.'

'How long do we have to do this for?' Kit asked, taking the envelope with his name on. 'Some of us have important napping planned before our panel later.'

'Oh, you're one of the first stops, so anyone who's serious about winning will have found you within the hour.' Marcus handed out the rest of the envelopes. Posy's felt heavy in her hands. 'Don't worry, it'll all be over before you know it. Now, I'd better go check that our murder victim is good and dead, and our detectives are finding the clues. Actors; places, please!'

With a swirl of his tail coat, he headed towards the front door, leaving the rest of them studying the contents of their envelopes.

The first card Posy pulled from hers read: *You are the murderer. Tell no one!*

She rolled her eyes, and shuffled the card to the back to read the instructions behind it.

Sit on the bench in the Murder Spiral, and wait to be approached.
When investigators ask where you were when the murder was committed,
tell them you were with your fiancé, and kiss him firmly for evidence!

'Apparently I need to go and linger by the Gate House,' Rosalind said, her tone dry with annoyance. Obviously she felt that a national treasure of her acting status was above such activities.

'Well, I'm at the cake stall,' Caro said, cheerfully. 'So that's all right by me. Have fun, everyone!' She departed with a small wave over her shoulder, her white gloves bright in the sunshine streaming through the window. Rosalind waited a moment, then followed.

'What's a Murder Spiral?' Kit asked, frowning at his own card. 'Because it doesn't *sound* like the ideal place for a romantic rendez-vous for me and my fictional fiancée.'

'I don't know, but speaking as the aforementioned fictional fiancée, at least we'll be risking our lives together.' Posy pulled the map from her bag and studied it, mentally clocking the distance between the Murder Spiral and the folly. 'Apparently it's in the gardens, behind the house.'

'I suppose we better go find it, then.' He gave her a wink. 'See if it's as cosy as it sounds.'

The Murder Spiral was easy enough to find; a large, printed sign with the convention logo and 'Murder Spiral' written on it had been attached to a curved wall segregating a circular garden from the rest of the grounds. Underneath that sign sat an older, more official plaque, that Kit stopped to read.

'Does it tell you why it's called a murder spiral?' Posy asked.

Kit tapped a finger against the edge of the sign. 'Apparently it's a circular garden planted in a spiral, like they used to do with herb gardens.'

'I'd sort of guessed the spiral part. What about the murder?'

He pulled a face. 'This herb spiral is planted with all the poisonous plants Lettice Davenport ever used in any of her books.'

'Of course it is.' Still, she checked over Kit's shoulder to make sure he wasn't teasing her. He wasn't.

Planted in 1976 to celebrate the release of her fiftieth book, the Spiral Garden is a commemoration of Lettice's place as the Princess of Poison in the canon of Golden Age Crime Writers.

They didn't call it the Murder Spiral, she noticed. Probably Marcus had added that to the maps for an added bit of death and danger.

'The investigators will be here soon.' Shading his eyes with his hand, Kit looked towards the house, but the path they'd followed was empty for now. 'I guess we'd better get in position.'

'Guess so.'

'Don't touch any of the plants, though,' Kit added with a grin. 'I mean, we've already lost one Dahlia Lively on this movie. Two could be considered careless.'

An uncomfortable feeling seeped through her at the reminder of everything that had gone wrong with the film so far. Was her blackmailer looking for the final nail for the film's coffin?

The path through the plants wound round in a steep curve, spiralling to the more open area in the centre, where an ornate metal bench stood waiting for them. Posy held her hands clasped in front of her, sticking to the centre of the path so no leaves or flowers could brush against her, and made her way to the bench. Probably a person needed to eat the flowers or leaves to be poisoned, but in a place like Aldermere, she wasn't taking any chances.

She sat, flipping her skirt out around her legs, and Kit settled beside her. The bench was uncomfortably small for two people, but

Posy supposed that was the point. She and Kit were supposed to be in love, after all.

Well, if they were going to be Dahlia and Johnnie, she'd have to get used to that. Especially if there was more than one movie, as everyone was hoping, and they kept going back to the 1930s for murder and romance.

She frowned. 'If Lettice was still publishing Dahlia Lively mysteries into the seventies, why is everyone here dressed like they're waiting for their sweetheart to come home from the war?'

'I take it you haven't read the books yet, then?' His voice was kind, rather than condescending, which made her feel slightly better about her ignorance.

'Not *all* of them.' Or any, really, yet. But she would.

'The books never moved on,' Kit said, with an easy shrug. 'They're all set back then, between the wars. Some go into the nineteen forties, and one is set around VE Day, but that's about it.'

Posy tipped her head backwards to look up at the bulky, square form of Aldermere House. Windows ran, evenly spaced, across the back of the building, above a large terrace outside. The roof was covered in chimneys, none of them belching smoke into the warm summer sky, although she imagined they would be in winter.

Under the eaves, there were smaller windows – an attic room. She blinked, as she realised. This was the bench that Clementine had been sitting on earlier that morning, when Posy had seen her talking to Hugh. Which meant those windows must be the ones to Lettice Davenport's study, from where she'd viewed Clementine.

Beside her, Kit was uncharacteristically silent.

'So how did you become such a fan of Dahlia Lively, anyway?'

Kit gave her a sideways look. 'Press answer or real answer?'

'Real.' She knew what that was like – having one answer to share with the world at large, and another that only a few got to hear. Kit would be handing out the press answer to anyone who asked on the panel later, she was sure. But if they were going to work together they needed to trust each other, and sharing a truth was the fastest way she knew to do that.

Perhaps Kit was aware of that too, because he nodded. 'Okay, then. When I was twelve or so, my mum was working two jobs to make the rent after my dad left. She didn't want me home alone, though, so every day after school I went to the local library to wait for her to pick me up.'

'You didn't hang out with your mates?' Posy asked.

'Sadly, at twelve, I was not the suave, handsome and personable soul you know today,' he said. 'Mates were not something I had to worry about.'

Posy thought back to when she was twelve. She'd just starred in her first big movie, after a few years as a recurring character on a TV soap. She'd been on the cover of every teen girl magazine, but her friends had mostly been the catering staff on set, and one of the director's dogs. 'I get that. Go on.'

'The librarian noticed I was spending a lot of time there, and sort of took me under her wing. I helped her shelve books instead of doing my homework, and she let me read books from the adult section in return. She knew I'd read all the kids' murder mysteries, so one day she handed me *The Lady Detective* and told me to see if I could figure out whodunnit.'

'And could you?'

'No. But I was hooked from then on. Even though the world they were written about looked nothing like mine, the characters were still people I could believe in. And the mysteries fascinated me.'

Posy could imagine a smaller, skinnier Kit curled up in a corner of a London library, devouring a stack of old paperbacks. Maybe Lettice hadn't written for their generation, who hadn't even been born when she died, but somehow her books still spoke to them. Dahlia Lively belonged to Kit Lewis as much as she did to the likes of Marcus and Harry and Heather.

Kit stared up at Aldermere again, and Posy finally figured out what was bothering him.

'You know, what Anton said earlier, at lunch . . . he was out of order,' Posy said.

'He wasn't wrong though, was he?' Kit's smile was melancholy. 'I mean, this place really *doesn't* have any precedent for a DI Johnnie like me, does it?'

'And that's why the new film has to bring it up to date,' Posy told him.

'Right. Yeah. That's the hope.' But he didn't sound convinced.

'Kit, what were you and Anton arguing about before lunch?'

'We weren't arguing,' Kit said, too quickly. 'Just . . . disagreeing.'

'About?'

He sighed. 'Look, Anton's a great director. I've worked with him a few times now, and he always gets a good job done. It's just . . . this curse.'

'You think there really is one?' Posy hadn't taken him for the superstitious sort.

'Not like that.' He rolled his eyes, his smile amused. 'We've been unlucky, that's all. The car accident that took out Layla before filming, the fire, even the fraud investigation, they were all freak events. Unfortunate timing, that's all.'

'But?' Posy pressed, sensing there was something more he wasn't saying.

Kit pushed up from the bench and paced across the small grassed area inside the spiral. 'The script. Someone leaked that, someone involved with the film. That wasn't an accident.'

Posy thought about the script page in her bag, the photographs, and the person who'd be waiting for her at the folly. 'No. I guess it wasn't.'

'I was trying to convince Anton he should be taking it a little more seriously, I guess. But he told me to stop worrying.' Kit looked out of the spiral, towards the lawn they'd walked across. 'Heads up. Detectives incoming.'

He managed to settle back on the bench next to her before they heard a loud, 'Aha!'

Harry and Heather emerged into the centre of the spiral, both lifting their replica jewelled loupes to their eyes as they spied Posy and Kit sitting together.

In an instant, Kit transformed into another person – one she'd seen on screen a time or two before. Wrapping an arm around her shoulder, he pulled Posy close against him. His shirt was warm against her skin in the August sunshine.

'Hey! Can't a guy get a moment alone with his girl in this place?' He didn't quite wink at the detectives who'd discovered them, but he was playing to his audience.

'I'm sorry, young man,' Heather said, beaming broadly. 'But a murder has been committed at the stables!' She paused, and Posy gave an obligingly horrified gasp. 'We're going to have to ask you some questions.'

'Of course,' Posy replied, remembering her role in this game. 'Anything we can do to help.' That was what a murderer would say, right? They'd try to throw suspicion away from themselves by being as helpful as possible.

'Where were you at the time of the murder?' Harry asked, in a serious voice.

Posy was about to reply with the answer on her card, but Kit got there first.

'Well, when was the murder committed?' he asked.

Heather and Harry looked stumped. Clearly this hadn't come up in the game so far.

'Um, I think about twenty minutes ago?' Heather said after a long pause. 'I saw Clementine – the victim, I mean – through the window, talking to another girl, not long before that, so it must have been around then.'

'In that case, I was right here with my fiancé,' Posy replied. Then, turning to Kit with her best, blinding, film star smile she planted a kiss right on his unsuspecting lips. 'Wasn't I, darling?'

Kit blinked at her. 'Um, yes?'

Heather and Harry were still waiting for something more, Posy sensed, but she had no more information on her card. She nudged Kit in the ribs, and he remembered the game.

'Oh, right. Um, I did see someone else heading away from the stables on my way here though. A man in a red hat.'

'Did you see which way he went?' Heather asked, eagerly.

'Towards the cake stall, I think,' Kit replied.

Posy waited until Heather and Harry were out of earshot before saying, 'I thought *Caro* was by the cake stall.'

'What do I know? The card said to send them after a man in a red hat.' Kit's gaze slid sideways to look at her. 'I suppose yours said to kiss me?'

'Afraid so.'

'Hey, I'm definitely not complaining.' He waggled his eyebrows at her. 'And Anton will be thrilled to have found an actress who takes direction without arguing.'

'These days I'm mostly grateful to have a job,' she admitted.

Discovering that being a world-famous child didn't automatically translate into being a castable woman had been a blow. Coming on the heels of the revelation that her parents had already spent all the money she'd earned from the movies she'd made as a minor, it had almost been the end of her acting career.

Even now, Uncle Sol's words echoed in her ears at every rejection. *You were a cute kid, but you're not hot enough for lead roles. Plus some guys feel weird about lusting after girls they watched grow up. Give it a few years. Get some work done. Maybe you'll be ready for a comeback by the time you're twenty-five.*

Dahlia was her comeback. She'd done it without her parents, without her famous film critic godfather, without even getting a nose job – even if it had taken a few more years than Sol had predicted. And she wasn't going to lose it because of a few stupid photos and some two-bit blackmailer.

Kit turned slightly to meet her gaze. 'Well, *I'm* glad you've got this job,' he said. 'I think we're going to have a lot of fun, Posy Starling.'

Posy smiled. At least someone was glad she was here.

'Incoming,' she murmured to Kit, as she heard a voice reading the plaque outside the Murder Spiral aloud. It sounded like Christmas jumper guy – Ashok.

'Are you going to kiss me again?' Kit asked.

'Is that a problem?'

'Hell, no. I just want to be prepared. I can definitely do better than last time, now I know it's coming.'

Eight sets of detectives – and eight kisses – later, the clock over the stables chimed quarter to three, and Posy knew it was time to make her move. She had to figure out how to do it without Kit tagging along with her.

'Where are you off to?' Kit asked, as she grabbed her bag.

'Do you think I've got time to nip to the portaloos before the next set of investigators arrive? We must be nearly done by now, right?'

'I'd wait, if I were you. Those things looked grim. At least inside the house is clean.'

Posy shrugged, and edged towards the exit. 'When you gotta go.'

Kit's eyes started to narrow with suspicion, and she bolted out of the spiral before he could stop her, hurrying past the deadly flowers with her hands clasped to her chest again.

'Wait!' His voice echoed after her, but she ignored it – instead grabbing a passing fan investigator and yelling, 'He's in there!'

The fan rushed into the spiral, followed by everyone else within earshot. Posy smiled to herself, and pulled her map from her bag, tracing her route to the folly. It took her across the West Lawn at the side of the house, where many stalls were set up, past the stables and then towards the river, and the alder trees the house was presumably named for.

She set out, keeping one eye on the people around her. She spotted a man in a red hat across the way, surrounded by more wannabe detectives. She saw Marcus, walking towards the Murder Spiral, and ducked out of view in case he tried to send her back. And she saw Caro, still regaling a few last detective fans by the cake stall, probably with more of her stories of TV series gone by.

Away from the main convention area Posy passed the stable block, surrounded with vintage vehicles on display. She paused for a second, watching the day visitors inspecting the impeccably maintained cars, and Caro's motorcycle.

Clementine was in the stables, pretending to be dead; if Posy popped in there now she could beg for her phone back. Call . . . someone for help with this whole blackmail thing. But who? Her parents? Uncle Sol? Her agent? Damon?

Hell, no.

Despite the anxiety eating up her insides, she wasn't that desperate yet.

She walked through the stable yard, though, and saw Clementine lying prone on her bale of hay, pretending to be dead. The illusion was ruined when Posy realised she was whispering to the last couple of detectives, telling them to head to the Murder Spiral.

'Most helpful corpse ever!' one of them said, gleefully, to the next detective heading in. Marcus's idea that it would be over in an hour or so seemed optimistic, if there were still people starting their investigations now.

Posy glanced up at the stable-yard clock. Nearly three. No time to talk to Clementine.

Past the stables, the manicured lawns and tidy gravel paths gave way to longer stems of grass, and tracks that were more dirt than stone, the further she got from the house. She'd only been walking for ten minutes or so, but already she seemed a world away from the chaos of the convention. The sound of water lapping sluggishly against the banks, and the reeds in the stream rustling in the breeze, were overtaking the laughter and chatter of the stalls and the convention goers. As she reached the river path, the stone tower of the folly rose against the trees and blue skies.

Nausea rose in her throat at the thought of who could be waiting for her. But what else was there to do but find out?

She covered the remaining steps in a few long strides, and pulled open the wooden door before she could have second thoughts. Then she blinked.

'You?' she said, in astonishment, just as Rosalind King said, '*You?!*' in a considerably more scathing manner.

'You didn't send me this note.' Posy pulled the script page from her bag and held it up with the writing facing Rosalind.

Confusion cleared from Rosalind's expression, and she reached into the deep pocket of her jacket to retrieve her own note. 'And you didn't send me this one.'

'No.'

'With it being on the back of a page of the script, I'd assumed my correspondent was somebody connected to the film,' Rosalind said, drily. 'But I never did imagine you.'

There was a thinly veiled insult hidden in there somewhere, but Posy didn't bother teasing it out or being annoyed by it. Because if Rosalind hadn't sent the note, that meant they were still waiting for someone else.

She spun around as she heard movement outside, her muscles tensing. Behind her, she felt Rosalind moving closer. Who would want to get both her *and* Rosalind King in the same place at the same time, and why?

The door rattled open again and a figure appeared, shadowed by the sun behind it until it was almost unrecognisable.

Almost.

'Well!' Caro Hooper said, one hand on her hip and the other leg stretched out to the side – her classic Dahlia pose. 'What the absolute heck are you two doing here?'

Chapter Eight

'I don't believe in coincidences, Johnnie.' Dahlia dropped the corpse's
hand back on to its chest, and stood up again, one hand on her hip
and one foot pointing out. 'When it comes to murder, it seems to me
that everything happens for a reason.'

Dahlia Lively *in* A Lively Take On Life
***By* Lettice Davenport, 1931**

'You got a note too, I presume,' Rosalind said, moving out from
behind Posy now it was clear there was no danger. National treasure
she might be, but it seemed to Posy that Rosalind King was a bit of a
coward.

'I did. Inviting me to a secret assignation.' Caro waggled her
eyebrows. 'Obviously I couldn't pass *that* up.'

Posy rolled her eyes at Caro in full Dahlia mode, but caught hold
of the door as she sashayed inside, propping it open. She didn't like
the idea of anyone else sneaking up on them.

'Now, let's take a look at these notes,' Caro said.

There was a rickety table underneath the far window of the narrow
turret, and one by one they spread their notes on it to study. The
wording was the same on each. *Meet me at the folly at 3PM,* scrawled
on the back of the script text.

Caro's right eyebrow jumped higher and higher as she read her
way across the table – another Dahlia affectation.

'Same handwriting,' she said, more to herself than to Posy and Rosalind, it seemed, as she flipped the pages over. 'And consecutive pages of the script, although not a particularly interesting scene. Still, we have to assume the same person sent all three.'

Posy looked between the two older women. 'Did either of you . . . did your note come with photos?'

Caro's sharp gaze snapped to Posy's face. 'You too, huh?'

'Mine as well.' Rosalind sighed. 'So it's blackmail, then.'

What secrets were the other two Dahlias hiding, Posy wondered? She didn't ask to see their photos, though. Not when she had no intention of sharing hers.

'Who would want to blackmail all three of us, though?' Posy asked. 'I assumed it had something to do with the film – with the curse. But—'

'But I'm not *in* the film,' Caro finished for her. 'Yet, anyway. No, I'm afraid it seems this is nothing quite so interesting as that. Just ordinary, prosaic blackmail.'

'You mean they want money,' Rosalind said flatly.

'That's my guess.' Caro shrugged. 'People always think celebrities are rich.'

Posy thought of the dwindling balance of her bank account, and all the money her parents had taken from her before she was old enough to manage her own finances. 'Then where are they? If they want our money, why aren't they here? It's past three o'clock.'

All three of them turned as one towards the door. In a movie, that would have been the perfect cue for the mysterious note sender to reveal themselves.

The doorway remained stubbornly empty, the folly silent except for the faint noises drifting on the breeze from the convention.

'I don't think they're coming,' Posy said. 'Whoever they are . . . they wanted the three of us here together. I don't know why. Maybe they just wanted to scare us?'

'Or perhaps there's something we're supposed to see here.' Caro tapped a finger against her lips as she surveyed the small room. In a flurry of movement, she darted under the table, checking for secrets.

Posy followed her lead, checking behind the door, under the windowsills, while Rosalind tried the handle of the other door inside the room, which presumably led to the stairs up the turret.

'Locked,' Rosalind reported, then returned to the table, leaving Posy and Caro knocking on stones and searching ledges.

'Nothing.' Caro hopped up onto the edge of the table, which looked like it might be considering collapsing, but a stern look from Caro persuaded it otherwise. 'This must just be some sort of prank.'

Posy shook her head. 'I still think it has to do with the film. Why send the script pages, otherwise?'

'You mean this supposed curse?' Rosalind asked, eyebrows raised in amusement.

'No. Well, not really. But things *have* been going wrong for the production. I wouldn't be here if they weren't.'

'And she has a point about the pages from the script,' Caro added. 'That has to mean something, right? Of course, I was kind of hoping it might mean a part for me, but it seems not.'

'I assumed the script page meant that someone wanted to use my influence for . . . something to do with the film,' Rosalind admitted.

'And I thought it was a threat,' Posy said. 'That someone was out to ruin the film.'

Caro gave her a knowing look at that. 'Your photos are that bad, huh?'

Posy didn't answer.

'Caro's right. It's probably a prank,' Rosalind said decisively. 'Best forgotten quickly before anyone starts laughing.'

Posy thought of those shots of her slumped over the railings outside Damon's house. Someone had gone out of their way to get hold of those, she was sure. She had the feeling that the others' photos weren't so . . . career ending. 'No. I don't think so. The photos . . .' she stopped before giving away too much, but her face felt hot at the memory.

Caro tapped a finger against her chin again. 'Marcus. It has to be. He wants us flustered and running about trying to catch a black-mailer, so he can laugh and tell us it was all another one of his games.'

'Do you really think so?' Posy asked.

Caro nodded. 'Besides, it was Clementine who delivered the notes,' she said, absently, as she hopped off the table. 'Probably on Marcus's orders.'

Posy stared at her, aware that Rosalind was doing the same. Caro looked up from gathering the notes and handing them back.

'What? Oh? Didn't I mention that part?'

'No. You did not.' Rosalind's voice was clipped as she grabbed her note and strode to the doorway. 'You can explain as we walk.'

'Where are we going?' Caro asked. 'Oh, to find Clementine, right?'

'The stables, then,' Posy said. 'That's where she was last.'

Rosalind eschewed the river path, and led them across the grass towards the house. 'So. You saw Clementine leave the notes?'

'Well, not all of them, obviously. But I was behind you two head-ing into the house, remember? I had to go park up Susie, and then Marcus and I were . . . reminiscing about old times. So you were both in your rooms by the time I came up. I saw Clementine pushing an envelope under my door, but she didn't see me. I imagine she'd already done your two by then.'

'And you didn't think this was relevant?' Rosalind said, through gritted teeth.

Caro shrugged. 'Relevant, yes, but not necessarily *important.* I mean, if you had notes you wanted delivered to somebody staying at Aldermere this weekend, what would you do?'

'Give them to Clementine to pass on,' Posy guessed.

'Exactly.'

'Which means she must know who sent them in the first place.' Rosalind shot another glare at Caro without breaking stride. 'Which means we could have been asking her instead of playing Guess Who in the folly for the last while.'

'Unless they were handed to her through a volunteer, or left at the desk with a note, or—'

'Still,' Posy, aware that Rosalind's cheeks were reddening, interrupted Caro. 'Speaking to Clementine is a good place to start, right? Whether this is real blackmail or a stupid prank, I want to know who is behind it.'

'Marcus,' Caro said, stubbornly. 'I told you, it's got to be Marcus. No one else could have had those photos. And this is *exactly* the sort of thing he would find amusing.' Posy wondered what Caro's photos had been pictures of, that Marcus would have them and find them funny, but she didn't ask. If they could put an end to this without having to admit what they'd each been blackmailed about, that would be *ideal* in her book.

'It could have still been Clementine herself, though,' Rosalind argued. 'If Marcus had the photos she could have taken them easily enough.'

'But why?' Posy asked.

'Money, I imagine. Marcus doesn't seem the sort to pay a fantastic salary, and like Caro said, everyone believes that celebrities are loaded.'

'Then why not meet us?' Caro raised that single eyebrow again.

'She could have been held up doing the murder mystery,' Posy reasoned. 'There were still investigators arriving when I passed here on my way to the folly.'

'She probably had a copy of the script, too,' Rosalind added. 'The dinner tonight is based on the one in the movie, so they'd have needed it for that.'

'Marcus or Clementine,' Posy said, as they reached the stables. 'Blackmail or prank?'

'Let's go and find out,' Rosalind said.

All the vintage car enthusiasts must have found somewhere else to be because the stable yard was empty except for the display vehicles when they arrived.

'Where was Clementine playing dead?' Rosalind asked.

Posy pointed to the stall at the far end. Once, Aldermere must have owned a whole herd of horses, if the number of stalls were representative. Now, much of the stables seemed to be used for storage.

'Clementine?' Posy waited until she was right outside to call, not wanting to give her a chance to escape. But when she entered, the stall was empty. All that remained was the scent of fresh straw, and an abandoned map of Aldermere, marked with footprints on the floor. 'She's gone.'

Rosalind glared at Caro. 'If only we'd come straight here, we'd have caught her.'

Caro rolled her eyes. 'She's staying in the same house as us. I think we'll have another chance to talk to her.'

'Still, we could have tied this whole thing up by now if you'd told us what you knew right at the start,' Rosalind said. 'But no, you just had to play Dahlia, examining the whole damn folly for clues when you *knew* who'd sent them all along!'

Posy followed the bickering Rosalind and Caro out of the stable yard towards the West Lawn, playing over the strange events of the afternoon in her head.

'We can still go find her now,' Caro said.

'If she wants to be found,' Rosalind snapped back. 'There are a million places to hide at Aldermere if she doesn't.'

'What would *Dahlia* do?' Posy interrupted.

'Oh, that's easy,' Caro replied. 'She'd find the script the pages came from.'

'And examples of Clementine and Marcus's handwriting for comparisons, probably,' Rosalind added.

'Then we should do that, shouldn't we?' Posy suggested. Rosalind and Caro looked at her like she was missing something obvious. 'Oh. I could do that.'

Even if it turned out that Caro was right, and this *was* one of Marcus's pranks, she didn't want any reviews that said, *Handed a mystery on a plate, fledgeling Dahlia Posy Starling ignored it completely.*

'I'll get on with that, then,' she said. 'Finding the script, I mean. You two search for Clementine.'

'Oh, I think you might have something else to do first,' Rosalind said, archly, as Caro cupped a hand to her mouth and yelled, 'She's over here!'

Posy turned to see a mob of fan investigators approaching, Kit at the front wearing a Sherlock Holmes deerstalker hat he'd found somewhere, grinning wildly as he said, 'There she is! Arrest her!'

Chapter Nine

*'You know, people think the most interesting investigations are
always murder enquiries,' Johnnie said, as he studied the files in the
desk drawer. 'But a really clever theft can be just as engaging, done
right.'*

*Dahlia gave him a disbelieving look, before waving the piece of
paper she'd found half burned in the fireplace at him. 'You probably
won't be interested in this death threat over here then, will you?'*

Dahlia Lively *in* Diamonds for Dahlia
By Lettice Davenport, 1958

Posy was swept up on both sides by eager fans, Kit grinning as the
crowd barrelled towards the front of Aldermere House.

'Nice try escaping,' he said, cramming the deerstalker a little more
firmly on his head. 'Was that on your card too, or were you just
improvising?'

'Uh, improvising,' Posy replied. 'For all the good it did me.'

The driveway was crammed with vintage buses strung with
ribbons and bunting, presumably preparing to return those of the
day delegates who weren't booked in for the evening events to the
station. But nobody was getting on them.

Instead, the entire convention was gathered by the steps where
Marcus held court, arms spread wide as he addressed them, his dinner
jacket open and flapping in the light summer breeze. Hugh Davenport

stood beside him, hands in his pockets, smiling amiably, as if not really sure why he was there. Posy vaguely remembered something about him presenting the prize to the winner.

'Your endeavours have brought us here,' Marcus intoned grandly as he spotted them. 'Without your assistance, your investigations – your genius – a murderer might have gone free today!'

'How did you know it was me?' Posy asked, as Kit took her arm and held it tight against his side, sending a warmth through her that their staged kisses hadn't managed.

Kit waved his free hand towards the gathered throng. 'Finest investigative minds in the fictional business here this weekend, remember? Of course they figured it out.'

Beside her, Caro clucked her tongue disapprovingly. 'Have you been a naughty girl?'

'Don't worry,' Kit told her cheerfully. 'We're performing a citizen's arrest.'

Caro clapped her hands together with glee. 'How perfect! Let's go, then.'

Marcus was still performing for his audience as Kit hauled Posy up onto the steps, Caro beside them, every inch the Dahlia Lively she wasn't, any longer. Rosalind followed behind them.

This isn't how this was meant to go, Posy thought, looking at the crowd. *She* was supposed to be the only Dahlia at this convention. The one who would win over the fans with her deductive skill, or her ability to look good in a 1930s evening dress, or *something*.

Instead, here she was, being mock-arrested for a crime that Dahlia would never have considered committing.

Not that the audience seemed to mind. They cheered, as Kit pinned both her arms behind her back – loosely, but making it look good all the same, she suspected.

'As so many of you intrepid detectives deduced, by process of elimination, our murderer today was indeed . . .' Marcus left a rather unnecessary dramatic pause, since she'd already been exposed and arrested. 'Posy Starling!'

A host of boos, worthy of a pantomime villain, filled the air around Aldermere. Marcus waited patiently for them to pass, a pleased smile on his face, before he spoke again.

'And so, I am delighted to announce that the winner of our competition is . . .'

Another dramatic pause from Marcus was ruined by the crash of the front door slamming open. Posy twisted in Kit's arms to find Isobel standing in the doorway behind them, her expression thunderstruck.

'Don't let anybody leave!' Isobel's voice was shrill, her alarm clear.

'Why? Whatever's happened?' Marcus asked.

'Somebody,' Isobel said, her blue eyes huge and damp as she looked at her husband, 'has stolen Lettice Davenport's jewelled jeweller's loupe!'

'What?' Hugh turned to Isobel, as a murmur went up throughout the crowd, spreading the news. 'How could you let this happen?'

'Uh, is that car supposed to be leaving?' Kit pointed over Posy's shoulder. She followed his finger with her gaze and saw one of the vintage cars from the display area driving along the path around the West Lawn and the convention stalls towards the main driveway.

She frowned. The figure in the driver's seat with the victory rolls and the mustard silk scarf was unmistakable. 'Is that Clementine?'

Where was she going? Why would she leave now, if she was the one blackmailing them? Unless she had the photos with her and was leaving to sell them . . .

'Somebody stop her!' Isobel shrieked, like Posy desperately wanted to do.

Hugh placed his hands on his wife's arm to lower her accusing finger as she pointed at the car. 'No, no, it's okay, dear. Clementine called me. Apparently she's had a message about some sort of family emergency. She asked if she could borrow a car to get to the station. Of course I said yes.' He gazed after Clementine as she beeped the ancient horn to part the crowd, and drove the vintage car over the lawns, around the waiting buses, and towards the main gates. 'I, uh, didn't imagine she'd take that one, though,' he added, with a nervous laugh.

'Well, she didn't tell *me* she was going,' Marcus grumbled. 'Though she did mention that she had family in the area. I can't imagine what kind of emergency would take her away from the convention now, after all the hard work she's put in to making it a success.'

A family emergency. Posy's heart rate started to return to normal. If that was true, it would explain why Clementine hadn't met them. She had more important things to worry about than blackmail.

It didn't stop the threat of those photos getting out hanging over Posy's head, though.

'I'm glad she didn't decide to take Susie.' Shading her eyes, Caro watched as Clementine passed the Gate House and drove onto the main road. Then she turned back to Isobel, one hand on her hip, one foot pointing out, and Posy could tell that she'd switched into full Dahlia mode. 'Now, what's all this about Lettice's loupe?'

'I told you. It's been stolen,' Isobel snapped. 'And nobody is leaving Aldermere until I am certain they haven't taken it. I want every bag searched before anyone gets on a bus. And if we don't find it, you can be sure I'll be calling the police and giving them the details of that car.'

Isobel glared at her husband, then looked pointedly at Marcus.

'Ah, right. I'll get on that now.' He lumbered down the steps towards the waiting buses to talk to the drivers.

'It must have been taken during the house tours!' Ashok said, excitedly. 'No one else was allowed upstairs in the house unless they were on a tour.' Apart from Clementine, of course, but that didn't seem to trouble Ashok.

'Which means it could have been one of us!' Felicity added. Instantly, they were discussing theories, Kit in the middle of it all adding alien conspiracies to the mix.

'That's a very conveniently timed emergency, don't you think?' Caro murmured from beside Posy. 'What do you reckon? Lost her bottle for blackmail and did a bunk with the magnifying glass instead?'

'Or maybe she realised what she was caught up in and decided to run before she got in any deeper,' Rosalind suggested.

'Either way, I think a lot of people would like a word with her. Me included.' Posy surveyed the crowds, humming with theories and questions, while Rosalind and Caro got drawn into the VIP debate about who could be responsible. It was probably time to get out of there before anyone remembered that she'd been on the tour too. She was already branded a murderer; she had no desire to add thief to her résumé for the weekend.

Posy headed into the hallway, pausing at the convention desk as she spotted Clementine's clipboard sitting there, abandoned. The front page was a copy of the day's schedule, liberally annotated in Clementine's handwriting; Posy had seen her jotting notes on it herself.

She picked it up. Then she unfolded the note from her bag, and compared the two.

The same handwriting. Clementine had written the notes all three Dahlias had received.

One question answered. So many more to go.

An hour later, Posy still didn't have any answers, but she was a little better educated on the life and times of Lettice Davenport, and why the China Room was so damn creepy.

Sixty minutes of solitude to skim through the books she'd accumulated gave her more confidence about the next item on her agenda, too. The film panel, in the main marquee out on the South Lawn. This time, she hoped she was ready for whatever the fans had to throw at her.

Making her way outside, her spirits lifted further as the festival-like atmosphere surrounded her. The tea and cake stalls had mostly given way to mobile bars, now that the evening programme was beginning. People sat on folding chairs clutching wine glasses and watching some sort of scene re-enactment going on in a quadrangle of grass between other food stalls. If she ignored the police officer talking to Isobel on the driveway, presumably about the missing magnifying glass, everything could be perfectly normal.

Posy passed a small queue waiting for a talk on the History of Poison in one of the fringe tents, and made a beeline for the big, white tent in the centre of the South Lawn. Outside stood Kit, hands in the pockets of his trousers, slouched against one of the wrought-iron lamp posts that lined the paths of the formal gardens. His nonchalant stance and teasing smile were drawing plenty of approving glances from the passing visitors.

'Where have you been hiding out?' he asked, as she approached. 'You weren't mad about the citizen's arrest thing, were you? I had to fend off another six sets of investigators after you left the Murder Spiral. You deserved to be arrested.'

'It's a hard life being a star. And no, I wasn't mad.'

He pushed away from the lamp post and followed her. 'So, want to tell me where you ran off to in such a hurry?'

'I told you. Needed the loo.'

'And you somehow returned from the opposite direction with Rosalind King and Caro Hooper in tow?' Kit's eyebrows arched with disbelief.

'Don't you know women always have to go to the bathroom in packs?' It was a stereotype she usually hated, but it served her purpose now.

Kit didn't buy it. 'Fine, you keep your secrets. Just . . . if it was anything to do with the film, you'd tell me?'

'Of course.' It wasn't really a lie, she justified to herself. The blackmail was personal, not professional.

The fact that the note was written on the script *could* be a coincidence, right?

A harried convention assistant in a waistcoat appeared in the doorway to the marquee, glancing around, obviously looking for them. Normally, Posy would have expected them to be fetched from the green room, ready for their appearance. But Marcus was so insistent on providing access to the stars of the event, she wasn't sure there *was* a green room.

She waved to the assistant, whose face relaxed with relief as Kit and Posy headed over. Almost before she knew it, they were sat on the long table on the stage, with Anton and Libby beside them.

This was what she'd come to Aldermere for, Posy reminded herself, as the nerves threatened to overcome her. To win over the many, many people who loved the Lettice Davenport books so much that the characters came alive for them, and the world felt real. Those people who wanted to be transported back to a simpler time, to experience danger and death from the safety of their own armchair, between the pages of a well-loved book. The people who dreamt of having the comebacks and insight of Dahlia, or the steadfast skills of Johnnie. Not to mention the wardrobes.

It was all about the fans.

And this was her best chance to convince them that Dahlia was safe in her hands.

'Welcome, everyone!' Marcus took the stage beside them, still dressed in his butler outfit. 'Welcome, to what must be the highlight of today's events!'

There was a half-hearted cheer at that. Posy shared a look with Kit. There was a long way to go with this lot.

'So much of this weekend is about appreciating the past,' Marcus mused aloud to the audience. 'About celebrating the world that Lettice Davenport lived in, as well as the one she created for us. But the joy of the Dahlia Lively mysteries, of the Lady Detective herself perhaps, is that they are timeless. Each generation discovers them anew and wonders at their cleverness, their ingenuity – and, of course, their inimitable style. And now, as we stride into the twenty-first century, almost a hundred years after Lettice started writing, it is time for a whole new generation of fans to discover the magic. And today, I am delighted to introduce you to the people working so hard to make that happen. Anton Martinez, our illustrious director!'

Anton stood and gave a little bow, earning himself a bigger cheer.

'Libby McKinley, one of the writers transforming Dahlia's adventures for the big screen!' Libby gave an uncertain little wave but didn't stand – probably because of the coffee stains on her skirt – and received a smattering of applause.

'Next up, our very own Detective Inspector Johnnie – Kit Lewis!' Kit stood, beaming, arms outstretched to welcome the much louder cheer that accompanied his introduction. After all, *he* was a household name, a rising star, someone everyone wanted to see more of.

Posy held her breath as she waited to hear her name.

She wasn't a rising anything, and there was a good chance that Uncle Sol had been right all those years ago, and people were tired of her already. *It's always sad to see a star past her prime trying to relive her glory days, and Posy Starling in The Lady Detective only proves that her best days were over before she finished puberty.*

'And finally, Dahlia Lively herself – Posy Starling!'

Posy stood, smile plastered in place on her bright red lips, her hands on her hips, like the picture of Dahlia on the cover of the first edition of *Never Underestimate A Lady* she'd picked up in Lettice's study, tea dress bedamned.

And the crowd bought it. They cheered, maybe not quite as loud as they had for Kit, but not far off. She'd still have to work to win them over, but they were giving her the benefit of the doubt, for now.

And that was all she needed.

Marcus chaired the panel. He threw a number of soft questions at them, most of which Anton grabbed and ran with. His answers didn't always have a great deal to do with what Marcus had asked, but he got across his favourite buzz words, so he seemed happy enough.

Then Marcus threw the floor open for questions. Anton fielded a lot of them again, and since few came to Posy directly, she was able to smile and nod and add the odd comment without embarrassing herself.

Answering a question from an aspiring screenwriter, Libby spoke softly but confidently about how she approached the challenge of transforming a book into a film script, focusing on her efforts to stay true to the original story and feel while still making it fresh and new, and not mentioning how she'd had to tear up the previous script and start again from scratch when she'd been brought on board.

'And is it true that you worked on the script for *The Two Doves*?' the girl in the audience asked, before the mic could be taken away for the next question. 'And *Gates of Hell*?' She'd named two of the most talked-about movies of the last couple of years, and that set a buzz going amongst the crowd.

'I did, yes,' Libby replied.

Anton grabbed the mic. 'You might not know this, and you might not always see her name in the credits, but basically every script you've loved over the last ten years, Libby has probably been involved with.'

The questioning moved on, but Posy didn't miss the surprised look Libby gave Anton after his praise.

Answering a question on how Anton's vision for the film was bringing Dahlia into the twenty-first century, Kit talked about how Anton's non-traditional casting had opened up opportunities for him and other actors of colour.

'I know that, for a lot of fans, Detective Inspector Johnnie will always be Frank Kaye, or Carl Richards,' he said, naming the actors who had played the role opposite Rosalind and Caro. 'And that maybe for some, he will always be white. And, in case you haven't noticed, I'm not.' There was a slightly awkward chuckle from the audience. 'I *am* British, though, not that it should matter. My dad's family come from Scotland originally, and my mum's grandparents moved here from Uganda.

'But I'm not here to talk about *me*, I'm here to talk about Johnnie and Dahlia. And I think the brilliance of Lettice Davenport's books is how each generation finds something new in them. They still speak to us, like, ninety-plus years after the first ones were written. She wrote for her audience back then, reflecting the world she lived in. So we're making this film for our audience now, and reflecting *our* world. Even if we are doing it in a period context.' He gave a small, self-deprecating laugh, which was almost lost in the whoop of support and cheers from the crowd. 'If that makes any sense at all.'

'Makes perfect sense to me,' the audience member who'd taken the microphone for the next question said. 'But what about the character itself? What are you looking forward to about playing DI Johnnie Swain?'

'Honestly? It's refreshing to play a male lead who doesn't have all the answers,' Kit said. 'I mean, he goes in there thinking he's going to solve everything, right? But eventually he has to learn to trust that Dahlia has much better instincts when it comes to murder than he does.'

That got another laugh.

'They're such opposites, it's going to be a fun dynamic to work with, I can tell. They don't like each other much at the start . . .' He snuck a flirtatious glance at Posy. 'But as the film goes on, they learn to respect and even like each other, long before they ever share their first kiss. I like that slow burn aspect of their relationship, and I'm excited to see how Libby works it into the script.'

'So you haven't read the final script yet?' his questioner piped up from the audience.

Kit laughed. 'I don't think anybody has! Well, apart from Anton, and the family. Libby? You said it's done, right?'

Libby nodded but didn't say anything else. Anton didn't respond.

Posy couldn't resist. Marcus was watching. If he had anything to do with her blackmail note . . .

'I haven't read the whole thing,' she said, suddenly. 'But I do have one page of it right here . . .'

She pulled the page from the bag at her side, then held it up in the air, making sure the crowd didn't get a look at the handwritten scrawl on the back. While the audience gasped at it – many trying to get a photo on their phone that they could zoom in on to read – Posy studied Marcus's reaction.

Nothing. Either he was a better actor than she'd given him credit for, or the script page didn't mean anything to him. Looked like it was all Clementine, then. And she was gone, on the run from the police. Surely she wouldn't try and do anything with the photos now? Not when it could lead the police right to her?

A lightness rushed over Posy at the thought, and she grinned. 'How much do you guys want to read this?' She laughed, and the audience cheered appreciatively. 'Sorry, sorry. No can do. It's top secret until the boss says otherwise.' She slipped the page back into her bag, ignoring the good-natured booing.

She'd been so busy watching Marcus, she hadn't been paying attention to the people sitting on the table beside her.

Anton was fuming, she could tell that without even looking directly at him. An aura of anger surrounded him, and she could feel the tension in his back, the popping of his jaw, all the way from the other end of the table. Angry because she'd seen the script before she was supposed to, or because she was teasing the crowd? Or for some other reason? From the way he was glaring at her, she had a feeling she might find out as soon as the panel was over.

Kit looked confused, and perhaps a little envious. Libby, though, looked scared. And given Anton's thunderous face, she didn't blame her.

'Okay, okay. Last question,' Marcus called, as the crowd calmed.

'What do you say to people who claim the movie is cursed?' The question rang out around the suddenly silent marquee.

Posy held her breath and waited for Anton's answer. Because of course Anton would be the one to answer this question – it was his movie.

Only, he didn't. He stayed silent so long, that Kit grabbed the microphone and responded.

'I think it makes a great story,' he said, earning a laugh from the crowd. 'I mean, it's a murder mystery, it's got a hell of a lot of history behind it, I can see why people want to believe in a curse. It adds a little extra magic, right? But in my experience, what looks like magic on the screen, or even curses in the media, is usually a lot of graft.'

That seemed to satisfy the crowd, even if it didn't satisfy Posy one bit. It made her think.

A lot of graft. Was he right? Was someone working to make it seem like the film was cursed? And if so, who? Why?

Marcus launched into his wind-up spiel, reminding visitors that the evening buses would be waiting to take them back to the station shortly, and to meet at the front of the house. Just like that, the panel was over, and she'd survived it.

Glancing across the stage she saw Anton and Libby deep in conversation, the director looming over Libby as he stood beside her, his face thunderous. Time to escape, before he turned that rage on her.

Posy made her way across the lawn, around the side of the house and skipped up the steps into the main hallway of Aldermere House, where she checked the schedule on the reception desk. She had an hour before she was due for pre-dinner drinks in the library, apparently.

She could corner Rosalind and Caro then, tell them they could stop worrying. She'd figured it all out. Clementine had sent the notes, then stolen the magnifying glass and done a runner – probably because she thought she was about to get caught by Isobel – so hadn't met them at the folly. Now the police were after her, they could leave it to the professionals, and get back to what they were there to do – playing Dahlia for the fans.

Posy was still congratulating herself on her deductive skills when she walked into the China Room and found Lettice Davenport's priceless jeweller's loupe sitting on the dressing table.

Chapter Ten

'Everyone has secrets. And until you uncover them all, you can't know which ones are worth killing for.'

Dahlia Lively *in* The Lady Detective
By Lettice Davenport, 1929

Posy entered the library for pre-dinner drinks, dressed in another of Anton's hideous tea dresses, but with diamante combs holding back her dark blonde hair, and freshly applied bright red lipstick giving her confidence. God knew she needed it.

After the initial shock of finding the stolen loupe in her room had worn off, it hadn't taken Posy long to take stock of her options – and realise she hated all of them.

The obvious thing to do was to return the magnifying glass to Isobel, and hope she believed her when Posy explained how it came into her possession. Except Posy had no confidence that she would. While the reputation she'd blazed for herself back in LA hadn't included shoplifting, she'd found that when people knew you'd committed one illegal act – say, drug taking – they always assumed you were capable of others. Posy couldn't imagine the Davenport family letting her star as Dahlia if they thought she'd tried to steal from them – which would be taken as another sign of the curse on the movie.

But she'd considered handing the loupe over, all the same. Until she'd realised something else.

If Clementine *wasn't* on the run with the magnifying glass . . . why had she left? Was it really because of a family emergency? Was this theft linked somehow to the blackmail photos she'd sent the three of them? Or was someone here at Aldermere trying to frame her? There had to be a reason it had been left in her room, didn't there?

Which led her to option number two: holding onto the stolen loupe and hoping it led her to some answers to the many questions she had about what was going on at Aldermere that weekend. She didn't like it, but she liked it more than being arrested for a crime she didn't commit or – worse – getting fired by Anton for bringing the film into disrepute.

And so, the magnifying glass was safely stashed in a shoe at the bottom of her wardrobe until she figured out what to do with it. The note that had accompanied it had joined the collection of clues she was carrying around in her bag.

NOT MY DAHLIA, it said, in block capitals so even and precise that she couldn't tell if it was written by the same hand as the other note, which had been lower case and joined up. It looked completely different, but maybe that was the idea. Maybe Clementine was still here somewhere, playing some game that Posy didn't understand.

There are a million places you can hide at Aldermere. What if Clementine was taking advantage of one of those places?

What if this was about something more than blackmail?

And if it wasn't Clementine who'd stolen the jeweller's loupe and left it for her, it had to be someone staying in Aldermere. Without one of those all-access-pass silver wristbands, they'd never have been allowed inside in the first place. Even the daytime convention staff, she'd noticed, were confined to the entrance hall, the kitchens and the rooms where meals were being served.

Which meant the thief was here, now, in this room.

She eyed the gathered crowd, all dressed in their finest vintage garb, pearls shimmering in the light from the wall lamps, feathers primped and eyes lined. She could have been looking at a film set. *Her* film set, or at least one of Caro's or Rosalind's. None of it felt real.

And yet, one of these people was a thief. And they were trying to frame her.

This didn't feel like a prank anymore, if it ever had.

Through the doorway from the library into the Sun Room next door, she saw Marcus's black butler's jacket and bald head. Marcus. And he was talking to Caro – Caro who had been so sure he had to be behind the photos she'd received. With Clementine gone, he might be the only person who knew what was going on.

Posy darted across the room, before realising that her sharp, speedy movements would draw more attention to her, not less. She slowed, taking one of those deep, mindful breaths her yoga teacher insisted on. She knew almost everyone in the room, she realised, by sight if not by name. They'd been around her all day – on the tour, at the panel, at lunch or coffee. Whoever was behind this, she *knew* them now. And that made it scarier.

Posy paused in the doorway, surveying the situation beyond. Most guests had stayed in the library with the pre-dinner drinks, so Marcus and Caro were alone, deep in conversation. About blackmail, perhaps?

Marcus spotted her first. 'Ah, Posy! Don't you look lovely?'

Caro turned to face her too. With her dark hair pinned up in perfect waves, and her gold and ruby-red evening dress clinging to her curves, Caro was every inch Dahlia again, down to the fan in her hand that she snapped closed as she saw Posy.

'Sorry. I didn't mean to interrupt.' Posy started to back away, but Marcus stopped her.

'No, no, not at all! Come and join us. Can I get you a drink?'

'Not for me, thank you,' Posy replied. 'I was just wondering if you'd heard from Clementine yet. I was supposed to, well, talk to her about something this afternoon.'

'Yes, she left me a *message,* blasted girl.' He fished his phone out of his pocket and checked the screen. Of course *he* wasn't bound by the no phone rule. 'Listen to this!'

He tapped the screen a couple of times, and suddenly Clementine's Scottish accent filled the room.

'Hi Marcus. So sorry I had to run. Bit of a family emergency, you see. I tried to find you. I'll come back as soon as I can and explain everything properly. Sorry again.'

'Can you believe it?' Marcus slipped the phone back into his pocket. 'And I can tell you now, Isobel is *not* pleased. Once we'd finished searching bags for the missing jeweller's loupe, she realised that one less person at dinner was going to mess up all her hard work on the seating plans, and got mad all over again.' He sighed. 'She was still reworking them when I came down for dinner. I suppose someone better go and check on her.'

'And that person should be you.' Caro gave him a little push towards the door. 'Come on, I'll protect you.'

Posy turned to watch them leave, and saw Libby backing away from the doorway, almost colliding with Rosalind. Her face was pale and troubled. Posy was about to follow her and ask if everything was okay after her stunt at the panel, when Kit slipped in through the doorway and handed her a glass of champagne.

'*There* you are. I need you to save me from the couple in tweed. I think they're trying to *collect* me or something.'

Posy placed the glass on the nearest shelf before she was tempted to take a sip. 'Collect you? I thought they were fundamentally opposed to the idea of you as Johnnie?'

'Obviously I won them over with my charm and rapier-sharp wit.'

'And now you're regretting it.'

'Yes.' Kit reached out and grabbed her hand. 'Come on. Let's go mess with the table plans so I don't have to sit anywhere near them.'

'I can't.' She smiled apologetically and shook her hand free, her mind whirring with thoughts that had nothing to do with dinner. 'I've got something else I need to do.'

She'd been led around like she was on a leash all day – from Anton dressing her, to the house tour, the note, the meeting at the folly – even Marcus's murder mystery and her arrest! Everything about the day felt staged, like she was an actress playing a part she hadn't even seen the script for.

And Posy was done with it.

'Okay, now *that* looks like a thinking face,' Kit observed. 'It's making me nervous.'

Posy shook her head. 'I'm done thinking.'

It was time for action.

So Posy asked herself again: *What would Dahlia do?*

The latest film version of The Lady Detective *is made all the more interesting by news of its star actress' descent into a life of crime . . .*

Uncle Sol's critique filled her head as she climbed the stairs to the second floor, but she pushed it aside. Posy might not have a great handle on the character of Dahlia Lively yet, but she knew one thing. If the Lady Detective was being blackmailed and framed, she wouldn't sit around waiting for things to get worse. And neither would Posy.

Clementine was her only real suspect – and Clementine was gone. But her stuff wasn't.

It had been easy enough to find out which room was hers from the list behind the reception desk. Now Posy hoped that nobody caught her breaking in.

Except, as she turned the corner at the top of the attic stairs towards Clementine's room, she discovered she wasn't the only person who'd had the same idea. Ashok, his Christmas jumper exchanged for a shirt and tie, twisted the handle to Clementine's door and pushed, humphing with frustration when it held firm.

'Lost your key?' Posy asked, wondering if he'd lie and claim that it was his room.

His dark eyes wide, he looked up at her, his hand falling away from the door instantly. 'Oh! Miss Starling.'

'Call me Posy, please.' Miss Starling made her sound like all those awful reviews in her head.

His face lit up for a moment at her invitation, then fell again. Shoving his hands in his pockets, he said. 'Um, it's not my room. I was looking for Clementine. I knocked, but there was no answer.'

'She's not here.' Posy stepped closer to the door. 'She left for a family emergency this afternoon, remember?'

'Yes, but, I thought she might have come back? And I didn't see her downstairs, so . . .' So he came to try and break into her room, she finished for him in her head. Or maybe that was her own guilt speaking.

'Why were you looking for her?' Posy asked.

'She, well, she has my phone. All of our phones, I guess.' Ashok looked both ways along the corridor then lowered his voice. 'She told me to find her this evening and she'd get it back to me.'

Since she'd told Posy more or less the same, she had no reason to doubt him. 'Well, it doesn't look like she's coming back tonight,' Posy said, and watched Ashok's shoulders droop. 'But she promised me the same thing, so I'm sure she wouldn't mind if we helped ourselves . . .'

She hadn't thought Ashok's eyes could grow any wider. She'd been wrong.

'But . . . the door's locked.'

Posy brushed past him and crouched in front of the keyhole. The door locks of Aldermere House were old, and easily manipulated from either side of the door. She'd checked hers after she found the magnifying glass, and realised that almost anyone could have broken in to leave it there. All it took was a little fiddling with one of the bobby pins in her hair, and the lock tumbled into place. Another skill learned on a film set put to good use.

Posy pushed the door open. 'Done. You wait by the door while I search.'

Ashok stood nervously in the open doorway as she scanned the room. All of Clementine's stuff seemed to be still there, which tied in with her phone message saying she'd be back soon. But Posy wasn't willing to wait.

There was no sign of their phones, or a lockbox for keeping them in, out in clear view, so Posy searched the drawers, wardrobe and bedside table, hoping to turn up, if not her phone, then some evidence of blackmail or *something*.

Nothing.

Next, she checked all the usual hiding spots – the sort of places she'd hid her diary or other private things in hotel rooms from her parents. The top of the wardrobe. Under the bed. It wasn't until she slipped her hand under the pillows that she found anything of interest at all.

The script for *The Lady Detective* was a big hunk of paper, bound with a simple card cover. Posy flicked through it quickly, knowing that Ashok was shifting from foot to foot in the doorway.

There. She stuck a finger in and opened it fully at the spot where the page numbers jumped. Where three pages were missing.

And stuck on the previous page, was a neon Post-it note that read: *Should we warn them?* in the same handwriting as the note she'd received with her photos. Clementine's handwriting.

'Posy? Are you nearly done?' Ashok's whisper from the door broke her out of her trance. She slammed the script shut and shoved it into her bag before hurrying out again.

'No sign of the phones, I'm afraid.' She hoped her words sounded relaxed, despite the terror racing through her veins. 'She must have stored them somewhere else.'

'Damn,' Ashok said. 'I really, really need to check my emails.'

'You and me both.' She flashed him a conspiratorial grin as they descended the stairs. 'Hey, could you, like, not mention this to anyone? The whole B&E thing?'

Ashok shrugged. 'Who'd believe me anyway?'

'You'd be surprised what people will believe when it comes to me.'

Chapter Eleven

'I always find that people say the most fascinating things when they believe no one is really listening,' Dahlia said. 'And inane dinner party chatter is the perfect *example of that.'*

Dahlia Lively *in* Dining with Death
By Lettice Davenport, 1954

Posy and Ashok went their separate ways as they re-entered the library. Pre-dinner drinks were still under way, which hopefully meant she had time to talk to Caro and Rosalind before they went through to the dining room. She needed to trust somebody, and they were in the same boat as her with the blackmail, at least.

'Posy, darling! You look as though you've seen a ghost. Where's your drink?' Caro asked.

'Oh, I don't have one.' At her admission, Caro raised an arm and in a second a waiter was beside them with a tray. Caro took a fresh glass for each of them, depositing her empty one on the tray and dismissing the waiter with a nod. Posy twisted to catch him and switch her own glass for an orange juice.

'What's the matter?' Marcus asked from beside Caro. 'Isobel been pestering you about that damn magnifying glass too?'

'It hasn't been found yet, then?' Posy asked, widening her eyes as if she was as clueless to its whereabouts as everyone else.

'No sign.' Marcus shook his head.

'Hugh is convinced it must have been one of the day visitors,' Caro explained. 'Even though none of them were allowed in the house unless Isobel was with them on the house tour.'

'And Isobel still thinks it was Clementine, of course,' Marcus added, with a heavy sigh. 'Which I have to admit is the most likely explanation, much as I hate to say it. She's already given the police Clementine's description, and the details of the car.'

'Tricky,' Caro said, but the gleam in her eye suggested it was more exciting than distressing.

'Everyone looks very fine tonight, don't they?' Posy said, looking around the library.

'Always the favourite part of one of these events, isn't it, Caro?' Marcus said. 'Everyone loves the chance to pretend they really are part of Dahlia's world.'

'Have you done many of these conventions together, then?'

'Oh dozens, haven't we, Caro?' Marcus nudged Caro familiarly, and her smile slipped for a second.

'Not quite *that* many, I don't think. But yes, I've appeared at a few of them that Marcus has arranged.' The fake fur stole around her shoulders – too hot for a summer night, but perfect for the dress she wore it with – slipped slightly, and Caro adjusted it to sit right. 'It's always a nice opportunity to meet the fans.'

'And slip back into the role of Dahlia again, right?' His elbow pressed against her arm again, and this time, Posy was sure she saw Caro flinch. 'Sometimes, I swear I don't know where Caro Hooper ends and Dahlia Lively begins!'

It was an observation Posy had made herself, but even she could see that Caro didn't appreciate it being made aloud.

'Were we not supposed to have gone through to dinner by now?' Posy asked.

Marcus rolled his eyes. 'Isobel is still fussing with the damn seating plans. Wouldn't let me help.' He checked his watch. 'It is getting on, though. I'd better go chivvy her along.'

'I need to talk to you,' Posy murmured as he walked away. 'And to Rosalind, too.'

Caro raised her eyebrows. 'Do you now? What about, exactly?'

'Dahlia business.'

Caro's eyebrows went from curious to a full, surprised arch, and she slipped a hand through Posy's crooked arm. 'Oh, well, in that case . . .'

They skirted the edge of the room to where Rosalind was in conversation with Anton, and looked meaningfully at her until she excused herself. 'What do you two want?'

Posy checked around them. Still too many people. 'I need to talk to you both. In private.'

Rosalind glanced at Caro. 'Come on, then. We'll go through to the Snug. That's where Hugh keeps the best drinks, anyway.'

The Snug was at the front of the house, looking out over the driveway.

'Have you been here often before?' Posy asked, as Rosalind set about fixing them cocktails from the drinks cabinet shaped like a globe that sat beside a trio of seating – two leather wing chairs and a chaise longue. 'Ah, not for me, thank you. I don't drink, actually.'

'A mocktail, then.' Rosalind reached for another bottle from the lowest shelf, and started mixing something else. She handed the resulting bright pink concoction to Posy, who frowned at the colour and sipped it cautiously.

'I'm an old friend of the family,' Rosalind said, answering Posy's question as she tipped the gin bottle a little more sharply into her own glass. 'I've stayed here often.'

'Plus she was engaged to the lord of the manor, back in the day. What?' Caro asked as Rosalind gave her a sharp look. 'It's hardly a secret now, is it? Practically common knowledge. They met on the set of the original movie, you see,' she said to Posy. 'Love at first sight, they say.'

'If it had been love, we'd have married.' Rosalind's tone was dry. 'As it was, we remained good friends for the last forty years, and that has served us both far better. And we're not here to talk about ancient history now, are we?'

'I suppose not.' Caro sounded moderately regretful about that as she took her drink. 'So, what *are* we here to talk about?'

'When I got back to my room this afternoon, after the film panel, someone had put the missing magnifying glass on my dressing table,' Posy said.

Caro and Rosalind were trained actresses, used to reacting to the unexpected as if they meant it to happen all along. Caro raised her eyebrows a little, and Rosalind took another sip of her gin cocktail.

'Interesting,' Caro said. 'Any note?'

Posy nodded, and pulled it from her bag to show to them. '*Not my Dahlia*. In block capitals.'

'No way to tell if it's the same handwriting as the first note, then,' Rosalind guessed.

Posy gave another, glum nod. 'I think someone is trying to frame me.'

'Then we need to find out who put it there,' Caro said, as if it were the simplest thing in the world. A warm feeling settled over Posy at the idea of not having to do this alone. But then the realities settled in.

'How?' Posy asked. 'I didn't exactly bring a fingerprint kit with me, you know.'

'We don't need it,' Rosalind said, sanguinely. 'Dahlia never had any of that stuff – no forensics, no DNA, not even fingerprints usually. She used her brain, and her knowledge of people. We can do the same.'

'There's more.' Posy pulled the script from her bag. 'I found this in Clementine's room.'

'You searched her room?' Caro looked impressed. 'You really are taking this Dahlia thing seriously.'

'I was looking for my phone,' Posy admitted. 'She told me to find her and get it back this afternoon. But look at the script. It's missing the same pages we were sent.'

'Another indication that Clementine sent the notes herself.' Rosalind took the script and ran a finger down the torn edge of the missing pages.

'Oh! And I compared the handwriting on the notes we received to Clementine's on her clipboard, and it was a match.'

'You have been busy,' Caro murmured.

'I figured that she'd sent the blackmail notes, then stolen the magnifying glass and realised she needed to run before she got caught so faked the family emergency, and that's why she didn't meet us. The jewels on that thing are probably worth more than she could get out of us, anyway.' Posy's shoulders sagged. 'But then I found the magnifying glass.' And her carefully worked out theory fell apart.

The three Dahlias sat in silence as they considered the evidence.

'Could she have stolen the magnifying glass and hidden it in your room to frame you before she left?' Caro suggested. 'And that's why she wanted us out of the way at the folly – as a distraction while she did it?'

Posy shook her head. 'It wasn't there when I went to my room after Isobel announced it was stolen. Only when I went back after the film panel.'

'Unless she doubled back after we saw her leave?' Rosalind said. 'But if she didn't, then we have to assume that she left because of an actual emergency and that's why she didn't meet us.'

'Even if that emergency was chickening out on blackmailing us,' Caro muttered.

'In which case, the thief is still here and wants me to take the fall for their crime,' Posy finished.

'Made any enemies lately?' Caro smiled brightly as she asked the question.

'I was hoping not,' Posy replied. 'But I guess it's possible that one of the fans just hates me because I'm, well—'

'Not their Dahlia.' Rosalind waved a hand at the note.

'I was going to say "me". But that, too.' Taking the script back from Rosalind, she flicked through to the missing pages. 'There was one other thing.'

Holding it open at the previous page, she pointed to the neon Post-it note.

'Warn us about what?' Rosalind asked with a frown. 'That we're being blackmailed? I think we sort of noticed that ourselves.'

'I was thinking that perhaps the photos *weren't* blackmail in themselves,' Posy said. 'Maybe Clementine wanted to warn us that someone other than her had that material and planned to use it?' And still might.

'Marcus was adamant it wasn't him when I approached him,' Caro said, which probably answered Posy's question about what they'd been talking about earlier.

'He didn't react when I showed the script page at the film panel earlier, either,' Posy said. 'Are you sure no one else could have got their hands on the photos he sent you?'

Caro pulled a face. 'God, I hope not.'

Somewhere out in the hallway, a gong sounded. Dinner time, Posy guessed.

'So we're back where we started.' Rosalind said after a moment's silence, as the door to the Snug opened to reveal one of the waiting staff come to beckon them in to dinner.

'I say we ignore it all, for now,' Caro said. 'Let's go and eat dinner. Things always make more sense after a good meal.'

Posy hoped she was right. Because right now, nothing made any sense at all.

The rest of the guests had already been shown through to the dining room, and were checking the seating chart that had been placed on a board by the far wall, when Posy and the others arrived.

'Tonight, we will be enjoying a recreation of the tasting menu served in the first Dahlia Lively mystery, *The Lady Detective*,' Marcus announced, from the head of the long mahogany dining table. 'And in honour of the book, we shall also do as the characters did, and swap seats between every course. There'll be a new chart put up with every plate.' Which explained why it had taken Isobel so long to redo the seating plans.

There was an excited buzz in the room at the news; this was what people had come to Aldermere for this weekend, Posy realised. The chance to be a part of something they'd loved from a distance for so long. To step inside the pages of a Lettice Davenport novel.

'Hopefully without the same deadly consequences, though,' Marcus added, with a wink.

A ripple of laughter ran around the room. Posy hadn't read the book, or done more than glance through the script she'd found, but she assumed the fictional dinner ended with a murder.

'Not sure I can recommend the after-dinner coffees, in that case,' Hugh joked to Posy as they took their places for the first course. 'Probably better to stick to brandy!'

Posy smiled weakly, and poured herself a water.

As the starters arrived Felicity, her blue hair constrained by a feathered band, kept up a steady conversation with Hugh from his other side about his aunt's legacy.

'She was the most magnificent auntie,' he said, fondly, over the single scallop they were served. Posy supposed that when you had eleven courses to get through, they all had to be fairly small. 'She'd set up games and treasure hunts all over the gardens when I was a boy. She spent a lot of her school holidays here, you see, when her parents were overseas, so she knew all the best hiding places.'

'But she never married, did she?' Felicity speared her scallop whole and popped it in her mouth. 'Do you think she never met anyone who lived up to Johnnie Swain in her imagination?' She flashed a smile at Kit, sitting across the table.

On Posy's other side, Juliette – now dressed in a sedate floral dress – prodded her scallop and muttered, 'How many courses of this do we have to sit through again?'

'Eleven,' Posy murmured, and even she could hear the despair in her own voice.

'Well, she wasn't entirely celibate, you know.' Hugh had a twinkle in his eye as he spoke and, even though he dropped his voice, Posy could tell that the whole table were straining to hear him. 'You've heard about her relationship with Fitz Humphries, right?'

'The hardboiled detective author?' Felicity nodded. 'But they always denied it.'

Hugh lifted one shoulder in an artless shrug. 'Who am I to say. But I do still have his autograph on several of my copies of his books from when he came to stay one summer.'

Juliette sat back in her seat, scallop untouched, apparently uninterested in her great-great-aunt's romantic affairs. 'I promised Oliver I'd call him this evening, but this is going to go on forever. He's going to think I bailed on him.'

'Boyfriend?' Posy asked.

'Was. Wants to be again,' Juliette replied, with a smirk.

Across the table, Kit leant forward, his elbows perilously close to the silverware. 'What about the stories of a romance with her editor?'

Hugh's eyebrows rose. 'You *have* been doing your research. Yes, there was talk of that, too. But if she did, I think it must have been over and done with before she moved to Aldermere permanently. I don't remember any stories of him ever visiting her here.'

'Such a shame she never married,' Heather said from beside Kit. 'No little Lettices to carry on the legacy.'

'My husband and I strive to carry on her legacy in every way we can,' Isobel said, obviously bristling. 'The name Lettice Davenport won't be forgotten while we have breath.'

After three movies, a thirteen-year TV series, a new film – not to mention nearly eighty books and stories – Posy was pretty sure that Hugh's Aunt Lettice was in no fear of being forgotten. But Isobel clearly felt responsible for her legacy, despite only being related by marriage.

'I heard there was only ever one man she *really* loved,' Marcus pronounced, from the head of the table. 'He broke her heart and she never recovered. That's the real reason she moved back to Aldermere during the war.'

'And I thought it was the bomb that landed on her building that brought her back here,' Hugh said, lightly. 'I think we can all agree that Aldermere House is a far nicer place to sit out a war than London at the height of the Blitz!'

That drew some laughter from around the table, but not much.

'And then after the war she bought the place from your father? Is that right?' Felicity asked.

Hugh stiffened beside her. 'Not exactly. A place like Aldermere costs an awful lot to run, of course, and since she was living and writing here, Aunt Letty contributed to the family finances. But the house has always belonged to the family, first and foremost. Now, what do you think of these scallops?'

Was it just the crassness of talking money at the dining table that offended him? Posy knew that the British upper classes could be funny about that – at least, that's what all the period dramas said. Or was Aldermere in financial trouble again? Relying on the latest reboot of the Dahlia Lively mysteries to save them? The threadbare table linens, and the draught through the rattling windowpane, suggested they might be.

Before Felicity could ask any more questions, the waiters cleared the plates and it was time to change seats. For the second course, Posy was shifted to the other end of the table, between Heather in what seemed to be a tartan evening gown and Ashok.

'Of course, in the book, the food is far more extravagant than this!' Heather reached for a second bread roll from the basket in the centre of the table. 'Her first book was published in 1929, so I suppose it was that between the wars luxury, before the rationing came in. It was all very free and easy then, wasn't it? And I'm not just talking about the food.' She nudged Posy in the ribs, and Posy forced a smile.

Was *that* what people wanted from Dahlia Lively and her mysteries? The freedom to let go of the real world and overindulge – food, sex, drugs, money. To let all morals fall away.

Posy had lived that life in LA, once her teen star career was over, and all she had left was her notoriety. It always sounded good on paper – the freedom to do anything without consequence. But Posy knew how it ended.

By the time they'd finished the eighth course, it seemed that Juliette had reached her limit.

'Where are you going, Juliette?' Isobel called, from the far end of the table, as Juliette stood and headed for the door. 'There's another three courses to go. And you don't want to miss pudding.'

'Grandma, I've already eaten enough food for a week,' Juliette said. 'And I promised Oliver I'd call him tonight before bed, and it's already nearly eleven.'

Isobel's face soured, a little, behind her smile. Hugh, sitting a couple of seats away from her, laughed. 'Let her go, Isobel. She's put up with us boring old folks a lot longer than most girls her age would.'

'I suppose so.' Isobel made an indulgent shooing motion with her hand, as if Juliette were still five, not nineteen. Juliette departed before her grandmother changed her mind.

For the ninth course, Posy found herself between Kit and Harry.

'A rose between two thorns!' Harry announced, plucking one of the yellow roses from the table centrepiece to present to her. Posy had no idea what she was supposed to do with that, so she smiled, and placed it beside her plate.

'Have you spoken to Anton tonight?' Kit asked, while Harry was distracted by one of Caro's more outlandish stories about filming a Dahlia Lively episode in Egypt.

'No. Why?' Posy's gaze darted to the far end of the table, where Anton sat beside Isobel.

'He's acting weird. Weirder than normal,' he clarified, off her look. 'He collared me before dinner, demanding to know where you were, and where you found that script page.'

Posy winced. 'What did you tell him?'

'That I had no idea. Because I don't.'

Posy gazed at Anton again, deep in conversation with Ashok, and suddenly a thought occurred to her. Perhaps she'd got this wrong from the start. Perhaps the truth was much simpler than she'd imagined, and the drama and the theatrics were just that – a fiction designed to entertain, and to distract.

I keep coming back to the film. And the curse. What if that was what everything had been about, right from the beginning?

Anton got to his feet, heading for the door. Without thinking, Posy rose to follow him.

'Where are you going?' Kit asked.

'Bathroom,' she lied, again.

Kit's gaze darted between her and the door Anton had just walked through. 'Yeah, right.' He didn't try to stop her, though. And Rosalind's raised eyebrows and Caro's urgent hand signals weren't going to, either.

It was time to find out what or who had really cursed the new Dahlia Lively movie.

Chapter Twelve

*'Sometimes, Johnnie, you just have to take the least bad option.
Take a leap into the unknown, and trust someone – or cut someone
out of your life. Even if it goes against everything you thought was
true.'*

Dahlia Lively *in* The Devil and the Deep Blue Sea
***By* Lettice Davenport, 1940**

'Anton.'

The director stopped at the bottom of the stairs, one hand on the bannister, then turned towards her. 'Posy.'

In the darkness of the hallway, lit only by wall sconces that were little better than candles, his heavy brows cast a shadow over his eyes, but she could still see his lips curved in a semblance of a smile.

'I wanted to talk with you. About the film.'

'And how you got hold of that script page?' Anton asked. 'Libby swears blind she didn't give it to you, and very few other people have seen it. So I must confess to being curious.'

'It was pushed under my door this morning,' she replied, honestly. 'But it's not the script I want to talk to you about. It's the curse.'

He scoffed. 'There is no curse.'

'Of course there isn't. Curses don't exist.' She watched him closely as she spoke her next words. 'But marketing campaigns do. And so do sabotage campaigns. So which is it?'

Anton blinked slowly, buying himself time to decide on his response. 'I don't know what you're talking about. But I will tell you that when I agree to take on a film, that film becomes my *life*. It's all-consuming for me. I eat, sleep, breathe and *live* that project. So—'

'Really?' Posy interrupted. She wasn't interested in hearing any more over-the-top sales pitches from him. 'Because you weren't exactly jumping to listen to Kit when he tried to talk about the curse earlier.'

'I thought we agreed curses don't exist.'

'Maybe not. But that doesn't stop people believing in them.' Posy leaned against the wall beside the dinner gong and considered the man in front of her. 'I did some research into you, you know, before my audition. All these articles about how you're a passionate – or angry – up-and-coming young talent. Except you can't stay up-and-coming forever, can you? Or young for that matter. What are you now? Forty? Forty-five?'

Anton's shoulders stiffened. 'What are you implying?'

'This is your big break, right? A mainstream movie with a loyal fanbase. One you could sprinkle with your trademark fairy dust – diverse cast, modern humour, edgy film techniques. Turn Lettice's books into an innovative Anton Martinez movie, rather than another retelling of the same old stories.'

'I've tried to be faithful to the spirit of the books with everything I've done,' Anton replied. 'I had to be.'

'Because the family retained the final approval of the script, right? And they didn't like the first one at all, did they?' The pieces were coming together, now.

Anton's laidback, handsome face contorted with frustration. 'It was a *great* script. Fresh, new, modern – and they dismissed it out of hand.'

'You leaked the script,' Posy said, a statement not a question. 'You put it out on the internet hoping the fans would love it, to try and get your own way.' They hadn't though. The articles she'd read had universally panned the original script. That was when the production company had brought Libby in to start over.

'What do the *fans* know? They'd keep everything exactly as it was in the originals, right down to the racism and the homophobia, if they could. They're stuck in the past!'

There was a kernel of truth in his words, enough to give her a pang of empathy. 'Maybe some of them are. But not all.' She thought about the VIP fans she'd met, and the questioners from the film panel. From what they'd said, she'd got the impression than most of the fans at Aldermere that weekend would be happy to have Dahlia's adventures brought up to date, as long as they kept the heart of the stories the same. The thing that *really* mattered to them.

'I thought that I could bring something new to the oeuvre of murder mystery films.' Anton slumped against the bannister. 'That I could do something innovative, something truly ground-breaking. But this ridiculous family weren't having any of that, were they? I was told I'd have full creative control – but in truth, they had the final veto on everything!'

'So you leaked the script, and the backlash was so awful the lead writer left town and became a virtual hermit.' Posy stared Anton dead in the eye. 'And instead of feeling guilt about that, you found a way to use it to your advantage. By spreading more talk of a curse.'

'Hey, you can't put all that on me,' Anton said, taking a hasty pace back up a step. 'Layla's accident, that was just bad luck. And the fire at the filming location, too.'

'But the fraud investigation on the investor?' Posy asked, and Anton shrugged.

He'd gone out of his way to make the curse a real thing. And Posy had a horrible feeling that she might have been a part of that.

'You promised the fans you'd cast a Dahlia who knew and loved the books,' Posy said, remembering what Ashok had said. 'Why did you pick me?'

'Because I wanted out. If I wasn't going to get to do this my way, why do it at all? Why not burn the whole thing down for another generation?'

'I was part of your curse.' Posy looked at her hands, trying to breathe through the nausea rising in her at the idea. 'Of course I was.'

If he'd quit, the production company would have replaced him. That wasn't enough for him, Posy realised. He wanted the family to pull the plug completely.

'You were perfect for ending this film once and for all. Everyone knows your story. How long could it be before you screwed up? I figured your first drugs or drink binge in the papers would be all it took for the family to decide you were sullying Lettice's reputation.' Now his secret was out, Anton seemed happy to revel in the drama, telling the tale of how his talent had been betrayed, and how he'd fought back. 'I even got photos, before we offered you the part. In case no one else bothered enough to follow you around with a camera these days. You, falling out of your ex-boyfriend's flat, high as a kite. Didn't take much to convince him to lead you astray one last time, I might mention. I was going to let you screw up here, alienate the fans, then release them next week to put that final nail in the coffin. But here you are! Wearing the god-awful tea dresses I was sure you'd baulk at, and reading Lettice's bloody autobiography!'

Posy's heart clenched at the casual way he threw her mistakes in her face. She'd been so scared of him finding out about her slip-up, when he'd orchestrated it all along.

Posy Starling as Dahlia was never going to fly, not for the fans and certainly not for the legion Hollywood nobility she's offended during her time on the scene . . .

No. Her nails dug half-moons into her palms as she shoved Uncle Sol's voice out of her head for the last time.

She'd read enough about the curse to know the truth. People hadn't hated the original script because it was modern or new. They'd hated it because it was bad. Because Dahlia didn't sound like Dahlia, and because DI Johnnie ended up solving the mystery.

'That's because you were wrong about me. And you were wrong about the fans, too. This film is about more than you and your vision. Everyone else involved *cares* about this film and we will make it the best we can, with or without you. If you don't want to be part of it, quit now. But Anton – just because the world isn't moving as fast as you'd like, doesn't mean it isn't moving at all. We *can* bring Dahlia into the twenty-first century, but not if we trash everything that she was about.'

'And you know what that is, do you?' Anton looked unconvinced.

'I'm learning,' she said, simply. But what she still didn't know was whether he was behind everything else that was happening at Aldermere that weekend.

'Tell me something. Did you give Marcus or Clementine those photos?' she asked.

'I didn't have to.' Anton's smile sharpened. 'It was all Marcus's idea, you see. *I* just asked him to make sure you screwed up publicly on the panel earlier, to get the fans bitching about you. But Marcus *really* doesn't like the idea of you as Dahlia, you know?'

'So he arranged the photos,' Posy whispered.

Anton shrugged. 'He sorted the photographer. I sorted your ex. I like to think of it as a joint effort. Not that he knew why I was doing it – just that it would get you off the movie.'

He sounded pleased with himself, but Posy wasn't listening. She was thinking. Hard. Marcus would have had access to her photos *and* to Caro's. Was it so much of a stretch to think he could have got Rosalind's too? And that Clementine could have found them and sent them to the three of them as a warning of what he had planned?

Maybe Marcus found the photos had disappeared, and needed another way to discredit her. One that would *definitely* get her fired from the film. Like stealing Lettice Davenport's jewelled loupe.

'So, what are you going to do now?' Anton asked. 'No one will believe you.'

Posy tilted her head to the side, listening to the laughter inside the dining room as she considered his question. 'You know, I think they might. Especially since I broke into Clementine's room earlier to retrieve my phone. I've been recording every word you said since I came out here.'

He stared at her in horror as she lifted her bag, her hand inside as if wrapped around the phone she didn't have. *Acting is just bluffing,* Uncle Sol had used to say. *Making people believe something you know isn't true, by making them believe that* you *believe it.*

'You wouldn't.'

She shrugged. 'Ask Ashok if you don't believe me. He was with me when I did it.'

Anton's throat moved as he swallowed. 'You release that and I'm finished. I release those photos and you're finished. Mutually assured destruction.'

'Or mutually assured success,' she countered. 'It's up to you. You need to decide to commit to the film or to quit. But I'm telling you, I'm all in. And if you release those photos, or let Marcus release them, or try to pin anything else on me—' She watched him carefully as she said that, but saw no reaction, no hint that the idea of framing her meant anything to him. 'I'll tell the world what you did, play them this recording, and they *will* believe me.'

They stared at each other across the hallway for a long moment. Posy kept her spine straight, her shoulders back and her chin high. She would not be brought down by this man, not now.

She was Dahlia Lively, whether he wanted her or not.

Finally, he nodded.

'Glad we got that straight.' She beamed at him, which only made him scowl more. 'Now, I think it must be nearly time for dessert, don't you?'

She returned to the table to find that everyone had moved around again, and the tenth course was already in front of her. A sorbet, thankfully.

The tenth course also sat her beside Caro for the first time.

'You were right,' Posy murmured under her breath. 'It's Marcus.'

'Told you so,' Caro replied, brightly. 'We'll confront him after dinner, yes?'

Posy nodded. 'Tell Rosalind.'

The final course was coffee and mints. Posy took her seat between Marcus and Ashok, and watched as across the table, Caro leaned in close to Rosalind and whispered something. Rosalind looked up, met Posy's gaze, and nodded. Not long now, and they'd have the truth from Marcus's own mouth. And all of this would be over.

A waiter leaned over to place a coffee cup before her, complete with a sugared blue flower next to the mint.

'Well, I guess this is where we find out fact from fiction,' Hugh joked, further along the table. He added cream to his coffee, stirred in a sugar, then reached for the sugared flower, popping it in his mouth. He took a sip of his coffee. 'So far so good!'

Posy tried to smile, but the tension knot in her stomach wouldn't let her. *I'm going to confront a blackmailer tonight.*

She looked across at Caro and Rosalind again. *At least I don't have to do it alone.*

'Right,' Marcus said beside her, dropping his own cup back into its saucer. 'Time to get this lot to bed before they drink tomorrow night's wine as well as tonight's.'

He lurched to his feet, one hand on the table to steady himself, and bellowed, 'If I may have your attention!'

The room quietened, gradually. Posy caught Caro's gaze and nodded. It was time.

'Today has been a marvellous celebration of the life and writings of Lettice Davenport.' Marcus swayed slightly as he spoke. Posy suspected it wasn't just the other guests who'd overdone the wine. 'Thank you all for being here, and being a part of it.'

Wait. Was he slurring his words, too? And beads of sweat were popping on his forehead, as his clammy hand clutched at the table.

'Tomorrow—' He stopped, and swallowed visibly. 'Tom- To—'

His other hand flew to his chest as he staggered backwards, and Ashok jumped to his feet to catch him before he fell into his chair.

'My pills,' Marcus managed, one hand pawing at his jacket pocket.

'Marcus?' Ashok asked, but the man's eyes were already fluttering closed. 'Marcus!'

'Where are his pills?' Isobel asked, her voice shrill as she jumped to her feet. 'He needs his pills!'

Gasps filled the air as people gathered close – calling for ambulances, doctors, or shouting well-meaning but useless advice. Ashok felt Marcus's pockets and pulled out his medication, but Marcus wasn't conscious enough to take any.

Because Marcus was dead. Posy knew that as surely as she knew there was a stolen, jewelled magnifying glass hidden in her wardrobe.

'It's just like in the book!' Felicity said, her whisper harsh in the suddenly silent room. 'Poison in the coffee.'

And suddenly, no one was talking about Marcus's heart condition or medication. In that moment, everyone around that dining table was looking at their companions with suspicion.

Her fingers trembling, Posy reached out and picked up Marcus's empty cup, sniffing it. She didn't know what she was smelling for, beyond Marcus's usual herbal tea, but that didn't seem to matter. It was what Dahlia would do.

There was no proof, no evidence, but somehow Posy knew in her gut that Felicity was right. This was murder.

The cup clattered back into its saucer, and she looked up to find Rosalind and Caro both watching her, staring at her, their expressions a mirror of her own. In the entrance hall, beside the family tree, and Lettice's dollhouse, the old grandfather clock chimed midnight.

This endless day was over. And Posy wasn't the same person who'd got on that train from London that morning.

She was Dahlia now. She'd seen a murder committed.

And she was going to solve it.

Sunday 29th August
Caro

Chapter Thirteen

'Everyone has their talents, Johnnie. Mine just happen to be considerably more useful than most other people's.'

Dahlia Lively *in* Death By Moonlight
***By* Lettice Davenport, 1937**

Caro looked at Marcus's body, slumped in his dining chair, vomit dribbling out of the corner of his mouth, and thought *Thank God.*

A surge of guilt followed hot on the heels of the thought, but she pushed it away. She'd been certain this whole weekend was another one of his games, a test or a tease. A way to control her, scare her. Certainly no one else could have been behind the photos Clementine had slipped under her door.

But apparently someone else had been playing with them after all.

Across the table Posy was sniffing Marcus's coffee cup, getting her fingerprints needlessly all over a possible murder weapon. Caro had no idea what she thought she was going to smell. All the best poisons were odourless, and ideally tasteless. The idea of a poison that was undetectable by science had gone out with the golden age of crime, sadly, but undetectable by the victim was still very much an achievable aim. Marcus probably never realised what was happening to him until it was too late.

'It must have been his heart,' Isobel said, stubbornly, ignoring Felicity's pronouncement. He'd had issues with it for years, and everyone had seen him take his medication. It was a reasonable assumption.

It wasn't one that Caro shared. And she was pretty sure no one else in the room did, either. It was too much of a coincidence, wasn't it? Him dying at the same moment as in the book?

What was the poison the killer used in *The Lady Detective?* Caro couldn't quite remember.

Funny how all those murders merged into one in the memory, three years or more after the last camera rolled, but the individual moments – the people she'd worked with, the fun they'd had on set – stayed with her, sharp as daylight. The Dahlia Lively mysteries had never been only about solving a crime. They were like this weekend – a chance to escape to another world, one that had been slipping away even when Lettice started writing.

Murders in Lettice's books were safe, almost. A puzzle, more than a loss.

Which brought her back to Marcus.

A crowd had gathered around him within moments, with Isobel yelling instructions to all and sundry while standing far enough back not to get her hands dirty. Heather, an ex-nurse apparently, was holding his wrist, while her husband dragged the vintage landline dial phone in from the library to call the ambulance. Ashok, meanwhile, slipped Marcus's mobile phone from his pocket, and found the emergency call setting well before Harry could turn the dial to the nine three times.

'Not that I think it'll do him much good now, poor lamb.' Heather ran her palm over Marcus's face to close his eyes.

'He always said he was one giant cheeseburger away from a heart attack,' Harry added, mournfully, as he set aside the phone.

'Better ask for the police, too,' Hugh said to Ashok, who nodded. Beside him, Rosalind stood wringing her hands as she watched him, apparently more concerned with Hugh's wellbeing than the man who had died. Did Hugh even realise that the woman he'd jilted all those years ago still loved him? Caro didn't know. But it did seem a damn waste. Idiot man.

'For a heart attack?' Kit asked.

'Unexplained sudden death,' Rosalind replied. 'The 999 operator will send them anyway.'

'We shouldn't touch anything, then,' Ashok said, putting Marcus's phone down beside the empty coffee cup after hanging up. 'Just in case.'

The tension in the air was a palpable thing, as they backed away from the table. A step or two, but enough. Enough to show that they knew there was something wrong here. Felicity might have been the only one to say the word poison, but Caro knew they were all thinking it.

Maybe tomorrow they'd have convinced themselves it was a heart attack after all. But tonight . . . tonight, they were wondering. And they were scared.

What had Marcus been thinking, recreating a murderous dinner party, at Aldermere of all places?

Caro allowed herself to study each of the guests in turn – noticing that they were doing the same. All eyeing their dinner companions, wondering who might have slipped something in Marcus's coffee. Who hated him enough to kill him? Who would take the risk, in a room full of people there to solve mysteries?

Caro had wanted the man dead as much as the next person, but she still wouldn't have done it.

In the books, it always came down to means, motive and opportunity. But in real life, it took something more. It wasn't enough to have a reason or a way or a chance to kill.

You had to be willing to do it. To take another life.

She didn't have that in her. But someone in this room did.

Caro took another circuit of the room with her gaze.

The Davenport family. Hugh and Isobel, standing solemn and scared. Thank goodness Juliette had gone to bed, and was spared seeing this.

The fans. Heather and Harry, clutching hands as they stood by the body. Felicity and Ashok off to one side, as if realising what they'd signed up for by coming here. *You and me both, kiddos.*

The film team – Anton, Kit and Libby. Anton looked like he might be taking mental notes for staging the film, but Libby had grabbed hold of Kit's arm, and he looked to be comforting her.

And the Dahlias. The other two. Rosalind standing silently at Hugh's side, Posy staring at the empty coffee cup on the table in front of Marcus. Her two doppelgängers. Her co-conspirators.

Twelve people – thirteen, if she counted herself. Twelve suspects, then.

And Caro wasn't ready to cross any of them off her list yet.

Sirens broke the silence in the dining room not long after, and Aldermere became a hive of activity again. By the time the paramedics and police were finished, it was well past two in the morning, and everyone was too exhausted to be traumatised by the idea of sleeping in a house where a man had just died.

Odds were, as Caro pointed out to Ashok, hundreds of people had died in this house over the years, anyway. Strangely, that didn't seem to reassure him.

The paramedics and police medical examiner seemed casually certain that the death was a result of Marcus's pre-existing heart condition, and the uniform officers were happy to agree if it meant they got home tonight. They bagged up Marcus's phone and pills from the table, sealed off his room, and took everyone's contact details. As the body bag was carried away, the medical examiner muttered something about a post mortem after the bank holiday.

'We should have told them,' Posy murmured, as the door shut behind the police officers. 'About the blackmail. That there might be more to this than it seems.'

'Based on what? Coincidence? The fact that his heart gave out at the same point as in the book?' Caro patted her lightly on the back, rubbing circles like her wife Annie did for her when she was stressed. 'They wouldn't have believed us, anyway.'

'Caro's right.' Had Rosalind ever uttered those words before? Probably not. Caro drank them in, knowing it could be a long, cold while before she heard them again. 'Did you see their faces? They think we're all nuts, being here in the first place.'

'Maybe not nuts,' Caro allowed. 'But they definitely think we're drama queens. Playing this up for extra theatrical excitement.' The older police officer had recognised her. He'd grinned and made a joke about leaving it to the professionals this time, eh?

Caro had no intention of leaving it to the professionals.

She was Dahlia Lively; if anyone was going to solve this murder it would be her.

Because whatever the *professionals* said, Caro was certain this was murder.

'We should get to bed,' Rosalind said, as Posy yawned. 'We can talk in the morning, over breakfast.'

'We've got that panel tomorrow,' Posy reminded them. 'The Three Dahlias event. If it even happens. I mean, Clementine's gone, Marcus is . . .'

'Dead,' Caro finished for her, as she turned towards the stairs. 'But I think it'll happen. Too much money at stake and too many people already here. So we'd better meet early. And someone needs to get in touch with Clementine.'

'Isobel will,' Rosalind said. 'She's good in a crisis.'

'Is it . . . is it all over now, do you think?' Posy asked. 'I mean, if Marcus or Clementine were behind the blackmail, it could be over. Couldn't it?'

Caro thought about the photos slipping out of the envelope she'd found in her room. Her own naked form, immortalised on film in a way she'd never agreed to do for money. The humiliation she'd felt at the reminder of it, the realisation that Marcus hadn't just photographed her, he'd secretly filmed the whole of their ill-advised night together, right after her divorce. The shuddering fear at the idea of a sex tape on the internet, at her age.

Once she'd believed that all publicity was good publicity. Now, it seemed, she'd found her limit.

'Perhaps,' Caro lied, realising that Posy was still waiting for an answer to what she'd hoped was a rhetorical question.

If Marcus really hadn't sent the notes, like he'd claimed – and now he was dead, Caro was more inclined to believe him – that meant that someone still had those photos, that film. Maybe Clementine, maybe not, if Posy was right about the notes being a warning. And until they knew who, it couldn't be over.

At the bottom of the stairs, the dollhouse was lit by a shaft of moonlight – or maybe a lamp on the porch, shining through the glass either side of the heavy front door. Caro peeked in, and saw another tiny body, lying on the miniature dining table – a copy of the real one they'd just eaten at. Had that been there when she came to dinner? She was almost certain it hadn't.

She reached in and plucked it out, holding it up to the others. With its round, red face and tiny black jacket, there was no doubt who it was meant to be.

Let the police think this was a heart attack. They knew better.

Blackmail. Theft. Murder. There was so much more going on at Aldermere this weekend than the authorities could even imagine. More than that, Caro's gut instinct told her they were connected.

And Caro always went with her gut.

But there was no need for them to rush the post mortem on a bank holiday weekend, as far as the authorities were concerned, and that suited Caro nicely. By the time the police realised that Marcus had been poisoned and launched an investigation, the convention would be over.

Which gave her until Monday night, and the end of the convention, to figure out who was behind it all. Who was playing with them.

Who knew her secrets, and what it would take for her to keep them.

And when she found the murderer, she could turn them over to the police, and prove once again that intelligent women who paid attention got a hell of a lot more done than the people who belittled and undermined them.

Dahlia would approve of that.

Caro couldn't imagine that anyone slept well that night – clear conscience or guilty. She wondered that more of the guests hadn't tried to leave yet, but she supposed it was down to human nature. The parts of them that didn't want to believe that Marcus could have suffered anything worse than a heart attack wouldn't, after that initial moment of terror, until the police confirmed it. For the fans, this was a long looked forward to weekend they didn't want to give up, and for the professionals like her, well, this was their livelihood. Easier to convince themselves there was nothing untoward going on than try and find transportation away from this place in the middle of the night.

Even she, who had Susie waiting for her in the stables, sidecar at the ready to carry her bags, wouldn't leave. She was living a real-life murder mystery. How could she walk away from that without solving it?

Which didn't mean that she'd slept peacefully – or much at all, after Marcus's death. And, judging by the dark circles under others' eyes at breakfast, neither had they.

Breakfast was being served on the terrace, looking out over the gardens where the event marquees and stalls stood, bright white against the green of the trees and the sharp blue August skies. Caro passed two tables pushed together, where Heather, Harry, Felicity and Ashok were sitting huddled over the coffee cups. She smiled and waved, receiving only weak greetings in return.

Continuing to the other end of the terrace, Caro found Rosalind and Posy seated together – somewhat uncomfortably – on a small bistro table, a pot of coffee on the surface between them, untouched. The basket of pastries, however, looked to be going down steadily.

'So,' Caro said, throwing herself into the third seat at the table. 'Where do we start?'

Neither Rosalind or Posy needed any context to join in the conversation. Caro liked that. It made her feel they were on the same wavelength, inhabiting the same character, even. Her wife, Annie, needed context clues sometimes, to catch up with the conversations Caro had been having in her head before she asked Annie to join in.

'First . . . are we *sure* it's murder?' Posy asked.

'No,' Caro admitted. 'We can't be *sure* until the post mortem comes back. But that could take days. And if it *is* murder . . .'

'We have to start asking questions now,' Posy finished with a nod. 'Okay. How?'

'We need to go over what we observed last night,' Rosalind said. 'Who sat where, when. Who left the room. That sort of thing. Between us, we should be able to recreate what happened last night, and figure out who murdered Marcus, and when.'

'It's simple deductive reasoning,' Caro said, cheerfully. 'Like Dahlia always does.'

'We're assuming the poison was in the coffee, I take it?' Posy asked, grabbing another mini pastry. 'Only, I checked last night, and the poison used in the book was aconite, which is apparently very fast acting in a large enough quantity. But the murderer could have used something else, something that would take longer to take effect, and added it to one of the earlier courses.'

Aconite. Of course it was. Caro knew that. Interesting that Posy had the book to go and check, though. 'Well, if it was earlier, it could have been anyone. Everyone sat next to him at one point or another – even us. But if it was the coffee . . .'

She squinted in the sunlight, trying to remember who'd been next to him at the end.

'If it was the coffee, it had to be someone sitting reasonably close to him at that time, or someone who stopped by to talk to him,' Rosalind summarised. 'Someone who could drop it in his cup, since no one else's coffee was poisoned.'

'Exactly. Which narrows it down to Ashok and Felicity on one side, and Posy and Harry on the other.'

'And Heather,' Posy put in. 'She stopped by to talk to Marcus about something or other around then, I'm almost sure.'

'Five people,' Caro mused. 'Four, if we discount Posy. But only if it was in the coffee.'

'We need to know if it really was aconite that killed him.' Posy pulled a face. 'How do we do that without a post mortem report?'

'Or how do we steal a post mortem report?' Rosalind asked and shook her head. 'Alternatively, we could leave this to the police.'

There wasn't a chance of Caro doing that. 'We need to know more about the poison. How it works, how it affects the body, that sort of thing. Aconite comes from a plant, doesn't it? Monkshood, I think. I'm no gardener, but there might well be some here.'

'It'll be in the Murder Spiral,' Posy said.

'The circular garden at the back of the house?' Rosalind asked.

Posy nodded. 'Kit and I were stationed there yesterday during the murder mystery. Apparently it has every poisonous plant Lettice ever used in any of her novels planted there.'

'Well, that sounds like a remarkably stupid idea.' Rosalind sniffed, and reached for a mini croissant.

'Were the plants labelled?' Caro asked, thinking. 'If they were, we could find out what this plant looks like, at least. Heck, but I miss the internet.'

'I reckon Dahlia would have solved half her mysteries a damn sight quicker if she'd had a smart phone,' Rosalind agreed.

Smart phones. What was Caro forgetting about phones? She followed the thought back through the last twenty-four hours, and found what she was looking for. Posy had told them she was supposed to be getting her phone back from Clementine.

An investigative mind at work was a glorious thing. 'Still no sign of Clementine returning this morning?' she asked Posy, enjoying Rosalind's look of confusion at the apparent non-sequitur. Not every-one was built to be a detective.

'Not that I've seen.' Posy pulled a face. 'The convention must be in chaos with her *and* Marcus gone.'

Down on the grass below, the group of waistcoated volunteers was getting larger and louder. Had anyone told them that Marcus was dead?

'Looks like it.' Caro moved to the edge of the terrace and looked down at the growing throng of volunteers.

'I wouldn't be surprised if Hugh shut down the whole thing,' Rosalind said.

'No.' Caro spun back to face the table. 'We can't let that happen.'

'Why not?' Rosalind asked, with an elegant shrug. 'Would get us out of this bloody panel later.'

'Because someone here could still be planning on blackmailing us,' Posy pointed out. 'Probably the same person who is trying to frame me for theft, and is responsible for murdering Marcus. We can't let anyone leave until we figure out what's going on.'

'And make sure it isn't going to come back to bite us,' Caro agreed. 'Well, if we want to keep this show on the road *someone* is going to have to take charge. And it doesn't look like it'll be Hugh or Isobel.'

Her gaze swept across the terrace. The fans were still talking quietly over coffees, but none of the Davenports had deigned to join them for breakfast. Unless . . . Caro beamed at the sight of a blonde head bobbing across the lawn below.

'Juliette!' The young woman looked up, and Caro beckoned wildly from the terrace until she hopped up the steps to join them. 'Pull up a chair.'

There wasn't room for three around the bistro table, let alone four, but it wasn't as if there were much of Juliette anyway. She had the tiny waist and waiflike physique of a naturally slender nineteen-year-old, which was basically cheating. The great injustice of life, Caro thought;

you never appreciated the body you had until you were too old to have it anymore. Of course, Caro suspected Rosalind, at sixty-odd, would say the same about her at forty.

'What's up?' Juliette asked. 'If you're looking for my grandmother, I think she's locked herself in her room. Granddad filled me in on what happened after dessert. Apparently it was 'traumatic' for her, even though she never even *liked* Marcus.'

'Still, watching someone die is never pleasant,' Rosalind said.

Juliette gave a careless shrug. 'I wouldn't know. I wasn't there. First interesting thing to happen at Aldermere in *decades,* and I missed it. Typical.'

'That's right. You went to call your boyfriend.' Posy looked thoughtful. Caro suspected she was adjusting her mental image of who was where when to reflect Juliette's absence. Caro would have to get her to write it all down later; she was rubbish at holding that sort of thing in her head.

That was what Dahlia had sidekicks for – whether it was Detective Inspector Johnnie Swain, or her maid Bess in the earliest stories. They held onto the details, Dahlia was responsible for the flashes of brilliance and insight.

'The thing is, with Marcus dead and Clementine not returned from wherever she drove off to yesterday, the poor convention staff are at a loss. They need a leader,' Caro announced. 'Someone to guide them through this difficult time.'

'And you want *me* to do it?' Juliette asked, brightening. 'Of course! I've been asking Granddad to let me do more around here, with the estate, but he still thinks I'm about twelve and doesn't trust me with anything.'

'Then this could be your chance to show him,' Rosalind said, fondly.

'I can definitely do that.' Juliette hopped up again.

'Your first job is to get in touch with Clementine, since you have the privilege of still having a phone.' She turned to Rosalind and Posy. 'You know, we really should see about getting ours back.'

'I'll ask Hugh,' Rosalind promised.

'What do you want me to say to her?' Juliette asked.

'Tell her to get back here,' Caro replied. 'The convention needs her. We can break the news about Marcus when she arrives.' And ask her some questions about those incriminating photos, too. Or if she might have found time to sneak back and poison her boss.

Whatever else had happened, Clementine was still their number one suspect, and Caro wanted her close enough to question.

Juliette nodded. 'I'll get the number from one of the volunteers. What else?'

Caro surveyed the volunteers below again. Since breakfast, however paltry, had been served, she supposed that Clementine must have instructed the catering staff before she left. They were professionals. They knew the job and got on with it.

The convention volunteers were a different matter. She knew from past events that Marcus lured them in to help with the promise of a free ticket, front-row seats at the panels and talks, and maybe some special access to the VIPs for photos and autographs. Then he worked them into the ground keeping everything running, while he swanned around in his butler's outfit.

They'd need someone to tell them where to go and what to do. Someone who knew how these things were supposed to work. Someone they'd recognise and listen to.

Basically, her.

'Next we talk to the volunteers.' Juliette was already halfway down the steps before she'd finished the sentence, clearly desperate for *something* to do. Grabbing a pain au chocolat from the basket, Caro turned to the other Dahlias, keeping her voice low in case anyone was listening.

'Right, Juliette and I are going to go sort this lot out. Posy, you go see if the Murder Spiral can tell you anything more about aconite as a poison. Rosalind, there was a book on poisons in Lettice's study yesterday. See if you can borrow it, will you? Then meet me in the dining room as soon as you're done. We need to recreate last night – with less murder.'

With that, she left the others to get on with the investigation, and went to save the convention.

Being Dahlia Lively was a full-time job. Whatever Annie said.

Chapter Fourteen

'The key,' Dahlia said, as she paced along the patio, 'is to create a picture. A living painting that tells us who was where, when. Opportunity! That's what we're looking for, Bess!'

Dahlia Lively *in* A Lady's Place
By Lettice Davenport, 1934

Rosalind and Posy were waiting for her in the dining room when Caro arrived. The room had been reset since the dinner the night before, the long mahogany table now bare except for a floral centrepiece. Caro placed her hands on her hips and surveyed the scene, trying to see in her mind who had sat where, when.

'It looks different, in the daylight,' she murmured absently, as Rosalind draped herself over the chair at the head of the table. Or perhaps it looked different now they were searching for a murderer.

'Oh! This might help.' Posy said. 'I grabbed the seating charts from the board last night.'

Caro smiled at her approvingly. 'Good thought, kiddo.'

She ignored the face Posy pulled at being called kiddo. Dahlia called *everybody* kiddo, although Caro wouldn't try it with Rosalind. 'We'll need those for reference.'

'I went to take a photo of them on my phone before I remembered I didn't have it,' Posy admitted. 'So theft seemed like the next best option.'

Caro had to admit to being mildly impressed. 'Works for me. Let's have a look.'

Posy pulled the sheets of paper from her voluminous handbag and laid them out on the table. Caro had no idea what else she was stashing in that thing, but it seemed larger than was strictly necessary for day-to-day life. *Dahlia* would never have carried something so unwieldly. But then, all Dahlia needed was her lipstick, her cigarettes, and someone to pay for the cocktails.

Caro frowned as they studied the seating plans, Rosalind leaning across the mahogany from her position at the top of the table. Caro had known, of course, that they'd moved around a lot last night, but she hadn't realised how comprehensively the seating plans had been thought through.

'No wonder it took Isobel so long to redo the seating plan,' she murmured.

'Nobody sat in the same seat twice, or next to the same combination of two people more than once,' Posy added, peering over her shoulder. 'Like in the book.'

'So, what exactly are you expecting us to do now?' Rosalind asked.

'We . . .' Caro paused. What would Dahlia do? 'We recreate the crime!'

'Are you planning on actually poisoning one of us?' Rosalind's dry, laconic voice made her skin prickle. 'Because I'd like to opt out of that activity, if so.'

Caro ignored her. 'We try to remember everything that happened last night, in order – who said what, who left when – by taking our places for each course.'

'I suspect this is going to make me hungry,' Rosalind said, sounding bored, but she did heave herself out of her chair and check the seating plan for her first location.

Posy, however, was clutching the book and biting her lip. 'Do you have unhelpful objections too?' Caro asked.

'No! No, I think it's a good idea.' Was that surprise in her voice? 'I just . . .' She reached into her bag and pulled out the script she'd found in Clementine's room, as well as a tatty paperback copy of *The Lady Detective*. 'I was thinking that we might want to compare the events of last night to the book – and to how it happens in the script, too. I mean, if someone was recreating the murder from the story, everything should be the same, right?'

Damn. Why hadn't she thought of that? Sidekicks weren't supposed to have useful flashes of inspiration, were they?

Except Posy and Rosalind weren't sidekicks. They were all Dahlias here.

'Right. Good plan. Positions, please ladies. Posy, you check against the book, Rosalind, the script. *I'll* direct.'

'Naturally,' Rosalind muttered. Caro continued to ignore her.

It took a couple of courses to get them into the swing of things. They each took the seat they'd occupied during the course, then Caro reminded them who had been sitting either side of them, then tried to remember who said what, in case there were any clues in it. At the same time, they checked the notes from the script and the descriptions on the page, with Posy jotting down any differences between them.

Unfortunately, most of the conversations they recalled seemed as boring and banal as all the dinner parties Caro had endured during her first marriage, and the changes and differences were minimal and insignificant. All they'd established was that, since they had been served eleven courses rather than the twelve in the book, Marcus had been recreating the film version of the dinner.

By the time they'd reached the eighth course, Caro was starting to doubt the genius of her idea. And so were the others, from their bored expressions and half-hearted answers.

'Ninth course!' Caro pointed to the relevant seats, and everyone moved around again, with sighs. 'Rosalind, you had Juliette and Marcus.'

Rosalind frowned. 'No I didn't.'

Caro checked the seating plan again. 'This says you did.'

'I didn't sit next to Juliette all night.'

'Because she left!' Posy chirped. 'She went to call her boyfriend, remember? She wasn't there for the next couple of courses.'

'That's right,' Caro said, slowly. 'She was the only person who left the table but didn't come back.' They'd tried to keep track of who had left the room and when, Posy scribbling notes on the seating plans to remind them later, for all the good it would do. With eleven courses and matching wine pairings, *everyone* had needed a bathroom break at some point or another.

'Maybe Juliette saw something when she left,' Posy said. 'We should talk to her.'

'If we're serious about doing this, we're going to need to talk to everybody, sooner or later,' Rosalind pointed out. 'The question is how to do that without raising any suspicions that we know more than we should.'

'A dilemma worthy of Dahlia,' Caro said. 'And one we'll solve after we've finished our recreation. So. Ninth course.'

Once again, there were no particularly enlightening conversations. Caro wasn't sure what she'd been hoping for. This sort of re-enactment always seemed to work better when Dahlia did it.

'Two more to go,' she said, her enthusiasm fading as she checked the seating plans again. Then she frowned. 'Posy, you were next to me – but you didn't show up until after the sorbet had been served. And when you did, you told me you were sure that Marcus was behind everything. Where were you?'

'I needed to talk to Anton.' Posy's reply was short and sharp, and she glanced away towards the door as she said it.

Dahlia would say that was a tell. A sign of a lie – or at least an omission.

'What about?' Caro pressed.

A muscle jumped in Posy's jaw. 'The curse on the movie. I don't think it's going to be a problem anymore. But he also confirmed that Marcus was behind the photos I was sent.'

There was a story there, and Caro wanted to hear it. But before she could ask for more details, Rosalind said, 'Next course.'

Which brought them, inexorably, to the coffee and mints.

'The book has the poison in the coffee cup,' Posy confirmed. 'They had wrapped mints on the saucers, just as we did, and coffee poured at the table. Dahlia reasons that the poison must have already been in the cup as a powder, before the coffee was poured in.' She shut the book. 'Except Marcus didn't drink coffee, did he? He drank that foul camomile and ginger stuff. He made a big deal about it at lunch. I'd almost forgotten. But when I sniffed his cup after he, well, afterwards, it wasn't coffee. It was tea.'

Now *that* sent Caro's investigative brain whirring. 'What does the script say? Anything about coffee, or the mints?'

Rosalind studied the script. 'The stage directions mention the mints, the coffee, the sugared flowers—'

'They're not in the book,' Posy blurted. 'The sugared flowers. They're not in the book.'

'Are you sure?' Caro asked, swinging round to stare at her. 'They're a new addition?'

Posy nodded. 'Definitely. Libby must have added them in.' She grabbed the script from Rosalind and flipped through the later pages, comparing it to the paperback in her hand. 'And in the film, the poison isn't in the coffee.'

Caro knew what she was going to say next before she said it. 'It's in the sugared flowers,' she said, in sync with Rosalind, who'd followed the same train of thought.

'Not in them,' Posy corrected. 'Every saucer has a sugared violet – except for the victim's. They get a sugared monkshood flower – aconite. Ridiculously poisonous, and acts almost instantaneously.'

'Someone switched Marcus's flower for a poisonous one. And they'd know which cup and saucer was his because he had tea not coffee.' The implications of that were huge, Caro realised.

'So it could be done before the teas and coffees were served,' Rosalind observed. 'The cups weren't on the dining table from the start – not enough space with eleven courses, I suppose. They were on the long table by the French windows, I think.'

'Anyone in the room could have switched his flower then,' Posy said. 'When the serving staff brought Marcus's cup over, it already had the teabag in – I was sitting next to him, remember? They gave him a little pot of hot water to go with it.'

'Ye-es,' Caro agreed. 'I saw it too – the teabag was there when the cups were on the long table. I remember stopping to look at them between a couple of the courses – not sure which ones, though. The breeze through the window was lovely, the room was so hot.' That, or she was starting to experience the hot flushes her mother had complained so bitterly about throughout her forties, and Caro refused to countenance that idea. 'I remember rolling my eyes when I saw Marcus's teabag – bloody awkward man, I've seen him order black Americanos in Starbucks plenty of times, when he's hungover. He likes to be different when people are watching.'

'Liked,' Rosalind corrected her. 'He *liked* to be different.'

The reminder made her insides squirm. For a moment, she'd forgotten a man she knew was dead. She'd been focused on the puzzle.

It's easier when you're not a part of the story. She'd said that line as Dahlia once, hadn't she? *When you're just an observer, solving a puzzle.*

'Yes. Right. The point is, we were moving seats all evening and we must have passed that table half a dozen times or more. Any one of us at dinner last night could have switched that sugared flower for a deadly one.'

The three Dahlias contemplated that idea in silence for a moment.

'It would take some planning,' Rosalind said, finally. 'The flower must have been sugared, not fresh. That takes time and effort.'

'Well, we were hardly thinking this was a spur of the moment killing,' Caro pointed out acidly. 'That's why we can be pretty sure none of the catering staff were behind it. This was definitely personal.'

Sugaring flowers sounded like something her ex-mother-in-law would have expected her to do, for perfect dinner parties to support her husband's career.

Needless to say, such events had never been high on Caro's agenda.

She'd bet that Rosalind had sugared a flower or two in her time, though. And Isobel *definitely* would have done. Another one for the suspect list.

'More than that, they'd have needed to have read the script.' Posy spread the script pages open again to the relevant scene. 'Otherwise they wouldn't have known about the sugared flowers.'

'It comes back to the script again, doesn't it?' Caro said, thoughtfully.

'The original script was leaked on the internet. We need to check if that had the flowers in too – if it did, anyone here could have read it. But if Libby added them in . . .' Posy let the sentence trail away.

'It narrows our pool of suspects down to the people who had access to it,' Caro finished for her. 'So we need to find out who those people were.'

Rosalind checked the slender golden wristwatch on her arm. 'As fun as this has been, ladies, we do have a panel we're supposed to be attending shortly.'

The Three Dahlias panel. Of course.

'Come on.' Caro gathered the script and thrust it at Posy. 'There's a few things I need you two to do before the panel. I've got an idea.'

Caro swept out of the door, and pretended not to hear Posy saying, 'Does that make you as nervous as it does me?' behind her.

After sending Rosalind and Posy off on their errands, Caro delegated her own task quickly, then headed to the main marquee and made friends with the volunteers scheduled to assist with the Three Dahlias panel.

Rosalind and Posy arrived back before the crowds of fans were allowed in. Caro caught them at the back door.

'What did you find out at the Murder Spiral?' she asked Posy.

'Monkshood is definitely planted there, and currently blooming in a beautiful purple colour, although I kept my distance.' Posy shuddered.

'And I borrowed Letty's poison book,' Rosalind said. 'Like Posy told us, it's a fast-acting poison. But also, it causes heart attacks, paralysis, nausea and some vomiting.'

Caro didn't need the vision of Marcus staggering backwards into his chair, or that dribble of vomit on his cold dead lips, but her brain presented it anyway. 'Sounds like we have our poison,' she said, her mouth dry. 'Any luck with the phones?'

Rosalind shook her head. 'I couldn't find Hugh. Isobel said she thought he'd gone for a walk, but she did confirm he has the phones locked in a safe in his study. I'll try and talk to him later.'

'Okay. Next job – finding a motive.' Caro gestured towards the stage.

'What, exactly, *are* you planning here?' Rosalind's eyes were narrowed as she studied the set-up on the stage of the marquee. One small table, with three seats for them, plus another longer one with five seats set up across from it. Both tables were angled so the audience could get a clear view of the people sitting at them. 'Isn't this supposed to be a simple Q&A?'

'And it still will be!' Caro widened her eyes in what she hoped was an innocent way. 'Instead of the VIP delegates throwing questions at us, like Marcus planned, we're going to ask them questions. A small interrogation.'

'Like in a court room,' Posy said, sounding uncomfortable.

Caro wondered how many court rooms Posy had been in during her short life. Maybe a few, given that whole affair with her parents that was in the papers a few years back – not to mention her own problems. She seemed stable, now, if a little sad. Not the diva starlet Caro had expected.

She almost liked her.

'That's the idea,' Caro said, encouragingly. 'I thought, since these good people are here to watch Dahlia Lively in action, that's what we should give them!'

Outside the marquee, a long queue was snaking around the formal gardens waiting to get in. Caro could only glimpse the start of it from the stage, through the open flap door, but the chatter and excitement that floated in on the breeze told her this was going to be one of the highlights of the convention.

Marcus would be so mad he was missing it, if he were still alive to care.

'And are the VIP delegates going to be okay with this?' Posy ran a finger along the length of the table, looking thoughtfully across at the other one with its five chairs.

'They'll love it! Each of us asking questions about where they were yesterday, what they saw, that sort of thing.'

'Investigating Marcus's death for entertainment? Isn't that a little bit crass?' Rosalind didn't add 'even for you', but Caro could hear it in her voice. Rosalind always had thought she was better than Caro, because her Dahlia made it to the silver screen, while Caro's was only on the telly. But millions more people worldwide associated Caro with Dahlia, thanks to syndication deals, so who had the last laugh?

'Of course we won't be investigating Marcus's death,' Caro said, with exaggerated patience. 'Apart from anything else, we don't have any proof he was murdered, yet. But we *do* all know that a magnifying glass was stolen yesterday, don't we? We can question everyone about their movements legitimately on that–'

'Without revealing where it is right now,' Posy interjected. She looked nervous, so Caro nodded and acknowledged the point.

'*Without* revealing that. Because what we're *really* interested in is who knew Marcus before this weekend, who spent time with him here at Aldermere – and who had a reason to want to kill him. We haven't been paying enough attention to our suspects so far this weekend, ladies.'

'Because we didn't know they *were* suspects,' Rosalind muttered.

Caro ignored her. 'It's time for us to up our Dahlia game.'

Rosalind and Posy exchanged a long look. 'It *could* work,' Posy said, eventually. 'If the VIPs go along with it.'

The tent flap that served as the back door for volunteers and speakers opened, and Caro grinned as Kit ducked through it, a fedora hat at a rakish angle over his dark hair.

'Oh, they'll go along with it. I've invited reinforcements to make sure of that.' She waved Kit towards the stage.

'You summon and I obey!' Kit sketched an elaborate bow. 'Now, where do you want me and why? Juliette wasn't exactly clear when she fetched me.'

'Just take a seat over there,' Caro told him. 'You're going to be playing suspect, rather than detective, today.'

Kit shrugged. 'Sounds fun. Bring it on!'

Chapter Fifteen

'I don't know why you police types get so worked up about interrogating suspects,' Dahlia said, lighting another cigarette. 'It's really just giving people a chance to incriminate themselves.'

Dahlia Lively *in* Twelve Lively Suspects
By Lettice Davenport, 1945

Caro watched as the VIP fans took their seats, and the delegates filed in to fill the audience. She smoothed down her favourite Dahlia outfit – a cream silk blouse she'd taken from wardrobe on the last day of filming, and a pair of navy linen trousers. Rubbing her lips together she hoped that her scarlet lipstick had survived breakfast.

Across the way, the VIP fans were looking decidedly uncertain about this new addition to their schedule. But as she'd planned, Kit's presence – and his relaxed, joking manner – was going a long way to setting them at their ease.

As the clamour in the audience died down after their introductions, Caro took the microphone and beamed at the audience.

Oh, this was why she kept coming back to Marcus, year after year. No one else gave her the chance to stand up and be adored like this. To know that she was connecting with people who valued her for who she was – well, who she *could* be.

Annie always tried to tell her that she was more than just Dahlia, more than an actress. That she mattered in her own right. But then,

Annie had never been to another convention after the one where they'd met, when she'd been accompanying her aunt for the day. Annie didn't know what *this* felt like.

'Friends!' Caro started, to cheers from the audience. Another of Dahlia's turns of phrase, that. Everyone was a friend – until she was demanding their arrest. 'Thank you for joining us today! As you can see, this is an historic moment. *Three* Dahlia Livelys all on stage at the same time!'

Another cheer, louder this time, that set the blood rushing through Caro's veins, pounding in her ears as she waited for enough space in the noise to speak again.

'Since this is such a novelty, we thought we'd use it to do something entirely new.' Better to make it sound like this was a joint decision, rather than something she'd sprung on the other two. 'We all know what Dahlia Lively does best, right?'

She threw the question out into the audience, ignoring the few, mostly indecipherable answers that came back and ploughing on with her own. 'Interrogations! Dahlia's skill at fast talking a suspect into incriminating him or herself is second to none, and today, we're going to recreate this for you here!'

A buzz had started amongst the audience. Because there was one thing every fan knew about Dahlia's interrogations. Eventually, the right person would tell her the wrong thing and she'd solve the case. But before it got that far, many other people – the red herrings – would confess to something else. Only Dahlia got to keep all her secrets.

With a broad smile and a hand to one side of her mouth, she gave the suspects a reassuring wink, feeling like a pantomime prince as she did so. 'Don't worry. This is just for show.'

Caro turned back to the audience. 'We've picked our VIP delegates to play our suspects, as they were here all day yesterday. And as some of you know, we have a very convenient crime to investigate! The theft of a jewelled magnifying glass.'

There was a satisfying gasp at that. Caro glanced at the suspects in case any of them were looking particularly guilty. They weren't.

'Now, I imagine we'll all look very silly when it turns out the glass has actually fallen down the back of a cabinet or something—' That earned a somewhat relieved chuckle from some audience members. '—but for the purposes of this exercise, it's perfect! All we're going to do is ask each of our suspects here to think back over the events of yesterday and see if they can remember anything suspicious . . .'

An 'Oooo' went up from the audience. She wondered if they thought this was a set-up, another part of the game they'd played yesterday with the fake murder mystery.

It took Caro a moment to realise that Posy had stood up and joined her in the centre of the stage. When she held out her hand for the microphone, Caro had little choice but to pass it over graciously. After all, this was the *Three* Dahlias panel.

'As you'll all know from the books,' Posy said, smiling out at the crowd, 'Dahlia is always looking for a chink in the armour of a story. Something that doesn't quite match up with the facts, or what some-one else has said. But of course, *we* know that our memories are fallible, and it's rare to get two people to agree on exactly what happened!'

Rosalind appeared at her other side, holding out a pale, elegant hand for the microphone. 'I'll start.'

Rosalind approached the suspects. From behind her, Caro couldn't see her face – but she'd place money she knew exactly the expression that was on it. The arch, slightly knowing look she'd perfected as Dahlia. The one that told the audience she knew something they didn't, yet, but if they stuck with her all would be revealed.

Caro had watched those old Lady Detective movies a dozen times, both before she landed the part and after, in that nervous waiting period before filming started. The period she supposed Posy was in, right now. Had she been re-watching the classics yet?

'Let's start with the basics,' Rosalind said. Even her voice sounded different. More clipped, clear – proper Received Pronunciation, rather than her usual relaxed version of a refined English accent. The sort she trotted out for period dramas and the like. 'Before you came to Aldermere this weekend, which of the people staying at the house had you met before?'

Caro smiled. A nice, easy question to start them off, but a useful one all the same.

'Well, I was already quite well acquainted with my wife,' Harry said, earning a laugh from the crowd that made his cheeks pink. 'Other than that . . . we knew Marcus, of course. Been coming to his conventions for years. And Felicity, for the same reason. We'd met Caro once or twice, too, not that I'd expect her to remember us . . .'

'Oh, of course I remember!' Caro lied. 'Now. Go on. Anyone else?'

Harry shrugged and looked at Heather, who shook her head. 'That's about it.'

Rosalind turned to Felicity next. 'Same as Harry and Heather, really. Oh, and I'd spoken to Clementine on the phone and by email, but we hadn't actually met in person before this weekend.'

'Ashok?' Posy asked, gently. 'Did you know anybody here?'

'Not a soul.' He gave a self-conscious chuckle. 'I'm actually, well, quite new to the Dahlia fandom, really. But it's taken over my life over the last year, and I couldn't miss this chance to actually stay at Aldermere!'

Caro shared a look with Rosalind. Interesting.

'And Kit?' Caro asked. 'How about you?'

Kit leaned back in his seat, his hands folded behind his head. 'Well, I knew Posy, of course.'

'We guessed that when we saw you kissing her in the Murder Spiral!' Harry barked a laugh, and another murmur went up among the audience.

'That was part of the murder mystery game!' Posy protested, but she was blushing, which rather ruined things.

'Of course it was, sweetheart,' Kit said, so unconvincingly that Caro knew there'd be rumours about the two of them on social media before the panel even finished. 'Anyway, other than that, I only knew Anton, our director, and our writer, Libby.'

'Okay, then.' Rosalind took back the microphone. 'Next, I'm going to recount the basic events of yesterday, and I'm going to ask you all to jump in if you remember anything unusual about it. Anything you saw, or heard, for instance. Posy, perhaps you might help me?'

Posy leaped to her feet, blinking, as Rosalind motioned to the flipchart and pens on the corner of the stage. Why hadn't Caro thought of that? It was perfect!

'First of all, the coaches arrived from the station from around 9AM.' Rosalind nodded at Posy and she wrote it down on the board, leaving space for any extra notes that came later.

'You were all met by Clementine, who gave you your wrist bands and your welcome packs. Then you were all shown to your rooms. Then we all met later by the dollhouse for Isobel's tour of the house.' Another nod at Posy, who scrawled 'House Tour' on the paper. Rosalind winced, presumably at Posy's handwriting.

She'd been holding court long enough, Caro decided. Getting up, she motioned to the volunteer to hand her the second microphone that was supposed to be used for audience questions.

'During the tour, we all handled the jewelled magnifying glass,' Caro said, ignoring Rosalind's glare. 'For those of you who don't know, this is the beautiful jeweller's loupe that Dahlia uses in the novels. A bejewelled version was created for the movies, and given to Lettice Davenport as a gift, after filming ended.'

'Thank you, Caro.' There was no gratitude in Rosalind's voice. 'As you say, the object was handed around everyone on that house tour when we visited Lettice's study. It was then replaced in the cabinet by Isobel, before we all left the room.'

'Was it locked?' Kit asked. Rosalind blinked at him. 'I wasn't on the house tour, see, so I don't know. Was the cabinet one with a lock?'

'That's a good question, DI Swain,' Caro said, with a slow smile. 'Did anybody notice?'

The VIP delegates shook their heads. Posy frowned. 'I was one of the last out, I think, and I didn't see Isobel lock it.'

'So it's possible that someone could have taken it on their way out, without being noticed. Or they could have crept back later to take it, now they knew where it was,' Caro surmised.

'After the tour we had lunch, and the convention murder mystery was announced by Marcus.' Rosalind's stride hitched a little there, as she fumbled for her next words. Posy, taking the microphone from her, stepped in.

'We went to take our places for the mystery – and you four set about investigating, along with plenty of other delegates.' She smiled at the suspects – a Hollywood smile that Caro could feel from across the stage. She'd had the real LA life, hadn't she? All the praise and the glory and the parts. She knew how to work a room, Caro had to give her that.

'Then there was the conclusion of the murder mystery where *I* was arrested – and Ashok, I think you won, didn't you?' Ashok blushed under the weight of Posy's smile.

Time for Caro to take over again. 'And that was when Isobel announced that the magnifying glass had been stolen. So we know it must have been taken between eleven, when we left Lettice's study, and five when Isobel made that announcement. Agreed?'

Everyone on the stage nodded, along with a lot of the crowd. Caro cast an assessing eye over the audience. A few people at the back were sneaking out again – this wasn't what they'd come for, after all. But the majority had stayed and looked engaged in the process.

'Of course, after that, whoever took it would have to hide it – since all our bags were searched – then retrieve it, too.' Rosalind had claimed the microphone from Posy. 'So we need to carry on into the evening. There was free time until the pre-dinner drinks, then dinner itself.'

Caro watched the suspects carefully at the mention of dinner. Every one of them glanced at their neighbours, reflecting on what had happened as that dinner, and the day, had come to an end.

'So now we get to the fun bit,' Posy said, into Rosalind's microphone. 'What you all noticed about the day.'

Posy nodded at the second microphone in Caro's hand, and she passed it to Felicity to start.

'Um, well, I think it basically went pretty much as you said.' She flicked her blue hair over her shoulder as she studied the flipchart. 'I was with Ashok when we did the murder mystery thing after lunch – Posy, you saw us together in the Murder Spiral, so you can be our alibi for that?'

'I sure can.' Posy's bouncy smile made Caro think of children's TV presenters. And not in a good way.

'Then after that we tracked down another couple of clues together, before splitting up for the last part – to see which one of us could win.' She gave Ashok a baleful look. 'I got caught up in an argument with a group of day delegates about how Dahlia solved the mystery in *Flowers and Feuds* without ever leaving the undertaker's parlour, so Ashok beat me.'

One of Lettice's sixties efforts that, although still set in the thirties. Not one of Caro's favourites to film, as she had to sit around with a fake corpse all day. But the ending *was* clever, she had to admit that.

'Then after that was over, and we knew the magnifying glass had been stolen, I was reading in my room.' Her cheeks took on a slight pink tinge. 'I know we're supposed to be having an immersive experience, no modern electronics and all that, but I smuggled my kindle in, you see, and I have all the Dahlia Lively books on it, as well as the hardbacks at home.'

'You wanted to check you were right about the ending of *Flowers and Feuds*,' Caro guessed. 'I can understand that.'

She kept her voice calm and soothing – more practice for those mum-part auditions her agent kept sending her on, even though she'd never had children, or any desire for them. Apparently that was what was available for women her age – parts where she stood in the background supporting others, always stirring something on a stove, or wrapping a scarf around someone's neck. And not even in a fun strangling way.

Caro could get behind playing a murderer, as long as it was a role where the script cared about what her character wanted, needed, more than what she could do for others.

But today she was still a detective, still Dahlia. And she'd got her first – albeit minor – confession. Felicity had smuggled in banned electronics. It wasn't much, but it opened the doors for the others to share their small secrets and shames, too, she hoped.

'Then there was the film panel, and later I met the rest of you for drinks and dinner.' Felicity looked thoughtful. 'I suppose I technically *could* have taken the magnifying glass when we were on the house tour together, and then hidden it when I say I was reading – but my bag was checked with all the others on my way into the house, so where would I have put it? Unless I hid it somewhere else on the house tour and retrieved it later?'

'And that's the fun of interrogating other detectives. They work out all the possibilities for you!' Caro threw the aside to the audience and received a gratifying laugh in return. 'What about at dinner? Assuming you *weren't* the thief, did you see anybody acting suspiciously?'

Felicity pulled a notebook from her bag and flipped through the pages. 'I've been trying to recreate everyone's movements from dinner. You know, just for investigative practice.'

Her eyes were wide and innocent as she said it, but Caro half expected her to give a knowing wink. Investigative practice indeed.

The Dahlias weren't the only ones investigating a murder, as well as a theft. That might complicate things.

'How useful,' Rosalind said. 'Anything you'd like to share? From your . . . notes.'

'Well, I did see Juliette – the teenage daughter of the house,' she added, to the audience, 'sneaking out the front door during dinner, when I went to the bathroom. I think she said she was going to call her boyfriend, but why would she need to do that outside?'

That *was* interesting – and given the questioning hum around the marquee, others thought so too. It was absolutely the sort of clue that would help Dahlia solve a mystery, although Caro couldn't see how.

'Of course, since the magnifying glass belongs to her family, and will one day belong to her, it's hard to imagine why she might want to steal it,' Rosalind said, drily. 'I hate to tell tales out of school, but I rather suspect she was sneaking out to meet her boyfriend! Now, who is next?' Rosalind moved on smoothly, while the audience laughed, but Juliette had risen to the top of Caro's mental list of people to speak to.

Next up was Ashok, who confirmed Felicity's story, and added that he'd also been in his room reading – 'an actual book, not a contraband electronic one' – between the film panel and dinner. But there was something about his manner that made Caro suspicious. She narrowed her eyes as she tried to figure it out, then smiled as she realised. His gaze was darting around the marquee, but there was one place it never landed – on Posy. Did the boy have a crush on their Hollywood starlet, perhaps?

Or was there something more to it?

'And are you certain there isn't anything else you'd like to share with us about your day yesterday?' Rosalind asked, mildly, from Posy's side.

All three Dahlias stared him down.

And Ashok broke.

'Okay, *fine.* I bribed those girls to distract Felicity with the argument about *Flowers and Feuds* so that I could win the tickets for next year's convention. Happy?' He threw himself back in his chair with his arms folded across his chest, his chin low and his eyes embarrassed.

Beside him, Felicity gasped, then whacked him on the arm with her convention guide. 'See if I share any more of my investigation notes with you!'

'But I also saw *you* arguing with Anton in the hallway during dinner.' Ashok pointed at Posy, who gave a somewhat tense laugh.

'Artistic differences, I'm afraid,' she joked. 'Rather than theft related.'

'And I did see Marcus heading towards Lettice's study in the attic, not long before you and I . . . bumped into each other on the landing before dinner,' he added, looking at Posy.

Or when she'd broken into Clementine's room and stolen the script, more likely. But what had Marcus been doing up there? At least it explained where he'd disappeared to, leaving her to try and talk Isobel down from her seating plan related hysteria.

'Interesting. Thank you, Ashok. So that's two confessions so far,' Caro said. The audience applauded dutifully. 'Let's see if we can get anything a little meatier from our next suspects, shall we?'

Harry and Heather had nothing new to add, but Kit happily took the floor to be thoroughly questioned for the last fifteen minutes of their session. By the end, Caro suspected he was making stuff up for dramatic impact.

'So let me get this straight,' Posy said, rolling her eyes good-naturedly at the audience. 'Over the course of yesterday, you saw a ghostly face at Lettice Davenport's study window from the Murder Spiral, a fight between two people dressed as Detective Inspector Johnnie Swain, our scriptwriter trying to bribe a conference organiser to get her phone back, and a small bear stealing jam from the preserves stand.'

'Yes,' Kit said, firmly. 'Well, some of those things, anyway. It's hard to remember because I'm hungry. Is it lunchtime yet?'

The audience laughed. By the door to the marquee, the volunteer in the waistcoat was tapping her watch. They were nearly out of time; Caro had better start wrapping things up.

'Yes it is,' Caro said. 'So we'd better finish there. Thank you all for helping us demonstrate a few key investigative points that I think Dahlia would be proud of! Firstly, that you never know which snippet of information will unravel the whole mystery. Secondly, that opportunity means nothing without – what else, everyone?'

'Motive and means!' the audience bellowed back, sending Posy a few surprised steps backwards.

Caro beamed. 'Exactly! And thirdly . . .' She gave the suspect panel a wicked smile. 'Everyone has a little secret or two to hide – even if it's just a contraband kindle. Thank you for joining us here today!' she added, over the laughs of the audience. 'We've been the Three Dahlias!'

'You make us sound like a circus act,' Rosalind grumbled, as Caro grabbed both her and Posy's hands and dragged them into a bow for the cheering crowd.

'Just giving the fans what they want,' Caro muttered, through her teeth, before realising what she had said.

Just giving the fans what they want. That was one of Marcus's sayings. He always claimed everything he did was all for the fans.

But had one of those fans killed him?

Chapter Sixteen

'You realise that this is illegal,' Johnnie said, mildly.

The window lock finally gave way under her efforts, and she pushed it open wide enough to fit through. 'I like to think of it as a creative interpretation of the law,' she replied.

'Let's hope the courts see it the same way,' Johnnie muttered, following her through the open window.

Dahlia Lively *in* The Devil & the Deep Blue Sea
By Lettice Davenport, 1940

The rest of the convention seemed to be carrying on to plan, despite the loss of its two main organisers. Caro grinned as she spotted Juliette – now dressed in a classic skirt suit and with a silk square tied around her neck – holding a clipboard and talking to some of the volunteers.

Caro motioned to Rosalind and Posy to wait for her, then approached Juliette, catching her eye but waiting until she'd finished instructing the volunteers to speak.

'Everything going smoothly, then?' she asked, as the volunteers left to carry out Juliette's orders.

'Perfectly. Clementine kept good notes, and the volunteers are pretty clued up.'

'Any luck getting hold of her?' If they could speak to Clementine, she could answer a lot of the questions that were hanging over them.

But Juliette shook her head. 'I called, but no answer – I guess the family emergency thing is still ongoing. I left a voicemail, and sent a text, so she's got my number.'

'And the volunteers are okay without her or Marcus here?'

'Yeah, seem to be.' Juliette smirked. 'Actually, they're mostly relieved that it isn't Marcus bossing them around. He wasn't the most popular guy around here. Everyone was happier when Clementine was in charge. She knew how things actually worked.'

Caro had suspected as much, but it was nice to have it confirmed by a source on the ground. 'Marcus always liked to be more of the ringmaster than a performer. Had you met him before? When he'd been to the house?'

A small frown line appeared between Juliette's perfectly groomed eyebrows as she thought. 'I don't think so. I mean, people are here visiting Grandma and Granddad all the time, but I don't remember him and I think I would.' She paused, her smile turning a little shy – not something Caro expected from the confident young woman. 'I wanted to say, thank you for trusting me with this. People . . . don't, generally. But Aldermere, Lettice and Dahlia . . . they're part of my family legacy too. And it's nice to be doing something that matters for once.'

Maybe Caro should audition for more Mum roles, after all. It seemed she was good at the teen mentoring thing. Or did that make her more of a cool aunt? There was a definite dearth of cool aunt roles on television at the moment. Perhaps she should write one. She could be writer, director *and* star of it. *That* would show Rosalind.

After she finished dealing with a murder.

'I'm glad you're enjoying it. I know yesterday wasn't much fun for you.' Caro looked both ways before giving Juliette a secretive smile. 'But did I see you escaping for a least a *little* bit of fun last night? After you said you were going to call your boyfriend?'

Juliette's eyes widened. 'Don't tell Grandma, will you?'

'Of course not!' As if she'd tell Isobel *anything*. Didn't Juliette know she was the cool sort of aunt? 'But just between us girls?'

'Oliver came here to meet me, by the stables. Grandma basically banned him from Aldermere for the weekend, but he really wanted to see me, so . . .' Her cheeks flushed a pretty pink that matched her neck scarf.

'Young love. I *totally* understand.' Well, she mostly remembered, anyway. Suddenly, that 'have to see you right now' feeling seemed a long way away. Had she felt like that about Annie, at the start?

Yes. Yes, she had. More than once she'd snuck away from a hotel on location and driven half the night to spend an hour or two with Annie, before driving back again for the following morning's early call.

'I don't suppose you saw anything . . . unusual, out there, did you?' There was a delicate line here. How to ask about a murder without actually letting on that there had *been* a murder.

'Like what?' Juliette asked. 'I mean, it was dark, and Oliver and I . . . well, we were kind of busy.'

I bet you were. 'Oh, I don't know. Just still trying to figure out where someone might have hidden that blasted magnifying glass, I suppose. And there was so much coming and going at the dinner, I wondered if someone might have slipped out to hand it to an accomplice.'

Juliette shook her head. 'Well, if they did, I didn't see them. Sorry. Although . . .' She frowned.

'Although?' Caro prompted.

'I went up to get changed before I went out to meet Oliver – I mean, I wasn't going out in the outfit I had to wear for the dinner, right? Anyway, when I was up there, I saw Ashok letting himself out of the China Room. And I thought that was weird because I was sure Posy was staying there?'

'She is,' Caro said, thoughtfully. And if Ashok had slipped out when Posy had and seen her arguing with Anton, like he'd told them on the panel, he'd have known that Posy wasn't in her room to catch him snooping.

Interesting.

Another volunteer approached, clutching a sheet of paper and with a questioning look about them. Juliette turned towards them, and Caro took the opportunity to back away.

'I'll leave you to it.' She headed back to Rosalind and Posy, still thinking.

'Well?' Rosalind asked.

'You were right; she was meeting her boyfriend.' Caro frowned. 'Although we should probably try to speak to him to confirm that.'

'Confirm that she *wasn't* in the room when the murder was committed?' Posy asked.

'It's what Dahlia would do,' Caro insisted, stubbornly. 'Rosalind, perhaps you can do that?'

'Why does she need an alibi anyway?' Rosalind said, crossly. 'She's a child, Caro.'

'She's nineteen. That's an adult,' Caro counted. 'And everyone needs an alibi. Right, Posy?'

Posy looked between them, considering her response. 'I was nineteen when I discovered that my parents had embezzled all the money I'd ever earned, and lost it all. I was nineteen when I walked away with nothing and, well, went off the rails. So, yes, nineteen is old enough to be an adult – if that means being alone in the world and making bad decisions. But I'm guessing that Juliette's nineteen looks different to mine.'

The pain in her voice caught at Caro's throat, robbing her of an answer.

Rosalind sighed. 'I'll talk to Juliette later, try to get her to call the boyfriend for me. Claim it's some sort of great-godmother thing.'

'So what do we do in the meantime?' Posy asked.

'I'd suggest stopping for a cup of tea, personally,' Rosalind replied, still sounding annoyed with Caro. 'I mean, we've asked questions all morning and the only secrets we've uncovered are an illicit kindle, a clumsy attempt to cheat at a stupid game, and a teenage love tryst. Why not quit before we're more behind? We're *actresses,* not detectives.'

'We can't be both?' Posy asked, eyebrows raised.

'Of course we can.' Caro gave Rosalind a hard stare. 'Dahlia wasn't a detective to start with, either. But she had brains and a talent for getting people to tell her things they'd probably be better off if they didn't. She solved puzzles and saw connections. And she knew *people.* Just like we do.'

It was only as she was saying it that Caro realised how true it was. They'd spent their careers pretending to be other people, learning what made their characters tick, why they made the decisions they did. Their biggest mistakes, their regrets, their passions – their motivations.

And that was what they were doing at Aldermere.

Rosalind sighed. 'Fine. So what do we do next? Since you seem determined to be Head Dahlia in this investigation.'

Caro tried not to preen too much. Of course she was Head Dahlia. She'd played her the longest. 'Well, the way I see it, we have two options.'

'Oh?' Rosalind's expression was bored, but Caro could see the flicker of excitement in her eyes. She was enjoying this more than she'd let on.

'Either we search Marcus's room for a reason someone might want to kill him, or we ask Ashok why Juliette saw him leaving Posy's bedroom during dinner last night.'

Ashok, it transpired, had gone straight from the Three Dahlias panel into another event in one of the other marquees, so they decided to search Marcus's room first. Although Posy did fill them in on Ashok's role in her searching of Clementine's room as they headed back to the house.

'And you didn't think to mention this earlier?' Rosalind asked.

Posy shrugged. 'He wanted his phone back. He played lookout. He never went inside the room. It didn't really seem important.'

Until it did. Wasn't that always the way with Dahlia's investigations?

For now Caro settled for keeping a mental running list of questions to ask Ashok when they caught up with him, and hurried up the stairs towards the China Room.

Marcus's room adjoining Posy's made things a lot easier than Caro had expected – but it did mean they had to pass through Posy's room to get there. The room was oppressively blue and white, and Posy winced as she opened the door.

'This room definitely worked better in fiction,' Caro observed, as they trooped inside. 'When we filmed it, we just had the one wall and the bedspread blue and white. I think viewers would have switched off to save their eyeballs, otherwise.'

'My eyeballs sadly continue to suffer.' Posy crossed the room to a door hidden in the wall by the matching wallpaper that covered it. It was only noticeable because of the heavy key sticking out of the keyhole.

'Wait!' Rosalind said. 'If Ashok was in here last night at dinner, that means he was looking for something. Shouldn't we figure out what?'

'The magnifying glass, I assume,' Posy said, with a small frown. 'But that's still hidden in my shoe in the wardrobe. I checked this morning.' She opened the wardrobe door and pulled out the shoe – and loupe – to prove the point.

'Either he's rubbish at searching, or he was looking for something else,' Caro said. 'But what?'

'I have no idea.' Posy glanced around her as if hunting for clues. 'The script? The blackmail photos and note? I had all those with me in my bag.'

'Maybe,' Caro said. 'Come on. Let's check Marcus's room.'

The Jack-and-Jill bathroom was soothingly white, and the door on the other side helpfully unlocked. Beyond it, Marcus's room was plainer than Posy's, or Caro's for that matter. Clearly designed as a Man's Room, there was little in the way of decoration besides two decorative guns on the wall, and an etching of a hunt by the window. The bed was covered with a tartan blanket, and a heavy wooden desk with a leather top sat along the wall beside the bathroom door.

'Where do we start?' Posy asked. The police had sealed off the doors to the room with tape, which they all ducked under, but otherwise left it untouched.

'You check the bed, Rosalind the wardrobe, I'll take the desk,' Caro said, decisively.

She had no idea what the others might find – she suspected Marcus had more secrets than she was privy to – but she also knew she stood the best chance of finding what *she* was looking for in the desk. Marcus was a creature of habit, after all, and while she might not have been in this particular bedroom before, she had been in others.

They moved quickly, none of them keen to stay in a dead man's quarters longer than necessary – or to be found there by someone else. Caro yanked open the desk drawers and found not much of interest; a paperback novel – not a Lettice Davenport – a blank pad of paper, and a few pens.

Then she reached *under* the drawers and felt the soft leather of Marcus's ledger. Small, square, stained and aged – much like its late owner. It was a simple thing to crouch down and prise it free, tucking it in the inside pocket of her jacket. Caro had an idea what she'd find in there, but she wanted to check it and be sure before she shared it with the others.

She hadn't expected Marcus to still have photographic evidence of their idiotic affair. Who knew what other evidence he was carrying around with him?

She double checked in case he'd hidden anything else there, and felt another piece of paper. Frowning, she tugged that free too, and brought it into the light.

It was a letter; creamy paper in a matching quality envelope, addressed to Anton.

Caro scanned the text as she stood up.

'What is it?' Posy asked. 'What have you found?'

'It seems that Marcus had been branching out,' Caro said, drily, as she held it up. She hadn't known about this part of his enterprise, but she wasn't surprised by it either. 'He didn't send *his* blackmail notes on script pages.'

'More blackmail?' Posy's eyebrows rose by degrees as she read the letter. 'But who was he blackmailing?'

Caro held up the envelope. 'Your boss. Was he really responsible for leaking the original script?'

Posy winced. 'And a few other things. What did Marcus want?'

'The usual. Money, plus a cameo in the new movie. Otherwise he was going to the investors with proof that Anton was behind the leak.' She checked under the desk again. 'Although, whatever proof he thought he had, he didn't have it here.'

'Anton is not having a very good weekend,' Posy said, a wide smile lighting up her face.

'This is what you were arguing with him about last night, isn't it?' Caro snorted a laugh. 'Artistic differences, indeed.'

Posy pulled a face, but admitted it all the same. 'He's responsible for all the talk of the curse.' She explained the row she'd had with the director the night before, and Caro grinned at the idea of Posy duping Anton by pretending to record his confession. She was turning out to be more of a Dahlia than Caro had expected.

She glanced at Rosalind to share the moment. But Rosalind was staring at the envelope in Caro's hand.

'No stamp,' she muttered. 'That's what was strange about it.'

Caro exchanged a look with Posy. Clearly they were missing something, but Rosalind was a consummate actress. She'd want to let the suspense build before she told them, and there was no point trying to rush her.

Finally Rosalind looked up, her eyes wide and her hands trembling. 'I saw a letter like this – or at least, an envelope, with this handwriting on it. It was sitting on the telephone table on Friday night, so I took it up to Hugh. At the time, I couldn't put my finger on what was strange about it, but I see it now. It had Hugh's full name and address on it – but no stamp or postmark.'

'It must have been hand delivered,' Posy said, thoughtfully.

'And Marcus was here at Aldermere that night,' Rosalind confirmed.

'So Marcus was blackmailing Hugh, and planning to blackmail Anton.' That opened up a whole new world of possibilities for motive.

'But what about?' Posy asked. 'I mean, I know what Anton was up to. But what was Hugh doing that was so blackmail worthy?'

Rosalind's face drained of all remaining colour. 'Isobel thinks . . . she told me she thinks he's having an affair.'

'An affair?' Caro asked. 'With whom?'

'She didn't say.' But Caro would place money that Rosalind had an idea.

Posy got there first. '*That's* why you were watching him and Clementine in the garden!' she said.

Rosalind glared at her. 'The tour wasn't exactly riveting.'

'Do you really think she could be Hugh's mistress? Maybe *that's* why she left.' Caro could feel more pieces slotting into place. 'I never bought that family emergency thing.'

'I don't know. I know Hugh. I don't think he would. Well. Not with Clementine. She's young enough to be his daughter.' Caro wasn't sure if Rosalind was trying to convince them or herself.

'Granddaughter,' Posy corrected, sounding disgusted. 'But yeah, I could see her running if Hugh was being blackmailed about their relationship. And it would explain why he let her take the car.'

'Was there anything else back there?' Rosalind waved a hand towards the desk. 'Any sign he was blackmailing anyone else?'

Caro hesitated. She should tell them about Marcus's ledger, she knew. But surely this was all to do with the blackmail? There was nothing worth killing for in the ledger.

'No. I think we have to assume that there might be more people he was blackmailing,' she said. 'This letter at least was never delivered, so perhaps Anton didn't know Marcus had him in his sights.'

'So he'd have no reason to murder him,' Posy finished. 'But Hugh did. He'd already received his letter.'

'But as Caro says, he might not have been the only one,' Rosalind added, hurriedly. She didn't want to believe her beloved Hugh could have been responsible. It was almost laughable how she still doted on him after all these years, and all those stories.

When Caro's husband had cheated on her, she hadn't sat back and played the scorned woman. She'd got out there and shown everyone that he couldn't break her. That she wasn't going to keep quiet and carry on as she might have been expected to in the past. The press had rather enjoyed the drama, too – especially in the early, raw, painful, pre-Annie days, when Caro's reactions to her more famous husband's infidelity had filled endless pages in the gossip columns.

And yes, she'd also been susceptible to too much wine in a hotel bar, and Marcus's dubious charms. But at least she could console herself that he'd been more of a catch back then. And she'd come to her senses pretty quickly, ended things and sworn off love and romance all together.

Until she met Annie. That had been something neither of them had expected or planned.

Rosalind, on the other hand, had reacted rather differently to being thrown over by Hugh when he married Isobel. She had fallen into the arms of her co-star, married him, and still spent high days and holidays being best buddies with her ex, and the friend everyone knew he cheated on her with. Caro couldn't claim to know the whole story, but Rosalind's grace under fire, immaculate manners and the way she'd held her head high and never badmouthed anybody prob-ably went a long way to explaining why she was a national treasure in the media, and Caro was a source of constant amusement.

But Rosalind had never known the satisfaction of setting Hugh's tie on fire while he was wearing it, like she had done to her ex-husband, so who was the real winner here?

'We need to get out of here before someone comes looking,' Posy said, breaking the silence. 'We can figure out who else Marcus might have been blackmailing in my room.'

'Do you think this is how someone got in to leave the magnifying glass?' Caro wondered aloud, as they turned to the bathroom.

Posy paused in opening the door. 'I hadn't thought about that. Could it have been Marcus who stole it?'

Rosalind looked to Caro as well, and Caro realised they were both waiting for her to answer. She was the one who had known Marcus best and longest, after all.

She considered. 'It *could*. I mean, I wouldn't put it past him to steal it. Marcus's sense of morality was always a little more elastic than some.'

'So we noticed.' Rosalind brandished the blackmail letter.

'Anyway, I think—' she started, but Posy cut her off with a slashing hand and a finger on her lips.

'There's someone in my room,' she breathed.

Caro inched closer to the door and listened. Posy was right. There was movement on the other side of the bathroom.

What would Dahlia do? Oh, well that was easy.

'Then let's surprise them,' Caro murmured, and shoved the door open.

Chapter Seventeen

'But is that really enough of a motive to kill?' Johnnie asked, looking up from the list he'd been making in his neat script in his small policeman's notebook.

Dahlia smiled. 'Oh, Johnnie. It's not for us to say what is motive enough for another person. What might be a minor annoyance to us could mean murder to someone else – and vice versa. A person's motives – and their emotions – are always unfathomable to those of us on the outside.'

Dahlia Lively *in* Flowers and Feuds
***By* Lettice Davenport, 1965**

Caro burst into the room hoping to surprise the intruder, but the bedroom door stood open. She was too late.

The China Room was dark, the curtains drawn. Whoever had broken into Posy's room had been there longer than they'd realised; the bathroom between them must have insulated the sounds next door.

Hurrying to the second open door, Caro scanned the hallway only to find the landing full of people. The VIP delegates were heading towards the stairs, a gang of four bound together by obsession and their own investigations. Hugh was descending the stairs from Lettice's study, and she spotted Isobel's pale hair disappearing around the corner towards her own rooms.

Any one of them could have been in Posy's room, then got lost in the crowd.

Caro shut the door behind her and turned to find Posy and Rosalind standing at the dressing table, staring at the small glass bottle in Posy's hand. It was opaque, the glass misty and dark, concealing the contents. But the skull and crossbones label with the word POISON printed on it solved that problem.

'Is that . . .' she trailed off as Rosalind nodded.

'The poison bottle from Letty's study.'

Posy looked up, her eyes wide with panic. 'Is someone trying to frame me for Marcus's death too? Is that really what's happening here?'

'It certainly looks like it.' Rosalind pulled a handkerchief from her pocket – and really, who still had hankies to hand these days? – and took the poison bottle from Posy and studied it.

'Oh God! Fingerprints!' Posy wiped her hands frantically against her skirt, as if that could vanish the prints from her fingertips, or her prints from the bottle in Rosalind's hand. 'Why didn't I think of that?!'

Because you haven't been Dahlia long enough, Caro thought, but didn't say. Tact, twice in one day. That might actually be a record, now she thought about it.

'Was there another note?' Caro searched the dressing table and turned up the expected piece of paper. Not on a script page, and not on the same creamy stationery that Marcus had used for his blackmail letters. It was a plain page of notebook paper, covered in block print writing.

USE THIS

Posy read it over her shoulder, then turned away in horror, yanking open the curtains and staring out at the gardens instead. As if the rest of Aldermere was any less threatening than Posy's new stalker.

'It's like a twisted version of Alice in Wonderland,' Caro mused. 'Well, more twisted, I suppose.' She'd played the Queen of Hearts in an immersive Alice experience a couple of years ago that became rather more immersive when they got a lost and confused stag party in one night, and the groom drank the glittery, gluey substance in the 'Drink Me' bottle. There were ambulances involved, but he'd been okay. Probably.

'Who was out in the corridor?' Rosalind asked Caro. 'Any clues who left it here? Could it be Ashok? We know he's broken in here before.'

Caro shook her head. 'It's Piccadilly Circus out there. Plus anyone could have ducked into one of the other rooms along the corridor before I came out.'

'Should we call the police?'

'And tell them what?' Posy spun back around from the window. 'That someone keeps relocating Lettice's keepsakes from her study to another room in the house that used to belong to her? I'm really not sure they could prosecute something like that.'

'That someone is trying to frame you,' Rosalind corrected her.

'For a murder that no one else knows happened? Right.' She gave a high, nervous laugh. 'I mean, that bottle probably wasn't even used in the murder! It was the sugared flower, remember? Unless we're all crazy and it was a heart attack after all . . .'

Posy was starting to lose it, that much was obvious. And they couldn't afford for one of them to freak out and go rogue, not now.

'Okay, I think we need to act fast,' Caro said, soothingly. 'Someone is trying to frame Posy and we're not going to let that happen, right?' She looked to Rosalind for confirmation, who took a beat too long to nod her agreement.

Caro resisted the urge to roll her eyes as Posy let out a squeak of something that sounded like fear and frustration rolled into one.

'What are you suggesting we do?' Rosalind asked.

'The only people who know that Posy has any connection to the poison bottle or the magnifying glass are us three, right?'

'And whoever put them there.' Rosalind's point was annoyingly accurate.

'Ah, but all they can do is tell someone to look for them here.'

'Which is when the police arrest me,' Posy pointed out.

'Not if the things aren't here when they search.' Caro grinned. 'Then, they have to turn to the person who gave them the tip-off and ask how they knew in the first place.'

'So you're saying we need to hide them?' The hope in Posy's eyes was encouraging. She needed someone to tell her what to do for the best, that was all.

Caro always knew she should have done more directing. She clearly had a natural talent for it.

'I'm saying we need to put them back where they came from.'

Caro left Rosalind to distract Hugh, and Posy standing guard in her bedroom with the door open, keeping an eye on the stairs to Lettice's study, while she returned the stolen items.

She crept up the stairs, praying they wouldn't creak too much, and turned the handle to the study, easing the door open to check that it was empty before she entered. The last thing she needed was someone catching her with a priceless jewelled magnifying glass stuffed in her bra and a poison bottle in her hand.

She was in luck; the study was empty. She pressed the door shut behind her, then leant against it. Strange to think that this was the place where Dahlia Lively had sprung into existence. Lettice had moved to London in her late teens, precocious as ever, moving in literary circles and selling her first novel at the age of nineteen. But the germ of it, that character, had first come to her in this attic room, according to her later interviews.

Caro's gaze fell on the desk in the centre of the room, in front of the window, as she imagined Lettice sitting there, dreaming up new challenges for Dahlia Lively and her friends.

'You'd have liked this one,' she murmured to herself, or maybe to Lettice. She wasn't sure.

She placed the poison bottle back on the shelf, then hurried to the glass cabinet where the magnifying glass had been kept. A shadowy outline on the felt showed where it belonged, the way that objects that remained long in one place left imprints even in their absence.

Caro fished the magnifying glass out of her bra and returned it to its place. Then she looked again, frowning.

It didn't fit.

It sat nicely enough against the felt, but its shape didn't quite match the outline left behind. The handle was a fraction too short, and the glass a few millimetres too big. It could have been some quirk of the storage, but instinct told Caro that wasn't it.

The same instinct that reminded her of Marcus's ledger in her other pocket.

Caro dropped into the desk chair, pulled out the little leather notebook and flicked through it. She'd have to be quick, but hopefully Posy would distract anyone heading up here. And Caro had a feeling this was going to be important.

It didn't take her long to find what she was looking for – what her detective's intuition told her must be there. Three months earlier, an entry marked *Aldermere* in Marcus's cursive hand. *Jewellers Loupe belonging to Lettice Davenport.* And beside it was the amount it was bought for – significant – and the amount sold for – significantly more.

Marcus had bought the original magnifying glass, and it had been replaced with a replica, which someone had then stolen believing it to be the real thing.

That was the more legitimate side of Marcus's business. Buying items of significant value to fans from the owners, then selling them on to collectors. He had all the connections he needed through the conventions he organised, and the memorabilia sales probably earned him more than any of the events did.

Sometimes the items were sold, openly and freely. Sometimes they were secretive, like with the magnifying glass. But what Marcus didn't advertise was that sometimes, when the owner didn't want to sell, or where the object was hidden away, undervalued by the current owner, he'd arrange for someone to steal it.

That didn't seem to be the case here, though. Next to the sale entry was the name 'Davenport'. Which meant that someone in the family must have sold it, then replaced it with the fake. And now they were claiming it had been stolen ... An insurance fraud, perhaps? Aldermere was starting to look a little worn around the edges. But then why hide it in *Posy's* room, of all places?

Something else she needed to figure out, if she wanted to solve the mystery before the police even realised there *was* one.

The only problem was, she wasn't solving this mystery alone. As much as she hated to admit it, she needed Rosalind and Posy. They were better as a team. Rosalind knew the family, and they were going to need that insight. Posy knew the film lot, and this murder had been following their script. But more than that, they saw more together – more connections, more clues – than they found apart.

She might be Head Dahlia right now, but she needed her sidekicks.

Which meant telling them the truth. And hearing theirs.

This whole thing had started with the blackmail photos they'd each been sent – the one clue none of them had been willing to fully share. But now it was time.

If she ever wanted to move on from her sins, she had to confess them first. Dahlia had been Catholic; she'd known all about confession.

But in confessing, she'd become Caro again, rather than Dahlia. And *that* scared her more than the idea of sharing a house with a murderer.

With a sigh, Caro turned to the ledger, and looked at the other names listed next to the jeweller's loupe. The buyers: VIP delegates, Harry and Heather Wilson.

Caro squirmed uncomfortably through another fork buffet lunch, knowing what had to come next. She had to confess, to Posy and Rosalind at least, if not the police, what she knew about Marcus's criminal activities. Which meant admitting to her part in them, something she'd only ever done to Annie, before now.

Caro distracted herself by observing the others. Harry and Heather were chatting away to Felicity in one corner, as if nothing amiss was happening. Rosalind and Hugh were nowhere to be seen, and neither was Ashok, now she looked for him. Posy, meanwhile, had been cornered by Juliette, taking a break from convention responsibilities.

Isobel was holding court with Anton, Libby and Kit in another corner, laughing and charming them all. Caro eased past them on her way to the buffet table for seconds, slowing enough to make out a few snatches of their conversation.

'Of course, if you let us film here at Aldermere, the disruption would be even worse,' Anton was saying to Isobel.

'Anton! You'll put her off!' Kit laughed. 'And then where will we be?'

'I always believe in being upfront about what people can expect from one of my projects,' Anton said, loftily. 'It's only fair.'

What would be fair would be giving Caro a part in the film alongside Posy and Rosalind, but she didn't stop to mention that.

Posy, however, paused her nearby conversation with Juliette and looked over long enough to give Anton a meaningful stare. One that made him look away and add, 'But of course, the authenticity of filming at Aldermere is hard to beat. And we'll do everything we can to stop it being too disruptive for you.'

Hmm, apparently mini-Dahlia's debate with her director the night before had left her with the upper hand. Excellent.

'Of course we'd be more than happy to have the filming take place at Aldermere,' Isobel said. 'Once you've agreed a fee – and the script – with Hugh.'

As she moved out of earshot, Caro realised that Libby the scriptwriter had peeled away from the group and joined her at the buffet table.

'I'll say one thing for Isobel, she knows how to find good caterers,' Caro said, as they both helped themselves to extra portions. She was pretty sure Isobel wouldn't have left something as important as the food to Marcus. 'Do you have any more events this afternoon?'

Libby shook her head. 'I only had the film panel yesterday. I wouldn't have come normally, but Anton insisted, even though there were only four places and plenty of other people he might have brought. I think he wanted me here in case the family had any issues with the script. He wants to get it wrapped up this weekend – you know, get the go-ahead to proceed, or—' she broke off, as if not wanting to tempt fate.

'Or the opposite, I suppose,' Caro finished for her. 'Have you heard anything yet?'

'Not really.' Libby sounded understandably glum about it. 'I know Hugh has read the script, but he's been avoiding Anton I think. Which doesn't bode well.'

Or just suggested that Hugh had other things on his mind.

'I'd love to see what you've done with the story,' Caro said. 'I mean, if you're allowed to show me?'

Libby gave a shy smile but shook her head. 'Sorry. After the last script got leaked on the internet, Anton's been really particular about who gets to see it.'

Caro held back a snort. Given that Anton had been the one who leaked the original script, being precious about the new one seemed a bit rich.

'I was curious about one thing, after last night's dinner. I noticed a few changes from the original book in the menu. Was it based on the script, then?' Caro attempted to sound as innocent as she could. Like the time Dahlia tried to infiltrate a debutante training session.

Libby nodded. 'It was! Anton let Marcus have the script early to arrange that. Then I'd made some last-minute changes – like adding in the sugared flowers and cutting one of the courses to make it flow better – and poor Clementine had to rush around with the caterers on Friday night making sugared violets at the last minute.' She pulled a guilty expression.

'Such a shame Clementine wasn't here to enjoy it,' Caro said, lightly.

'Yeah. Anyway, it was nice to . . . I'd better . . .' With an apologetic smile, she moved away, back towards Isobel, Anton and Kit.

Caro didn't try to stop her. She'd already learned what she needed to know.

The sugared flowers were a late addition – and Clementine herself had been involved in making them. Well.

She looked up and saw Rosalind and Hugh enter the room, standing too close – then separating the moment they were through the doorway. Hugh headed straight to Isobel – every bit the guilty spouse, in Caro's opinion – and Rosalind approached Caro, and the buffet table. Posy peeled away from what looked like some flirtatious banter with Kit at the same time, and joined them.

'How did it go?' Rosalind asked, in an undertone, as she helped herself to food.

'Everything back in place,' Caro replied. 'And I found some interesting new information I need to share with you, too. Two lots, actually. But not here.'

Posy, glancing over her shoulder, nodded. 'Agreed. Too many ears. Where then?'

'Let's get outside,' Caro suggested. 'Maybe some fresh air will help.'

Chapter Eighteen

'I think everybody feels better after a good confession session, don't you?' Dahlia asked.

Johnnie looked sceptical. 'I think it usually depends on whether that confession is likely to get them hanged.'

Dahlia Lively *in* A Very Lively Trip
By Lettice Davenport, 1942

The Murder Spiral hadn't been what she'd had in mind, but Caro supposed it was fitting. Mindful of eavesdroppers, she sat on the bench with Rosalind, while Posy hovered nearby. Caro told them everything she'd found out in Lettice's study – and about her discovery of Marcus's ledger in his desk.

'Why didn't you tell us you'd found this when we searched his room?' Posy asked, her forehead creased with confusion as she looked down at the little book in Caro's hands.

Caro ducked her head a little. 'Well, we were focused on the blackmail letters.'

'No, that's not it.' Rosalind looked at her thoughtfully. 'Did you think it might implicate you?'

Caro winced. 'Not exactly. It's just . . . I've known Marcus a long time. And, well, he had things he could hold over me – you know that from the blackmail notes. I thought they were from him for a good reason. And I needed to know what was in his ledger before I shared it, that's all.'

'And what was in it?' Posy asked.

'A record of all the Golden Age of Crime memorabilia he has bought and sold over the years. And some that he didn't buy, too.'

'You mean stole.' Posy's expression was stony, and Caro remembered, too late, that Posy had been stolen from by people she trusted before. 'Did you steal for him? Is that why you didn't want to tell us?'

'No! Well, not recently.' Rosalind's eyebrows went, and Caro sighed. 'It was right after my divorce, when I was still working on the TV show. Marcus appeared in a few episodes as a recurring character, and we got to talking. We'd go to the pub together after filming finished for the day, drink too much and . . .'

'Wake up together?' Rosalind guessed.

'Once or twice.' Caro sighed. 'It was mistake. I knew it was a mistake at the time, but I didn't know how much. Because then he asked me to "borrow" a few items from the set for him, once his role was finished. Little things to start with, things that no one would miss, but that he could sell on.'

'And it was put down to extras taking mementos,' Rosalind said, echoing Caro's words from the day before.

'Exactly. Until he wanted me to take something bigger, and I said no.'

Posy scowled. 'Let me guess. He blackmailed you?'

'No,' Caro said, slowly. 'He didn't. He could have, for certain. But he didn't.'

'Why?' Rosalind asked.

'I think because . . .' God, how was she only seeing this now, so many years later, when the man himself was dead and she couldn't yell at him for it? 'It gave him more power, this way. If he'd blackmailed me, I might have done what he asked but I'd have hated him, and eventually I'd probably have cracked, if he'd asked for too much.

But this way . . . I've spent the last seven years waiting for the other shoe to drop. Playing nice with him, going the extra mile for his conventions, keeping his secrets, everything. Because he never let me forget that he knew mine, too. And he could share them with the world anytime he wanted.'

'Typical male power move,' Posy grumbled. 'He's as bad as Anton.'

Rosalind straightened her back as she sat on the bench, looking Caro in the eye. 'So. Truth time. Did you steal the magnifying glass?'

'No. I didn't need to. Someone in this house had already sold it to Marcus and replaced it with a cheap replica. It's all in the ledger – including who he sold it to.' She held the book out to Rosalind, who took it.

'Oooh, who?' Posy asked.

'Heather and Harry – that old couple in tweed with the fake magnifying glasses,' Caro said. 'Or, now I think about it, perhaps not *both* fake.'

'Harry did say that he and Marcus went way back.' Rosalind thumbed thoughtfully through the ledger. 'This was obviously what he meant. It looks like they've been buying memorabilia from Marcus for years.'

'Hard to think of a reason that Harry or Heather would want to kill him, then,' Caro said. 'If he was their supplier of precious items. And if they were such good buyers, he probably wouldn't risk black-mailing them, either. Not when he could fleece them on sales.'

'And he was definitely doing that.' Posy pointed over her shoulder to the discrepancy between how much Marcus had paid for the magnifying glass, and how much he'd sold it for.

Rosalind snapped the ledger shut. 'So. What do we do now?'

'We still need to speak to Ashok,' Posy reminded them. 'He wasn't around at lunch. I think he might be avoiding us.'

'Sensible man, especially if he's got something to hide.' Caro watched the other two, trying to guess how they'd react to what she said next, before deciding it didn't matter. She needed to say it anyway. 'Before we talk to him . . . I think we need to be honest with each other.'

'You mean you have more illegal activities to share with us?' Rosalind asked, eyebrows raised.

'No. I mean we need to each share what was in the photos we were sent yesterday.' She could trust Rosalind and Posy, she thought – well, hoped she could, anyway – but a dose of honesty from each of them would help. 'They're another piece of this puzzle and, to be honest, I think we need all the pieces we can get. I didn't ask before, because—'

'Because you didn't want to share your secrets either,' Rosalind finished for her. 'The same reason I didn't, and I imagine it was Posy's reason too. But you're right. It's time.'

'But it's not just the photos.' Posy's voice was low and steady, her shoulders stiff as she stared them down. 'You both have history with this place, with these people. I want to know everything you two know before we go any further. I'm sick of secrets.'

'Darling, I've been alive for sixty-plus years,' Rosalind drawled. 'If I live to be a hundred I don't have time to tell you everything I know.'

Posy stood her ground. Caro had to admire that – even if she didn't like what she was asking.

'Everything that's relevant to the case, then,' Posy countered. 'And that's everything to do with Aldermere, the victim, or any of the suspects.'

'In which case you need to tell us everything you know about the film and the people involved in it,' Rosalind said, sharply.

Posy's jaw tightened. 'Fine. Caro, you start. Since this is your idea.'

'I've already given you my secrets, and told you everything I know about what Marcus was up to.' Caro jumped up and paced to the edge of the Murder Spiral's inner sanctum. 'The photos I received were of Marcus and I. In bed. Seven years ago, now. And there was a note on one of them warning that there was video footage, too.' She turned to face them, her back against the monkshood's purple flowers — but carefully not touching — and crossed her arms over her chest, her right eyebrow raised and red lips pursed. Her favourite Dahlia look. Ah, it was good to be back. 'Which rather means it's over to you two, don't you think?'

'I told you earlier that Anton was behind the talk of a curse on the movie.' Posy's voice sounded suddenly smaller. She'd folded in on herself, her arms wrapped around her middle, her hair falling over her face as she looked at the ground. 'He leaked the original script, and I think he called in a tip-off that started a fraud investigation on one of the investors. And, before he cast me as Dahlia, he paid my ex-boyfriend to invite me over to his flat and get wasted. Which I did, because I was an idiot, and I thought . . .'

'You thought your ex wanted to get back together?' Caro guessed. After all, she knew about stupid post break-up behaviour. Marcus was proof of that.

'Yeah.' Posy sighed. 'Apparently my desperate need to be loved was stronger than two rounds of rehab, two and a half years of sobriety, and a hell of a lot of counselling.'

'Maybe not,' Rosalind said. 'I mean, you're here, sober, aren't you? So you slipped up. We've all done that before. We just have to pick ourselves up and move on.'

Caro gave her a look. 'That's surprisingly generous of you, Rosalind. Kind, even.'

Rosalind sniffed. 'I have my moments. Just not often around you.'

'The point is,' Posy said, loudly, drawing them back to the matter at hand. 'I *would* pick myself up and start over. Except Marcus and Anton had a photographer waiting outside when I left, so now there are photos out there just waiting to be shared with the world.' Posy ran a hand through her hair, dislodging a clip. 'He was planning to leak the photos if I didn't screw up all on my own soon enough. He figured that kind of scandal would be enough to get the family to pull out of the movie all together.'

'He really wants out of that film, doesn't he?' Caro said. Funny, when almost everyone else wanted in.

'Those were the photos that you got sent yesterday?' Rosalind asked, and Posy nodded.

Caro saw what Rosalind was getting at, almost immediately. 'So Clementine must have taken them from Marcus, same as mine. And, presumably, Rosalind's.'

'That's what I figured.' Posy's eyes were wide as she looked up at them at last. 'Marcus must have been planning to blackmail us too, and Clementine sent us the notes as a warning. But why?'

'And who did she write that Post-it note to?' Rosalind asked. 'It wouldn't have been Marcus.'

'Which means, if we're right about this, that someone else here knows what's going on,' Caro finished. 'But who?'

Rosalind and Posy returned blank looks, and Caro sighed.

'We need to talk to Clementine, family emergency or not.' She had a sneaking suspicion that Marcus's assistant knew *exactly* what was going on at Aldermere that weekend. Which was probably why she'd left. 'I'll get her number from Juliette and we can call from the house phone. But first . . .' She gave Rosalind a meaningful look.

'All right, all right.' Rosalind tapped her perfectly polished fingernails against the arm of the bench, filling the air with an annoying, tinny rhythm. Caro wanted to ask her to stop, but she wanted to hear her secrets more, so she stayed quiet. 'I've been having an affair with Hugh for the last thirty years. The photos showed us together in London, kissing, some time last year. Is that what you want to hear?'

Yes! Caro had *known* they had to still be together. Her deductive skills were second to none.

'It's not about wanting to know,' Caro said, sagely. 'It's about having all the information we need for our investigation.'

'You were together before he married Isobel, right?' Posy asked. 'You said earlier that Isobel thinks Hugh is having an affair – does she know it's with you?'

Rosalind shook her head. 'I don't think she'd have mentioned it to me if she did. But Hugh denies there's anything going on with anyone else.'

Caro snorted at that. 'Well he would, wouldn't he?'

That earned her an annoyed glare from Rosalind. 'I don't think he's lying to me.'

'But you can't be sure.' Posy shrugged apologetically as Rosalind turned the glare on her 'You can't. None of us can ever really be sure that someone else isn't lying, can we?'

'But we can be sure when they are, if we know the truth,' Caro said, thinking hard. 'That's what Dahlia always does – she deduces what the truth must be, then tricks the liar into admitting the lie.'

'How, exactly, are we supposed to prove that something *didn't* happen?' Rosalind's eyebrows arched in a way that almost looked like Dahlia, but not quite.

'I haven't figured that part out yet,' Caro admitted. 'But give me time.'

'What else?' Posy focused on Rosalind, her stare pressing for more secrets, more answers.

Rosalind shrugged. 'That's my big secret. The one that would ruin my reputation, my friendships. What else can you possibly want to know?'

'*Their* secrets,' Caro answered. 'Isobel, Hugh, the whole family. What do you know about them that they wouldn't want others to know? Hugh was being blackmailed, remember. Maybe it was about another affair, but maybe it wasn't. If you're right, then there must be something else.'

Eyes wide, Rosalind shook her head. 'I honestly don't know. I mean, there was everything with Serena, Juliette's mother . . . but Isobel wasn't able to keep that a secret, anyway.'

'What happened?' Posy asked.

'Serena ran away from home when she was seventeen,' Rosalind said. 'Moved to London, mixed with a bad crowd, all the usual clichés. She was . . . she is an addict. She fell pregnant and called Isobel. They got her into rehab, brought her home, and brought Juliette up ever since. Serena . . . struggled, even after she got clean. Depression, more than anything. She's relapsed a few times over the past seventeen years, and never really been able to hold down a job or anything else in between. She's in rehab again right now.'

Posy looked at her hands; Caro suspected she was thinking of her own experiences with rehab.

'Sad,' Caro said, so Posy didn't have to say anything. 'But not a scandal. Not when it's more or less public record. What else?'

'I don't know!' Rosalind protested. 'Um, there was the phantom pregnancy, but that was almost forty years ago. Nobody would care about that, now.'

'We care,' Posy said, shortly. 'Tell us.'

Rubbing a hand over her heart, Rosalind stared past them both, before she started talking. 'Like I said, this was forty years ago. Hugh and I were engaged to be married. I was filming the second Lady Detective film. He . . . we were both young. I know his family thought he was too young to marry, even though he was a good five years older than me. Perhaps age was an excuse. The only one at Aldermere who liked me was Letty, and that might just have been because she enjoyed being contrary. Anyway, it didn't much matter in the end.'

'Because he married Isobel,' Posy prodded, after a long moment of silence. Caro got the impression this wasn't a memory Rosalind wanted to relive, even for them.

'Because he got Isobel pregnant, while he was engaged to me. At least, he thought he did.' Caro had never seen Rosalind with anything but perfect posture. Now, it looked as if she were collapsing into the bench. 'Turned out he'd been cheating on me for months. Isobel was my co-star in the movies – she played Bess, Dahlia's maid, or assistant really. She was two years younger than me, but she already had Serena by then, and a single mother actress was probably even less palatable to the Davenports than I'd been. But she told Hugh she was pregnant, and that was that.'

'She lied?' Posy asked.

'I never knew for sure.' Rosalind glanced up, her hands clasped in her lap, her smile weak. 'On my more charitable days I think she was genuinely mistaken. Some days I think she must have lost the baby, and try to find sympathy for her. Others . . . well. Hugh would never have married her instead of me if she hadn't been pregnant. Everyone knew that.'

Caro dropped to the bench beside her, her jaw tight as she processed the story. 'How can you still be friends with her? And how can you still love him? When my husband left me—'

'You set fire to his tie,' Rosalind said with a watery chuckle. 'God, I remember reading that and wishing I'd had your guts.'

'Or my lack of control over my temper.'

'Did you regret it afterwards?' Rosalind asked.

Caro considered. 'Not really.'

Rosalind laughed, properly that time. 'Well then.'

Posy crouched in front of the bench. 'Caro's right. How could you stay friends with them? After what they'd done?'

The laugh fell away from Rosalind's lips. 'Hugh came to me, on set, and I could tell that something terrible had happened. He wasn't white, he was almost grey, but he was sweating, and his jacket was wrinkled, like he'd been scrunching it up in his hands.'

How many times had Rosalind relived this moment? Caro would bet it was hundreds, more, over the years.

Some moments in time never left you.

'He told me that I was his soul mate. That I'd always be part of his life. But that he couldn't marry me.'

'Bastard,' Caro muttered, not entirely under her breath.

'Yes. But I loved him. Despite everything.' Rosalind gave a small shrug. 'He begged me not to make a fuss, or a scandal. Not just for himself. For the family reputation. For the movies we were making, too. After all, who would cast me again if I had a reputation for causing trouble on set.' The bitter edge in her voice was clear. Maybe this had been a viable argument back in the early eighties, but it sucked now. And still, Caro could imagine men using it. 'I had my reputation to think of; the Dahlia movies were winding down, but Hugh was still an influential figure, and had struck up a great friendship with the director. I wanted more work, and that meant making sure I was someone that others would want to work with.'

'That's just . . .' Posy shook her head in apparent disbelief. But, thinking about what Caro knew of Posy's career – the rise, the fall, the scandal and the disappearance – she wondered if the problem was actually that Posy believed it all too well.

Rosalind had taken the high road that Caro herself had been unable to walk. And what had it gained her? A thirty-year lie of a love affair.

And a thriving career, Caro supposed. A place as a National Treasure.

Was this really how it worked? Women could have their place at the table as long as they suppressed their rage and their pain?

Well. That just wasn't good enough.

'Seems to me that Hugh got everything he wanted out of this deal,' Caro said.

'Except he did have to spend the rest of his life married to Isobel,' Posy pointed out, with a wicked smile. 'Surely all those perfect twin-sets and pearls must get old pretty soon?'

'Perhaps. That's my confessions done, anyway.' Rosalind straightened her spine and looked up, her hands still folded in her lap. 'So. We know each other's secrets now. Whose do we want to find out next?'

Chapter Nineteen

Dahlia slammed her hands down on his desk and stared at him hard across the wooden surface. 'You've arrested the wrong person.'

'He confessed,' Johnnie pointed out, mildly.

Dahlia shook her head. 'Doesn't matter. I'm right and he's wrong. Trust me on this.'

The worst part, Johnnie thought, as he pulled out the files to go through them again, was that he did.

Dahlia Lively *in* To Catch A Fly
***By* Lettice Davenport, 1970**

Ashok was still top of their list for interrogation, but on their way back towards the house they found Heather and Harry at one of the stalls on the West Lawn, inspecting jars of chutney.

'You know you won't eat that one,' Heather was admonishing her husband. 'It's got chilli in it. And you know what that does to your digestion. No, it'll sit in the fridge, going mouldy, until I throw it out or Jenson comes by to eat it.'

She sounded so like Annie, reminding Caro that she *shouldn't* eat things with green peppers in, that Caro felt a sudden pang of longing to be home with her wife, only worrying about fictional murders again. Or the lack of any acting jobs involving fictional murders, mostly.

Posy nudged her in the ribs, and Caro nodded to her and Rosalind. They'd take their investigative chances where they found them – and this one was ripe for the questioning.

Grumbling under his breath, Harry put the jar back, and the couple turned away from the stall – and right into the three Dahlias.

'Heather, Harry!' Rosalind, smiling her most delighted smile, took Heather by the arm before she could protest.

'Just the people we were looking for,' Posy added, taking Harry's arm. From the pink spots on his cheeks, he didn't mind being escorted by a beautiful twenty-something actress.

That left Caro following behind, but it was okay by her. Charm and tact had never been her strong suit.

But investigations . . . well, that was where she was going to come into her own.

They followed the path that led to the folly, pausing at a bench overlooking the crumbling stone fake ruin so Harry could catch his breath.

'You said you were looking for us.' Heather's forehead was creased with suspicion. 'Why, exactly?'

Rosalind and Posy looked to Caro; she was the lead investigator, it was only natural. With a steadying breath, Caro considered what Dahlia would do in this situation.

Would she obfuscate, like she did in *Rosemary and Remembrance,* pleading ignorance until the suspect confirmed all her suspicions in their attempt to exonerate themselves? Or would she come at it blunt like a hammer, as in *The Devil and the Deep Blue Sea?*

The latter, Caro decided. Dahlia was always at her best when she was being brutally honest with people.

'Here's the thing, Heather. Harry.' Caro perched on the warm wooden arm of the bench, one hand on Harry's as he sat beside her.

'We have reason to believe that Marcus's death might not have been entirely natural.'

She'd expected a gasp of horror, or at least a little surprise. But Heather just nodded sharply and said, 'I thought as much. Aconite, you think? Like in the book? Probably in the coffee, I suppose.'

'That's our best guess,' Posy said, glancing between Rosalind and Caro but not mentioning the sugared flowers. 'We won't know for sure until the post mortem is done.'

'If they bother to do one at all,' Harry said. 'Those police seemed happy enough it was his heart.'

'We've been talking about it with the others,' Heather went on. 'You know, figuring out the timelines, who was where when, and the motives of course. I assume that's what you three were *really* doing on the panel this morning.'

'The point is,' Caro went on, standing up and pacing in front of the bench, 'someone must have really wanted Marcus dead. And given some of the things he was up to, that's hardly surprising. Now, we know that you were in business with Marcus, before his death—'

'I wouldn't call it *business,* exactly,' Harry interrupted. 'More . . . sometimes he had things for sale, and we bought them. That was all.'

'And you never, say, asked Marcus to procure you something in particular?' Rosalind's eyebrows were raised in disbelief as she stared at the jewelled magnifying glass hanging at Heather's waist. 'Something that might not have ordinarily come onto the public market?'

Heather shifted so that the magnifying glass fell behind her jacket. 'I don't know *what* you're talking about.'

Caro sighed. 'Heather, we have Marcus's ledger. We have the details of everything he ever sold you – as well as who he bought it from and what price was paid. Including the occasions where he paid nothing for them at all.'

Heather's face lost its pinkness, fading to bone white. Harry's complexion, meanwhile, had turned bright red and bullish. 'I'm an honest businessman – a *retired* honest businessman. Never been a whiff of scandal about any of my business dealings. So I don't know what you're insinuating—'

'That you asked Marcus to arrange for certain items to be stolen and given to you in exchange for a fee.' The truth sounded so sordid in Rosalind's clipped tones.

'We certainly did nothing of the sort,' Heather blustered. 'I won't deny that we've bought some nice pieces of memorabilia from Marcus over the years, there's nothing wrong with that. They're our nest egg, see. What we're going to retire on.'

'As long as this new movie of yours is a success, anyway,' Harry added. 'We need Lettice's star to rise again so we can sell them off for a good price. That's just good business.'

'Everyone's got a lot riding on this movie,' Posy said, mildly. Caro figured they'd better hope Anton stuck to whatever deal Posy had enforced on him to make it a success.

'So you're saying that you *never* asked Marcus to steal any items of memorabilia for you?'

'No,' Heather said, quickly. Too quickly.

'Or bought any items you knew to be stolen?' Rosalind clarified.

No fast answer this time. Harry and Heather exchanged a look that spoke volumes.

Caro sighed – her impatient, 'I-know-more-than-you-think-I-know' Dahlia sigh.

'We could always ask the police to check out that magnifying glass at your waist,' she said, nodding towards Heather's middle. 'I saw how surprised you both were to see it sitting in its case yesterday.' A lie, but a believable one. 'And without Marcus's ledger, there's no way to prove you didn't steal that yesterday, like Isobel thinks someone did.'

Posy shook her head sadly. 'A terrible blow to your respectable reputation, that would be.'

Caro watched as the reality of that settled over Heather and Harry. They had one of those old married couple wordless conversations, where they each made their own arguments with nothing more than a quirk of an eyebrow or the twist of a lip.

She and Annie were getting good at those. She'd never had that sort of rapport with her first husband. That should have been a sign that it was going to end with ties on fire, shouldn't it?

Heather and Harry came to some unspoken conclusion, and Heather gave a sharp nod. 'Fine. What is it you want from us?'

Posy hopped over the arm of the bench and sat next to Harry, a broad smile on her face. 'We want you to tell us everything you know about Marcus. *Especially* if it has anything to do with why someone might want to kill him.'

'Did you talk to him yesterday, for instance?' Caro asked. 'I thought I saw the two of you together in the library, Harry?'

Harry shuffled uncomfortably on the bench. 'Well, yes. Rather awkward that, actually. I needed to talk to him about a piece he'd procured for us. And I *did* talk to him about the jeweller's loupe, too, as it happened.'

Caro tried to wait patiently for him to continue, and failed. 'And?'

For a man who'd spoken for a full forty minutes about his latest dentist appointment at dinner the night before, Harry was strangely reticent. Caro looked to his wife for elaboration.

Heather huffed a loud sigh, and dropped onto the bench on the other side of Harry. With three of them sitting there, things looked a little cramped, but Posy didn't move.

'Marcus sold us what was supposed to be the only surviving original signed script from Lettice's play of *Murder Misdiagnosed*,' Heather said. 'There was a fire at the theatre, you see, before the end of the run. This script only survived because Lettice had brought it back to Aldermere with her.'

'I take it there was a problem with it?' Rosalind said. 'What was it? Fake signature? Missing pages?'

'Nothing like that.' Harry shook his head. 'In fact, it all checked out. Authentic, as far as we could tell.'

Heather scowled. 'But then we saw another copy being sold on an internet auction site. And another through a Dahlia fans social media page.'

'All sold by Marcus, I take it,' Caro said. Oh, Marcus. It seemed such a stupid risk to take. What had driven him to it? The same thing that drove him to blackmail, she supposed.

'Yup,' Harry said with a nod. 'So of course, I had to ask him about it. And, after seeing the jeweller's loupe in her study on the house tour, I had even more doubts.'

'At least we can confirm that one is fake, if it helps,' Rosalind said, drily. 'What did Marcus have to say for himself?'

'That we had the originals. That there must have been a mix-up. You know what Marcus was like,' he said, turning to Caro. 'All charm and promises when you're with him, but who knows what he said behind our back. But he assured me ours were the real deal, and that he had nothing to do with the copies.'

'So who did, then?' Posy asked. 'You said they were being sold in his name?'

'He hinted that it might have been his assistant,' Heather said. 'That Clementine girl? Branching out on her own initiative, apparently.' From Heather's tone, she hadn't completely believed him.

'We were going to get our items independently valued after this weekend,' Harry added. 'Just to be sure.'

'If you thought that Marcus was up to something shady, like selling fakes, why not go to the police?' Posy asked, before answering her own question. 'Oh, because they might have been stolen in the first place. I see.'

'Catching on quick,' Caro murmured to her, with a smile.

'And that's all we know.' Heather pushed up off the bench and moved away. 'So if you don't mind, we're going to get back to enjoying what's left of this disaster of a convention. Come on, Harry.'

'One more thing, before we let you return to the jam selection.' Caro smiled to herself as Heather and Harry obeyed, pausing on the path. 'Did you see anyone else talking to Marcus? About anything that mattered, I mean.'

Harry frowned thoughtfully. 'Well, when I went to talk to him in the library, he was busy talking to Ashok, so I had to wait a minute or two. Ashok seemed quite insistent on getting an answer about something or other – I wasn't close enough to hear what. Then Marcus did his usual thing of talking a lot without saying anything at all, and hurried off to do something else.'

'Do you know what he was talking to Ashok about?' Posy asked.

'No idea. Probably something to do with the convention, or Aldermere. He's always got a question or two, that Ashok. He was bending Clementine's ear at lunchtime yesterday too. He spotted her through the window and headed out to chase her. Almost missed pudding.' Harry rolled his eyes. 'At least it stopped him telling those stupid Christmas cracker jokes.'

Ashok, again. Caro was starting to get suspicious about their Christmas Johnnie wannabe. 'Anything else you've noticed about Ashok this weekend?'

'I don't think so.' Harry frowned. 'Apart from the fact he was hanging around outside your room earlier.' He nodded at Posy as he spoke. 'Pretended like he was waiting for us, and joined us when we walked past.'

'When was this?' Rosalind asked, sharply.

'Must have been before lunch, I think.' Harry turned to his wife. 'Before lunch, wasn't it?'

'Yes. Before lunch. *Now* can we go?' Heather radiated impatience, and annoyance. Caro almost wanted to think of another question to call her back for, but she suspected they'd got all they could out of the couple. She nodded, and Harry hurried to catch up with his wife.

They reached the main path before Heather looked back at them, her arm linked with Harry's, and scowled. 'You three want to play at really being Dahlia Lively instead of pretending for the cameras? Fine. But don't expect the rest of us to forget that you're a washed-up child star with issues; a tired, old actress who doesn't know when to retire; and a two-bit wannabe who only ever played one part and can't even get a part in the latest movie, when *everyone* else who has ever been connected to Dahlia Lively has a cameo.' With a cruelly sympathetic smile, Heather shook her head. 'Really, Caro. What would Dahlia think of *that?*'

Caro wanted to respond, wanted to take Heather down as comprehensively as she'd just destroyed the three of them. But the words dried up. All those years of perfecting Dahlia's putdowns and sharp comebacks in the mirror, and they'd deserted her now.

Because Heather was right. Dahlia wouldn't have been used by Marcus, the way she had been. She *wasn't* Dahlia, wasn't anywhere close to her hero. Why was she still trying to pretend she was?

'I've always thought that the worst kind of fans are those who think they're owed something. Don't you, Posy?' Rosalind drawled.

'You mean, the kind who want to police who is allowed to like a book or a film? Who think they're better than other fans, and so deserve more?' Posy replied.

Caro blinked, raising her eyes from the ground as the warmth of their words started to fill her. They were *supporting* her. Almost like friends.

'Exactly. Those vampire fans who suck the fun out of loving anything. Who try to buy up everything connected to a show so they can keep it for themselves, just to show off because they can afford it. Who make the fandom a smaller, more exclusive place to be.'

'Rather than the open, inclusive place it's *meant* to be,' Posy finished. 'Yes, they definitely are the *worst* kind of fans.'

Heather's face was puce with rage, but she didn't say anything more. Her lips tightened to a thin line, she whipped Harry around and hurried down the path, leaving the three Dahlias alone.

'They're not wrong,' Caro whispered, once they were out of earshot. 'I mean, I did steal for Marcus. I *did* betray the character Lettice created. Maybe I don't have the right to call myself Dahlia Lively anymore.'

'You made a mistake,' Posy said, with a shrug. 'Hell, we've all made those. Me more than most.'

'And you're not making it anymore. That's what matters.' There was a note of reflection in Rosalind's voice as she stared towards Aldermere House. Caro wondered what mistakes she was contemplating giving up.

'Well, if you're right, then we still have a murder to solve.'

Rosalind's attention snapped back to them at Caro's words. 'Yes, we do. Which means we *really* need to find Ashok. Wherever he's hiding.'

They found Ashok interrogating Anton and Kit in the Drawing Room, alongside his partner in crime, Felicity.

'And you don't remember anything else?' Felicity tapped her pen against the page of her notebook, as she waited for Anton's answer.

'Anything at all, however small,' Ashok added.

'Like Dahlia always said, it's the little details that others overlook that often matter most.' Felicity smiled knowingly, probably trying to ape one of Caro's own Dahlia smiles. Like Dahlia Lively would *ever* sport blue hair.

Urgh, Caro was starting to sound like Heather and Harry, even in her own head. Was growing more judgemental a side effect of hitting early peri-menopause?

Caro exchanged a look with her real Dahlia sisters, and hoped they understood. Kit and Anton backed away, clearly done with being investigated, and Caro stepped in, keeping her back towards Felicity, to cut her off from Ashok. As she'd hoped, Rosalind and Posy moved to distract her with questions about her notes, leaving Caro to tackle Ashok alone.

Perfect.

'Conducting a little investigation of your own, huh?' she said, smiling, as Ashok frowned and glanced around the room, uncertain what had happened. *Get used to that feeling, kiddo.*

'We were, uh, asking some important questions.'

'Right. As it happens, I've got a few questions of my own. If you have a minute.' Without waiting for an answer, she guided him towards the door and into the entrance hall. 'We could take a little walk.'

Ashok glanced over his shoulder, but Felicity was preoccupied with the book Posy had handed her, pointing out something of note. 'I guess.'

Outside, the August sun warmed the paths that wound around Aldermere Hall, although there were darker clouds on the horizon. Well into its second day, the convention felt established, and Caro found it hard to imagine the gardens and lawns without the white marquees, stalls and crowds. Overhead, a Spitfire rumbled past – a visitor from the local air museum, according to the convention timetable – swooping low and causing people to stop in their tracks, shading their eyes as they stared into the skies.

'You said you had questions?' Ashok shoved his hands in the pockets of his cord trousers. 'What about?'

'Mostly about you.' Caro looped her hand through his arm, as if they were out for a jolly walk together. Just like Dahlia would have done. And then she levelled with him. 'Here's the thing, Ashok. You don't make sense here.'

'Because I'm not a white, middle-aged, pureblood Brit?' Caro was disappointed to hear resignation in his voice, rather than anger.

'No,' she said, firmly. 'Never that. Dahlia is for everybody.'

'Then what?' He sounded genuinely confused and, for a second, Caro began to doubt her deductions.

Then she remembered that she was Dahlia Lively – for this weekend, at least – and there was no room for doubt when it came to murder.

'You admit you'd never read the books until this year, you had no connections with anyone at the convention, and yet you paid what I believe was a significant sum of money to get a place as a VIP delegate.'

Ashok shrugged. 'I've always been an all or nothing sort of person. When I find a new interest I become obsessive for a while. I've learned to roll with it and enjoy the experience.'

'And then, once you arrived at Aldermere, you started asking questions,' Caro went on. 'You were seen quizzing Marcus about something before his death, and racing out to ask Clementine questions at lunchtime, too.'

'There's a lot to learn, as a new fan, and Marcus and Clementine were the ones in charge. Of course I went to them.' Ashok stood back as a fan approached, asking shyly if Caro would have a photo taken with her. 'Let me take that for you,' Ashok said, with a smile.

That was the worst of it, Caro decided. Ashok seemed like a genuinely nice guy. Young, inquisitive, enthusiastic . . . and hiding something. If it wasn't for that last bit, she was pretty sure they could have got along nicely this weekend.

The fan moved on, and Caro went for the kill. 'And then there's the way you were hanging around outside Clementine's door the first night, even though we'd seen her leave that afternoon.'

'I explained that to Posy at the time. I was hoping to get my phone back.' He gave her a sideways look. 'And it was *your* friend who broke into the room looking for them. Perhaps you should be questioning her about what she was really doing there.'

'I know what Posy was doing there,' Caro said, calmly. 'But I don't know why you were seen leaving Posy's room last night, or loitering outside it again today. Care to tell me?'

Ashok's face stayed blank. Perhaps he'd had acting training, or something in his past had taught him how to school his emotions. Either way, he wasn't giving anything away without a fight.

'I don't know what you're talking about.'

Ah, the classic 'I have no defence' defence. That never flew with Dahlia.

'I think you do,' she said, keeping her voice soft so Ashok needed to stay close to hear. 'I think you came to Aldermere this weekend for a reason. I think you know all about the blackmail notes we received the first day, and that perhaps you were responsible for stealing the jeweller's loupe and hiding it in Posy's room, as well as the bottle of poison she found there this afternoon. Or that you at least know who *was* responsible. And I think you know that Marcus was murdered, and maybe even why. Maybe because you're the one who murdered him.'

She watched his face carefully, so she saw the moment he decided to tell her the truth.

His grip on her arm was surprisingly strong as he yanked her off the main path and behind one of the stalls, where they were sheltered by bushes on two sides and the canvas of the stall on the other.

'Look, I don't know anything about the jeweller's loupe, or the poison bottle. And I'm not even sure about the blackmail notes. But . . .' Ashok dropped her arm and ran a hand through his hair, looking suddenly older. More worldly, perhaps. The whole weekend, he'd seemed to be a naive, excitable puppy, staring wide-eyed at all the wonders of Aldermere.

Now . . . now, his eyes looked more like the ones she saw in her own mirror. A little bit jaded.

'But you do know *something*,' she surmised. 'About Marcus's death? You think it was murder too, don't you?'

'I don't . . . I'm not sure. The man had a heart condition. It could have been coincidence that he dropped when he did.'

'But you don't think it was,' Caro guessed. 'Why?'

He sighed. 'Because I know things. About Marcus.' Hands in his pockets, slouching slightly, Ashok looked like a different person. Like all they'd seen so far was the character he'd been playing. 'I'm not here at Aldermere because I'm a fan of Lettice Davenport's books – although I did read them all in preparation for this. I'm here because I was hired to investigate Marcus Fisher by a client of his who believes he has committed fraud.'

'You're a private investigator.' *Now* the pieces were starting to fall into place.

'Yes. And I'm a good one, usually. But Marcus ... he was slippery.'

'He'd been at this a long time.' Caro thought about Harry and Heather, and their concerns about fake memorabilia. Looked like they weren't the only ones being conned by Marcus. She looked Ashok up and down. 'What about you? First case, or have you been at this a while, too?'

'Don't let the baby face fool you. I got my licence when I was twenty-one, and I know what I'm doing.'

Caro had a head full of questions she wanted to ask about his career choices, but they'd have to wait until later. Right now there was only one that mattered. 'Who were you working for?'

'I can't tell you that,' Ashok said, fast enough that she guessed he'd been prepared for the question. 'Client confidentiality.'

'Hmm.' More secrets. Just what they didn't need. 'Why should I trust you if you won't trust me?'

Ashok sighed. 'I can tell you it's an overseas collector with a vested interest in the upcoming movie. Will that do?'

'I suppose so.' For now.

'The important thing is, I'd almost convinced his assistant, Clementine, to testify against him.' Ashok scowled. 'Before she disappeared for that conveniently timed family emergency.'

'You think Marcus was behind that, too?' Caro asked.

'I think she was scared, and it wouldn't have taken much. I've been trying to get in touch with her since – I didn't give up *both* my mobile phones on arrival, obviously – but she's not replying to my messages or taking my calls. That's why I was at her room that first night; I wanted to see if she'd left me a note, or anything.'

'If you were only here to investigate Marcus, why stay once he's dead?' she asked. 'Why not go find Clementine, or wash your hands of it all and report back to your client?'

'Because it wasn't just the fraud I was investigating,' Ashok admitted. 'My client was also being blackmailed by Marcus.'

'He wasn't the only one,' Caro muttered.

'So I've discovered,' Ashok said. 'And yeah, I wouldn't be surprised if one of his victims *did* kill him. But that's not what I was here to investigate. I was under instructions to find the evidence Marcus held, or find enough evidence *against* him to discredit him completely.'

'What evidence were you looking for?' she asked. 'What was your client being blackmailed over?'

Ashok gave her a pitying look. 'Ms Hooper, you know I can't tell you that.'

'Client confidentiality,' she chorused with him. 'I know, I know. Can't blame me for trying though.'

All the same, another section of the jigsaw that was this weekend was coming together in Caro's head at last. Why, if Ashok was behind the magnifying glass and poison bottle in Posy's room, he'd been seen leaving there *after* the first was hidden and before the second, and the magnifying glass had stayed undisturbed both times, for instance.

'You weren't searching Posy's room that night, were you? You were going through it to search Marcus's.' Like they had done, earlier that day.

Ashok nodded. 'The lock on his door was a newer, sturdier one. But I knew from the floor plans I'd studied before I came here that the rooms were connected by a bathroom. Posy's lock was much easier to pick.'

'Well, you didn't search it very well,' Caro told him. 'He always hid his most important stuff *underneath* the desk drawer in his room.'

'I heard a noise out in the corridor before I could finish searching,' Ashok admitted. 'Had to get out of there fast.'

'That would have been Juliette, going up to change clothes. She saw you, by the way.'

He winced. 'So much for being stealthy. I was sure whoever was outside had gone past; I guess I didn't bank on her coming back again so soon.'

'Is that why you went back again today? To finish the job?' Ashok looked confused at the question, so she explained. 'Harry and Heather said they saw you outside Posy's room before lunch.'

'No. No, I was waiting for Felicity. Posy had asked to borrow her kindle, and left her door open so she could leave it in her room without anyone seeing. Felicity said that Posy was feeling self-conscious about how little she knew about Dahlia, and wanted to read up on the books without having to ask to borrow them from the library here.'

'I see.' It was a good excuse, a plausible one for sure. Ashok had certainly bought it. But Caro also knew for a fact that it was a lie. *And Felicity just took the number two slot on my 'would most like to interrogate' list.* With Clementine still gone, that effectively made her number one. Unless Rosalind and Posy had already finagled the truth out of her.

'She came out just after Harry and Heather passed me, I guess,' Ashok said. 'We caught up with them on the stairs.'

As Caro had seen. 'You like Felicity.' A statement, not a question.

Ashok's cheeks turned a little ruddy. 'Yes. She's . . . interesting. Different. With the tattoos and the hair, she has plenty of people saying she doesn't belong here, either. Did you know her parents are both doctors, as are her two brothers? All famous in their fields. We bonded over being the odd one out in a family—'

'You told her you're a PI?' Caro asked, interrupting his flow of Felicity worship.

'No, no. She thinks I'm in insurance.' Ashok looked serious. 'But I haven't let getting to know her distract me from my investigation.'

'That's the important thing.' Caro patted his arm reassuringly, and decided not to puncture that bubble of self-belief just yet. 'Now, one last question.'

'Go for it.' Ashok folded his arms across his chest and waited.

'How sure are you that Marcus was the one behind the fakes and the blackmail? Could it have been Clementine, hiding behind his name and reputation? Because this all seems to be a huge step up from his usual activities.' Even though they'd found the blackmail letter in his room . . . perhaps Clementine could have planted it there? She'd know his habits as well as Caro did, after working for him for six months.

'You mean, she sent the letters pretending to be him? And made the sales through his account, then killed him and ran with the money?' Ashok frowned. 'I don't know. It's possible, I guess. She told me that she wasn't involved. Said that he'd been taking more and more risks over the last few months, after his doctor gave him some bad news about his heart condition. Like, he wanted to make the most of the time he had left, and he needed money to do that.'

'And he'd be dead before he had to worry about the consequences of his actions.' Well, on that part he'd been proved right.

'But the way she ran . . .' Ashok shook his head. 'I don't know. I keep getting the feeling that there's more to this case than I bargained for when I got here.'

Caro gave him a sympathetic smile. 'You and me both, kiddo.'

Chapter Twenty

The door slammed in their faces. 'Well, that went well,' Johnnie muttered, sarcastically.

Dahlia tapped him on the arm with her bag. 'Really, Johnnie, don't you know anything? If someone hates being interrogated that much, it means we're on the right track!'

Dahlia Lively *in* Home for Murder
***By* Lettice Davenport, 1956**

Caro returned to the house to find the drawing room empty, save for a helpful waitress clearing coffee cups who told her that her friends had gone upstairs to prepare for dinner.

She caught up with Posy and Rosalind as they reached the China Room.

'What did you learn from Felicity?' she asked, without preamble.

Posy pulled a face. 'Not much. She disappeared almost as soon as you did – something about an interview she was supposed to be conducting for the fan club newsletter.'

'Or she was avoiding your questions,' Caro said.

'Most likely,' Rosalind agreed, as Posy opened the door. 'I assume you got more from Ashok, given how long you were gone?'

Caro checked over her shoulder and, spotting Harry and Heather coming up the stairs, just nodded.

'Well, at least there are no more surprises waiting for me in here tonight,' Posy said from inside the room, scanning the surfaces for stolen objects. Caro followed her gaze, then shuddered at the sight of the China Room wallpaper. It didn't get any less migraine-inducing on further acquaintance.

'Having ascertained that, may I suggest you two gather your things and we retire to a room more suitable to talking and thinking at the same time?' Rosalind winced as she glanced around her. 'My room has blissfully little in the way of pattern. We can get ready for dinner together there.'

'Like getting ready for a girls' night out,' Posy joked, but her smile was a little sad. Caro wondered when the last time was she'd had actual fun with friends. 'Just with more murder talk.'

There was a sudden flash outside the windows looking over the gardens, followed shortly after by a roll of thunder. The light dimmed for a moment as the rain began, lashing against the windows as if the earlier, perfect summer day had never happened.

'Ominous,' Caro said. 'Come on.'

Rosalind's room was at the opposite diagonal corner of the house to the rooms Caro and Posy had been allocated, looking out over the front driveway as it curved around the house.

'So there were definite perks to arriving early,' Caro said, examining the room.

With the large bay window with a window seat built in underneath, not to mention the king-sized bed, sitting area and desk, it had to be the largest and nicest of the guest suites.

Rosalind glanced at her surroundings as if seeing them for the first time. 'I suppose so. This has always been my room when I stay at Aldermere.'

Posy dumped an armful of clothes and her make-up bag on the pillowy sofa in the sitting area. 'We'd better get ready for dinner. I don't think we should risk being late – who knows what we might miss?'

'True,' Rosalind agreed. 'Caro, you can fill us in on what young Ashok had to say while we change.'

She did so with relish, drawing out the revelations to get the responses she wanted from her audience, who were gratifyingly impressed and surprised.

In some ways, it was just a performance. Dressing for dinner, applying lipstick next to Rosalind in the mirror in the en-suite, helping Posy do up the zip of another hideous dress and watching her pull a face at her own reflection . . . it was almost like being backstage at one of Caro's early forays in the theatre. Shared dressing rooms, doing their own make-up, and the buzz of excitement that she only ever got from live performance.

Of course, when she'd been backstage the chatter had been about which critic was in tonight, or whether the lead actor had been drinking before curtain-up again, that sort of thing.

Tonight, it was about murder.

Or it was, until they stood back and looked at their reflections together. Caro caught Rosalind's eye, and saw her shake her head.

'You're right,' Caro said. 'It'll never do.'

Posy looked between them, confusion creasing her brow. 'What?'

'You can't be Dahlia dressed like that,' Rosalind explained. 'It's embarrassing.'

'Especially if you're hoping to snag the attention of your Johnnie.' Caro pantomimed a leer at Posy in the mirror. 'That Kit of yours is quite lovely.' She was married to a woman, but that didn't mean she couldn't appreciate a good-looking man when one stopped by. And Kit's looks hadn't hindered his rise to stardom one bit.

'It's not like that with me and Kit.'

'Doesn't mean it couldn't be. Theirs is a slow burn romance in the books . . .'

'But it might burn out if you go down to dinner dressed like that,' Rosalind added.

Posy looked at her dress and scowled at it. 'Well, this is all I have, unless you want me in jeans. Anton purposefully didn't tell me that it was a dress-up weekend so he could lumber me with these awful dresses on the train. All part of his master plan to screw up my chances of winning over the fans as Dahlia.'

'Stupid man,' Rosalind muttered, which Caro thought was putting it mildly. 'Well, we'll just have to see what we can do, won't we?'

'I brought a couple of tops.' Posy grabbed some slippery fabric from the sofa. 'I thought maybe one of them over the dress might be less awful.'

Rosalind and Caro exchanged another look. 'Oh, I think we can do better than that, don't you, Rosalind?'

It took a bit of trial and error, a couple of safety pins – Posy's slender figure was a few inches smaller than either of theirs – but eventually they had something that worked. Rosalind's skirt, Posy's top, and Caro's beaded vintage jacket over it, looking slightly more oversized on Posy than it did on her. It meant Caro would need to find something else to wear over her dress for dinner, but Posy's smile as she studied her reflection made it worth the effort.

She swished the pleated, silvery skirt that hit her mid-calf, her own black top tucked neatly into it, and grinned. 'It looks good. And the shoes I have will be fine with it, I think.'

'Unless you want to squash your feet into something of mine, I think they'll have to,' Caro said. 'Now, have you mastered the eyebrow raise, yet?'

'The eyebrow raise?' Posy asked.

Caro demonstrated in the mirror, amused that Rosalind did the same. 'Right eyebrow only, raised sceptically like this.'

'It's *the* signature Dahlia move,' Rosalind added.

Posy raised both her eyebrows. Then she frowned a lot, and one eyebrow jumped a fraction before falling again.

'We'll practise,' Caro promised.

'Later.' Rosalind checked the delicate silver watch on her wrist. 'Come on, we need to get to dinner.'

'And question Felicity.' Posy grabbed her bag. 'Let's go.'

'I'll meet you down there,' Caro said. 'I need to get a jacket.'

She dashed back across the landing to her own room, flipping on the lights and reaching into her wardrobe for the first appropriate thing she could find to wear over her dress. Then she hurried towards the door and her friends – and almost missed the tiny doll sitting on her bedside table.

Caro paused, her breath suddenly loud in her ears. She picked the figure up between two fingers, studying it carefully. A woman, of course, in trousers and shirt. It *could* be her, but it could also be almost any woman at Aldermere this weekend. Apart from the stream of red blood that ran down her miniature face.

What would Dahlia do?

Dahlia would say that if someone was scared enough of their investigations to try and threaten her with a doll in her room, that meant they had to be doing something right.

Her heart rate almost back to normal, Caro slipped the doll into the pocket of her jacket and headed down to dinner.

This time, Posy distracted Ashok while Caro and Rosalind descended on Felicity.

'What do you think?' she asked Rosalind, as they waited for Posy to sweet-talk Ashok into showing her something or other across the room. 'Charm or blunt force?'

'Let's show her the respect of assuming she's not an idiot,' Rosalind said, after a moment. 'She's been asking questions all day as much as we have.'

'Blunt force it is then.' Caro nodded in agreement, then they stalked across the room to where Felicity stood alone.

'We were hoping you might join us in the Snug for a moment,' Rosalind murmured softly, as she took Felicity's left arm.

'We have something of importance to discuss with you.' Caro smiled her best Dahlia smile, relieved Felicity of her wine glass, and took her other arm.

'It seems you've made my mind up for me.' Felicity sounded more amused than she'd expected, but Caro didn't let her smile slip as they headed for the door.

The Snug was fortunately abandoned once more. They sat Felicity on the chaise longue, while Rosalind prepared the drinks again, and Caro took the seat opposite their suspect.

'So, what do you want to talk to me about?'

Rosalind placed her glass on the side table and leant forward. Caro could only see her hard, Dahlia stare out of the corner of her eye but, she had to admit, she did it perfectly. 'You stole Lettice Davenport's jewelled magnifying glass, and a bottle of poison, and put them in Posy's room to frame her for the theft. We *know* this. What we don't know, and what you are here to explain to us, is why.'

It was a bit of a stretch from what Ashok had told her, but it was the explanation that made the most sense. What else could she have been doing in Posy's room?

Felicity glanced between Rosalind's stony expression and Caro, as if trying to figure out who was playing good cop and who was bad cop.

Neither, kiddo. We're both Dahlia, and you're in trouble.

There was a long silence, the only noise the summer rainstorm battering the windows outside.

Finally, Felicity spoke. 'I don't . . . what did Ashok tell you? I know you spoke to him earlier.' She looked rattled, and Caro allowed herself a smile. They had her.

'That you told him Posy had asked to borrow your kindle, and left her door open so you could put it in her room,' Caro said. 'Except we know that she didn't. So, care to explain what you *were* doing in Posy's room?'

'I wasn't . . . it started as a game. A way to get back at Marcus, really.'

Rosalind blinked, twice. 'At Marcus? Why?'

Clearly she hadn't known Marcus as well as Caro and Felicity had.

'Why, I can understand,' Caro said. 'It's how that's tripping me up. How did stealing the magnifying glass get back at Marcus?'

Felicity's smile turned a little bit wicked. Caro couldn't help but approve. She was pretty sure Dahlia would have too, if she'd ever met Marcus.

'He was so caught up in his own genius about the murder mystery game – like he hadn't ripped half of it straight from Lettice's interviews where she talked about devising one for the family here at Aldermere. He wouldn't stop going on about it, how *he* was the one who kept the Dahlia fandom going.'

'While you and Clementine were doing all the actual work,' Rosalind observed.

'Exactly!' Felicity was clearly thrilled at the vindication. 'I knew he wanted to crow about what a success it would be, and that he'd be holding court over us for the rest of the weekend, going on about it. And I wanted, well, I wanted there to be a bigger, better mystery for people to solve.'

'Because it was a *real* mystery,' Caro said, and Felicity nodded.

'I figured I'd take the magnifying glass and hide it, then we could spend the weekend investigating the theft. I thought it would be fun!'

'What were you planning to do when Isobel called the police and had you arrested?' Rosalind asked, mildly.

'I didn't think she'd go *that* far,' Felicity admitted. 'I don't know. Maybe I wasn't thinking at all. But I saw it sparkling there in the case, and I thought about that first Dahlia short story – you know, the one with the jewels at the dinner party that show up in the soup?'

'"Sapphires for Supper",' Caro supplied, helpfully.

'Yeah. And I guess I thought it would be like that.' Felicity sighed. 'That we'd team up in pairs to find the missing jewels and it would be a big game. But obviously, it wasn't.'

'So you hid the magnifying glass in Posy's room to avoid getting caught,' Rosalind guessed.

Felicity nodded. 'I'd planned to put it back where I got it, but then I heard Hugh coming down the stairs from the second floor and I panicked. The locks on these doors are so feeble, I twisted the nearest one and stumbled in. The fact that it was the China Room seemed kind of appropriate. And when I realised it was Posy's room . . .'

'You decided to frame her.'

'No! Well, not really. I . . .' Felicity's brows twitched down into an angry frown. 'She's not Dahlia. She can't be. Anton promised us he'd only cast someone who truly *understood* the books, and I don't think she's even read them!'

'She's working on that,' Rosalind murmured, but Felicity was on a roll and didn't seem to hear her.

'She's completely wrong for the part! I mean, her history, the stories about her – and all she's ever played are stupid, whiny popular girls in American teen movies. She's every girl I ever hated growing up. Every perfect girlfriend my brothers ever brought home.' Felicity sucked in a breath. 'She's like . . . the anti-Dahlia!'

Rosalind raised a knowing eyebrow in the direction of Felicity's bright blue hair. Felicity stared back. 'Appearance isn't character, you know.'

'She has a point,' Caro allowed.

'You don't understand.' Felicity took the jewelled satin headband from her hair and placed it in her lap, rubbing at her temples. 'For me, Dahlia is more than just a fictional character. She was my escape. My rebellion, even.' She huffed a laugh. 'My parents didn't care whether I dyed my hair or got full sleeve tattoos. They only cared about academic achievements.'

'But you didn't,' Caro guessed, remembering how Ashok had said that all of Felicity's family were doctors, except her.

'No. I wanted to be free to do something – anything – else. Something that was *mine,* you know?' She looked up, searching for understanding in their expressions. 'I'd always loved the Dahlia Lively stories – wanted to be Dahlia, as a kid. And when I saw the job come up working for the fan club, just when I thought my PhD studies might break me, I knew it was a sign. I dropped out before Marcus even formally offered me the job.'

It was strange, Caro thought, to think of Dahlia Lively as an alternative heroine for the twenty-first century, but that was what she seemed to have become – for Felicity, at least, and she probably wasn't the only one.

The joy of Dahlia was that she never cared what other people, or even society, thought about her. She did what she considered was right. She used her brain when half the world she lived in seemed to think she shouldn't have one. She never played down her brilliance to make men feel better. And she never pretended to be anything less than what she was.

'When I heard there was going to be a new movie, that Dahlia would be brought up to date for my generation . . . I was so excited. But then Anton cast *her* and I knew that he didn't understand who Dahlia was at all.'

Maybe Felicity was right. The Posy Starling the world thought they knew from her teen acting career and her exploits in the gossip pages *wouldn't* be right for Dahlia Lively.

But that wasn't the Posy that Caro had got to know over the last two days – even if it was the one she'd expected to find.

'I think you're wrong about Posy,' she said, softly. 'But go on. Tell us about the magnifying glass.'

Felicity blinked, twice, then reached for the drink Rosalind had poured her and took a sip, some of the wind seemingly gone from her sails. 'I realised where I was – the freaking *China Room* – and that *she* was staying there, while I was up in the servants' quarters in a tiny single room next to the shared bathroom, and I . . . I wanted to show her that she wasn't my Dahlia. That some director guy *telling* us she was Dahlia didn't make it so. You know?'

'I can understand that,' Caro admitted. 'So you left the magnifying glass and the note.'

Felicity nodded. 'I wasn't trying to frame her, exactly. I figured she'd find it, then make a huge scene about it, you know? Freak out and run away, or whatever.'

Rosalind smiled, slow but amused. 'Except she didn't. Did she? She decided to investigate instead. And she asked us to help her.'

'So you doubled down by putting the poison bottle there, to really scare her,' Caro surmised. 'Nefarious.'

'It was a *game*,' Felicity stressed. 'One a *real* Dahlia would have understood.'

'The real Dahlia would have hauled you off to the police already. Or at least to Isobel,' Rosalind pointed out.

'So why haven't you?' Felicity asked. 'I mean, you've solved your mystery. Justified that whole trial by audience panel thing this morning. Why not turn me in and claim the glory?'

'Because the theft of a magnifying glass is the least of our worries this weekend.' Caro downed the last of the cocktail Rosalind had given her. '*This* was a distraction. We're more concerned about solving an actual murder, rather than a pretend theft.'

Felicity's hands shook as she put her glass on the table. 'Murder? You don't really think—'

'That Marcus was murdered?' Rosalind raised her right eyebrow. 'Of course we do.'

'And so do you, or you wouldn't have been investigating it so hard all day,' Caro said. 'Unless you thought that was a game, too?'

'Sort of,' Felicity admitted. 'I mean, not that he was dead. But it was a heart attack, right? I figured it was a spooky coincidence that he died when he did. I know it's not like there aren't enough people here this weekend who'd be happy to see the back of him. But everyone knows about his heart bypass last year, and he wasn't a picture of healthy living, was he? So, yeah, Ashok and I played detective, and so did Harry and Heather. But I don't think any of us thought we were trying to solve a real murder.'

Harry and Heather did, though. They'd said as much earlier. And so did Ashok, after their conversation earlier. But they knew the shady stuff Marcus was up to. Felicity might not have liked the man, but she probably wasn't aware of all his flaws and illegalities.

'You still investigated it as though it was.' Rosalind wasn't ready to dismiss that as game playing. 'What did you find out? Who did you decide did it?'

'Clementine,' Felicity said, promptly. 'I mean, it was obvious. She disappears and Marcus dies? Had to be her.'

'Except she *did* disappear.' Caro had her own suspicions about Clementine, but the fact she hadn't been seen since hours *before* the murder made the logistics a little trickier. 'She drove away from Aldermere right when Isobel announced the theft.'

Felicity rolled her eyes. 'Yeah, she drove away – when everyone was looking, because Marcus was announcing the murderer from the mystery game, which she'd have known he was planning, right? And *he* didn't know she was going, did he? And he didn't buy that family emergency story. I saw him between two of the courses at dinner that night, calling her, leaving a message asking what the hell was going on.'

'Did you, now?' *That* was interesting, given he'd already played Clementine's voicemail to Caro and Posy before dinner.

'Besides, what's to say she didn't come back?' There was something about the confident way Felicity folded her arms across her chest, that told Caro this wasn't a guess.

'When did you see her?' she asked. 'And where?'

'When I was in the China Room that afternoon,' Felicity admitted. 'I slipped out of the film panel to hide the magnifying glass because I figured the house would be quiet.'

'She was in the house?' Rosalind sat up straighter, and cast a surprised look Caro's way.

Felicity shook her head. 'No. I saw her out of the window. She was walking towards the Gate House from the river. I figured she must have ditched the car by the woods then headed across the river and hidden out at the Gate House until it was time to sneak up and poison Marcus's coffee – probably disguised as one of the waitresses. I mean, if he really was murdered.'

'You had quite a complex plan figured out for not believing he was murdered,' Rosalind observed.

Felicity shrugged. 'I like mysteries, and finding solutions to them.'

'Doesn't everybody here this weekend?' Caro leaned forward and looked Felicity in the eye. 'But I'll tell you one thing. Dahlia Lively would never try to frame or shame another person for her own entertainment. And I think you know that.'

She watched the red flush up Felicity's neck to her cheeks before Caro stood and turned for the door, knowing that Rosalind was right behind her.

'So, what now?' Rosalind murmured, as they left the room.

'We need to search the Gate House.' If Clementine had been there, she'd have left a clue, or something. And Caro was the person to find it. 'Come on. Let's find Posy.'

Chapter Twenty-One

'The important thing to remember, Bess, is that a cornered criminal is a dangerous one,' Dahlia whispered, as they approached the build-ing, the sense of dread building all around them.

Dahlia Lively *in* A Lively Take on Life
***By* Lettice Davenport, 1931**

Before they could do more than fill a waiting Posy in on the basics, they had to get through another dinner.

'If we *could* all take our seats, please?' Isobel's usual bright smile looked a little testy, Caro thought, as she and Rosalind slid back into the room. 'We have been waiting rather a long time for this meal to start already.'

Caro found herself sitting next to Harry and Heather, who point-edly ignored her and tried to start a conversation with Kit and Libby across the table, which was fine by her. She settled back for some people watching, instead.

Dahlia had always said – well, she supposed Lettice had said it, really, through Dahlia, but the point stood. She'd said that she learned more about people by observing them with others than in a hundred interrogations. Caro had never bought that, because in truth, it was always the interrogations that got her the information to solve the crime. But it was generally a good way to get people to leave her alone and let her be nosy in peace, which seemed more a Lettice trait than a Dahlia one, from what she'd learned of the author from documentaries and such.

Sitting at the dining table, watching her suspects as they tucked into their lamb and dauphinoise potatoes, Caro could see Dahlia's point.

Everyone around the table had secrets and fear in their eyes. Probably most of them had nothing to do with murdering Marcus, and everything to do with their own little lives, their own little lies.

Isobel held court at the furthest end of the large, rectangular table, closest to the doors that led to the inner hall and the kitchen stairs. Hugh, returned from wherever he'd disappeared to earlier, appeared happily ensconced at the other end, in conversation with Posy and Anton, although the director was looking less comfortable than his host. Hugh also appeared oblivious to the worried looks that Rosalind was sending him from several seats away.

Did Rosalind think her lover was involved in the murder? Caro couldn't rule it out. In her head, the three Dahlias were a team, but did Rosalind and Posy feel the same way? Or were they playing along for their own reasons, to keep their own secrets? How was Caro supposed to know?

Outside, there was another crash of thunder, and Caro wished that she'd thought to bring an umbrella for tonight's adventure. One could never trust an English summer.

'Say, Hugh, did I see that your car was back in its spot in the stables this afternoon?' Harry asked, along the table.

'The one Clementine borrowed?' Libby asked.

Kit gave a low whistle. 'That is one beautiful car. Any chance I can borrow it next?'

'Yes, well,' Hugh said, with an awkward chuckle. 'I, uh, picked it up from the station earlier today, as it happens. 'Clementine let me know she'd left it there, when she went to visit her family.'

'Did you speak to her?' Posy asked, a little overeager, in Caro's opinion.

'Oh, uh, no. She sent me a text message,' Hugh said. 'Anyway, it was such a lovely day, I walked down to collect it.' Another crash of thunder punctuated his words, and he laughed, sounding uncomfortable. 'Well, it *was* a lovely day, anyway.'

'Whenever *I've* tried to call her, her phone's been off,' Juliette grumbled. 'And I have *so* many questions about what Marcus had planned for the grand finale tomorrow.'

'Grand finale?' Isobel asked. 'He didn't mention anything to me. What does the schedule say?'

Juliette shrugged. 'Not much. Just that there'd be a closing ceremony, or something. But some of the volunteers told me that he'd been talking for days about how it was going to 'knock everyone's socks off' or something equally stupid. But I can't find anything about it in Clementine's notes.'

Caro glanced across the table at Rosalind, then Posy. Something else to look into. But first, the Gate House.

As soon as this interminable dinner was over.

Finally, the miserable group retired to the library for digestifs and conversation. It was easy for Caro to manoeuvre her way to Posy and Rosalind and decide which back way out to take.

'There's a side door on the lower ground floor, from the kitchens,' Rosalind murmured. 'We'll go that way.'

'We can't all leave at once,' Posy argued. 'Won't that be suspicious?'

'I don't think anyone is going to want to linger too long over drinks tonight,' Caro said. But Posy did have a point. 'We'll make our excuses and retire, then meet in the kitchens. Okay?'

With three nods, they separated to make brief conversations with the other guests. Rosalind spoke with Hugh and Isobel, before retiring with a faint smile – the sort that suggested she was an older lady who needed her rest after a challenging day. It was a lie, of course, but people bought it because that was what they expected.

That could be a problem. People who knew *her* expected Caro to be the last one propping up the bar on a night like this. She was not one to walk away from a free drink, let alone a fully stocked drinks trolley.

Posy disappeared next, with a whispered conversation to Anton, Libby and Kit, and a furtive look in Caro's direction. They weren't the only ones to leave, Caro realised, as Libby and Anton also made their excuses.

'Another?' Hugh asked Caro, holding a bottle up for inspection.

'Do you know, I don't think I could,' Caro said with an apologetic smile. 'Today has pretty much taken it out of me.'

'I'll have one, Granddad,' Juliette said, popping up beside them with an empty glass. Her cheeks were flushed and her eyes glassy.

'I think you've had plenty,' Hugh replied. 'Besides, you know I don't waste my good brandy on people who don't appreciate it.'

Juliette rolled her eyes. 'And how am I supposed to learn to appreciate it if you never let me drink it?'

Caro used their argument as cover, backed away, and darted out of the door into the hallway and towards the kitchens where she found Rosalind and Posy waiting for her.

The rain had started to lighten, but it was enough to make her hair frizz and skin damp. Caro wrapped her jacket tighter around her shoulders and wished that the sturdy boots Dahlia wore most often had gone with her cocktail dress. In retrospect, while the outfit she'd picked for the evening was perfect for giving her Dahlia's investigative confidence, it was less ideal for doing the investigating.

'What did we think about Hugh retrieving the car today?' Caro asked, as they set out into the rain.

'Explains where he was all morning, at least,' Rosalind said. 'The station is a fair old walk from here.'

'Interesting that he and Clementine are so in touch, though,' Posy observed. 'I mean, he was the one she called to say she was leaving—'

'Because she needed to borrow a car,' Rosalind put in.

'And the only one she's been in touch with since that call to Marcus on the first night,' Posy finished. 'Definitely hints at that connection between them, don't you think?'

Apparently, Rosalind didn't want to think about that as she quickened her pace, leaving the others to catch up.

They took the long and the winding path around the back of the house from the side door, past the stables and the West Lawn, where the stalls were set up, until they joined the main driveway by the fountain. The same way Clementine had driven out the previous afternoon, Caro realised. They weren't too worried about anyone looking out for them, either from the big house *or* the Gate House. In this weather, Caro could barely see her hand in front of her face through the rain and gloom, and she was grateful for the torches Rosalind had found in the kitchen drawer on their way out. The lights from the windows of the main house wouldn't reach to the Gate House, but someone *might* notice if they turned on the ones inside. They didn't want to be interrupted tonight.

The Gate House stood, as one might expect, by the huge iron gates that formed the entrance to Aldermere Hall. Beside it, the river that edged the western side of the property curled around. The far bank was covered with the same alder trees that gave the house half its name, while from here the river became more of a sluggish stream clogged with reeds – the mere that provided the other half.

If this was one of Lettice's books, Clementine would be waiting inside, ready to give them the history lesson that explained everything that had been happening at Aldermere that weekend. Caro didn't think they'd be that lucky, but she'd settle for a decent clue or two.

'Let's get inside and have a look around,' she suggested, reaching for the front door.

'Wait!' Posy hissed. 'What if someone is still here?'

'You mean, Clementine?' Caro whispered back. 'I reckon she'll be long gone.'

'Just in case, though,' Rosalind said. 'Let's go slow.'

Caro eased the door open, her breaths short and shallow. Nothing. She peered inside at the darkness of the room.

'Looks empty,' she said, and reached for the torch in her pocket, clicking the button for full beam.

The torch's warm glow filled the main room of the small, red brick cottage. It was furnished with a small wooden table and chairs, two armchairs in front of a wood-burning stove, and open plan to a tiny kitchen with a sink, oven, fridge and microwave. It had a cosy, homely vibe, from the cross-stitched sampler on the wall, to the blankets laid over the arms of the chairs. There were even blue and white striped jars on the kitchen counter holding baking staples, although Caro couldn't imagine why anyone would choose to cook there instead of in the main kitchen.

Another doorway appeared to lead through to a small bedroom, and an adjoining bathroom. It seemed an ideal, tiny holiday home for a night or two. An extra guest house, she supposed – not that Aldermere, with its countless bedrooms, needed it.

'You're right. No sign of Clementine here tonight,' Rosalind commented. 'If she was ever here at all.'

'Felicity seemed pretty sure.' Caro peered around the bedroom door, but found only darkness.

'Felicity is an excellent liar.' There was a decided bitterness in Posy's voice.

'Come on,' Caro said. 'We need to search the place. I'll take the bedroom, Posy in here, Rosalind, the kitchen.'

In the bedroom, she flung the door open and began searching through drawers, yanking the covers from the bed, looking for something, anything, that would explain what Clementine had been doing here, after she supposedly left Aldermere.

There was a small wardrobe, built in between the window and the bathroom door, with a deep drawer underneath it. She pulled it open, her heart almost beating out of her chest. Here, she knew, would be the answers she was looking for.

She blinked. At the bottom of the drawer sat a bundle of clothes, wrapped in a mustard-yellow scarf. A scarf she recognised.

A scarf she'd last seen Clementine wearing as she drove away from Aldermere.

This was it! Proof that Clementine *hadn't* left after all. That she could still be here, in fact . . .

The thought made her look up, as a breath of air from an open window brushed across the nape of her neck.

Why was the window open? And when had the bedroom door closed?

Caro turned, too slowly to make out many details of the figure in front of her, as a hard, heavy object connected with her temple, and the room went dark.

Monday 30th August
Rosalind

Chapter Twenty-Two

'The problem with you policemen is that you do rather get in the way of a good investigation.'

Dahlia Lively *in* **Never Underestimate A Lady**
By Lettice Davenport, 1930

They didn't hear a scream.

Later, Rosalind would remember the scene with Caro screaming, but in truth, there was no scream. Maybe she was hit too quickly, unconscious before she had time to react. Maybe she was too stubborn to give her attacker the satisfaction. That would be like Caro.

While Rosalind searched the kitchen, she heard a thud through the adjoining wall to the bedroom, as clearly as she heard Posy stop searching the living areas and call, 'Caro?'

Rosalind told herself it was the lateness, the darkness outside the pools of torchlight, the strangeness of investigating a real-life murder, all these years after her last fictional one. Those were the only reasons for the heavy feeling in her stomach, her sudden awareness of the beating of her own heart.

She placed the sugar canister on the counter, a little pile of spilt, white crystals surrounding it, and turned from the kitchen, moving without thinking towards the bedroom, and Caro.

Posy got there first, pausing by Caro's fallen body, before jerking away towards the window. 'They went out that way.'

'Who was it?' Rosalind dropped to her knees at Caro's side, ignoring the spike of pain in the left one that always came when she moved suddenly. She was mesmerised, instead, by the small trail of blood that trickled from the base of Caro's victory rolls, over her temple and down her cheek, a perfect match for the red lipstick that stood out against her pale, bloodless face.

'I couldn't see.' Posy levered the window further open and threw one leg over the sill. 'I'm going after them.'

'What? No!' Torn between helping Caro and stopping Posy doing something stupid, Rosalind swung her head up to meet Posy's gaze. 'It's not safe. You can't.'

'You look after Caro.' And then she was gone, out of the window and into the night.

Caro stirred beside her. 'Wha— Rosalind?'

'I'm here. Don't try to move.' She stroked a comforting hand down Caro's arm. 'Did you see who attacked you?'

Caro shook her head, then winced at the movement. 'Where's Posy?'

'Gone after your attacker,' Rosalind said. 'No, don't try to sit up. Stay there. I'm going to try to find a phone and call for an ambulance.'

Caro ignored her, and struggled into a sitting position. 'You need to go after her.'

'I can't leave you here alone.'

'You can't leave her out *there* alone.' Caro tried to shuffle towards the wall, pain contorting her face under the blood as she moved. Rosalind reached out to help her, but Caro shook her off. 'I'm serious. *Go!*'

Rosalind's days of climbing through windows were long over, but she knew she didn't need to. If Caro's attacker was headed away from

Aldermere, they'd have to go around the edge of the Gate House, and past the front door.

She only looked back over her shoulder at Caro once as she raced for the door.

Outside, the ground that had been baked hard that afternoon was now slick with mud. There was no sign of anyone running through the rain on the main driveway up to the house and, given the lights from the windows, Rosalind was almost certain she'd have seen them if there was.

She turned the other way, towards the road, and found Posy racing towards the gates from the back of the house.

'Where did they go?' she called to Rosalind. 'I can't see them!'

Rosalind shone her torch beam down the road, but there was no sign of anyone out there escaping from Aldermere.

It made no sense. Unless they weren't running away . . .

'The river,' she said. 'They must have taken the woods to the river path.'

From there, they could follow the river as it curved around the edges of Aldermere, past the Boat House and the folly, before coming back over the South Lawn and through the gardens. It was dark enough that they could probably make it to the house and in the side door unseen, if they were clever.

And whoever they were chasing, they seemed clever.

'Caro woke up,' she told Posy, as they ran for the trees, and the river path. Rosalind knew that Posy would be faster without her, but she didn't want either of them to be alone in the dark with whoever was out there. 'She didn't see who attacked her.'

'Felicity,' Posy said, panting. 'Or Clementine. Felicity was the one who told you about seeing Clementine at the Gate House. Maybe she's in league with Clementine, and this was a trap all along. But one of them must have hidden out there and waited for us.'

'Maybe.' Rosalind couldn't think through the options right now. Not while her hips ached, and she concentrated on keeping her weight balanced so her bad knee didn't give way. Not with Caro still bleeding back at the Gate House.

They slid their way down towards the river bank, grateful that she'd brought the torch. It gave them enough light to follow footprints in the mud. Rosalind gritted her teeth and grabbed a tree branch for support as her knee weakened.

God, what was she *doing* here? What had possessed her to join this strange midnight adventure to the Gate House in the first place? She should have stayed in the library with Hugh, having a nightcap together after everyone had gone to bed. Like they'd done together for years.

'I think they went this way,' Posy whispered, nimbly picking her way along the mud and leaf-strewn ground, while Rosalind lumbered behind.

The point was, she decided, as she clumped through the undergrowth between the Gate House and the river path, she wasn't the woman who got into scrapes like these. That was Caro, or Posy – jumping in without thinking, or being led astray by their impulses and inability to say no.

She was Rosalind King. She shouldn't *be* here.

But Caro had been right. She couldn't leave Posy alone with a murderer.

The rain had started up again, a relentless drizzle that Rosalind was sure would wear off before morning. She wiped her eyes, blinking away the droplets as she tried to focus in the darkness. How were they supposed to find anybody out here?

The path that ran alongside the river bank seemed even blacker than the trees and undergrowth they'd struggled through to get there. Hands on hips, Rosalind looked both ways along the path – the one that led off the Aldermere Estate, following the river as it made its way towards the nearest village, then back again at the path that led to the folly, and the house.

'Which way do we go?' Posy asked. 'Do we split up?'

'No!' That was definitely *not* the plan. 'If they wanted to get off the estate, they'd have taken the main road, or hidden and waited for us to pass then made a run for it.' In which case, they might be chasing no one at all. 'If they're still here, they'll have gone towards the house.'

If they were right, and the murderer was one of the people staying at the house, they'd want to get back there before they were missed, so they could pretend they'd been there all along. Except Clementine hadn't been back to the house since Saturday.

'Come on, then.' Posy set out along the path towards the house, leaving Rosalind trudging behind, still thinking.

There had been sugar on the counter, in the Gate House. If Clementine had been hiding out there she could have made the sugared poison flower, then snuck up during dinner to place it on Marcus's saucer – disguised as one of the waiting staff, like Felicity had suggested. Nobody had really looked at their faces, Rosalind would bet, and they'd all had those little caps covering their hair.

But if she had, she wouldn't be heading back to the house now, would she? Unless she wasn't done. Unless there were more deaths to come . . .

A shiver crept up Rosalind's spine. She stopped on the path, suddenly certain that she was being watched. She could feel someone's gaze on her, as clearly as she knew when she held the audience in her thrall on stage.

Clementine.

She hadn't gone back to the house. She hadn't escaped to the village. She was waiting, watching, to see what they did next.

Posy was several paces ahead of her, but Rosalind didn't try to catch up.

Slowly Rosalind turned around, her ears pounding with the sound of her own heartbeat as it melded with the sluggish trickle of the river and the wind in the reeds. The darkness surrounded her, moonlight flickering between the alder branches as the clouds rushed on overhead.

She was alone. There was no one there.

Her gaze fell to her hands, twisting around each other at her stomach, bone white in the night.

And then she saw the eyes watching her from the reeds.

Rosalind screamed.

'It looks like she'd been there for some time. At least a day or more, we think. We're going to need to speak with everyone staying at the house.'

Rosalind tugged the blanket tighter around her shoulders and reached for the cup of hot tea – with a shot of whisky in it – that Isobel had given her. She felt like she'd been awake for days, even though the sun was still a way off rising. Her heart rate seemed to be returning to normal, at least her blood pulsing in her ears didn't muffle all other noises and conversation. That was progress, she supposed.

Posy had turned back and found her on the path, staring at Clementine's bloated, grey, naked body in the river. From there, things were a blur, but Rosalind vaguely remembered Posy's voice as she dialled 999 from the phone in the Gate House, demanding an ambulance and police, then the sound of the sirens as they came up the driveway.

The police had taken over, and they'd been guided back to the library up at Aldermere House, while Hugh and Isobel were woken up.

And then there'd been tea. They were still in England after all.

Dahlia would be so proud.

Caro's head injury had been checked by a paramedic, and they'd been told to keep an eye on her overnight, but that there didn't seem to be any concussion.

'I suppose this means we have an answer to where Clementine went,' Caro murmured, still watching the officer in charge as he spoke to Hugh.

'And why she didn't come back,' Posy added, from Rosalind's other side. Rosalind liked that; being flanked by her sister Dahlias. As if their presence could hold the ghosts at bay.

'It couldn't have been Clementine that attacked you at the Gate House, though.' Rosalind's voice sounded croaky, like she hadn't used it for too long. Except for the screaming. She'd screamed for some time, she was sure. 'She'd been dead . . . longer than that.'

At least a day or more, the DCI had told Hugh. Detective Chief Inspector Larch, that was his name. He'd introduced himself when he arrived. Given the bank holiday, Rosalind was surprised how fast the police had secured the scene and got a senior officer on site.

'I heard him tell one of the uniformed officers that this was officially an "unexplained death",' Posy said.

'Isn't that the truth.' Rosalind looked up at Larch and Hugh. Men talking about men things, despite Hugh probably not having the first idea of what the hell had been going on at Aldermere that weekend.

At least, she hoped he didn't. Because, if he did . . .

'We need to befriend the detective,' she said, quietly, aware that Posy and Caro were watching her, like she was some timid animal they'd coaxed in from the wild. Had she still been screaming when Posy found her? Possibly.

Caro nodded, then winced at the movement. 'Good plan. Dahlia always got on side with the detectives working the case.'

'Yes, but that was mostly Johnnie, wasn't it?' Posy said. She was watching the door, Rosalind realised, waiting for anyone else to arrive. The police hadn't exactly been quiet, but then, Aldermere was a big place. Those on the second floor might not have been disturbed.

'It was also fictional.' Rosalind suspected that didn't make much difference to either of them, but it felt like something that should be highlighted. 'We need to get in with DCI Larch because otherwise nobody is going to tell us a damn thing.'

'Do we . . . I mean . . .' Posy swallowed, and started again. 'We could leave it to the professionals. Now they're here. Tell them what we've found out and let them handle it.'

'No.' The word came out louder than Rosalind intended, and Hugh and the DCI looked at her in surprise.

Rosalind lowered her gaze and waited for them to forget about her again.

'We can't stop now,' she said, after a moment. 'Whoever attacked Caro knows we're onto them, and the police aren't going to solve this fast enough to keep us out of danger.'

'But we're *not* onto them,' Posy whispered back. 'Are we? We thought it was Clementine, hiding out in the Gate House.'

'We're closer than the police are, even if they believe everything we tell them,' Caro said. 'But we could ask them for protection. Go home and hide out, make it clear we're not a threat.'

They wouldn't, though, Rosalind knew. They were in too deep to walk away now.

'There's the blackmail photos to think about,' Rosalind said. 'If Clementine and Marcus were behind those, then who has them now? Finding their killer – or killers – might be our best chance of keeping the photos from seeing the light of day.'

She didn't mention her other reason for continuing their investigation. She didn't want to plant the idea in their heads. But if Hugh was involved, somehow . . . she needed to know first.

'We've got another day here,' she said. 'If we can't find the killer before we leave Aldermere, we'll give up and hide. But we'll stay one more day. Agreed?'

She looked from Caro to Posy. They nodded.

'We're Dahlias,' Caro said, sounding more resigned than pleased at the idea. 'We can't bottle it now.'

'Who is going to speak to Larch?' Posy asked.

'I'll do it.' Rosalind let her blanket fall to the floor as she stood and handed her tea to Caro. 'After all, I'm the one who found . . . the body.' And she wouldn't sleep without knowing all the facts.

Hugh had moved away to stand at his wife's side, talking to one of the police officers over more cups of tea, so Rosalind inserted herself into his place opposite Larch with a smile.

'Detective Chief Inspector.'

'Ms King.' His eyes were wary, and his gaze darted to where Posy and Caro sat, watching attentively. Neither of them knew the meaning of the word 'subtle'. 'To what do I owe the pleasure? I don't suppose you or either of your friends have remembered some vitally important fact about this weekend that you'd like to share with me?'

He hadn't been completely satisfied with their reasons for being in the Gate House that evening. Of course, they'd been lying, so she

259

couldn't blame him. Even if 'we saw someone down there and went to check' was probably the sort of idiot thing he expected ageing actresses like her to do.

Rosalind pushed her memories of the evening aside and smiled, warm and welcoming. Her *trust me* smile. Dahlia's smile. It felt good to slip into her skin again after so long.

Dahlia didn't freak out at dead bodies. Dahlia didn't care if anyone thought she was intrusive, or abrasive. Didn't care if the papers labelled her difficult. Didn't shy away from causing trouble.

It was liberating.

Maybe Caro had it right all along. Who wanted to be themselves when they could be Dahlia?

'I was rather hoping you might have something you could share with *me*, actually,' she said.

His greying eyebrows rose. 'Oh? And why is that? I'm sure you, of all people, Ms King, must understand the importance of confidentiality in an ongoing investigation. Especially in these early stages.'

'Please, call me Rosalind.' She tripped over her own name, just slightly, but she could see that Larch caught it. He was smart, this one. She'd almost said Dahlia. 'And of course, I understand completely. It's just that the events tonight . . .' She shuddered, delicately. 'They've left my friend, Caro, quite shaken. I think it would help her sleep tonight if she could understand a little bit about what happened, and why.'

Larch looked sceptical, but Rosalind had been playing poor, meek, scared older ladies for years now. She knew how to sell it. As long as he didn't turn around and see Caro's eager expression as she leant forward, trying to eavesdrop on their conversation.

He sighed. 'Like I said, I can't tell you much. We have someone examining the body right now, but you saw it.'

She had. She wasn't going to forget it any time soon. 'It was . . . bloated.' The words she'd overheard another member of his team telling him came back to her. 'Like it had been in the water for a while, then got tangled in the reeds?'

Tight-lipped, Larch nodded confirmation.

'So she drowned?' Rosalind pressed. 'Only, I thought I saw . . . something else. The back of her head . . .' She blinked to try and clear the image from her mind's eye. It didn't work.

Larch's gaze darted sideways, towards the window and the water. 'We think she was killed by a blow to the head before she went in the water.'

'Oh. That . . . that probably won't make Caro and her head injury feel much better.'

'I wouldn't imagine so, no.' At least he was straight and to the point. 'And that's already more than I should have told you. Are you sure none of *you* have anything more to tell me about why you were there tonight in the first place? Did you tell anyone that you were going?'

Rosalind shook her head. 'No. It was a . . . spur of the moment thing.'

He gave her a long, disbelieving look. 'Here's the thing, Ms King. While I appreciate that you and your friends here this weekend believe yourself to be detectives, my team and I have actually *trained* to do this work. We have experience. We know what we're doing – and what *not* to do – based on the actual law, rather than fiction. So I'll tell you now, things are going to go better for all of us if you tell us what you know and let us do our jobs, rather than playing Miss Marple or Dahlia Lively or whoever and screwing up my investigation. Okay?'

Thank goodness he'd said that to her, rather than Caro. Setting a Detective Chief Inspector's tie on fire wouldn't be a good way to start a working relationship.

Rosalind gave him her coldest look, her tone icy as she said, 'Believe it or not, DCI Larch, even *actors* are capable of telling the difference between real life and the roles they play.' She wanted to tell him they'd known it was murder long before his team had even suspected. That if he had any sense, he'd be buttering them up for information, rather than scolding her. But she didn't. 'I'm sure you and your team are more than capable of solving this murder without our help, so we shall leave you to it. I assume you will want to question us all in the morning?'

'You assume correctly,' Larch said. 'Now, if you'll excuse me—'

'One more thing.' Rosalind reached out and rested a hand on his arm. He looked up at her, and she could see his patience waning in his eyes. 'Just tell me . . . Clementine. You said she'd been hit on the head, like Caro, before she went into the water. How much before?'

His jaw tightened, and she could sense his reluctance to share the information.

'Your team out there were already cordoning off the ground either side of the river all the way upstream before you even arrived,' she pressed. 'So you don't think she was killed where I found her, do you?'

Frustration flared across his face but she could tell he was going to answer her all the same. Maybe he hoped that by confirming what she'd already figured out, he'd persuade her to tell him anything she knew. Or perhaps he thought she was befriending him because she was responsible, somehow.

Either way, after a long moment he said, 'Our guy thinks she was already dead by Saturday evening. Looks like she'd been in the water over twenty-four hours. There's no obvious sign of blood other than a few drops of your friend's at the Gate House, or of any other struggle, so odds are good she was killed somewhere else, then moved at night, perhaps, when the coast was clear.'

'Except we were all up for hours that night, too,' Rosalind replied. 'Because Marcus . . .'

'Died here that night too. Yes. We're hoping for some more information about that soon.' Larch stepped away, and Rosalind's hand fell to her side. 'I'm afraid your convention is over, though.'

'You'll let me know if you find anything?' Rosalind said, coolly.

'Not unless I think you did it,' Larch replied, before striding off towards the front door, where he was intercepted by Isobel.

Rosalind watched him go. That could have gone worse. Even if she might now be more of a suspect than she was before.

She was already dead by Saturday evening.

Before Marcus was poisoned. *That* had to mean something.

Chapter Twenty-Three

*'Sometimes, Johnnie, we need to move backwards to move forwards,'
Dahlia said, looking uncharacteristically reflective. 'Sometimes, the
answers we're looking for lie in things we've already done, or seen.'*

Dahlia Lively *in* Poisoner's Delight
***By* Lettice Davenport, 1986**

By the time they were all done, the sun was almost up over the horizon. Rosalind and Posy followed Caro to her room, but Rosalind turned around and headed back into the corridor. 'Come on,' she said. 'Grab what you need – half your stuff is in my room anyway. *And* it doesn't have head injury aggravating wallpaper,' she added, before Posy could offer up her own room.

Rosalind's room was the nicest of Aldermere's guest rooms, and had enough space for the three Dahlias to sleep there comfortably while they kept an eye on Caro's head injury. It was a logical decision, that had nothing to do with the fact that every time she blinked Rosalind saw Clementine's staring eyeballs behind her own lids.

She opened the door, dropped her bag onto the dressing table, and stopped, staring. Propped against the mirror was a tiny doll wearing a floral tea dress.

'Is that meant to be me?' Posy pulled a face at the thing as she picked it up. The silver skirt Rosalind had lent her was splattered with mud, and the jacket she'd borrowed from Caro was missing a few beads, presumably torn off by the branches they'd fought their way through.

Caro took the doll from her calmly. Apparently they'd used up their capacity for shock this evening. 'It's got the right hair. And the dress.' She handed it to Rosalind for inspection.

'Do we think it's a warning?'

'I think the heavy object that whacked me on the head was a warning.' Caro touched the bandage at her temple gingerly. 'I think this is a taunt.'

Posy was still frowning at the figure in Rosalind's hand. 'But why me? *Caro* hasn't had a doll, and she's the only one who has been attacked by a murderer so far.'

'Actually . . .' Caro fished in her jacket pocket and pulled out another miniature figure. 'It was waiting for me when I went back to my room to get my jacket, before dinner.'

There was a long pause while they both stared at the dolls. Rosalind wondered if they were thinking the same as she was. *Why haven't I got one yet?*

Or maybe there was something else planned for her.

Rosalind yanked open the bedside drawer and tossed the Posy doll inside. After a beat, Caro did the same with hers.

'Something else to worry about tomorrow,' she said.

'It *is* tomorrow,' Posy pointed out.

'After we've got some sleep, then.' The dolls could join a long list of questions Rosalind hoped to answer before the end of the day.

Before they left Aldermere behind.

'Wait. Are we supposed to keep you awake all night?' Posy asked Caro, with a yawn.

'God, I hope not.' Caro dropped onto the bed, bouncing slightly. 'As much as I love talking all night at a girly slumber party, this bed is too comfortable to waste not sleeping.'

It felt reassuring, but strange to have others in the room as Rosalind prepared for bed. She removed her earrings, placing them on the dressing table, then reached up to unlatch her necklace. Stranger than it had been dressing for dinner. Perhaps because that was a performance; this was personal.

Posy curled up on the window seat, hugging a cushion to her chest. 'I don't know if I can sleep. I keep thinking about Clementine.'

White skin in the moonlight. Those bulging, staring eyes. Rosalind swallowed.

'Do you think whoever killed her was in the Gate House tonight?' Posy went on. 'That the person that attacked Caro killed Clementine? And Marcus? Why?'

Why?

Wasn't that always the most important, and infuriating question? The one that drove everything else. Rosalind had asked Hugh '*Why?*', all those years before, and so many times since. She'd never had a satisfactory answer to that question, either – why, if he loved her, he'd slept with Isobel. Why he'd married her, stayed with her when it became clear there was no baby.

Maybe that was why she kept coming back, why she'd orbited him so tightly through the years. If she'd had an answer to her why, maybe she'd have moved on.

'Perhaps Clementine *was* behind the blackmail and the fakes after all,' Caro suggested.

'Was there anything in Marcus's ledger we might have missed? Anything about Clementine?' Rosalind asked.

Caro frowned. 'I don't think so. Hang on.' She fished the small, brown leather journal from the overnight bag she'd brought from her room and paged through it. 'I can't see anything, but then I might be concussed. You try.' She tossed it to Posy, who caught it easily, dropping her cushion to do so.

Posy leafed through the ledger more slowly, taking the time to check every page. Rosalind returned to the bathroom to smooth night cream into her skin, and by the time she'd finished, Posy was done.

'Nothing I can see. Nothing that makes this make sense.'

The three women absorbed the information in silence. Rosalind turned the facts over in her head, but she still couldn't find a way to make a coherent story.

They needed to find the missing links, or else they'd never know why someone here this weekend turned to poison. And bludgeoning.

She frowned. Something else that didn't make sense.

'Clementine was hit over the head before she was dumped in the river,' she said, thinking aloud. Posy closed the ledger and gave her full attention, which was gratifying. Caro was less attentive, but Rosalind forgave her because of the possible concussion. 'And the killer tried to do the same to Caro tonight.'

'I was there,' Caro grumbled, rubbing the side of her head. One of her victory rolls had come unpinned, and a long dark curl hung down the side of her face, while the other remained pinned and pristine. 'I remember.'

'That doesn't seem the same sort of death that Marcus suffered, does it?'

'No, it doesn't.' Posy's spine was straight as she sat up on the window seat, alert and keen despite the lateness – or earliness – of the hour. She reminded Rosalind of an Irish setter her father had been particularly fond of when she was a child. 'Marcus's murder – that was planned. Coordinated, even. Someone had to take the time to find out about his special tea, to get hold of the poisonous flower and sugar it . . . that's not like whacking someone on the head.'

'They took advantage of the set-up, too,' Caro mused. She'd pulled herself up to rest against the padded headboard of Rosalind's bed, looking like a worn 1930s shop girl after too good a night out. 'The whole multi-course tasting menu, like in the book. They'd planned this.'

'But it might not have been the same person who attacked Caro tonight.' Posy didn't make it sound like a question, more a confirmation that they were all on the same page.

'Whoever it was, they probably did do for Clementine, since they found her body near the same place they tried to whack me,' Caro said, matter-of-factly. 'But not Marcus. That's a whole different M.O. Right?'

'Right,' Rosalind agreed. 'Which means, our investigation isn't over yet, like we agreed. Detective Chief Inspector Larch might want to take over this whole debacle, but I'm not sure I trust him to get it right, are you?'

Posy shook her head.

'Dahlia wouldn't be,' Caro said.

'So neither are we three Dahlias.' Rosalind smiled, feeling the muscles in her cheeks move as it stretched, wide and real, across her face.

Three Dahlia Livelys. Working together.

It felt better than she'd imagined it could. As if she were stepping out of her own history at Aldermere and into something new and exciting.

Something deadly, admittedly. But something.

'I guess we'd better try to get some sleep, then, if we're going to solve a murder in the morning.' Posy shifted from the window seat to the sofa and stretched across the cushions. 'At least the wallpaper's more restful in here.'

She was asleep in moments, the sleep of the young, the unburdened. For all the tabloid stories about her exploits, she still seemed impossibly innocent to Rosalind.

'Put a blanket over her?' Caro said, in an oddly maternal voice. 'She'll get cold. No insulation on her, is there?'

'No.' Rosalind picked up the satin coverlet from the end of the bed and laid it over Posy, then turned to Caro. 'I suppose it's too much to hope that you don't snore?'

'A lady never *snores,* darling.' Caro shimmied down the mattress, pulling more than half of the duvet over to her side and wrapping it around her. 'They merely breathe a little louder.'

Rolling her eyes, Rosalind settled onto the other side of the bed. She hadn't expected to sleep much, anyway. She had murder to think about.

And, she thought, as Caro's first snore broke the silence, at least if she was snoring, she knew that the head injury couldn't be too bad.

They would need her encyclopaedic Dahlia knowledge if they were going to solve these murders. Because Rosalind had a feeling it had more to do with Aldermere, and Lettice, and the Davenports, than either of the other two had guessed.

Breakfast was served late – very late – the next morning. But it wasn't like any of them had to rush off. The police had made it clear that the current guests and occupants of Aldermere House should stay in residence until they'd had a chance to talk to everybody, but they'd closed off the grounds completely. An outer cordon at the gates, then an inner one following the path of the river, enclosing the banks on either side.

It was bank holiday Monday, on what should have been the final day of the convention. The sun had returned, and the only sign of last night's storm was the odd patch of muddy grass.

But everything else had changed.

The buses with day delegates had already arrived – and been turned away by the police guard at the Gate House. From where they sat eating pastries on the terrace, Rosalind could see the empty marquees and abandoned stalls, the festival atmosphere of the last few days washed away in the rainstorm of the night before.

This should have been Marcus's triumph. His climax to a thrilling three days of murder, mystery and a little light blackmail.

Instead, the news about Clementine's murder had been common knowledge by the time they'd had their first cup of coffee. There was an officer stationed at the house, as well as the specialist teams working along the river, although Detective Chief Inspector Larch had disappeared for now. Rosalind wondered how long it would take him to figure out what she, Caro and Posy already knew.

They should probably make the most of their head start while they still had it. Especially if they didn't want photos of their indiscretions displayed as evidence in a court room in the future.

Juliette dropped into the fourth seat at their table, scowling.

'I can't believe they've cancelled the whole thing, right when I had everything under control!' Juliette pouted, and reached for a mini pain au chocolat from the basket.

Rosalind hid a smile as she took her seat. Yes, she was definitely Isobel's granddaughter, if murder was more of an inconvenience to her fledgeling career in the events industry than a terrible shock.

But then she looked up at Rosalind, eyes wide. 'Sorry, Auntie Rosalind. Grandma said it was you who, well, you know. Found her.'

'Yes, it was.' She must make sure to spend more time with Juliette. She'd failed badly as Serena's godmother, but maybe she could do better by her daughter. Whatever happened next, they were family – more or less all the family she had left, these days.

'At least you don't have to worry about whatever Marcus's big plans for the closing ceremony were,' Posy said.

'That's true. But to think I've been texting a dead woman for the last day and a half!' Juliette shuddered. 'At least she never replied. That would have been so creepy.'

But Clementine had texted Hugh, Rosalind remembered suddenly. She'd messaged him about the car, long after she must actually have been dead. So who had Clementine's phone?

'I don't know what I'm meant to do now,' Juliette said, a hint of a whine in her voice.

'Well, there's still the clean-up.' Caro pointed to a volunteer with a clipboard loitering by the edge of the terrace, obviously waiting to ask a question.

Juliette sighed, but jumped to her feet. 'Tidying up is always my least favourite part.'

As she descended the terrace steps to help the volunteers, Isobel appeared beside their table in her place, her beautiful face looking older, drained of its usual pink and white colour. 'Rosalind. Do you have a moment? Please?'

Rosalind took a final sip of her coffee, then followed Isobel down the terrace steps onto the path that wound around the gardens.

'At least DCI Larch cancelled the rest of the convention,' Rosalind said, after a few minutes of silence. It would seem Isobel needed to work up to whatever it was she wanted to say. 'That's the last thing you needed to deal with today.' Rosalind may have found the body, but Isobel had to live here, forever, where the woman had been killed.

'Yes. Not surprising, really. But he also informed me that I have house guests until he tells me otherwise.' Isobel sighed. 'He seems to think this will be a quick job to solve. Although I can't imagine why . . .' she trailed off, shaking her head.

'Is there anything I can do to help?' Rosalind tried not to sound reluctant in offering. Friendship had to come before investigations, she supposed. Although if she found herself having to put on some sort of Dahlia skit with Posy and Caro to entertain the guests, she might rethink that.

Isobel glanced over her shoulder towards the terrace, even though they'd walked far enough to be sure no one could overhear them. Her hands were clasped in front of her stomach, the skin around her pale pink nail polish red and raw.

'I need you to . . . I need you to talk to Hugh.'

A cold, creeping sensation started in Rosalind's stomach, winding its way towards her throat. 'What about?'

'Clementine.'

Her body froze. Rosalind hunted for a reply, but her tongue didn't seem to be cooperating. *Why am I surprised? I already knew, didn't I?*

But knowing it and accepting it were different things. While no one had said it aloud, she could pretend it wasn't happening. *Forty years, and it's the same damn thing all over again.*

Except it wasn't. Because Clementine was dead.

This wasn't about Hugh cheating on her – on them. This was about murder.

Isobel didn't seem to need a response to carry on. The floodgates were open now.

'I told you I thought he was having an affair.' Isobel's hands twisted again, her forget-me-not blue eyes wet and worried.

'Clementine . . . they met when Marcus first came to talk about the convention. Hugh showed her around while Marcus and I discussed menus and they were gone, well, a long time. But I thought . . . I thought he was being solicitous.'

'Maybe he was.' Even though she didn't believe it any more than Isobel did.

'They've been in contact since,' Isobel went on, determination in the line of her jaw as she forced the words out. 'I overheard them talking on the phone, last week. And before that . . . there was a voicemail on his mobile from her. I think he met up with her when he went to London last month.'

'You've been checking his phone?'

'Wouldn't you?'

If they'd had today's mobile technology forty years ago, Rosalind probably would have. 'Did you ask him about it?'

'In a roundabout way.' Isobel gave a shrug. 'You know what it's like.'

Yes. She did know. Except last time it had been Isobel that Hugh had been disappearing off with behind Rosalind's back. And then the other way around. And now . . .

Now a girl was dead.

'The thing is . . . there's a lot riding on this movie,' Isobel said, and Rosalind blinked at the sudden change of subject. 'Financially, I mean. Things are . . . well, the location fee for the movie would certainly help, not that Hugh will admit it. He wouldn't approve the script, because he felt it wasn't true to Letty's vision, and now there's all *this*.' Isobel spread her hands wide, as if to encompass murder, adultery, financial ruin, and all the other disasters the world had to offer. 'So you see, don't you? Why I need you to talk to him?'

'About the affair or the film?' Rosalind asked, confused.

'Both.' The ferocity in Isobel's eyes surprised her. 'They're connected, somehow. I mean, the first script really *was* a disaster, but he was *fine* with the direction of the new one until Clementine showed up. Then something changed. *He* changed.'

She knew that moment, too, Rosalind realised. From before. When there'd been nothing she could put her finger on, but she'd known there was something wrong. And then he'd told her about Isobel . . .

'Why me?' Rosalind rubbed a hand across her forehead, a poor salve against the headache forming there.

'You're his oldest friend—'

'You're his wife!'

Isobel shook her head. 'Yes. But you're . . . you've always been . . . something more.'

The cold hit Rosalind's lungs, stealing the warm summer air she'd been breathing.

They'd never talked about it. Never even hinted at it. If Isobel knew of the relationship between Rosalind and Hugh and had not once given her a clue that she suspected . . . she was a better actress than Rosalind had given her credit for.

'You matter to him. He trusts you, and he *listens* to you.' Isobel's smile was sad. 'It has to be you. He'll tell you the truth.'

But what if I don't want to hear it?

Rosalind let out a long breath, and nodded.

'Thank you,' Isobel said, relief in her voice. 'I know . . . of course he had nothing to do with, well . . . the important thing is that you make sure there's nothing for the police to find out. Right?'

Her shoulders relaxed, instead of hunched up around her jaw, Isobel turned to head for the house, her hands swinging loosely at her sides.

274

Rosalind hesitated. 'Isobel?'

She turned, her usual smile back in place, seemingly surprised that there was anything more to say.

'Do you . . . do you really think Hugh could know anything about Clementine's death?' Even now, she couldn't bring herself to say 'involved with'. Let alone 'caused'. 'Or are you worried the police might think he did?'

Because that made more sense. Isobel's attachment to the family reputation, their social standing . . . any hint that Hugh might have been having an affair with a young murder victim would put all that at risk. She might be more concerned about that than the fact he was having an affair to begin with, now she thought about it.

But Isobel's reply went one step further. 'Does it matter? The important thing is that nothing gets out.'

Rosalind watched her walk away, more unsettled than ever.

'Murder makes everyone selfish.' Dahlia's words, but she heard them in Caro's voice, not her own, and she saw Posy's melancholy eyes as she spoke them.

But then the VIP delegates descended from the terrace to intercept Isobel, and Rosalind hurried to catch up, in time to hear Heather demanding, 'We want our phones back. Now.'

Chapter Twenty-Four

'What are you doing?' Johnnie asked.

Dahlia replied without opening her eyes. 'I'm investigating.'

'You look like you're taking a nap in an armchair.'

With a sigh, Dahlia sat up, opened her eyes, and reached for her glass of whisky. 'Sometimes, thinking your way through what you already know is the only thing that can help you figure out what it is that you don't *know.'*

Dahlia Lively *in* Twelve Lively Suspects
By Lettice Davenport, 1945

Isobel hadn't been able to smile or sweet-talk her way out of their demands – not least because they were perfectly reasonable.

'Whatever we signed up for when we agreed to hand in our phones, it definitely wasn't this,' Felicity said, and the others had nodded.

Isobel had led them through to the library, and the safe hidden behind one of the paintings. 'We'll have to wait for Hugh, though,' she said. 'He's got the combination memorised.'

'What did Isobel want?' Caro murmured to Rosalind, as they waited by the door.

'She wants me to talk to Hugh.'

Posy raised her eyebrows. 'About?'

'Clementine, and the film.' Rosalind spotted Hugh arriving, and waited for her heart to do its usual double beat on sight of him. 'I'll explain later.'

The three Dahlias kept a close eye on everyone's faces as they got their phones back. Word had got around quickly, and Kit, Anton and Libby had soon joined the queue.

The VIP delegates seemed relieved to have restored contact with the outside world, quickly checking their messages and social media feeds. Kit, on receiving his phone, hugged it like an old friend, then planted a loud kiss on the screen. 'I'll never leave you again!'

Anton, brow furrowed, muttered to himself as he glared at the screen. Libby, meanwhile, slipped her phone into her pocket and hurried out of the room. Either she didn't have anyone she expected to hear from, or she wanted to check her messages in private. Rosalind wondered which one it was.

Rosalind assured herself there was nothing she needed to worry about on her emails, then put her phone away. Caro muttered something about calling Annie, and stepped outside.

Phones distributed, Hugh and Isobel left the room together. Rosalind watched them go. Would Isobel bring up any of the things she'd talked to her about this morning? She doubted it. Isobel preferred to smile and pretend that everything was okay, while someone else dealt with the harder issues. She always had.

Rosalind glanced over Posy's shoulder as she flicked through what seemed like a dozen different apps in record time, then she smiled with relief. 'No sign of the photos showing up anywhere.'

'That's good. That means we have a little more time.'

'So what do we do next?' Caro walked into the room, slipping her phone into her pocket. Whatever she'd needed to talk to her wife about, it hadn't taken long.

'We were going over what happened last night while you were talking to Isobel,' Posy said to Rosalind. 'And what we already know.'

'How far did you get?' Rosalind asked.

'Not very,' Posy admitted.

'It's too complicated.' Caro dropped into one of the leather armchairs. 'It's getting like that awful fifties book, the one in eight parts that doesn't make any sense until the last page.'

'*Forever Summer*,' Rosalind supplied. 'Nobody liked that one. It was Letty getting experimental.'

'I preferred the one she wrote from Johnnie's point of view,' Caro grumbled. '*To Catch A Fly*. That was good experimental.'

'Let's go back to basics,' Posy said. 'What would Dahlia do?'

'She'd figure out the facts in hand,' Caro replied. 'That's something we haven't done – looked at the facts of Clementine's death.'

'Because we don't know them.' Caro glared at Posy, and she rolled her eyes before continuing. 'Okay, fine. We know that she was pretending to be dead in the stables before three o'clock on Saturday, because I saw her there. And we know she drove away from Aldermere just after five, because we *all* saw her do that. And we know that she showed up dead in the reeds at midnight the next day, and had been dead over twenty-four hours, so she probably died *before* Marcus was murdered.'

'We can also assume she came back at some point between those last two events,' Rosalind said. 'If Felicity is telling the truth about seeing her that afternoon.'

'And left her clothes in the Gate House, where I found them,' Caro added. 'But why pretend to leave then come back and hide if it wasn't to kill Marcus? And what happened to the clothes she put on instead? Unless the killer stripped her *then* hid her clothes there?'

Another thing that didn't make any sense.

'Caro, tell us again what happened at the Gate House last night.' There had to be a clue in there somewhere, but for the life of her, Rosalind couldn't see what it was.

'I told you. I went in to search the bedroom. I opened the drawer under the wardrobe, and I saw Clementine's clothes.'

'How did you know they were Clementine's?' Posy had a pen in hand and was scribbling notes.

Caro shrugged. 'I recognised that mustard scarf she was wearing when we met her. Anyway, I went to pull them out and someone whacked me over the head and everything went black.'

'Where did the attacker come from, though?' Rosalind wondered aloud. 'They couldn't have been in the room when you came in, and no one went past Posy and I to get to the bedroom. The window was open?'

'Yes. But I don't think they came through it.' Caro frowned, as if trying to remember. 'I think . . . she must have been behind the door when I entered.'

'Which means she was already in the Gate House before we got there.' Posy dropped her pen and looked up. 'Wait. It was definitely a woman?'

Caro nodded, slowly. 'I'm pretty sure. I couldn't get a good look at her in the dark – I dropped my torch. But she didn't *feel* like a man. You know? You can tell, can't you, when the threat is male.'

The strangest thing was, Rosalind knew exactly what she meant.

'So we need to figure out which of the women could have been in the Gate House at midnight to whack Caro over the head, then we've got our killer.' Posy grabbed her pen again. 'So that's Heather, Libby, Isobel, Juliette and Felicity. Anyone else?' Caro and Rosalind shook their heads. 'That's five women we need to talk to, get their alibis for midnight last night.'

Rosalind's mouth felt dry. Even if it was a woman in the Gate

House, she wasn't willing to write off the involvement of all the male occupants of Aldermere just yet.

'You two handle that,' she said.

Isobel was still in the entrance hall, talking with her housekeeper, but she paused to tell Rosalind, 'Hugh's in Letty's study, if you're looking for him.'

Rosalind nodded, and was rewarded with a relieved smile from her friend.

She lingered at the dollhouse at the bottom of the stairs, postponing the moment of seeing him again, painfully aware of how different this felt to even three days ago. When she'd found him there on Friday night, even after what Isobel had told her, she'd wanted to be in his arms.

Now, she was almost afraid of what happened next.

She peered closer into the replica of Aldermere, and spotted another figure, this time in Letty's study. Her fingers moved towards it without thinking, lifting it out and holding it up to the light.

To her surprise, it was a man. *Not me.* Then she registered the grey hair, the cord trousers, and the bottle of poison clutched in its hand. *Hugh.*

Maybe it had been left for her, after all.

The figure still clenched in her fingers, Rosalind climbed the stairs to the first floor, then the second, narrower staircase to the attic floor, and Letty's study. She could feel her heart thumping too fast in her chest, as if her body were preparing itself for another shock.

She pushed open the door, and found Hugh sprawled over the armchair beside the bookcase reading one of Letty's earlier mysteries. Hugh had always said his aunt's books were comfort reads for him. 'It feels like she's talking to me, even now she's gone,' he'd told her, when she visited for Letty's funeral and found him in the same place.

Rosalind cleared her throat, and Hugh looked up, his face brightening under the anglepoise floor lamp behind him. 'Well, this is a nice surprise. Managed to break away from your sycophants, did you?'

'My what?' Rosalind raised her eyebrows as she drifted over to the case where the jewelled magnifying glass sat.

Hugh sat up straighter, closing his book on his lap. 'Oh, you know. Every time I've seen you this weekend you've had those other two following you around like ducklings to your mother duck. Caro Hooper, of course, and the American. Posy. I assumed they were trying to cash in on your popularity.'

'Posy's British. She just grew up in America. And I think Caro has always been the most popular Dahlia Lively,' she replied, keeping her voice mild.

'Only to the plebs with no taste.' She hated it when he was like this: aloof and above everyone. When they'd met, so long ago now, he'd seemed different. Privileged and wealthy, but aware of it, perhaps. Compared to Rosalind's upbringing, he'd seemed like he'd arrived from another world – but one he'd been eager to welcome her into.

As the years went on, after he welcomed *Isobel* into it instead of her, that had changed. Rosalind's star rose, she married, moved up in the world – financially and socially. And Hugh started to treat her as if she'd been there all along, saying the sort of things about those with less that he never would have done when they met.

When *she* was the one with less.

It might not have bothered her so much to hear him talking down Caro before this weekend. In fact, if she was brutally honest, she knew it hadn't. She'd heard his words and believed it was his way of defending her, of declaring his love for her without saying it out loud in front of others.

But now it sounded different. Defensive. Jealous. As if she'd taken a part of his aunt's legacy that he wasn't willing to give up.

Eager to change the subject, she nodded to the glass case. 'I see you found the magnifying glass?'

Hugh glanced over, placing his book on the shelf beside him, then pushing up on the arms of his chair to cross the room and join her. 'It was the darndest thing. Just showed up there again yesterday – no idea where from. I half wondered if Isobel had hidden the cursed thing herself to cause a scene.'

'Why would she do that?'

Hugh shrugged. 'Who knows, with Isobel. Probably to punish me for agreeing to hold this blasted convention in the first place. Given everything that's happened since, maybe she thought I'd been punished enough. But I have to tell you, I'm happy to see the thing again. Worth a fortune, that is. Could have claimed on the insurance, I suppose, but that's just money, isn't it? And Aunt Letty was always so fond of it.'

The original was worth a fortune, of course. But that wasn't the original. Did Hugh know? Had he sold it to Marcus himself? Or was Isobel right, and he wouldn't acknowledge how bad the financial situation at Aldermere really was?

'Why did you?' Rosalind asked. 'Agree to have the convention here, I mean.'

She thought she knew, but she wanted to hear it from him. If Marcus was blackmailing him, maybe he'd wanted more than a cash payout. Aldermere House had been saved by Letty's money – Hugh's grandfather had been almost bankrupt before Letty's fame and fortune came along. She'd never married so all her money had gone into the estate, even before she died and left everything to Hugh – the last of the Davenports.

'Oh, I don't know,' Hugh said, with what sounded like forced casualness to her. 'Marcus had been asking for years. And this place, Aldermere, it *is* Letty, in so many ways. I've had it to myself for years; I suppose I decided it was time to share it with the fans. And with the new movie coming up, the publicity never hurts. Bring Dahlia Lively to life for a new generation of readers, and make sure those royalties never dry up.'

It was perfectly reasonable and reasoned. It made perfect sense. So why was Rosalind so certain he was lying? *Because I know him. And I know what he sounds like when he lies, because usually he's lying to his wife about me.*

If he could pretend nothing was wrong, so could she. She ran a fingertip across the shelves, and moved along the rows of books and keepsakes, clocking each one as she went, just in case.

'They're saying that Marcus was killed because he was blackmailing people, you know.' She kept her voice as light and inconsequential as she could, but her gaze was trained hard on him, so she saw the way his jaw tightened, his shoulders stiffened. 'Clementine was his accomplice, I assume.'

'Are they? I hadn't heard that. Have you been sweet-talking Larch to get extra information? I saw you two talking last night.' Hugh raised an eyebrow. 'I suppose I should be grateful you weren't giving up all my secrets to him.' He laughed, but there was no humour behind it.

She couldn't spill Hugh's secrets, Rosalind realised, because she didn't know them. Not all of them, anyway. Not the ones that mattered right now.

'You were watching me, were you?' She forced a smile. 'Nice to know I still have your attention.'

'Always. You know that.' He stepped towards her, his arms going around her waist automatically. Hers responded in kind, but she couldn't settle into the embrace. Her mind was too busy working, even as her gaze darted across the shelves behind him.

There was something missing.

She blinked, and refocused.

It was like Kim's Game, the memory game she'd played as a child. Rosalind scanned the shelves, trying to figure out what wasn't there. Because there *was* something missing, but what?

The dolls from the dollhouse. Letty's hat. The magnifying glass. Her awards. The poison bottle—

The poison bottle. That macabre gift from a fan to Letty – actual poison in a skull and crossbones labelled bottle. Like the one in the hand of the doll she'd found downstairs.

Where was it? Caro had brought it back when she returned the magnifying glass, hadn't she?

Which meant someone else had taken it again.

She needed to get back downstairs, to tell Caro and Posy. Warn them. Warn Larch, as well, so his officers could protect people—

Hugh's arms tightened, and he pulled his head back from where it rested on her shoulder to look her in the eye, his chin dipping as he lowered his mouth to hers.

And as she kissed him, she forced herself to focus on what she knew.

Hugh had been talking to Clementine in the Murder Spiral before her death. Clementine worked for Marcus, who was blackmailing Hugh. Marcus, who had to die. Clementine knew everyone's secrets.

And Isobel thought Hugh was having an affair with her. Was she right?

It was a story that made too much sense in Rosalind's head. She could see it playing out in the movie theatre of her mind.

She didn't want to watch the ending.

Rosalind broke the kiss and pulled away.

'Isobel is worried, you know. She asked me to talk to you.'

That seemed to surprise him. 'Isobel asked *you* to talk to me?'

'Because of how long we've been friends.' Rosalind thought about mentioning Isobel's money worries, but if she got him riled up about the finances, she might never get to ask the more important questions. She took a breath, and dove in. 'She thinks you were having an affair with Clementine.'

'Well, you know she's wrong about *that*.' He gave her a knowing, secret look. The same look he used to give her across the dining table, their spouses oblivious to what it meant. *Meet me, later.*

Except now it meant something else. It meant *I know your secrets too, remember. Bring me down, we both go.*

She fought to remain calm in spite of the shiver crawling the length of her spine.

'Do I?'

'You really think I was having an affair?' Hugh asked, incredulously. 'When would I have time for something like that? Between you and Isobel, I have plenty of women on my hands, thank you very much.'

'You wouldn't be the first man to want something younger, prettier, at your stage in life.'

He rolled his eyes. 'Rosalind, I barely even met her! Isobel sorted the catering and such, I stayed out of the way as much as possible. I doubt I shared more than a handful of words with her the whole time.' His words were light, but she could feel the fear under them.

She was almost certain it wasn't an affair he was worried about being accused of. It was murder.

She'd loved him almost her whole life. And now she couldn't even trust him.

'Except I saw you with her. In the Spiral Garden. The day she died.'

He shrugged. 'I bumped into her in the gardens. Spoke about the flowers. That doesn't mean anything.'

She'd watched them, seen the intensity of their conversation. But even if she hadn't, the beads of sweat forming on Hugh's forehead would have told her all she needed to know.

'Rosalind King. I've never loved another woman the way I love you.' Hugh's eyes were dark and serious, his shoulders hunched as he reached out for her.

She stepped out of his grasp.

'I want to believe you. But Hugh . . . if there is something you need to tell Isobel, you should tell her.' Even if it destroyed everything she'd spent years protecting.

'That's surprisingly good advice, Mr Davenport.' They both jumped at DCI Larch's voice, dry and humourless from the hallway. How long had he been there? 'I'd suggest you follow it. And request that, if there *is* anything you're keeping secret, you also share it with me and my team.'

Hugh's face paled to bone white, but he remained silent. Rosalind relied on her training to appear self-assured rather than rattled. Shoulders straight, smile in place, glide as she turned . . .

'Detective Chief Inspector. Was there something more you needed Hugh to help you with?'

He studied her face before he answered, and she kept it as expressionless as she could.

'Actually, Ms King, I was hoping to speak with you.' His gaze flicked across to Hugh. 'Privately.'

Oh, hell. 'Of course. Let's go.'

Because really, what else could she do?

Chapter Twenty-Five

*The policeman leered across the interview table at her. 'Not so much
fun when you're on the other side, is it, Miss Lively?'*

Dahlia Lively *in* The Devil and the Deep Blue Sea
***By* Lettice Davenport, 1940**

Rosalind led the DCI to her own rooms, deciding that home turf
would be easiest for this confrontation. Except, she'd forgotten that
her room was still strewn with the remnants of their 'girlie sleepover'
the night before.

'Take a seat.' She gestured to the large sofa, and winced when
Larch picked up Posy's leopard print bra between two fingers and
placed it delicately on the coffee table before him.

One thing she'd learned from Isobel, it was always better to brazen
these things out. Even when they'd shared that terrible flat on the
northern end of the tube line, the one with the slugs in the bathroom, Isobel had greeted guests with a tea tray complete with sugar
bowl and lace doilies, as if they'd been invited to the palace.

Rosalind ignored Posy's lingerie, and Caro's make-up bag spilling
across the coffee table, and took her own seat opposite the policeman.

'You wished to speak with me?' She raised her eyebrows to suggest
she couldn't possibly imagine what about.

'Yes.' He shifted uncomfortably on the sofa, and she hoped he
hadn't found any more of her friend's unmentionables to sit on. 'I

know my officers took your statement last night, about finding the body. But it seems to me on second reading that there were some notable omissions I hoped you could clear up for me.'

'Oh?'

'Like why you went down to the Gate House in the first place.' He'd pulled out his notebook to consult his scribbles on the matter, but he didn't look at them before asking.

'I told you last night. It was a spur of the moment decision.'

'Only when I spoke to one of your fellow house guests, Miss Felicity Hill, she suggested it might have been because she told you she'd seen the victim heading to the Gate House on the afternoon of her murder.' Another long, expectant look from the DCI, punctuated by him tapping his pen against the paper.

If he was expecting her to sound guilty, he'd misjudged this situation rather badly.

'She did tell us that, yes,' Rosalind admitted. 'And since we were concerned about Clementine, we discussed it between the three of us and decided – on the spur of that moment – to go and check if she was still there, and if she needed anything.'

'You were concerned about her.'

'Yes.'

'Were you concerned she might be dead?'

'No!' Rosalind stared at him in horror. 'If anything, we were concerned that she might have been involved in her boss's death.'

'So you went to the Gate House, on the spur of the moment, to confront a woman you suspected of being a murderer.' Larch shook his head. 'You understand that doesn't make this situation any better.'

'Yes, I see that now,' Rosalind snapped. 'Have you had the results of Marcus's post mortem back yet?'

He looked up from his notes, and met her gaze, like he was searching her eyes for secrets. 'We have.'

'Poison? Aconite, right?'

He paused, his pen still where it rested on his notebook. 'Yes. How did you know that?' For the first time since they'd met, Larch managed an expression other than weary disappointment. It wasn't quite surprise, but it was enough to make Rosalind feel a flare of triumph.

'Because that's how it happens in the script. Marcus had recreated the dinner scene from *The Lady Detective*. Eleven courses, then murder over coffee.' She shrugged. 'Very unoriginal, in fact.'

'*That's* why you suspected murder. Because of a film.' Larch's tone was flat, disbelieving.

'We suspected murder because we understand character. Narrative. Opportunity. And because we know, when it comes to murder, there's no such thing as coincidence.'

Larch rubbed a hand across his forehead. Apparently this conversation was giving him a headache. Good.

'Marcus wasn't a nice person.' She had to tread carefully if she wanted to avoid giving away all of their secrets. 'It wasn't a massive stretch to guess that someone had used his convention set-up to get rid of him.'

'How?' Larch asked.

'I assume you noticed the spilled sugar in the Gate House?'

He looked confused, so Rosalind explained about the sugared violets at dinner that night – and how one of them was not a violet. Which led to explaining about Marcus's tea.

'Hmm,' DCI Larch said.

'Is that all you have to say?'

'Would you rather I question you as to why you didn't share this theory with us earlier?' he asked.

'It's not a theory. It's what happened.'

'You believe.' Larch put down his notebook, and rested his arms on his knees as he leant forward. 'Or perhaps you'd prefer that I ask you about your relationship with Mr Hugh Davenport.'

Rosalind froze. 'We've been friends for over forty years – I'm friends with him *and* his wife. I'm godmother to their daughter. What else is there to know?'

Larch got to his feet, looking down his long nose at her as she sat. If he'd been wearing glasses, he'd have looked like a mildly annoyed librarian. 'I don't have to give you another warning on the perils of lying to the police. Or pursuing your own, amateur investigation, instead of helping us with ours. Do I, Ms King?'

'Of course not,' she replied, primly. 'I've already told you everything we'd figured out about the poison, haven't I?'

'Well, if you think of anything else—'

'I'll tell you. In the meantime, may I ask . . . did you find the murder weapon? I mean, whatever someone used to kill Clementine?'

'Not yet.' He sounded almost as annoyed by that as by her stories. 'But we're still looking. Aldermere is a large place.'

'It is.'

'And we have at least managed to find a record of her next of kin – a cousin, I believe – thanks to Miss Hill's staff records.'

Of course. As secretary of the fan club, Felicity would have access to all the records Marcus did. Why hadn't they thought of that?

Larch paused by the door. 'In fact, you might be able to help me locate her. She's here this weekend, I understand. A Miss Libby McKinley.'

After assuring the DCI that she had no idea where Libby might be at this time, Rosalind raced to the library to find Posy and Caro.

'You're here!' Posy beamed at her as she dropped into one of the free chairs.

'Where have you been?' Caro demanded.

Rosalind rolled her eyes. 'Where I was supposed to be. I spoke to Hugh – and then DCI Larch collared me for a Q and A. Now, what did you two learn?' She'd save her big reveal for the end. She was sure that, after they learned that Libby was Clementine's next of kin, they'd be dropping all the other investigative threads for a while anyway.

'Isobel was in here, with Hugh, Heather and Harry until late last night – they'd only just gone up when the police arrived. So it couldn't have been any of them in the Gate House attacking Caro,' Posy said.

Caro nodded. 'Heather said the same. What about Juliette?'

'Confirmed,' Posy answered. 'She stayed with them for a while, then went up to bed to call her boyfriend, but she still couldn't have got down to the Gate House before we did.'

'What about Felicity?' Rosalind asked. 'She knew where we were going. Could she have beaten us down there?' Realistically, she couldn't imagine who else could have, with Clementine already dead, and Felicity was the one who'd given them the tip-off that led them there. But she'd also told *Larch* that she'd done that, which was risky if she was the one who'd been lying in wait.

Caro made a wobbly motion with her hand. '*Maybe.* But she'd have been pushing it. She was with Ashok and Kit when we left, the three of them heading up to bed, but they stopped and talked for a while on the landing, it seemed, and Anton joined them. I confirmed that with the guys, too.'

Posy looked down at her notes. 'Libby's the only one I couldn't find. But I'll keep looking.'

'You're not the only one looking for her.' Rosalind waited for them to look at her before offering her prize. 'Larch wants to speak to her. Apparently she's Clementine's next of kin.'

That stunned the pair of them into silence for a few seconds, which was fun. But nothing kept Caro quiet for long.

'Perhaps she'll be able to answer Posy's question for us then, when we find her,' she said, with an air of 'we know something you don't, too'.

Rosalind looked at Posy. 'What's your question?'

'There was something bothering me about the clothes Caro found at the Gate House,' Posy explained. 'I got a good look at them while we were waiting for the police, and there was something missing. Her locket.'

'I can solve that one.' Rosalind's mind filled with the memory of Clementine's bloated face bobbing on the edge of the reeds. 'It was still around her neck. I saw it.' It had rested on the shining white skin of her chest, glinting in the moonlight.

She couldn't have forgotten that if she tried.

'Did it look like this?' Posy shoved the paperback book in her hands under Rosalind's nose.

It was the biography of Lettice Davenport she'd been reading the other day. She held it open at a full-page photo of Letty, wearing that same hat that Caro had passed around the study only two days ago, even if it felt much longer. And around her neck was a heavy, silver locket, engraved with flowers.

Rosalind closed her eyes and swallowed. 'That's the one.'

'So, do we think it's a fake – another replica, like the magnifying glass?' Caro asked.

'Hard to tell,' Posy said, frowning. 'It could be, I suppose. Especially if Clementine *was* involved with Marcus's business arrangements.'

'But if we assume it isn't, and that it has something to do with her death, the question becomes . . . how did Clementine get her hands on Letty's locket?'

'And when?' Posy flicked through the photo section in the middle of her book. 'She's wearing it in every photo before the mid-forties, but never afterwards. So what happened to it?'

'Oooh, good question!' Caro sounded gleeful at the idea of another mystery to solve.

Rosalind was afraid she'd already solved it.

'Tastes change,' Posy said thoughtfully. 'Or maybe it had bad connotations of a love affair gone wrong. Hugh was talking about enough of those at dinner.'

'Or maybe she put it away and forgot about it, and the family found it again after her death.' Caro looked meaningfully at Rosalind, who sighed.

'You mean, you think Hugh gave it to her.' Rosalind bit her lip before continuing. 'I told you Isobel thinks Hugh and Clementine were having an affair. But it's more than that. She's afraid he had something to do with her death.'

'That's what you didn't want to tell us this morning.' Caro gave her an astute look. 'You talked to him. What do you think?'

'He's hiding something,' Rosalind admitted. 'I don't know what. I pushed him on seeing him and Clementine together in the Murder Spiral, but he claimed they'd just bumped into each other. And then Larch showed up before I could get any more from him.'

'But he could have given her the locket,' Posy said. 'That much is clear.'

Rosalind nodded. 'They met up in London, Isobel thinks, at least once.'

'And how do you feel about that?' Caro's eyes were wary, like she was waiting for Rosalind to explode. Maybe burn some fetching wardrobe items, like she would have done.

But Rosalind couldn't seem to feel anything much at all.

Oh. That probably meant something, didn't it?

'I think we should find Libby,' she said, and Caro nodded.

'I've been trying!' Posy said. 'She's nowhere. We were talking about it while we waited for you. Caro and I think we need to go back over the last couple of days and block out Clementine's movements.'

Caro jumped in. 'You know, figure out where she was and when and hope it gives us the lead we need to solve this thing.'

'Sounds like a plan,' Rosalind said. 'And if we're lucky, it might lead us to Libby, too.'

Hopefully before DCI Larch found her. Because Rosalind was almost certain that whatever Libby knew, it was what *they* needed to know for this whole thing to make sense.

After all, she'd written the literal script for this weekend.

'So, where do we start?' Posy asked.

Rosalind jumped up. 'On the first page. Come on.'

'We need to get inside Clementine's head,' Caro said, as they stared at the frontage of Aldermere House. 'Imagine every interaction she had with others from her point of view.'

'Find her motivation.' Posy's mouth stretched in a half-smile. 'Well. At least we've had practice at that.'

'I reckon this whole thing centred around Clementine somehow,' Caro said. 'I mean, she was the first one killed, wasn't she? She knew our secrets, and either she was trying to blackmail us with them, or warn us about someone else planning to.'

'The Post-it note on the script.' Posy scrabbled around in her bag and pulled it out. '"*Should we warn them?*" You think Libby was the other side of that *we*?'

'It was her script,' Caro said, with a shrug.

'We'd better get started.' Before Larch caught them up. 'So, everyone arrived on Saturday morning and Clementine was here to greet them. What happened next?'

'We met Marcus,' Posy answered promptly. 'He was kind of skeevy with Clementine, which made me wary of him.'

'Did you notice anything between Clementine and Libby?' Rosalind asked.

'No. Nothing to suggest they knew each other. Then you came out, and then Caro arrived, and Clementine showed us all inside and she took me up to my room.' Posy stepped forward, up the stairs to the house, and into the hallway.

Caro followed her. 'Did she say anything strange, or that stood out?'

Posy shook her head. 'Mostly we talked about my phone. How the family didn't want anyone taking photos inside, so Marcus set up this immersive experience thing.'

They climbed the stairs to the China Room, still following in Clementine's footsteps.

'She must have slipped the note under your door after she left you here.' Caro pointed to the door of her own room, next to Posy's. 'She was just leaving mine when I got up here from parking Susie in the stables.'

'Did Marcus see her too?' Rosalind asked, remembering that he was the one who'd shown Caro where to leave her motorcycle. 'And did she see you?'

Caro shook her head. 'He wasn't with me when I got up here, so I was alone when I found the note. And I hung back so Clementine wouldn't know I'd spotted her. What about you, Rosalind?'

'I went up before Posy. I found the note on the floor by the door when I was leaving.'

'So that all ties up.' Posy made a note on her pad, and Rosalind tried to imagine what the gossip magazines would make of her now, a pencil tucked behind her ear, wearing another hideous floral tea dress, more focused on murder than any of the vices that had so fascinated her fans for so long.

They'd probably put it down to method acting, she decided. But Rosalind had a feeling that *this* Posy, the one she'd got to know this weekend, might be the real one after all. She'd never been given a chance to get out, before.

'Where next?' Caro asked.

'Back downstairs,' Posy answered. 'Next up was the house tour. Clementine was there when it started, but then she disappeared.' Her gaze darted to Rosalind.

'To meet Hugh in the Murder Spiral,' she finished for her. 'Come on, then.'

The gardens seemed strangely quiet without the fans bustling around. The abandoned stalls still stood on the lawn, as did the huge white marquee for the main events, a reminder of what the weekend should have been.

From the middle of the Murder Spiral they stared up at the window to Letty's study, and Rosalind had the strangest sensation of being in two places at once. Both there on the ground, and up in the window looking down on Hugh and Clementine again.

Except this time the window was empty.

'*What* were they talking about, here?' Caro paced as she mused.

'Do you think Libby would know?' Posy asked. 'I mean, they were obviously close if she was on Clementine's HR record as her next of kin, right? But I don't remember seeing them talk to each other since we arrived. And Libby didn't mention it on the train, either. Did Larch tell you how they were related? Could they be sisters?'

'Cousins, I think,' Rosalind said.

'But they were keeping the connection hidden.' Caro tapped a finger against her bright red lips. 'That makes sense. If they were both here to do something.'

'Like kill Marcus?'

'I'm not sure.' Rosalind shook her head. 'Why would Clementine end up dead in the river if she was Marcus's murderer?'

'True.' Posy flipped through the pages of her notebook. 'But Libby is the only one who could have attacked Caro in the Gate House last night. Unless someone else is lying.'

'I'm almost positive that most of them *are* lying,' Rosalind said. 'Maybe they weren't working together, then?'

'You mean, Clementine could have been trying to stop her cousin from murdering Marcus, and that's why she killed her?' Caro was frowning. Something about it didn't feel right, even if Rosalind couldn't quite put her finger on what.

'Perhaps. Or . . .' She tried again. 'What if Libby was there for the same reason we were? Not because she *was* the murderer—'

'But because she was trying to catch one! Or at least find out what had happened to Clementine.' Posy clapped her hand to her notebook. 'Yes! That makes sense. I mean, if they were family, if *Clementine* had a family emergency, doesn't it make sense that she would have spoken to Libby first? But I saw her face when we heard that voicemail from Clementine on Marcus's phone. She was . . . shocked.'

'You think she was investigating what had made Clementine run away?' Rosalind said. 'And if she suspected Marcus's death was murder she might have been scared something had happened to her.'

'Doesn't explain why she felt the need to try and knock my brains out,' Caro said, rubbing the side of her head.

'Maybe she thought *you* were Marcus's murderer, come to hide the evidence you left behind,' Rosalind suggested, which earned her a deadly stare from Caro.

'If we hurry up and find her, we can ask her,' Posy said. 'What happened next?'

'Lunch,' Caro said, promptly. 'I don't remember seeing Clementine at that, but Libby was there, wasn't she?'

Posy nodded. 'She spilled her coffee then disappeared. I thought she was getting changed – but she still had coffee stains on her skirt at the panel later that afternoon.' She paged through her notebook, muttering something under her breath about an app with tags. 'Ashok spoke to Clementine around then, he said. About Marcus. She must have been on her way down to the stables for the murder mystery.'

'Then that's where we go next.'

They headed down the path that led around the West Lawn, towards the stables.

'Kit said he saw Libby asking Clementine for her phone back outside the stables,' Posy said, as they walked.

'Kit also said he saw a bear stealing jam,' Caro pointed out.

'Yeah, but I think the phone thing was more likely.' Posy had a small half-smile on her face that made Rosalind wonder what she thought of her new co-star. 'Especially since Heather and Harry also told us they saw Clementine talking to another woman at the same time when Kit and I saw them in the Murder Spiral.'

'So she talked with Ashok and Libby – and dozens of wannabe detectives taking part in the murder mystery,' Caro said.

'And she was there when we went down to the folly, but not when we came back,' Rosalind added.

'Then she called Hugh and asked to borrow a car to get to the station for a family emergency, and drove one of the vintage ones out the front gates,' Posy finished. 'And that was the last anyone saw of her.'

'Except the murderer.' Caro frowned. 'And Felicity, who saw her headed to the Gate House that afternoon.'

It wasn't until they were approaching the stables that they spotted the police presence around the Boat House. They'd cordoned off a large area either side of the river, all the way from the Gate House down to the Boat House, which was now surrounded by police crime-scene tape.

'Oh God. Do you think . . .? Caro trailed off.

'What?' Posy asked. 'Is there another body?'

Rosalind shook her head. 'I don't know. But if I had to guess . . . Larch said they were looking for the murder weapon. There was no sign of it, or a struggle, at the Gate House, so she probably wasn't killed there.' They bypassed the stables, and carried on down the path.

Posy's eyes were huge and round as she stared at the Boat House. 'So she ditched the car after she drove out, then walked back around to the river path where she met her murderer?'

The same path they'd walked the night before.

'There's a private road – more of a track – on the other side of the bend in the river, over a stone bridge,' Rosalind remembered. 'She could have driven around to there, then crossed the footbridge to meet someone at the Boat House.'

'That's it, then,' Caro said. 'She pretended to leave, but drove up the track to the other side of the river, hidden by the alder trees. She called Marcus and left that voicemail about a family emergency. Then she met someone at the Boat House, they argued, and someone killed her.'

'They must have pushed the body into the river, to sink in the reeds.' Rosalind's mouth felt dry, like she was breathing in ashes. 'It could have stayed there for days. Months. Longer. Except . . .'

'It rained that night,' Posy finished, and suddenly Rosalind could feel the water droplets hitting her skin as Clementine's dead eyes stared up at her. 'The storm must have dislodged the body. Sent it down river towards the Gate House.'

'What about the clothes?' Caro asked. 'The murderer must have stripped her naked, taken her phone, and then hidden her clothes at the Gate House. No, wait. Felicity said she saw Clementine heading to the Gate House after she left. So she went there and got changed? When? And why? That's the part that doesn't make sense.'

'Not the only part,' Posy said. 'Why not meet us when she'd arranged to at the folly? There was plenty of time for her to do that *before* she left Aldermere.'

'Still so many questions.' Rosalind looked away, towards the folly, and saw a flash of movement.

Libby.

'Let's go and find some answers,' she said.

Chapter Twenty-Six

'Looks like his past came back to haunt him,' Johnnie said, looking down at the body.

'Doesn't everybody's, in the end?' Dahlia asked.

Dahlia Lively *in* Violet Murder
***By* Lettice Davenport, 1964**

'Why would Libby be at the folly?' Caro asked, picking her way along behind her. 'What's there?'

'Nothing,' Posy answered. 'We looked, remember? Unless you think Clementine hid something we didn't find?'

Rosalind shook her head. 'It's not what's there. It's what you can see.'

They took the last bend, and Rosalind heard the assenting noises from behind her and knew that Posy and Caro had caught on, at last.

From the folly's raised position, the new police cordon around the Boat House was even more clearly visible. Uniformed officers milled around, presumably recording the crime scene or searching for clues or something. Rosalind wasn't interested in them. She was interested in the woman watching them from the folly window.

'Come on,' she said.

Rosalind pushed the door open, and Libby half turned from where she stood by the window, her body tense with alarm.

Then she relaxed. 'Oh. It's you three.'

'Who were you expecting?' Rosalind asked.

'A murderer, I guess.' Libby smile was sardonic. 'There seem to be plenty of them around this weekend. Whoever killed Marcus. And whoever killed—' She broke off, staring out towards the Boat House.

Rosalind hadn't been sure on the way down. She'd had two stories in her head, uncertain which one this scene was going to follow. Would Libby be the victorious killer, gloating over her achievements? Rosalind hadn't *thought* so, but she knew better than to commit to a vision of the scene without knowing for sure what the other actors, or director, wanted.

Or, in this case, the writer.

But watching Libby stare with longing at the place her cousin had died, seeing the regret and the pain in her eyes, she knew.

'DCI Larch is looking for you,' Rosalind said. 'Something about wanting to speak to Clementine's next of kin.'

Libby's gaze fell to her hands. 'Oh.'

'She was your cousin?'

'Yes.' Libby didn't look surprised at the question. 'Sort of, anyway. She was a lot younger, but we grew up together, all the same.'

'You were close,' Caro said. 'You knew she was going to be here this weekend.'

Libby huffed a small laugh. 'Actually, I didn't. Not until it was too late. If I had . . . I don't know. Maybe I could have done something more to stop this.'

'Did she know you were coming?' Caro asked.

'No. I wasn't supposed to be, you see.' She looked at Caro. 'I'm afraid I lied when I told you Anton wanted me here. *I* was the one that insisted on coming in the publicist's place. Once I knew Clementine was here . . . I called him late on Friday night and convinced him that I was the only one who could sell Hugh on the script.'

'Why did you want to come?' Rosalind's nerves were humming with anticipation.

'Because I thought Clementine was in danger.' Libby glanced back out of the window. 'And I was right.'

Caro was as blunt as ever. 'Do you know who killed her?'

Libby shook her head. 'Not for sure, anyway. But I think . . . I think I know why.'

'Why?' All three Dahlias asked the question at once.

Libby looked between them, her gaze jumping from one Dahlia to the next, as if trying to decide whether she could trust them with the truth.

Finally, her eyes fell closed and she said, 'Because she was Lettice Davenport's granddaughter.'

Silence. For a long beat, all Rosalind could hear was the birdsong outside the window, and the river rippling over stones.

'Lettice never married,' Caro said, slowly.

'But that doesn't mean she couldn't have had a child,' Posy pointed out.

Rosalind perched on the rickety table under the window. She had a feeling she'd need the support. 'I think you'd better start from the beginning.'

Libby swallowed hard enough that Rosalind could see her throat move. She nodded, and when she opened her eyes Rosalind could see a steely determination in them.

Finally, they were going to get some answers.

'Clementine's father was Lettice's son,' Libby said, after a deep breath. 'She gave him up at birth, though, and he was adopted by my Grandma Joy. He never told Clementine. But after his death, at the wake, my mum – the woman we all thought was his sister – got a little tipsy and told us the whole story.'

It wasn't a pretty one. Libby told them how, during the war, Letty had come home to Aldermere from London and, while there, formed an attachment for her cousin, Freddie.

'She thought they were going to marry. But when she fell pregnant . . .' Libby trailed off.

'He broke it off?' Rosalind guessed.

Libby nodded. 'Apparently he had a longstanding arrangement with the daughter of his father's friend. She was a more *appropriate* lady for Aldermere. But Lettice had the baby anyway.'

'Here at Aldermere?' Rosalind asked, surprised.

'No,' Posy said, pulling her book from her bag again. 'She ran away to Scotland with her maid, Joy, didn't she?'

'My Grandma Joy,' Libby confirmed, with a nod. 'She was Scottish, you see, and ready to go home. She agreed to take Lettice's baby and pretend he was her own. She'd tell everyone she'd got married down south to a man who had died in the war. Her village wouldn't know any different. So they escaped to Scotland before Lettice was showing, and hid out in a rented cottage not far from the village. Once Uncle Ron was born, Lettice set Grandma up with a house in the village and sent money every month for his upbringing. She gave her locket to Grandma Joy, as a memento. Then Lettice went back to Aldermere to wait out the rest of the war. By then, Freddie had gone off to fight, too.'

'But then there was all that fuss about the missing maid,' Rosalind remembered. 'So Joy had to come back to prove she was still alive.'

Libby smiled. 'Yes. Grandma Joy always liked to tell the story of how she rose from the dead. But she never told us the reason she'd left in the first place. I don't think she even told Granddad Jack – she married, a few years later, you see, and had my mother. But she kept Lettice's secret her whole life – the only person she told was Ron, just before she died.'

'And he never did anything about it?' Posy asked. 'I mean, he was Lettice Davenport's *son*. From what I've heard, the money from her books is the only thing that's kept Aldermere in the family the last few decades.'

Libby shrugged. 'Clementine and I never knew, but apparently he came here some time back in the nineties, after Grandma Joy and Lettice were both dead. He spoke to Hugh but, according to Mum, he didn't believe him. Threw him out of the house.'

'Okay, skip ahead to now. Why was Clementine really here?' Posy asked.

'She'd been in touch with Hugh, months ago,' Libby explained. 'She wrote, first, but got no response. So being Clemmie, she called him. Told him who she was and he didn't believe her.'

'Just like her dad,' Caro said, and Libby nodded.

'But then she told him she had Lettice's locket, and that she'd be willing to take a DNA test. She threatened to go to the papers if he didn't meet her.'

'So they met up in London,' Rosalind guessed, remembering Isobel's fears. At least she didn't need to worry about an affair anymore.

'Yes. But Hugh kept stalling, telling her he needed more time to put things in order.' Libby laced her fingers together, then separated them. 'It was around the same time I was approached about being script doctor for the new movie. Clementine figured he was holding out on her until that was all sorted. So she went looking for Lettice's will.'

'Could she just do that?' Posy asked. 'Go get a copy of her will, I mean?'

'Wills are public record after probate,' Rosalind said, absently, remembering those bewildering conversations with lawyers after her husband died.

'The will was . . . imprecise. The lawyer Clemmie spoke with last month in London said she might have a case to contest it even after so many years, if she had DNA proof of her identity.'

'And that would bankrupt Aldermere.' Rosalind shook her head. 'Oh, Hugh.'

'I'm still not seeing how Marcus comes into all this,' Caro said. 'Or why he was murdered.'

'When Clemmie realised that Hugh was stalling, she wanted to find another way in. So she went to Marcus and asked for a job.'

Posy's eyebrows shot up. 'And he gave her one?'

'That's what I said.' Libby's smile was sad. 'Clemmie wouldn't admit it, but I think she gave Marcus something in return for the job.'

'Like, sexual favours?' Posy's nose wrinkled at the idea.

'No,' Caro said. 'She gave him information. Right? She told him who she was.'

Libby nodded.

'Marcus said something when she drove away,' Posy said. 'He said he knew she had family in the area.'

'I think we can assume he knew who she was,' Caro said, with a sigh. 'That's the sort of "I know something you don't know" brag that Marcus *would* make, if he was in on a secret.'

'And Marcus used that information to blackmail Hugh.' Another piece of the puzzle slotted into place in Rosalind's head.

'And got himself poisoned for his troubles,' Posy murmured.

'I don't know about that,' Libby admitted. 'Possibly. I know that Marcus was involved in some shady things. Clemmie didn't tell me everything, but . . . she was scared, I think.'

And she'd been right to be, Rosalind thought.

'So she got the job, and she came to Aldermere – more than once, because she was here for the planning meetings, too.' Posy had her notebook out again and was flipping through the pages. 'She was putting pressure on Hugh.'

'Not pressure,' Libby insisted. 'She just . . . she wanted to be a part of the Davenport family so much. She wanted him to acknowledge her. It wasn't about the money for her, not really.'

'But it was for Marcus.' Rosalind could see how easily this one secret had spiralled.

'Which brings us to this weekend,' Caro said. 'Clementine sent the three of us notes on pages from your script, with photos that it would be . . . unfortunate if they were seen by anyone else. Why?'

'I think she knew she was in too deep, and she needed help.' Libby looked up, gazing at each of them in turn. 'The script, I imagine was the one I gave her. The photos she stole from Marcus. She told me . . . When I spilt my coffee, that lunchtime, it was because she was beckoning to me through the window. I needed an excuse to slip away and speak to her, where no one would see us.'

'Except Kit did,' Caro said. 'He told us you were arguing about your phone.'

'He caught the start, then,' Libby said. 'We were arguing about how it wasn't safe for Clementine to stay at Aldermere. She'd messaged me on Friday night and told me she'd been approached by a private detective. He'd told her Marcus was a blackmailer, and she'd searched Marcus's room to see if he was telling the truth. She found photos and files and stuff – including ones of you three. She sent me a photo of some of them with a Post-it note message on the top.'

'*Should we warn them?*' Posy said. 'We found it in the pages of her script.'

'Why send the notes on the script pages though?' Caro asked.

Libby shrugged. 'So you'd know this was connected to Lettice and Dahlia, of course. That there was more to this than just the photos.'

'But why didn't she meet us, then?' Caro's forehead creased up in a frown.

'She definitely planned to.' Libby sounded more certain about this than a lot of her story. 'She told me that much at lunchtime. You three were her insurance policy.'

Rosalind exchanged looks with the other two Dahlias. 'How, exactly?'

'She was going to share her secrets with you, knowing that you'd have to keep them, because she knew yours too,' Libby explained. 'Marcus . . . he'd threated Hugh that he'd tell the world about Clementine if he and Isobel hadn't paid up the money he'd demanded by the end of the convention.'

'His grand finale,' Posy whispered. '*That* was what he had planned.'

'She wanted our help to stop him?' Caro guessed.

Libby nodded. 'Like I said, she wanted to be part of the family more than she wanted the money. And if Marcus ruined Hugh . . .'

'She'd never be truly welcome at Aldermere,' Rosalind finished for her.

'I think she hoped that giving you the photos would help you trust her.' There was a hint of a smile as Libby looked down at her hands. 'She grew up watching you. We both did, in a way. Rosalind and Caro as Dahlia, and Posy in all those teen movies. I guess she felt like she knew you. Trusted you. It's funny, isn't it? How you can feel you know a person when all you've ever seen is them pretending to be someone else.'

That shiver was back, at the base of Rosalind's spine. Because hadn't they all been acting, for all these years?

She and Hugh, acting like they weren't in love. Isobel acting like her best friend, then stealing her fiancé. Even poor Letty, acting as if she hadn't loved her cousin, hadn't given up her baby.

And this weekend! Hordes of people pretending that it was the 1930s again, that murder was a game, that the past was a better place than the present.

Aldermere was nothing but an act. Dahlia Lively might be the most real thing in it, and she was entirely fictional.

Or she had been, until now.

'Clementine was going to meet you and tell you everything. That's what she promised me when we spoke at the stables. And then . . . I wanted her to get away from Aldermere, fast.'

'Did she agree to go?' Caro asked.

'Clementine never agreed to anything she didn't want to do,' Libby admitted. 'That's why I was worried when she left without telling me – and surprised when I heard that message on Marcus's phone. If there'd *really* been a family emergency, I'd have known about it. But I hadn't expected her to do as I'd asked, either. I supposed that something must have happened that scared her into taking my advice.' She flashed a quick grin. 'Although I should have guessed she'd do it in her own flamboyant style, taking Hugh's vintage car.'

Cogs were whirring inside Rosalind's head, pieces clicking together faster than before. 'Hugh said she called and asked him if she could borrow the car.'

'I guessed she'd threatened him to get him to agree,' Libby said.

'And it was definitely her talking in that voicemail Marcus got? You're certain.'

'Absolutely.'

Something didn't add up. Something to do with phones . . .

But before Rosalind could grasp the wisp of a thought that was starting to form, Caro plunged on.

'So Clementine left, and you carried on like normal because you thought she was somewhere safe, and couldn't call because you didn't have your phone. Until – and I'm guessing here – you overheard Felicity telling us that she'd seen your cousin heading to the Gate House *after* she drove away.'

'Almost right,' Libby said. 'I heard you telling Posy, before we sat down for dinner.'

Caro's cheeks turned a little pinker at that, but she carried on. 'You headed down there first and lay in wait for us, then whacked me over the head with a – what was it you hit me with, anyway?'

'Bedside lamp. Sorry.' She did look truly apologetic, Rosalind thought. Whether Caro would appreciate it was another matter. 'But I wasn't lying in wait – I was looking for Clemmie, or some sign that she'd been there. I found her clothes, but nothing else, and I started to worry. The curse of the writer's imagination – I had every possibility swirling round my head. And then I heard the front door open and . . . I started to panic. I hid behind the bedroom door to start with, but then I realised that meant I was trapped in there with you. The last people my cousin had spoken to at Aldermere, as far as I knew. Clemmie was gone and I didn't know where or why and . . . I just knew I had to get out of there. I had to get away before anybody saw me, I had to get out of whatever Clemmie was mixed up in so . . .'

'You hit me over the head with a lamp.' Caro wasn't letting go of that any time soon.

Libby winced, and nodded. 'Sorry. I wasn't really thinking very clearly.'

Posy frowned. 'Where did you go? I followed you out of the window.'

'I know. I, well, I hid behind the nearest tree and waited for you to run off. Then I checked on Caro through the window without her seeing me, and once I was sure she was okay, I ran back to the house up the main driveway. I was already in bed when I heard the— the sirens.'

Libby's voice faltered on the last couple of words, and Rosalind knew they'd got all they could from her for now. Posy put her arm around the scriptwriter, murmuring sympathies to her. Caro moved to her other side to do the same.

But Rosalind couldn't. She was too busy thinking.

And she didn't like any of the answers she was coming up with.

'Who do you think killed your cousin, Libby?' Rosalind asked, after a moment.

'Hugh Davenport,' she answered, immediately. 'It had to be. He was the one who . . . who knew everything. And who had most to lose.'

Caro and Posy looked up to see how she reacted, so Rosalind made a point of not reacting at all. She wanted to tell them they were wrong. That the man she loved couldn't do such a thing.

But how could she when she knew there was a corner of her heart that doubted?

Why couldn't it have just been a horrible, sordid love affair?

In her pocket, she rolled the miniature doll with the poison bottle between her fingers. If Letty had written this weekend, there would be one more twist in the tale. She'd want them to investigate all avenues. To do Dahlia's clever, unpredictable mind credit.

But most of all, she'd want them to catch the right guy.

Which meant Dahlia – or three Dahlias, to be precise – had to solve one last murder.

Chapter Twenty-Seven

'The thing about the past is, it so rarely wants to stay buried.'
'Like bodies,' Johnnie replied, glumly. 'They seem to keep on
pitching up everywhere this week.'

Dahlia Lively *in* A Rather Lively Murder
***By* Lettice Davenport, 1932**

Dinner was being served when they returned to the house.

They hadn't talked much on the walk back from the folly, and as they took their seats at the table, Rosalind saw that Libby hadn't joined them. Was she still watching for her cousin's ghost? Or hiding from her cousin's family that didn't know she existed?

More likely, she was talking to DCI Larch, at last. Which meant the detective would soon know almost as much as them.

Tonight's meal was a shadow of the banquet of the first night, and not even a match for last night's catered dinner. With the additional staff Marcus had hired gone, but her guests staying on an extra night, Isobel had called in reinforcements from her usual household staff and managed to put on a simple casserole that felt unsuited to the warm summer evening.

There were no starters, and only coffee and mints for afters, but nobody seemed sorry not to linger too long at the dinner table. Everyone knew this wasn't over yet. Rosalind hadn't seen Larch since he'd questioned her that afternoon, but she had no doubt that he was around somewhere, poking at secrets to see if they yelped.

In fact, everyone seemed to be viewing each other with suspicion. Someone around the table – more than one, perhaps – was responsible for two deaths. She thought about the dolls they'd found – Caro, Posy and Hugh. Were they really a warning? Was someone planning another murder?

If the murderer was killing to keep Clementine a secret, too many people knew now. But with her dead, and unable to fight for her inheritance, might they kill again to avoid justice?

Rosalind let her gaze land on Hugh. His smile seemed forced as he told another amusing anecdote about his Aunt Letty to an attentive Ashok. Was she supposed to be keeping him safe, or protecting her friends from him?

The knot in her stomach tightened as she realised she had no idea.

The day had run late from the start, and it was later still once dinner was finished. Rosalind nodded to the other Dahlias to follow her as people bade each other good night and headed for their rooms.

The Snug was mercifully empty when they returned to it.

'So, have we solved it?' Caro dropped into the armchair nearest the fire. 'Should we call Larch and tell him everything we know, let him arrest the culprit?'

'Who is?' Rosalind asked as she took her own seat on the chaise longue. She knew *her* conclusions from Libby's confession, but she wanted to know what her fellow Dahlias thought before she committed to it.

'Hugh,' Caro said, promptly. 'Obviously.'

Posy glanced at Rosalind. 'It could be Isobel,' she said, but Rosalind couldn't tell if she was saying that to make her feel better.

She sighed. 'Let's take this one at a time. Caro – make your case.'

Caro jumped to her feet, pacing as she talked, ticking points off on her fingers as she made them. Posy, meanwhile, stole her seat.

'We know that Hugh knew Clementine was Lettice's granddaughter, and potentially entitled to a lot of the money that he inherited, right?' She looked up for confirmation, and the other two nodded. 'He had a copy of the script, so he'd have known about the sugared flowers. It sounds like he was stalling for time in giving Clementine anything, and he didn't tell anyone else about her as far as we can tell, which is suspicious in itself, right? So he planned to kill her when she arrived for the convention, and there were lots of people and fuss around to cover it. But then he discovered that Marcus knew too, so he had to kill him as well. He had access to the flowers in the Murder Spiral – he was there that morning with Clementine – and to the Gate House, and the Boat House. He knows Aldermere better than anyone, so would have known the reeds would hide her body, hopefully long enough for any connection to him to be hidden – although he got unlucky with the rainstorm. He might be older, but he looks strong enough to shift a body – especially one as slight as Clementine's. Plus he owns all those cars – he could have driven her out in one of those when he said he was collecting the car from the station yesterday morning.'

'You seem to have it all worked out,' Rosalind said. There'd be time enough to indicate the flaws in Caro's argument after Posy had put forward her thoughts. 'Posy? Why do you suspect Isobel?'

Caro, realising Posy had taken her chair, sat on the other, less comfortable one to listen.

'Isobel stood to lose just as much as Hugh,' Posy argued. 'She knew Hugh had been in contact with Clementine, but maybe that wasn't all she'd found out. She'd seen a copy of the script to sort the menu for the dinner, and I bet you she knows how to sugar a deadly flower. Everything about knowing Aldermere still stands for Isobel as much as Hugh. And as for moving the body, well, maybe she told Hugh what she'd done and he helped her, which makes him an accomplice, not a murderer.'

An accomplice. That was one thing Rosalind was certain was right – whoever committed these murders had help. They'd have to.

'How long does it take to sugar a flower, anyway?' Posy asked.

'No idea,' Caro admitted. 'But that's a good point. If this had been planned for ages, wouldn't they have done it ahead of time? I mean, Isobel and Hugh *both* had access to the Murder Spiral and the script before the Saturday.'

Posy shook her head. 'Libby only added the flowers in the last draft.'

'Still, it *could* have been someone else. Someone who only got to Aldermere this weekend,' Caro said, thoughtfully. 'Except why would they care about Clementine being Lettice's granddaughter?'

The conversation pinged back and forth between the two of them, and Rosalind didn't even try to keep up.

'Maybe they didn't. Maybe the person who killed Marcus was doing it because of the blackmail, and it's just coincidence that they both died this weekend.'

'"No such thing as coincidence when it comes to murder",' Caro quoted, and Posy rolled her eyes.

'What do you think, Rosalind?' Posy asked.

I wish I'd never come to Aldermere this weekend.

Was that true, though? In some ways, it felt like she was seeing clearly for the first time in her adult life. The first time since she'd met Hugh, and been swept up in the glamour of his world. Of being Dahlia Lively.

She'd been orbiting this place for decades. It was time to step out of its shadows at last. When she left Aldermere later again, it would be for the last time. This part of her life was finally, belatedly, over.

Once this murder was solved.

It was starting to come together in her mind. All the little things that people had said, or that she'd observed, over the course of the weekend that meant nothing at the time were starting to make sense. Libby had filled in many of the blanks, but not enough to explain everything. Although when she put it together, a picture was forming of how events had really gone over the last few days.

It wasn't a picture she liked.

'I think we're still missing something.' Something that would tell her for sure if she was right. Rosalind pulled the Hugh doll from her pocket. 'I found this in the dollhouse this afternoon, lying dead in its attic. And the poison bottle is missing, again.'

'You think the murderer is going to try to kill Hugh?' Caro asked. 'Why?'

'For money. And for love. And maybe for power, too.' Rosalind gave a small smile, that felt like it twisted her lips. 'Why else?'

'Do you know who it is?' Posy asked.

'I hope not.' She sighed. 'In fact, I really hope I'm wrong. But if I'm not . . .'

'We need to tell Larch,' Caro said. 'Whoever you think did it, we need to tell the police.'

Rosalind looked at her in surprise.

'I know, I know. I've been the one wanting to play detective all along,' Caro admitted. 'But even Dahlia knew when to call Johnnie for backup.'

'Not just yet,' Rosalind said. 'We need to be sure. I need to talk to

Hugh again. And there's something else I want to check, up in Letty's study. But I think I've got a plan.'

She hoped it was going to work.

It was dark outside by the time Rosalind found herself making her way up the stairs to Letty's study. Hugh was already there, as she'd expected. What she hadn't predicted, though, was the panicked look in his eyes.

His silver hair was disarrayed, as if he'd been running his hands through it in frustration, and the shadows under his eyes were almost purple. When he reached for her, his hands were shaking.

'Rosalind. Thank God. You've got to help me.'

'What's happened?' Her hand clutched the doll in her pocket.

'That detective. DCI Larch. He was up here asking me all sorts of questions.' Hugh's gaze met hers, distorted with horror. 'He thinks I did it. He thinks I killed that girl.'

So does your wife. 'Did he say that?'

Hugh scoffed. 'Of course not. They never *say* that, do they? Not in all the books. He'll hold his cards close to his chest until he has proof—'

'How can he find proof?' Rosalind asked. 'If you didn't do it?'

He stared at her for a long moment, and Rosalind found herself thankful for the desk between them. She needed the distance.

'You think I did it too,' Hugh whispered. 'How can you . . . *you,* of all people. You know me. How can you think that?'

'I didn't say I did.' She knew that wasn't any more of a denial than his own. 'But you did know Clementine. Who was she to you?' One last chance for him to tell her the truth.

'Nobody!' Hugh said. 'I'd never met the woman before this bloody convention thing started up!'

'Maybe that's why Larch suspects you,' she said. 'If you told him the same lie as you're telling me.'

Hugh's head snapped back as if she'd slapped him. 'What do you mean?'

Was the surprise in his voice because she knew he was lying, or because she'd called him on it? So many lies over the years that she'd let go. Every time he told her he loved her more than anything, then went home to his wife. When he proposed to her, but was already sleeping with her best friend.

So many lies. Lies he told her and lies she told herself to enable her to carry on doing what she wanted without the weight of her conscience dragging her down.

But now she needed the truth from him. Just this once.

Rosalind sank into the visitor's chair opposite the desk. 'You'd been in contact with Clementine before Marcus spoke to you about the convention. In fact, she was probably one of the reasons you agreed to hold it here, wasn't she?'

'Rosalind, I—I don't know what you think you know.' He raked his hands through his hair again, until he looked more unhinged than unkempt. 'But I had nothing to do with her death. And the fact that you think I might have done . . .' He looked pained, shaking his head at her. As if she were the one in the wrong.

'Clementine was Letty's granddaughter, by blood. And you knew that.'

Hugh froze, his hand halfway to his head, his eyes bulging as he stared at her. 'How did you find out?'

Rosalind gave an enigmatic Dahlia shrug she thought Caro would be proud of. 'Better question. Why didn't you tell me?'

Hugh collapsed back into his desk chair. 'I didn't . . . I hoped it wouldn't be true. That she'd be another gold digger trying to cash in on some tenuous connection to Letty.'

'But she wasn't.'

'No.' He looked down at his hands. 'I thought the DNA test would put her off. But . . . it was conclusive. Or as conclusive as these things can be, I suppose. She is – was – a Davenport.'

'But you were avoiding her, weren't you? Stalling, trying to get the movie money before she could claim anything. Did you have an offshore account set up? Somewhere to hide it where the courts couldn't touch it?'

'I was going to do the right thing!' Hugh protested, but it sounded weak to her ears. She'd heard too many promises from this man over the years to believe them now. 'I . . . she was family, whether I liked it or not. She was a true Davenport. Not just Letty's granddaughter. My father's, too. She was my niece.'

'And now she's dead.' Rosalind sat back and crossed her legs. 'You can see why DCI Larch might find that a little suspicious.'

Hugh's head jerked up as he stared at her. 'You can't tell him. You *wouldn't* tell him. Would you?'

Would she? She wasn't sure. 'It doesn't matter. Her DNA will be on record – if they search her house, or your emails, I'm sure they'll find it. Besides, I'm not the only one who knows.'

'The other two. The *Dahlias.*' He spat the name, and she flinched. 'You've been thick as thieves with them since you got here. Maybe I'd have told you what was going on if you weren't so preoccupied with your new friends.'

Rosalind pushed the rising anger deeper into her stomach. He was trying to start a fight, that was all. Get her angry so he could apologise and they could kiss and make up and she'd forget what they'd been talking about in the first place.

It was the same way he'd got out of every discussion that mattered for years. Any time she mentioned changing the way they lived their lives. Coming clean. Being together.

She'd stopped seeing it, after a while. Stopped asking.

But now . . . everything seemed clearer this weekend.

Including the fact she didn't have to play the game his way any longer.

'You didn't tell me because you knew it would incriminate you if *anybody* knew. Which I assume is the same reason you didn't tell Isobel, and why she believed you were having an affair with Clementine.'

'I told you I wasn't,' he snapped. 'You should have believed me.'

She got to her feet. 'I believe in finding the truth,' she said, feeling more like Dahlia than she ever had on a film set.

'Rosalind, wait.' Hugh grabbed for her hand across the desk, all his bitter anger gone, replaced with an earnest, loving smile. One she might have believed, before today.

'This could be what we've been waiting for. An opportunity for us.' His thumb brushed lightly against the back of her hand, caressing it, as he spoke. 'I mean, with this murder, everything is going to come out, you're right, of course it is. And as long as we stick together, we can help the police find the real culprit, yes? And then you and I . . . maybe it could be our time, at last.'

'You'd leave Isobel?' Never, in forty years, had he come out and said that. Oh, he'd hinted, he'd given hope, but he'd never said it.

'Of course I would. For you. We need to weather this storm together, that's all. Make sure Larch understands what really happened here this weekend.'

'That's what I want too.'

She met his gaze, held it for a long moment, drinking in the last of the love that she saw there.

Then she pulled her hand away.

'I honestly don't know if you were involved in this or not,' she said, stepping back. 'I don't think you killed Clementine or Marcus yourself. I don't think you could. But I don't think you're crying over either of them, either.'

'Rosalind—'

'I don't want you to leave your wife.' She felt the truth of the words as she spoke them. 'I want to find out the truth.'

His face darkened, ruddy with an anger she wasn't used to seeing from him. All his charm, his affection, had been stripped away, and she could barely look at the man left behind.

'And you wonder why I married Isobel instead of you,' he said, low and bitter. 'At least she has stood by me, these forty years. She'd never betray me like this.'

Rosalind considered him for a moment, then crossed the room to the glass display case and opened it. 'You should know that this is a fake. And if you *don't* already know that, then that means Isobel sold the real one.' She held the jeweller's loupe out to him. 'You might want to ask her what she did with the money.'

Hugh stared at her, like he wasn't sure whether to believe her, for a long while. Then he snatched the miniature magnifying glass from her hand and stalked out of the study.

Leaving his phone sitting on the desk, as she'd hoped.

She waited to hear his footsteps disappearing down the stairs, then picked it up. The passcode was easy – he'd used the same one for everything forever. She hoped he hadn't had the foresight to delete what she was looking for.

She scrolled through and found it, her pulse pounding as she lifted the phone to her ear and listened.

And then she knew for sure.

In the end, agreeing on a plan was easy.

Caro said, 'What would Dahlia do?'

'Dahlia would catch the killer,' Posy replied.

'Dahlia would let the killer catch themselves,' Rosalind corrected her, thinking of all the times Dahlia had brought a murderer to justice. 'She'd make them confess everything.'

'She'd also have Detective Inspector Johnnie on standby to arrest them,' Caro pointed out.

Rosalind sighed. 'Yes. She would.'

'You'll speak to Larch?' Posy asked. 'You've connected with him most.'

Apart from the bonding session he'd had with Posy's bra, she supposed that was true. 'I'll speak to Larch. *After* we put everything else in place.'

'What do we do?' Caro asked.

And together, they hammered out the details of the plan.

'The signal will be the gong,' Rosalind repeated, as they went over things one last time.

'Just after midnight,' Caro confirmed. 'Nobody will miss that.'

'As long as they don't miss these.' Posy waved the envelopes she'd finished addressing in the air. Good to know that the writing desk in the Snug wasn't just for show – it had been equipped with almost everything they needed for their plan.

As if Lettice Davenport herself had prepared the ground for what was to come.

Rosalind supposed that, in a way, she had. Without her, none of this would have happened. She'd started this mystery, and now she was going to end it. What had begun with script pages from *The Lady Detective,* and that fatal dinner, would end with a variation on Dahlia's *J'accuse* plan from the end of *Poisoner's Delight.* They'd changed only enough so that, hopefully, their target wouldn't realise what they were doing until too late.

'We're ready?' Rosalind asked. Caro and Posy shared a look, then nodded. 'Let's go catch a murderer.'

Posy left first, handing them the envelopes before heading for the main staircase. It was late, and dark, and though they heard her saying goodnight to the policeman stationed at the front door for the night as she passed, otherwise the house was in silence.

'Think she can do it?' Caro asked. 'I mean, patience isn't exactly a virtue for her, is it? She gets twitchy whenever she sits still for too long. Always tapping that pen or doodling or whatever. Probably displacement activity from missing her phone. Never known not having one, has she?'

Except she'd had it back almost all day, but she seemed to prefer her pen and paper.

'Do *you* remember life before mobile phones?' Rosalind wondered if Caro even realised how much she fidgeted – and babbled – when she was nervous. They all had their own tics, she supposed.

'Vaguely,' Caro admitted, with a grin. 'It's just . . . we're asking a lot.'

'She's up to it,' Rosalind said. 'All she has to do is stay still and not screw things up.'

'Like I said, that's a lot.'

'Which is why she's doing it, not you.' No way that Caro would have the patience to hold back until the right moment. But Rosalind had a feeling that Posy understood the importance of timing. After all, she'd timed her own comeback perfectly. 'Come on. We've got a job to do too, and she'll be up there by now.'

Caro nodded. They split the envelopes between them, then made their way up the stairs together.

The hallways and landings of Aldermere House were silent in the darkness, the faces of the Davenport ancestors in their paintings invisible on the walls. But Rosalind knew that at least one person would be waiting up tonight – other than them.

Because if they were following the books, so was the murderer. And that meant they could use Letty's stories to predict what the murderer would do next.

Caro took the bedrooms on the first floor, slipping the first envelope under a door as Rosalind padded around to the next staircase. Blind in the darkness, she felt her way up along the wall, watching for any glimmers of light ahead.

Nothing.

There were five bedrooms to deliver to on this floor, and Rosalind slipped notes under each of them as quickly as she could, before darting back down the staircase to her own room. She caught a last glimpse of Caro, heading down the main staircase, as she arrived, and braced herself for what was coming.

Rosalind held her breath.

And then the dinner gong started to sound.

Tuesday 31st August

Chapter Twenty-Eight

*'Why do you always have to make such a production out of it?' Johnnie
handed her his cigarette as he leaned against the car, watching their
suspects file into the country house one by one, following Dahlia's
summons. 'This whole "I've gathered you all here today" thing. Can't we
just go and arrest the culprit and let the others get on with their lives?'*

*Dahlia, perched elegantly on the bonnet, took a long drag on the
cigarette. 'That would never do. People expect a grand finale from
Dahlia Lively. And besides, this isn't just for me. It's for all of them.'*

'How do you mean?' Johnnie asked.

*'Well . . . I suppose it's . . .' Dahlia frowned, searching for the right
word. 'I think it's cathartic for them. They've all lived under suspicion for
days, weeks, longer. They've all had every secret of their lives exposed.
They've lost trust in their friends, their family. They might even have
started to question themselves. It's only fair that they get a moment, a real
ending, to close the book on that. To name the villain and watch them
submit to justice. That's what allows them to move on with their lives.'*

Dahlia Lively *in* A Lively Mystery for Dahlia
By Lettice Davenport, 1978

Posy

It was a plan worthy of Dahlia Lively – or possibly stolen from her.

Posy's heart had been hammering as she'd eased her way up the staircase to Lettice's study. The stairs were drenched in darkness, and she

didn't want to advertise her arrival, so she'd made sure to stand on the edges of the steps, so they didn't creak. Rosalind had been firm on that.

She'd found the study itself in darkness, too, but that was part of the plan, so Posy hadn't turned on a light. The moonlight through the window was enough to illuminate the shelves, the desk, and the armchair in the corner.

But now, alone in that blackness, tucked behind the long curtains covering the last window, she wished she had more light, something to make the night less oppressive. The phone in her pocket had a torch setting, but she couldn't risk it. Any moment now, people were going to start arriving. Hopefully, one person first of all. And she had to be able to see them without them seeing her . . .

Outside, Posy heard the clocktower chime midnight, a few minutes late, as usual.

'We need to find a reason to get our suspects together, where we can pin them down,' Rosalind had said.

'Oh, that's easy,' Caro had replied. 'We do a classic Dahlia – you know, an "I've gathered you all here today" thing. When she makes everyone think she's accusing them, before turning on the actual culprit at the last moment.'

'That could work.' Rosalind had looked thoughtful. 'But how can we do it without the police interfering? I don't want them involved until I'm sure. And I definitely don't want Larch arriving before we're ready for him. Before we've got our confession. He doesn't know these people like we do. He'll trample about and ruin everything.'

Rosalind wouldn't tell them *who* she thought was responsible, which Posy didn't like. The idea that she could be trapped in a room with a murderer and not know about it was not exactly relaxing. But then, she supposed she'd been in that position all weekend.

Only this time they were going to do something about it.

'We do it tonight,' Posy had replied. 'Larch must have gone home for the night by now, there's only one officer stationed at the front door. We get everyone together tonight, away from the entrance hall, and we put an end to this. We can send Larch a message at the last moment, so he won't have time to stop us.'

After that, it had all come together. Right now, Caro and Rosalind would be leaving notes with tiny blue – non-poisonous – flowers, similar to the ones they'd eaten sugared that first night, under everyone's doors. Nipping out the back door to pick the flowers while the other two waited in the Snug had been a little terrifying, under the circumstances, but Posy had got away with it.

It was late, but the people they wanted to talk to wouldn't be sleeping tonight, Posy was sure. And even if they were . . .

A loud, clanging, crashing noise ran through the house, and Posy smiled. Bang on cue.

She couldn't hear the conversation that must be going on downstairs, but she could imagine it. The policeman rushing in to find Caro staggering against the gong in the entrance hall, drunkenly apologising as she headed for the stairs. The family, and guests, opening their doors and looking into the hallway to find out what on earth was going on at Aldermere now. Caro slurring her words as she told people not to worry, had a touch too much of the after-dinner brandy, going to her room, everyone should go back to sleep.

And she could picture them shutting their bedroom doors – and finding the envelope waiting for them on the floor with its little blue flower.

By now, they'd know they were invited to a meeting, tonight, in this very room. In less than half an hour's time.

An 'I've gathered you all here today', as Caro described it. Rosalind called it a *J'accuse,* which was pithier.

A reckoning, Posy named it in her head.

And that meant, any moment now . . .

The door to the study creaked open. She hadn't heard footsteps on the stairs, but then, she wouldn't. The person she was waiting for knew Aldermere as well as anybody, and those stairs better than most.

In her hiding place, Posy held her breath. Through the tiny gap in the curtains, she saw someone enter the room and place something – the poison bottle, if they were right – on the shelf. Then the figure glanced around the study, turned, and walked away again.

But not before the moonlight from the open window behind the desk landed on their face, enough for Posy to make out their identity.

Posy swallowed a gasp. But as the murderer left, the same pieces that Rosalind had put together earlier moved into place for Posy.

They *were* right. Everything was going to plan.

Rosalind would be pleased.

Caro

The echo of the gong still ringing in her ears, Caro raced up the stairs towards Lettice's study. Everyone had their notes. Whoever had committed the murder had to know they were onto them. But with Posy watching the back door from the study window, and the policeman at the front door, where were they going to go?

Worst case scenario, nobody showed up for her big reveal. But Caro didn't think that was going to happen.

She knew these people, or knew people like them. There was too much drama for them to miss out. And even the guilty would want to appear innocent by playing along. The person who'd been taunting them with miniature dolls for days wouldn't want to miss a chance to see them get this wrong. Their killer was overconfident, convinced they were beyond suspicion. *That* was what would bring them down.

It always worked for Dahlia.

Caro slipped silently into the study, and flicked on the lights. 'Posy?' she whispered, and at the far end of the room a curtain moved. 'Did you see them?'

'Yeah.' Her voice was muffled by the fabric. 'Should I come out?'

Caro considered. Her first instinct was that she'd like to have Posy at her side when the suspects arrived – not as a sidekick, or a supporting actress, but as a Dahlia.

This was Caro's chance to take the limelight, to show everyone that *she* was the quintessential Dahlia Lively. And now she wanted to share it? She smiled to herself. Annie would be impressed. She'd tell her all about it when she got home.

But for now, she needed Posy where she was – for dramatic effect, mostly, but also for practical reasons.

'No, stay there – we need you to keep an eye on the back door, remember?'

The curtain nodded.

There was a tread on the stairs, and they both froze. Quickly, Caro took her place in front of the desk, leaning back on both hands, her ankles crossed, her bottom just perching on the edge of the wood. She'd taken a moment earlier, knowing what was coming tonight, to change into a shirt dress with hints of military stylings. It wasn't *strictly* vintage, but it had enough echoes of the period to work as Dahlia, and it made her feel like herself.

Herself. A small smile tickled her lips. Not Dahlia, but Caro. They had a lot in common, for sure, but for the first time Caro realised she wouldn't be playing a part this evening – for all it might appear that way to the audience of suspects.

She wasn't doing this as Dahlia.

She was doing this as Caro Hooper. Because Caro Hooper was every bit as mighty as Dahlia was, and *she* had the advantage of not being fictional.

The door opened, and Libby appeared, her forehead creased with worry.

'I got your note.' Ducking inside, she shut the door behind her. 'Is this about Clementine?'

'It's about all of it,' Caro said, mysteriously. 'And you're not the only one who needs to hear it. But I did have one question for you. When Clementine spoke to Hugh for the first time, what was his excuse for not replying to her initial letter?'

Libby blinked. 'Uh, he said he never received it.'

So, Rosalind was right again. Caro smiled. 'You might as well leave the door open. There are a number of others joining us.'

And they came, one at a time, or two at most. Each tentatively peering around the door, then looking confused at the growing party inside.

Ashok, wearing his Christmas jumper over his pyjamas. Heather and Harry in matching tartan dressing gowns. Anton, in a black sweatshirt and jeans, Felicity in leggings and a t-shirt, and then Kit, in low-slung grey lounge pants and a white shirt.

'Well, this is quite the party, isn't it?' he said, eyebrows arched, as he dropped into the armchair nearest Posy's hiding place. 'I should have worn a hat. Ah!' He reached up to grab Lettice's felt cloche from the shelf above him. 'Problem solved.'

Caro thought she saw Posy's curtain shake with laughter, but none of their other guests seemed to notice.

Juliette arrived in skimpy satin pyjama shorts and camisole in a fetching shade of rose pink. Isobel followed, in a more substantial silk nightie and matching dressing gown. And Hugh, still dressed in trousers and shirt, but without his ever-present jacket.

And that was everybody. The Aldermere Ten. Eleven, if you included Rosalind, who breezed in behind Hugh.

Caro pushed away from the desk, clapped her hands together, and smiled as attention fell on her. 'I think that's everybody. Juliette, would you close the door, please?'

It shut with a satisfying thunk. And the game was on.

'I've called you all here tonight—' Caro started, only to be immediately interrupted.

'*You* sent those notes?' Hugh's face was already turning red. 'I'll have you know I don't much appreciate being ordered around in my own house—'

'*Is* it your house, though?' Caro asked, sharply, silencing him. 'That's one of the things I've called you all here to discuss. So I suggest you listen carefully.'

Hugh wisely shut up.

'Ooh, is this a gathering of the suspects, like in the books?' Kit asked, excitedly. 'Where Dahlia goes through sort of accusing everybody, until she finally lands on the person who actually did it? We should be filming, Anton.'

Caro smiled. 'It's exactly like that.' No point mentioning that, as of now, she didn't know for sure who had done it. Rosalind hadn't shared her suspicions yet.

This wasn't about an accusation. It was about gaining a confession.

Getting proof.

Caro really hoped it worked.

With a deep breath, she drew her Dahlia confidence through her body. 'Let's get started.'

Chapter Twenty-Nine

'Damn it, Dahlia. Don't you realise that investigations like this can be dangerous?' Johnnie ran his hand through his hair with frustration.

She gave him a wicked smile. 'But Johnnie. Isn't that what makes them fun?'

Dahlia Lively *in* **A Lively Mystery for Dahlia**
By **Lettice Davenport, 1978**

Rosalind

Caro had taken the floor perfectly.

She was every inch Dahlia, without irony, without pretence. She brought the fierce intelligence of Lettice Davenport's greatest creation to bear on their suspects, leaving Rosalind free to observe their reactions – and confirm her hunches.

If she was right . . . well, it was too late now, anyway. Wheels had been set in motion. One way or another, this would all be over soon.

'When we arrived at Aldermere this weekend, we were told to expect three days of murder, mystery and fun,' Caro announced, her bright gaze moving from suspect to suspect as she talked. They were all in this together, that was the message. She even managed not to smile as she looked at Rosalind.

'While we were delivered the first two, the third has been sadly lacking.' There were a few murmurs of agreement. 'Since we arrived, two people have been murdered – both of them by someone in this room.'

Caro raised a finger, pointing into the mid-air between the suspects, who began to whisper and object more loudly. Caro waited for them to calm down before continuing.

'Marcus set the scene for his own death – or rather the script for your new movie did, right, Anton?' She pointed at the director who shrank back against the bookcase behind him. 'The script perfectly details the first murder in the film, as performed at the dinner Isobel had so lovingly recreated for us that first night.' Her gaze swung to Isobel, who stood firm under it. 'All the way down to the tiny blue sugared violets with the coffees. The violets that never appeared in the book. Did they Libby?'

She turned to the scriptwriter, and Libby jumped with surprise at being asked to contribute to Caro's monologue. 'Uh, no. I think it's sugared almonds, in the book, and the poison is actually in the coffee. But I thought the flowers would look better on film, and since aconite comes *from* a flower it, well, it made sense to me.'

'Except somebody at dinner that night replaced one of those violets with a sugared monkshood flower from the Murder Spiral, placed on Marcus's saucer beside the special tea everyone knew he drank.'

Pacing up and down the narrow space in front of the desk, her hands clasped behind her back, Caro held their attention. It was good that everyone at Aldermere that weekend was well versed in the way of murder mystery novels. Regardless of how these things were solved in the real world, no one questioned Caro's – or Dahlia's – right to conduct her own investigation.

Although, Rosalind had a feeling that might change when they got to the accusation part.

'And so the murder happened, exactly as it did in the script. And while the police ascribed Marcus's death to his heart condition, we all suspected differently, didn't we? I questioned all of you, with a little help from my friends – some of you, so subtly you might not have noticed we were doing it.'

There were a few sceptical looks. Caro ignored them, and Rosalind commanded her lips not to smile.

'I learned about Anton's attempts to disentangle himself from a film project that wasn't going the way he wanted, by trying to invoke talk of a curse. I learned how the stolen magnifying glass had not, actually, been stolen – but sold, some months before, to Marcus by somebody in this house, and replaced by a fake so the sale wouldn't be suspected by the rest of the family. That discovery led me to learn of Marcus's sidelines in blackmail and theft – and which of you had suffered or benefited from it.' The censorious eye she cast over the suspects left them squirming.

'Wait. The stolen magnifying glass wasn't even the real one?' Felicity sounded personally offended that she'd taken a fake.

'No.' Caro met Isobel's gaze. 'Would you like to explain how and why you came to sell Lettice Davenport's jeweller's loupe to Marcus?'

Hugh crossed his arms over his chest. 'I'm still waiting for that explanation too. Or maybe you'll be more inclined to answer the police's questions when I report it stolen.'

Finally, Isobel's perfect, smiling composure cracked. 'We're married, Hugh. That magnifying glass was as much mine as yours. That's what marriage *means*.'

'And that's the only reason you married me, isn't it? For what I could give you. You were a struggling, single mother actress and I *saved* you.'

'*You* saved *me?*' Isobel scoffed. 'Who do you think has been keeping this place running all these years? Stretching those dwindling royalties from your beloved aunt's books to keep a roof over our heads?'

'You mean keeping your junkie daughter in rehab,' Hugh shot back, and Rosalind winced, as she saw Juliette bring her hands to her mouth at his description of her mother. 'That loupe was my Aunt Letty's! A prized possession!'

Hugh's face was bright red, the fury clear. Rosalind had never seen him this way before. With her, he was always sweetness and charm. Isobel seemed unmoved, though, standing her ground opposite him.

Was she used to this? Was this how their marriage had been, behind the scenes? Filled with bitterness, betrayal and anger?

It seemed astonishing that, if it had, she'd never seen it. Perhaps Hugh and Isobel were better at playing the roles they'd signed up for than she'd imagined.

'Because that's all you care about! All you've ever cared about!' Isobel spat back at her husband. 'The legacy of the damn Davenports. You care more about them than your living, breathing family! As if anybody would care who any of you are if it wasn't for Dahlia Lively!'

There was a moment of silence, as Isobel's words sank in.

'And that,' Caro said, timing it perfectly, 'is why Clementine and Marcus had to die.'

All eyes were back on her, Rosalind noted with satisfaction. Had any of them noticed that Posy wasn't there? The youngest Dahlia, in some ways the most famous – or notorious – of them all, hadn't lived up to her reputation for sowing chaos and disruption. She'd been so meek and mild, Rosalind had wondered if Anton had brought the wrong girl.

But perhaps she'd made the same mistake there. Believing that the way a person presented themselves to the world was who they were inside. The stories of Posy's wild youth were years old, and people were allowed to change.

She should know that more than anyone. She was changing now. She could feel it inside her.

'Because what I discovered during my investigations was a secret so explosive it could tear apart the whole Davenport family.' Hyperbole, perhaps, but Caro seemed comfortable with it, so Rosalind didn't interrupt. 'It started with Lettice's will.'

It hadn't, of course. It had started with Libby, and the locket, and the picture in Posy's book. But that wasn't as dramatic.

Rosalind stepped forward, out of the crowd of suspects, to share the telling of the story. 'Lettice Davenport left everything she owned to her nephew Hugh – and asked only one thing in return. That he kept Aldermere House, and her legacy, in the family. But Hugh has no children of his own, no one related by blood. He's the last of the Davenport line, the last name inked on that family tree in the hall that Isobel showed us that first morning. So everything would go to Isobel, Serena and Juliette.'

'Until a young woman arrived at Aldermere, years after Lettice herself had died, claiming to be her granddaughter. And she had proof; a birth certificate, a locket, and a willingness to take a DNA test.' Caro's smile was crocodile sharp. 'If Clementine had proved to be Lettice's granddaughter, to honour his aunt's last wishes, Hugh would have to write Isobel and the others out of the will.'

Hugh stared at Caro in horror, and Rosalind could almost see the cogs turning in his brain. She'd told him she wasn't the only one who knew, but she didn't think he'd realised what that meant.

Until now.

'But nobody knew about that. Nobody. Clementine promised.' Hugh sounded desperate, the anger drained away like the colour in his face.

'Clementine lied,' Rosalind said, succinctly. 'She told Marcus. And she told one other person, who told us.'

'Who?' Hugh asked, but Rosalind shook her head. It wasn't time for that yet.

'Clementine wrote you a letter, didn't she?' Caro asked Hugh. 'Explaining who she was and asking you to contact her. But you claimed you never received it.'

'I didn't! If I had . . .' Hugh shook his head, sadly. 'I regretted my behaviour towards her father. Not immediately, I'll admit that. But as I got older. As it became clear that, well, that a family of my own blood wasn't on the cards for me.'

Rosalind watched the faces of his wife and step-granddaughter as he spoke, noting the tightening around Isobel's eyes, the way Juliette's jaw hardened as she stared towards the window. How must it feel for them to know that he never really considered them his family, all because of a little bit of blood?

'If I'd known that Clementine existed, and wanted to know me, I'd have got in touch this time. Will or no will,' Hugh added, firmly.

'But you didn't,' Caro said. 'Because someone took that letter. Someone who had reason *not* to want you to contact Clementine.'

'That person must have been horrified, on Saturday morning, to see – as I saw – you sitting with Clementine in the Murder Spiral, talking together.' Rosalind motioned to the window, remembering how she'd felt, after Isobel's talk of an affair, seeing Hugh with such a pretty, young girl, having what was clearly an emotional conversation. 'And maybe they cornered Clementine later that day. Perhaps they just wanted to talk. Or maybe they went in there knowing they wanted to kill her. We can't be sure. But we *do* know she ended up dead before the sun went down on Saturday, and one of you threw her body in the reeds and hoped it sank.'

339

'And that could have been the end of it,' Caro said. 'If it wasn't for something Marcus said as we all stood on the steps, watching Clementine drive away in that vintage car. He said that he knew she had family nearby. Because, being Marcus, he couldn't know something and not hint at it, tease others with it – or use it. I suspect he came to you afterwards – or maybe you even approached him – and asked what it would take to keep him quiet about Clementine's existence?' She stared at Isobel and, after a moment, Isobel flinched.

'He wanted money to keep the secret,' she admitted. 'I said I needed to talk to Hugh.'

Her husband gave her a strange look. 'You didn't, though. You never mentioned it to me.'

'Because he was dead before I got the chance!' Isobel's frustration leaked out in her angry words. 'He had a heart attack! He had heart problems! And I, for one, do not appreciate this amateur hour, mock interrogation. We are not supporting actors in your film, nor are we idiots. Nothing you say here has any weight, and none of you have any proof. I've half a mind to fetch the policeman from the front door and have you all thrown out!'

'No need, Mrs Davenport.' Detective Chief Inspector Larch lounged in the doorway to the study, unseen until he wanted to be. Rosalind didn't bother trying to hide her smile this time. He was early. 'And I'd quite like to hear the rest of what our Lady Detectives have to say.'

Isobel scowled but stayed silent.

'The point is, you had a woman who could steal your inheritance, and now a man who knew that secret – and would blackmail you or blow the scandal wide open. Either way, you had to keep him quiet.' Caro started pacing again. 'You all knew, because it had been planned by Isobel, that the first night banquet was a replica of the one in the new film of *The Lady Detective*. The script was sitting up here on Hugh's desk, so you knew about the sugared flowers, too – even though they weren't in the original book. And from here, you can see the blooming monkshood in the Murder Spiral, the same dark blue as the sugared violets that were drying downstairs in the kitchen. It's easy to see how the plan came together.'

'And the spilled sugar in the Gate House confirmed our suspicions,' Rosalind added. 'Obviously you made your own, deadly version – carefully, I imagine – and added it to Marcus's saucer at the last moment. He was eating in a room full of people he was either blackmailing, taunting, or whose secrets he knew. There were plenty of suspects for you to hide behind – and with aconite being such a fast-acting poison, plus his well-known medical history, it was likely his death would be ascribed to a heart attack, like it would have been in the past.'

'Our medical teams are rather more accomplished now than they were in the thirties, though,' Larch drawled from the doorway.

'But the murder was spotted,' Caro continued, ignoring Larch's interruption. 'And the rainstorm the next night meant that Clementine's body was found, too. And when we started to investigate *her* death, that was when things started to fall into place.'

Rosalind took up the narrative again. 'The part that threw us off for the longest time was the phone calls. Clementine called Hugh to ask to borrow a car to leave for a family emergency – an emergency her family have no knowledge of, incidentally. And then she called Marcus and left him a voicemail explaining the same thing, later that evening.'

'Except Clementine was already dead by the late afternoon,' DCI Larch added. 'According to my guy.'

Rosalind nodded. 'I'd guessed as much. You see, we posited that Clementine pretended to leave Aldermere, but then drove around the track on the other side of the river, left the car and crossed the bridge to meet her killer at the Boat House.'

'But Felicity told us she'd seen Clementine crossing the lawn to the Gate House later that afternoon,' Caro put in. 'And when we searched the place last night, we found the clothes she'd been wearing earlier that day, but no other sign of her except that spilled sugar.'

'It took me a while,' Rosalind admitted. 'Maybe longer than it would have taken Dahlia. But in the end there was only one explanation that made sense. And when I checked Hugh's phone this afternoon, it confirmed my suspicions.'

'My phone? When did you——?' Realisation dawned on Hugh's face. He didn't look happy about it. 'That's why you told me about the jeweller's loupe. To make me mad enough to leave you alone in here. You manipulative——'

'Clementine never called you that afternoon,' Rosalind interrupted, not wanting to hear how he'd finish the sentence. 'I imagine that when you saw her driving away, you were scared for what she had planned, or the questions that might be asked about her taking your car, so you covered as best as you could on the spur of the moment. Am I right?'

Hugh gave a stiff nod. 'I called her, repeatedly, afterwards, but she never answered.'

'Because she was already dead,' Rosalind said.

Gasps went up from the assembled group. Kit, she noticed, was leaning forward, his forearms on his knees, taking in every moment of the drama. Libby, however, was looking faintly sick.

'Clementine never left the stables after the murder mystery,' Caro explained. 'Not alive, anyway. Her murderer confronted her there and, in their argument, hit her on the head and killed her. Then, the person stripped her, shoved her into the boot of Hugh's favourite vintage car, put on her clothes and drove away from Aldermere disguised as Clementine, while we were all stood on the front steps to see it. Then, I imagine, this person left the car on the other side of the river, pushed the body into the reeds to sink, and raced back across the bridge to the Gate House to change and sugar a flower to kill Marcus that night.'

'But what about the voicemail Marcus got from Clementine?' Libby asked, her brow furrowed. 'That was *her voice*. I was certain.'

'It was,' Rosalind reassured her. 'That was another thing I found on Hugh's phone: a voicemail from Clementine, dating back a few months to after their meeting in London. In it, she apologised for having to leave suddenly. Apparently there had been a family emergency.'

'The words weren't exactly the same,' Caro said. 'But it would have been easy for the murderer to take a recording of the message on their own phone and edit it with an app to say what they needed it to say, then call Marcus from Clementine's mobile when they knew he couldn't answer and play the message to his answerphone.'

'Same with the text messages people have received from Clementine since then,' Rosalind said. 'They were all sent from the murderer.'

'So, the two main threats were dead. But with the discovery of Clementine's body, and the post mortem on Marcus that would show up the poison, now our murderer had a problem. They needed to throw suspicion away from themselves, and onto the one person with the opportunity, the motive and the means.' Caro held up the tiny figure of Hugh that Rosalind had found in the attic of the dollhouse.

'What? No!' Isobel gasped.

'These little dolls have been showing up all over the place this weekend – designed, I imagine, to scare us away from our investigation. But this one . . . this one was a warning, wasn't it?' Caro didn't speak to anyone directly, her gaze sweeping from face to face. But the feel of the room grew heavier with the switch to the personal.

The murderer was no longer an abstract 'They'. The murderer was in the room with them.

'You planned to make it look like suicide, I imagine,' Rosalind said. 'Maybe even pen a touching note about his guilt, and the family scandal. But with Hugh dead, along with everyone else who knew Clementine's secret, everything would be tied up with a neat bow – and all the money would come to you, wouldn't it? You even took the poison bottle from the shelf to use as a potential murder weapon – to make it look as though Hugh had used his aunt's own poison to kill himself.'

Everyone's gaze swung to the poison bottle with its skull and crossbones label sitting on the shelf, obviously unstolen once more.

'That's why we added the warning in our notes asking you here, telling you that the police would be searching everyone's rooms tonight, while we met,' Caro explained. 'It was a lie. We knew that, beyond anything else, would make the murderer return the bottle to its rightful place, before this meeting. And they did.'

'Luckily, someone was here to see who did it.' Rosalind raised her voice a little, mostly for dramatic effect since she imagined Posy could hear her perfectly well from her hiding place. 'Posy, dear?'

Posy stepped out from behind the curtain, and smiled – slow, and sure – and Rosalind knew they had solved this case for real.

Then, with a roar of frustration, Juliette burst forward and grabbed the poison bottle from the shelf, ripping the stopper out, and hurling the contents into Rosalind's face.

Chapter Thirty

'I always feel such a sense of triumph when we catch the bad guy,'
Johnnie said. *'Don't you?'*

Dahlia, watching the policeman lead Mr Jenkins away in hand-cuffs, sighed. 'Honestly? It always makes me feel a little bit sad.'

Dahlia Lively *in* Forever Summer
***By* Lettice Davenport, 1952**

Posy

It all happened very quickly after that – so fast that, later, Posy wasn't sure about the order of events, or who shouted what.

What she *did* remember was the wrench in her shoulder as she shoved Rosalind out of the way, sending her stumbling into Caro and the desk.

She remembered closing her eyes, tight, as the contents of the poison bottle hit her in the face. Remembered bracing herself for pain, stinging acid pain.

And she remembered opening her eyes to find silver glitter falling to the ground around her, as Juliette let out a howl of fury.

Glitter. It was only glitter.

There was no poison, just a bottle with a label that lied. Another fiction, dreamed up by the author who made murder feel safe.

Posy's body hadn't yet realised the danger had passed, though, as her heartbeat thumped against her ribcage so hard she though the bone might crack. Her breath came harsh and fast as, around her, the assembled crowd took in the full meaning of what had happened.

'This is all your fault!' Juliette leapt for Rosalind again, but DCI Larch wrapped his arms around her waist and held her back.

'Juliette.' Hugh's voice broke on his step-granddaughter's name. 'What have you done?'

She turned her pretty, snarling face towards him. 'What have *I* done? What about what *you've* done, *Granddad*?'

Behind her, Isobel stood frozen, watching the tableau unfolding before her.

'I saw you kissing her.' Juliette ripped her arm from Larch's grasp to point an accusing finger at Rosalind. 'I saw you two together. And I tried to tell Grandma, but she wouldn't listen, so I searched your study – and that's when I found the blackmail letter. The one from Marcus. It told me everything I needed to know, along with that voicemail from Clementine on your phone. And *still* Grandma wouldn't listen, so when I saw you talking to Clementine, I had to do *something*. Don't you see?'

Posy saw, all too well. 'They were taking your life away from you,' Posy said, softly. 'Everything you thought you had, that you'd earned. Your place in the world.'

Posy knew how that felt. When it happened to her, she'd turned to bad choices, the wrong people, and self-destructive coping mechanisms. She'd almost destroyed her own life.

Juliette had destroyed two others, instead, to try and keep what she thought was hers.

'*Yes.*' Juliette gave her a sharp smile. 'You understand.'

Posy shook her head. 'No. Not really.'

'I knew, you see,' Juliette went on. 'I knew he never really cared about me, or my mum. We weren't real family to him at all, because our blood wasn't the same as his. 'Not Davenport blood,' that's what

346

he said. I heard them arguing, about whether or not to pay for Mum's rehab this time – to give her the help she needed. He had all this!' She threw her arms wide, encompassing the study, Letty's legacy, the whole of Aldermere. 'And he couldn't give any of it up to help someone who needed it – but he'd give it away to a total stranger. To some girl who was lucky enough to have the right blood. That's why Grandma had to steal the stupid magnifying glass. To pay for my mother's rehab, because *he* wouldn't.'

Maybe she could understand, a little bit, Posy thought. 'What happened next?'

DCI Larch gave her an approving look. They'd have a full confession, soon enough. Now Juliette had started talking, she didn't seem to want to stop.

Then it would be up to his team to find the hard evidence to back it up in court.

'I cornered Clementine in the stables. After the fake murder mystery thing. But she kept trying to ignore me, too, saying she had somewhere else to be. She wouldn't *listen*. So I made her stop. I made her listen.'

'You pushed her and she hit her head, right?' Caro said. 'You made the fiction real.'

'I did! I—' Juliette faltered, the fight fleeing her body as she relaxed into Larch's hold. 'I did. She fell back and hit it on the edge of one of the metal rails. And then . . . she didn't move anymore.'

'So you put on her clothes and put her in the boot of your grand-dad's car, like we thought, didn't you?' Posy suggested. 'You dumped the body in the reeds, then drove the car to the station, so you could text Hugh from Clementine's phone the next morning, and tell him to collect it.'

Juliette nodded, and any uncertainty or regret that had coloured her expression faded, replaced by a slow, pleased smile. 'And not one of you noticed a thing. I even *waved* to you, and you didn't know. I'd rewritten the whole story, and you had no idea.'

'I bet that felt good.' Rosalind took a step closer to Juliette. 'And it was certainly very clever.'

In a diabolical way, Posy supposed. But it was the right thing to say. This girl, this *child,* so starved of loving kindness in this house, drank it up.

'I knew people would ask questions though, so I stole Granddad's phone and made a copy of the message from Clementine. It was so *easy* to fake up that voicemail for Marcus.' She gazed around at the assembled company. 'Well, easy for me, anyway.'

'And then you set about murdering Marcus,' Caro said. 'Because he knew Clementine's secret, too.'

Juliette nodded. 'I figured, what was one more, now? And all those poisonous flowers were *right there.* Like they were waiting for me to use them. All it took was a bit of egg and sugar and it looked like the other ones on the saucers. Well, if you didn't look too closely. And Marcus had been drinking all night, I knew he wouldn't.'

'You left the dinner that night early,' Posy said. 'You went and got the flower? How did you get it onto Marcus's saucer?'

'Easy,' Juliette said, with a shrug. 'The window was open. I slipped the flower onto the right saucer, then went to bed.'

And in one day, she'd killed two people. Posy shuddered at the casual way she admitted it. Like death, and life, and other people, were characters in a book to be manipulated any way she wanted.

'And none of you even knew!' Juliette eyes were bright with triumph. 'Even the police thought it was a heart attack. I'd killed two people and nobody noticed.'

'You wanted them to, though, didn't you?' Rosalind said, quietly.

'That's why you started leaving the dolls. To taunt us. To show us how much cleverer than us you were.'

'I wanted to scare you,' she said, baldly. 'Marcus had been putting them in the dollhouse, that first day. So after he was gone, I carried on. You lot might think you're *detectives*. But you're not. You're old, washed-up actresses who don't know when to quit. I was right here, helping you, and you never realised. If it wasn't for that storm washing the body free of the reeds, you'd never have known.'

'I don't know,' Caro said, thoughtfully. 'I think something else would have given you away. Something always does, in the books. And that's what you were following, wasn't it? The books? I mean, that whole "driving away pretending to be the victim" thing was right out of *Death by Moonlight*.'

'That's what this place is about, isn't it?' Juliette shot a contemptuous look at her grandfather. '*Her* books. Well, now you're all living in one. Just like you wanted.'

Posy looked around her at the faces of the others, people she'd come to know over the last few days. Nobody looked like *this* was what they'd wanted.

'You managed it all very cleverly,' Rosalind said, again. 'But there's one thing I don't quite get. Perhaps you can explain it for me.'

'Perhaps.' Juliette's superior smile as she echoed the word suggested that it might be past the understanding of an old woman like Rosalind.

Posy hid a small smile. Over-confidence. That was what caught them, every time.

'Sugared flowers take hours to dry. If you didn't plan to kill Marcus until *after* you killed Clementine, how did you have time to dump the body and the car *and* make a poisonous sugared flower, before dinner?' Rosalind asked.

'And you needed us to be on the steps to see you driving away as

Clementine,' Caro pointed out. 'How could you make sure that we were watching? If it hadn't been for the stolen magnifying glass – which we know *you* didn't steal – Marcus would have announced the winner and people would have been getting on buses. One more car leaving wouldn't have been noticed.'

They both already knew the answer to their questions, Posy realised. But it wasn't until Isobel spoke that Posy realised she did too.

'Juliette. You shouldn't say any more.' Isobel's words were sharp, cold. Maybe she was disapproving of her granddaughter's murderous actions, but Posy didn't think so. 'We'll call the family lawyer. You mustn't say anything else until he gets here.'

'It was you,' Posy said, hearing the amazement in her own voice. 'You were her accomplice. You helped her move the body – she'd never have managed that herself, she'd have needed a second person, we always knew that.' Even when she'd argued the case with the other Dahlias, she'd never *really* thought that smiling, composed, hostess extraordinaire Isobel could have been behind the murders. That *definitely* breeched etiquette rules. 'Then she met you at the Gate House after to plan how you were going to kill Marcus, too.'

'Don't be ridiculous,' Isobel snapped.

'I don't think it's *so* ridiculous, Mrs Davenport.' DCI Larch held up a mobile phone that Posy would bet once belonged to Clementine. 'We did search the rooms as it happens. And we found this in yours. Now, I think you and your granddaughter should both come with me. Don't you?'

'Isobel.' Hugh put a hand against the wall behind him for support, his face grey. 'You didn't. How *could* you?'

The last vestiges of Isobel's mask of civility vanished. 'What? Are you worried about your precious family reputation? I wouldn't fret. We're not *blood* after all, are we?'

Wrenching away from the policeman who tried to take her arm, she stalked across the room towards her husband. The others, Posy noticed, shrank from her as she passed.

'I gave you everything – I was the perfect society wife you needed, the one *Rosalind* could never have been. I worked all these years to be what you wanted me to be. And all I asked in return was security, for me and my girls. *And you were going to take that away.*'

'You'd already planned to kill Marcus, hadn't you?' Caro said. 'You had that sugared monkshood all ready to go from the moment the menu changed on Friday night. Maybe you had one for Clementine, too, or perhaps you had another plan for her. *Two* heart attacks might have been a bit suspicious, even for Aldermere. But Juliette solved that one for you, didn't she?'

'Solved it?' Isobel scoffed. 'She almost ruined everything! Everything I'd been planning ever since I found that first letter from Clementine and burned it before Hugh could read it. But luckily for her, I've always thought fast on my feet. And after forty years surrounded by the legacy of Lettice Davenport, I've learned a lot about murder.' She turned to Rosalind, her face contorted into a scathing expression. 'I suppose he's yours now, like you always wanted.'

Rosalind looked her best friend in the eye. 'I never wanted any of this.'

Larch jerked his head towards Isobel, and a police officer appeared from the hallway to caution her and lead her away.

'I think we've heard enough here,' Larch said. 'I'm going to take these two down to the station, but I suggest you all stay at Aldermere until I've had the chance to speak to you tomorrow. In case we need any more information.'

He looked meaningfully at Posy, Caro and finally Rosalind, before turning and leading Juliette out of the door. Posy suspected that might mean they were in some sort of trouble, but right then, she couldn't bring herself to care.

They had solved the mystery behind two deaths and they'd done it together. The three Dahlias.

And finally, with the surge of satisfaction, justice and horror that rushed through her, Posy knew *exactly* how to play Dahlia Lively. It wasn't just about the murder or even the investigation.

It was restoring the balance of the real world that came after.

Dahlia made the world feel right again. And that's what she would do.

Caro

Hugh collapsed against the wall, slumping down to the ground as Isobel and Juliette were led out of the room. Most of the other guests followed the police down the stairs, chattering in low voices as they went. Even Kit had nothing to say, placing Lettice's hat solemnly back on the shelf before he left. The drama was over; there was nothing more to see beyond the destruction of a family.

Outside, the clock chimed one o'clock. The last half an hour ran on a loop in Caro's head, as if her brain were still trying to process it all.

Juliette was their killer. Juliette and Isobel. Should she have seen it sooner? She'd *trusted* Juliette with the convention. Even asked her to try and contact Clementine . . . God, no wonder she'd been mocking them with those dolls. They must have been hilarious to her, bumbling around trying to be Dahlia.

No, trying to be detectives. And succeeding. Because they'd caught her in the end.

But nothing about that seemed funny.

Hugh looked up, focusing on Rosalind first, perhaps unsurprisingly.

'You knew, Rosa? You knew all this – and you didn't talk to me first?'

Caro felt Rosalind freeze beside her. 'I couldn't be sure,' she said, her voice stilted. 'Not until Juliette confessed.'

'But if you even suspected—'

'It could have been you,' Posy interjected. 'We knew there were two people involved and one of them could easily have been you. We couldn't risk showing our hand until we were sure.'

Hugh's head dropped, his chin against his chest again. 'How did I miss this? How could I . . . I might not be much of a husband, but this . . .'

None of them had an answer. Caro looked from face to face, searching for someone to say the right words, but there weren't any. From the way Posy was biting her lip, though, Caro suspected she was holding in some wrong ones. Perhaps words Hugh wasn't ready to hear.

Caro's gaze landed on Libby, pale but resolute, still there, almost as if she was waiting for something.

Waiting to say more.

And Caro knew, then, that there was one last secret to be spilled.

Lettice gave the locket to Joy, *not her son. And Joy gave it to her granddaughter.*

'There's more, isn't there?' she said, staring at Libby. She *thought* she knew what that final missing piece of the puzzle was but, if she was right, it was up to Libby to share it.

For a moment, she thought Libby might deny it. Might keep her last secret and let everything end here and now.

But then she nodded. 'Clementine lied.'

Hugh looked up at Libby's words, his legs wobbling underneath him. 'You mean this was all for *nothing*?'

'Not nothing.' Libby's voice was soft but strong. 'She wasn't Lettice's granddaughter. *I* am. Clementine was my cousin. It was *my* DNA she took for the test.'

'Why?' Posy asked. 'Why did she pretend? And why did you let her?'

'And why did you lie to us in the folly?' Caro added.

'I . . . Let me tell you the whole story. The *real* one, this time.' Libby sank into the chair Kit had vacated, the events of the last few days overtaking her. Rosalind opened a cupboard, below one of the bookshelves, and pulled out a bottle of whisky and four glasses.

Libby took a moment to compose herself, before beginning. When she spoke, her voice was soft but clear – and full of sadness. 'Clemmie . . . she was in love with the worlds Lettice Davenport created from the start. When we were kids, she always wanted to play Dahlia and Johnnie. Knowing that Grandma Joy *knew* Lettice, well, that made us feel pretty special, whenever there was a new Dahlia Lively on telly and people were talking about it. We grew up in a small village, and our connection with Lettice made us minor celebrities.'

'I know how that feels,' Caro murmured, raising a small smile from the others. But not from Hugh.

Rosalind poured the whisky and handed out the glasses, skipping Posy with an understanding smile.

Libby took a drink and continued. 'When Dad died, and we found out who he really was – who *I* was – Clemmie became obsessed. She researched everything she could about the family, about this place, about Lettice herself. And then she wrote to Hugh.'

'Did she tell you she was going to?' Posy asked.

Libby swallowed, and shook her head. 'We'd argued about it before. She wanted me to contact the family, tell them who I was.

But I wasn't interested. It wasn't about money, for either of us, you understand. For Clemmie, it was a chance to be a part of something she'd loved from the outside. But I already *had* a family. I wasn't interested in another one – one my father and I hadn't been good enough for from the start.'

'But Clementine went ahead and did it anyway,' Caro guessed. 'Pretending she was you.'

'Yes. What I told you in the folly, about what she did, that was all true. I just didn't know about it until later. And when I found out, I was so angry . . . but by then, she'd already met with Hugh. In fact *I* was the family emergency she had to run out on Hugh for in London. She was staying with me, you see, while she was working for Marcus. That morning, the DNA results she'd sent away for came back – turned out she'd already had them by email, which was why she was meeting Hugh. But they sent a letter, too, and as soon as I saw the name of the company on the envelope . . . I knew. So I opened it, and then I called her and told her to meet me.'

'Was she sorry?' Posy asked. 'For lying to you? Stealing your life?'

'She said she was.' Libby's voice sounded sceptical. 'She said she planned to come clean, to introduce me to the family once they'd got used to the idea, as if that wouldn't have made things even weirder. But I don't know if I believed her. She was so caught up in it all . . . I think she started to believe it really *was* her who belonged here, not me.'

'Aldermere has a way of drawing people in,' Rosalind murmured softly, her gaze on Hugh rather than Libby.

'She had birth certificates,' Hugh said, confusion in his voice. 'Hers and her father's. And the DNA test . . .'

'Getting samples for my DNA was easy,' Libby said, with a shrug. 'We were living together, remember? She could have taken hair from my hairbrush. Or nail clippings after we did manicures together one night. And the certificates were simple enough to amend or fake. They wouldn't have stood up in court, but just to convince you?' Hugh looked embarrassed at being tricked so easily.

'I told her she had to stop,' Libby went on. 'That she had to back away from the family, or tell them it was all a lie. She said that she would, and I believed her. Until she texted me from here on Friday night, scared about what Marcus had got her involved in, and I realised she hadn't given up at all. That's when I knew I had to be here this weekend too.'

'Why were you shocked to see her here on Saturday morning if you already knew she was here?' Posy asked. 'That was what surprised you when we arrived, right? Not the fountain, but your cousin.'

'Because I'd told her to get out. As soon as she told me what Marcus was up to with the blackmail, and when she admitted that she'd told him she was Lettice's granddaughter . . . I told her to get as far away from Aldermere as she could and leave things to me.' Libby gave a small shrug. 'She was my little cousin. I was used to looking out for her. I figured I could fix everything – tell Marcus it was all a lie, get him to drop it.'

'But she didn't leave,' Rosalind said. 'Why?'

'She was stubborn. And she was scared. When I spoke to her that lunchtime, she told me she'd found another way. That she'd sent notes to the three of you, and together you'd catch Marcus and set everything right.' There were tears glistening on Libby's cheeks. 'It was all just another Dahlia Lively adventure to her, I think. And she was gone before I could convince her otherwise.'

'Were you ever planning on telling the family the truth?' Caro asked. All these lies and subterfuges were making her head hurt – or maybe that was the residual head injury.

356

Libby thought for a long moment before replying. 'I don't know. If I'd known what would happen, how far things would go . . . if I could have saved Clemmie's life I'd have spoken up in an instant. I'll always regret not speaking up to stop this sooner. But . . . you asked why I lied to you at the folly . . .'

'You thought you could walk away and start over. Right?' Posy guessed.

Libby nodded. 'I knew my cousin was dead, and I had no idea who I could trust. I didn't know if the murderer would be found at all, and if the truth came out – if people knew it was me, not Clemmie, who was descended from Lettice, then I'd be at risk too, wouldn't I. So I lied. I'm sorry for that.'

'You shouldn't be,' Caro said. 'If things had been different, that lie could have saved your life.' She'd seen the madness in Juliette's eyes that night. If she'd known there was another threat to her future, Caro had no doubt that Juliette would have dealt with it the same way she had the others.

Rosalind topped up Libby's empty glass, the sound of the whisky glugging out of the bottle too loud in the quiet room. Caro didn't think *any* of them had anything to say to fill the silence.

Apart from Hugh, it seemed.

Pushing himself from the wall, he staggered towards Libby, kneeling in front of her. 'But now the truth is out and you're here. You're home, with your *true* family. You're my heir, my only blood relative. My niece, as well as Letty's granddaughter. You're the continuation of the Davenport line, when I thought all hope of that was gone.'

He reached forward to touch her hand, reverence glowing from his face, but she snatched it out of his reach.

'No,' she said, quietly but firmly. 'I told you, I was ready to walk away from it all. I am Libby McKinley, not Davenport. Leave me Lettice's books in your will if you want, I'll be proud of her legacy. But you, this family, cost me my cousin. I want nothing to do with you ever again.'

She downed her second glass of whisky, slammed it onto the table beside her, and got to her feet. 'Thank you, ladies, for helping to find justice for my cousin.' She looked at Caro, and winced. 'And I'm sorry again, about . . .' She waved a hand near her head to indicate Caro's painful wound.

Caro shrugged. 'No harm done. Well, not permanently, anyway.'

'Good luck,' Posy said. 'With everything.'

'You too,' Libby replied. 'And I'll see you on set for the film, I'm sure.' She shot a look at Hugh. 'I won't let this family take away from my *real* legacy. The pleasure that Lettice Davenport brought to millions of people through Dahlia's stories.'

'I'm glad,' Rosalind said.

As Libby left the room, the three Dahlias turned to Hugh, who still sat on the floor, looking more broken than Caro had ever seen a man.

Rosalind heaved a sigh, then crossed towards him, helping him into the chair. She spoke softly to him, but Caro couldn't make out the words. She wasn't sure she wanted to.

'Should we go?' Posy whispered beside her. 'Leave them to it?'

Caro brushed her hands against her dress to try and get the last of the glitter off them. Damn stuff got everywhere. Like secrets.

But she couldn't help but be impressed that Posy had thrown herself in front of a bullet – well, poison – for Rosalind. Even though she knew they'd probably tease her about it later. That was the Dahlia way.

After Caro had got some sleep, and the memory of this weekend wasn't so raw and terrifying.

'I think our work here is done,' she said, as she headed for the stairs.

Another Dahlia Lively mystery solved. She couldn't wait to tell Annie about it.

Epilogue

'What will you do now?' Johnnie asked, concern in his voice. 'Where will you go?'

'Oh, I imagine I'll go wherever I am needed,' Dahlia replied. 'After all, there are mysteries to be solved in every corner of this world. And I think, at least for some of them, I am the exact right person to solve them. Don't you agree?'

Johnnie smiled. 'I do.'

Dahlia Lively *in* Poisoner's Delight
***By* Lettice Davenport, 1985**

Rosalind

'Are you sure you won't stay?' Hugh's blue eyes looked tired and old in the late afternoon sunlight. Like he'd aged a decade or more over one long, terrible night. He slouched against one of the vintage cars waiting to take the remaining guests to the station, as if his bones couldn't hold his body up any longer.

From the driveway, Rosalind could see the blue and white police tape fluttering in the distance, towards the Boat House. Up at the Gate House, everything was in darkness.

DCI Larch had spent the morning speaking with each of the exhausted Aldermere guests, before allowing them to leave. Caro was still packing up her bag, and Posy was hammering out final details with Anton and Kit about filming schedules, before they said their goodbyes. It gave Rosalind a moment in private with Hugh, for which she was grateful. Last night, he'd been beyond conversation. It had been all she could manage to get him to bed – aided by another whisky – before she dropped, exhausted, into her own.

But they did need to talk. And she didn't want this conversation to be overheard, if she could help it.

'I can't stay, Hugh.'

'Because of Isobel? Or Juliette? Because, quite frankly, when you reach a certain point of reputational ruin, what's one more scandal?' he asked. 'You know it'll all come out in the trial. About us, I mean.'

Rosalind couldn't see any reason why Isobel or Juliette would keep it quiet. The papers would love it, of course – her adoring but judgemental fans probably less so. They could probably get away with it, though, now that Hugh's wife turned out to be an accomplice to murder.

But that wasn't the point. It just meant she didn't have any excuses to fall back on.

After forty years, she owed him the truth, even if he'd never given her the same courtesy.

'I'm not staying, Hugh, because I'm done with this. With Aldermere, with us – with you.' Oh, it felt good to have those words out. To feel the freedom flooding in to fill the places where the pain had lived.

'You don't love me anymore.' Hugh's words were slow but sure.

'I don't.' *I'm sorry.* She withheld the last two, automatic words. She didn't owe him an apology for her feelings. 'Goodbye, Hugh.'

He grabbed her arm. 'Forty years, and that's all I get? My life fell apart last night, Rosalind! Even as a friend, you should be standing by me.'

'We were never friends, Hugh,' she said, tiredly. 'And to be honest, after all these years, I've had enough of you telling me what I *should* do.'

She looked up to see Caro and Posy emerging from the front door of Aldermere House, descending the steps to the driveway. Libby, she knew from DCI Larch, was long gone.

She wondered what Lettice Davenport's legacy would be, once it finally fell into Libby's hands. She couldn't know for sure, but it gave her a hopeful feeling.

Aldermere, the old stories, were crumbling. Dahlia Lively was stepping out of the ruins and into the twenty-first century. Starting with Libby's new script, and Posy's new film.

'Are you ready, Rosalind?' Posy called. 'The car to the station is here.'

'Goodbye, Hugh,' she whispered again, and he dropped her arm.

Rosalind strode across the driveway towards Caro and Posy.

'Everything okay there?' Caro asked, with a surprising level of tact, for her.

'It will be,' Rosalind replied. 'For now, at least. My secrets will be all over the papers in no time, but yours are still out there somewhere too.'

Caro shrugged philosophically. 'Now Marcus is dead, I suspect the general public is even less interested in my historical sex life than before.'

Rosalind looked to Posy, and spotted the small frown line between her eyebrows. 'I don't think Anton will make my photos public, not without risking his own career. But even if they *did* get out . . . perhaps it wouldn't be the end of the world.'

'Not if we handled it right,' Caro agreed, and Rosalind smiled at her assumption that they'd deal with it together. The three Dahlias.

'Maybe it could be an opportunity,' Posy went on. 'A chance to show people that change is a process, and we're always changing. That a setback isn't a failure, and it doesn't mean you can't move forward again.'

'That sounds like good advice to me,' Rosalind said, not looking back towards Hugh. 'Now, which is our car? I'm ready to get out of this place.' For good, this time.

'I'm off to fetch Susie.' Caro jerked a thumb towards the stables. 'I've got my own ride, remember?'

'So, I suppose this is goodbye.' Posy looked so uncertain, so naive, even dressed in what Rosalind assumed were her normal clothes of choice – jeans, a top that could only cover one shoulder at a time, and her hair up in a messy bun on the top of her head.

'Oh, I wouldn't say that,' Rosalind said. 'I mean, hopefully we've still got a film to make.'

Posy brightened. 'That's true.'

'And I fully expect to accompany *one* of you to the premiere,' Caro added.

'It's a date,' Posy promised.

'And besides,' Rosalind added, looking up at Aldermere rather than her friends, because some emotion was best kept to oneself, wasn't it? 'We're the three Dahlias. The only three in the world. It's sort of like a club.'

'Then we'll have to have another club meeting, won't we?' Caro said, a knowing smile growing on her lips. 'Sometime soon.'

'I'd like that.' Posy grinned, and the sun came out from behind a cloud, lighting up the roof tiles and chimneys of Aldermere House.

Rosalind smiled. 'So would I.'

Five Months Later

Caro Hooper was balancing on a kitchen stool, trying to reach a rogue Tupperware lid on top of one of the cupboards with her wife's favourite feather duster, when her phone rang. Holding the duster between her teeth, she fished it out of her pocket, pressed speakerphone, then dropped it onto the counter.

'Caro? Caro! Can you hear me? This line is rubbish.' Posy's voice rang perfectly clear.

Caro rolled her eyes, and resumed her retrieval operation. 'I can hear you. Must be all the egos on set messing with the reception at your end.' Not that she didn't wish she was there with them. Annie reckoned Caro's ego could give some of theirs a run for their money. 'What's up?'

'We need you. Can you come up to Wales? We're filming in some old National Trust-type place since Aldermere's up for sale.' Posy's voice caught a little on the word Aldermere. Even Caro paused, the dust bunnies on the top of the kitchen cabinets forgotten.

'I did a god-awful indie film in a swamp of a woods in mid-Wales in the early noughties. Swore I'd never go back.' Although she had to admit, even Wales sounded more fun than the cleaning schedule Annie had stuck to the fridge, and was insisting they follow with relentless attention to detail. 'Unless Anton has suddenly found a part for me in the film . . .'

'Not that I know of,' Posy admitted. 'But Caro, we really do need you. Me and Rosalind.'

'Why on earth would you need me?' Caro asked. An unemployed, forty-something actress who hadn't even been able to nail the 'Mum in a cereal advert' audition she'd been up for last week.

'Give me that thing.' Rosalind's voice sounded in the background, growing louder as she wrestled the phone from Posy's grip. 'Caro Hooper, get yourself to Wales. Now.'

'Hello, Rosalind. How lovely to hear from you. How are things in the middle of nowhere?'

'There's been a murder,' Rosalind said, bluntly. 'Well, an attempted one, anyway.'

'Haven't we done that one already?' Caro asked. All the same, she could feel her pulse kicking up a gear at the idea of another investigation. 'Don't want to get typecast now, do we?' Not that she'd been given the choice so far.

'Yes,' Rosalind replied. 'But this time, we think they're trying to kill me.'

Acknowledgements

For all that writing is a solitary job, turning a book from an idea to a finished, readable thing really does take a village. And because of that, I have many, many thank yous to say.

Thank you to my agent, the inimitable Gemma Cooper, for emailing me at three in the morning with the germ of an idea that eventually became *The Three Dahlias*. Also for the endless text messages through lockdown, as we escaped the real world for a while imagining Aldermere and the world of Dahlia Lively instead.

Thank you to Dave Carter, for advising me on all things police – and allowing me a little dramatic license! (It goes without saying that all mistakes or misinterpretations of police procedure, unintentional or otherwise, are my own.)

Thank you to the whole team at Constable, for believing in my Dahlias and bringing them to print so beautifully. Most especially: thank you to Krystyna Green, for taking a chance on this book, to Martin Fletcher for expertly editing it, and to Amanda Keats for guiding it through the publishing process.

Thank you to Hannah Wood, for creating such a gorgeous cover for my story, and to Liane Payne for taking my very rough floor plans and maps and turning them into something that actually makes sense, and looks pretty, too.

Thank you, always, to my family. To Simon, for debating poisons with me, and for his general unending support. To Holly and Sam, for simply being the best children anyone ever had. To my parents, my brothers, my cousins, my aunts and my uncles, for being so encouraging and excited at the idea of me writing a murder mystery. (Special mention to Uncle Al, who has been asking me to write one for a decade, and now gets to have this one published just in time for his birthday. Happy birthday, Uncle Al!)

And thank you to my friends, my readers, and everyone – online and in person – who has cheered me on to the finish line of publication day.

I couldn't have done it without you all, and I wouldn't have wanted to.

NEW IN 2023

Keep reading for a sneak peek at Katy Watson's second book in the
Dahlia Lively series,
A Very Lively Murder . . .

Chapter One

'Look at them all, Johnnie,' Dahlia said, gazing around the gathering with disdain. 'Any one of them could have killed the old beggar then poured themselves a cup of tea afterwards, perfectly certain that they'd only done what was right and proper, under the circumstances.'

Dahlia Lively *in* All the World's a Stage
By Lettice Davenport, 1938

Posy

Posy Starling gazed out of the window at the glitter of snowflakes starting to fall from the leaden January sky. The clouds were so low that the tips of the Welsh mountains surrounding the house were hidden, and even though it was only mid-afternoon, it felt as if night was falling fast.

She felt a million miles away from London, in time, as well as place. Perhaps it was the weather – or more likely the grandeur and feel of the Art Deco mansion she stood in.

With one last look at the fattening flakes, Posy turned back to the room behind her. It was dominated by a large, mahogany dining table with high-backed chairs, and by the immense crystal chandelier that hung above it, sparkling in the light from the cheering fire that roared in the large fireplace. Over the mantelpiece hung a large oil painting of the house itself, showing how it would look in the summer months.

Tŷ Gwyn lived up to its name – the White House – as it shone in the sunshine of the painted landscape, with its curved windows reflecting brighter still above matching balconies. Posy hadn't had a chance to explore the whole house, yet, but just from that painting, and her impressions as she'd arrived through the wrought iron gates, she thought this place had to be bigger than Aldermere. More luxurious, too, if the glimpses of the rooms she'd passed were representative. There was nothing shabby or faded about Tŷ Gwyn.

Everything here was both shiny and new looking, but also of the perfect vintage for the shooting of a Dahlia Lively film. As if they'd travelled back in time to the actual 1930s, rather than bother trying to recreate it with antiques.

It would be perfect for the movie.

Posy just hoped she could live up to her surroundings.

Because right now, she didn't feel shiny or new. She felt the weight of her past, her experiences, hanging heavy around her shoulders as the occupants of the room all sized each other up. This was the first time the cast of the new movie had been all together in the same place, ahead of filming beginning next week. Today, they would do a full table read of the script, and start to get a feel for each other as actors.

She just hoped the other cast members wouldn't let their preconceptions of her as a person get in the way.

The wind howling outside the walls, rattling the window frames and screaming down the chimney didn't seem to disturb any of her new co-workers, many of whom were already chatting like old friends. Probably most of them were, she realised. Brigette, their casting director, had assembled a cast comprised of big names, familiar faces and a few up-and-comers. Posy wasn't entirely sure where she fitted into that mix, and hadn't really wanted to ask. But the chances were, most people in this room had worked together on some show or film before, except her. They had history.

She had a past. And that, she'd learned over the years, wasn't at all the same thing.

Posy glanced down at the table. A name card with *Dahlia Lively* written in perfect black calligraphy denoted her place, beside a stack of bound paper.

The Lady Detective – Shooting Script.

Inside that script lay her professional future. Her place here. After all the months of setbacks – and the occasional curse – it was finally time for the movie that was going to rebuild her career to start filming.

She looked along the table and spotted one of the few members of the cast she did already know. Rosalind King, the first actor ever to play Dahlia Lively, in the original 1980s movies, was back on set to play a different part, this time – Dahlia's Great Aunt Hermione, the last murder victim in the film.

Rosalind shifted to look at her, a small smile on her face. And in that moment, Posy ventured she could read her co-star's mind perfectly.

Look at them all. You don't need to worry about what they think. None of them *solved a murder last summer, did they?*

She might not have acting history with the rest of the cast, but she *did* have history with Rosalind. That was something. She wasn't alone here. She belonged.

That was what she needed to remember.

Unfortunately, her brain had other ideas.

The delight of seeing Rosalind King on screen again is dimmed only by the realisation that, even as a Lady Of A Certain Age, King still projects more Dahlia Lively spirit in her limited scenes than Starling manages in the full hundred and eight minutes.

Posy clenched her jaw as the mental review ran, unchecked, in her mind. She'd thought she'd rid herself of her inner critic – the one who always sounded like her Uncle Sol, famous film reviewer and her godfather – but apparently he was back with a vengeance now filming was starting.

Just what she needed.

At least Caro Hooper wasn't in the movie, too. After starring as Dahlia Lively for twelve whole series' on TV, she was by far the most synonymous with the character. For Posy to attempt to play the Lady Detective on screen next to *two* Dahlias would just be too much.

But it did seem strange to be back in another large country home with Rosalind, but without Caro and her encyclopaedic knowledge of all things Dahlia.

Posy's gaze slid across the room to Kit Lewis. Her only other friend on set, he would be playing DI Johnnie Swain in their revival – having weathered the initial outcry from certain quarters that the role should have gone to yet another white actor, just like the last two to play the part. He stood near the fireplace, the flames behind the grille making his dark eyes flicker amber against his skin.

She'd seen Kit since they'd left Aldermere last summer, although not as often as either of them would have liked. He was a hot commodity these days, and had two other projects to finish up or promote before heading to Wales to film *The Lady Detective*.

The rest of the cast were all new faces to her – albeit many of them familiar from the big screen. She'd googled those she didn't know the moment she'd got the cast list. Now, she watched them each in turn, connecting names with faces and faces with films or shows. Caro's words, from her good luck phone call the night before, echoed in her mind.

Remember, kiddo, you're the star there. You're *Dahlia. And that means you're the boss, whatever that director of yours thinks.* You're *the one who needs to pull the team together, to encourage them when you've been filming in the rain for three days straight, or when craft services have run out of the good sandwiches. You go in there and show them that you're a team player all right – but that it's* your *team, okay?*

Posy wasn't sure how well that would go down with some of the big stars present. But Caro was right; she had to try. And remembering everybody's name would be a good start.

She tested herself now, as she leaned against the back of her chair and observed them all.

There, talking softly to Kit, was Nina Novak, the Croatian-British actor playing Dahlia's maid and sidekick, Bess. This was her first film role, as far as Posy had been able to tell, although she'd done quite a bit on stage. Nina fidgeted with her long, dark hair as it hung in a braid over her shoulder. She'd definitely need to befriend Nina; if this movie went well, they could be working together on any number of sequels. Bess had appeared in most of the Dahlia Lively books, serving as Dahlia's sidekick and someone to whom she could explain her theories.

With them was Tristan Haworth – another one of the actors she'd needed to Google, although she'd instantly recognised a handful of shows she must have seen him in. He was playing Charles, the man Dahlia's Uncle Francis hoped she'd marry – and to whom Dahlia had no intention of shackling herself.

Tall and lean, with short, pale hair and striking blue eyes, Tristan definitely looked like the classic British aristocratic type Dahlia's uncle *would* want her to marry, Posy decided. Brigette had done well finding him.

Tristan said something that made Kit throw his head back with laughter, and even the nervy Nina Novak smile and giggle up at him. The satisfaction on Tristan's face told Posy that he was going to be the joker on set, although the slow smile he gave her when he caught her watching suggested he might be the cast flirt, too. The idea made the nerves in her stomach kick up a gear, as she thought about how all the personalities on set needed to work together perfectly to avoid issues between the cast. Something that was even more important than usual on such an isolated shoot.

She could almost hear Caro murmuring beside her. *A worse flirt than Kit? Kiddo, you* are *in trouble.*

Maybe she did wish Caro was there, after all. Life was a lot more fun with Caro Hooper around. And at least it would be one more voice out of her head . . .

Posy broke away from looking at Tristan, and turned to look down the other end of the room. Over by the window that framed the view across the river, Keira Reynolds-Yang had just arrived and fallen immediately into discussion with Bennett Gracy, Moira Gardiner and Dominic Laugharne. None of *them* had required any internet searches, of course. The last three were old establishment actors, famous in Britain and Hollywood alike for their long, distinguished careers. Bennett and Moira were just there for the day, to participate in the table read. Their scenes were few, and involved filming away from Tŷ Gwyn, so Anton had scheduled them separately. At least that was two big egos not to have to worry about on set.

Dominic, of course, would be playing her Uncle Francis. In recent years, that seemed to be his preferred sort of role – dominant patriarch types, of varying eras and styles. He had to be in his sixties now, but he retained the good looks that had made him a star in the first place, while the years added an authority that suited him. Recently, he'd been playing the corrupt billionaire CEO of a family business in a long-running TV series where he yelled at people and then arranged to have them made bankrupt or worse.

Prior to that, Posy recalled, he'd had a spell in the wilderness not unlike her own – although his had been due to his behaviour around his young, female co-stars. The TV role could have been a step down from his previous movie stardom, but after a few years of being blacklisted, she suspected he'd had to take it. And actually, it now seemed to have his star back on the rise.

From what she'd read of the script, Dominic would mostly be red faced and blustering in this movie, while she got to be cool and cutting. Posy was quite looking forward to that.

Despite being decades younger than the three big name actors she stood with, Keira was just as famous in her way – for her social media follower count, her modelling career, her newly burgeoning movie career, her ex-boyfriends . . . and most of all, her parents.

She'd be playing Dominic's younger – *much* younger – second wife. Posy wondered how Keira felt about that thirty-plus year age gap, under the circumstances.

The final two cast members, Scarlett Young and Gabriel Perez, had joined Rosalind at the table, sitting either side of her. Gabriel was playing Dahlia's cousin, Bertie, with Scarlett his wife, Rose. There was at least a ten-year age gap between them, too, Posy guessed – with Gabriel in his mid-thirties, and Scarlett only twenty-two, according to her profiles. He had a fairly established line in supporting roles in Hollywood while she had, until very recently, been appearing in a well-known British soap opera.

Posy didn't know either of them personally, although she was almost sure she and Gabriel had met at an awards ceremony or similar over in the States. Given how Swiss-cheesed her memories from those days were, perhaps she'd better hope that *he* didn't remember the encounter, just in case.

Outside in the hallway, raised voices caught her attention. Posy shifted slightly behind her chair, so she had a direct line of sight into the entrance hall as Anton, their director, and Brigette came into view.

'I'm just saying—' Brigette was cut off by Anton before anyone could learn *what* she was just saying. He was, by all accounts, a brilliant director – but in Posy's experience, not the most patient of men.

'And *I'm* saying that if you don't like it you can— Yes? What is it?' he snapped at someone standing just out of view. Posy leaned forward, and caught the edge of the bright pink hijab that Rhian, the manager of Tŷ Gwyn, was wearing.

She spoke too softly to be heard at a distance, but as Anton turned to give her his full attention, Brigette threw up her hands and turned away, only to be intercepted by Keira, who had slipped out of the room, presumably also intrigued by the drama in the hall.

'I say it *has* to be Moira.' Bennett's American accent cut across the room, his voice projecting just enough for everyone else to pause their conversations and listen, as Posy was sure he'd intended. It certainly caught her attention.

'Oh, no, really,' Moira demurred, but there was a glow of pride about her that spoke of a well-appreciated compliment.

'I'm sure it does,' Tristan said, moving to merge their small groups of chatter into one larger one. 'But what, exactly, has to be Moira?'

'Why, the murderer, of course,' Dominic replied, with a dramatic waggle of the eyebrows to accompany his 'I was in the RSC, don't you know' delivery. 'It's *always* the most famous guest star in these things, isn't it?'

Ah, that explained Moira's glow. And the slightly sour expression on Rosalind's face.

For such a classic novel, Posy would have thought the question of whodunnit was easily answered. But of course this was a reboot, and Hollywood seemed to have a thing for rewriting the rules on endings recently. It was entirely possible that Anton would follow suit and change the murderer for his version of *The Lady Detective*.

She was pretty sure it wouldn't be Moira, though. Her character of Uncle Francis's neighbour was barely in it – and scheduled to die in the opening scenes. Posy was looking forward to filming those. She got to burst into the room and derail Kit's investigation by announcing that 'Only an idiot would think this was suicide. You're not an idiot, are you, Detective Inspector?'

That was going to be fun.

Posy looked up as Keira slipped back into the room. Out in the hall, she saw Anton and Rhian still in conversation – the former's expression growing more impatient by the second. Behind them, Brigette held her phone to her ear and, frowning, opened the door to the room opposite and stepped inside, closing it tight behind her.

'Don't fancy the "most famous guest star" title for yourself, Dom?' Gabriel joked. 'We've all heard the rumours.' A slight pause, just enough for Dominic's smile to tighten. 'About this year's awards, I mean.'

'Ah, but Dominic *can't* be the murderer – he's the victim,' Kit pointed out. As a Dahlia fan himself, he'd know exactly who was supposed to commit the crimes – and who suffered them. 'Same goes for Moira, and for our illustrious Rosalind King.' He shot a fond smile towards the head of the table at that, and Posy noticed that Moira's glow had dimmed a little. 'So who does that leave?'

'I'd think perhaps they'd want to go for a . . . fresher take, for the new movie,' Keira said. 'Fame doesn't mean what it used to, does it?' Her voice was sweet, but Posy could hear the poison in her words all the same, as she smiled at Scarlett, who looked away.

A tension that hadn't been there earlier pulled the air in the room tight, until Posy longed to open a window.

'I'd think the solution to the argument was fairly self-explanatory,' Rosalind said, raising one eyebrow the way she had on the big screen as Dahlia. Something Posy had been practising in the mirror for four months and *still* couldn't get right.

When Rosalind didn't continue, Posy realised that her friend had given her the opening to fix this. To lead, the way Caro told her she needed to. Posy suspected that Rosalind might have got a call last night, too.

They'd all been given scripts before today, of course, but not the finished article – and if hers was anything to go by, they'd all been missing the important, final scenes where the killer was unmasked.

Was the killer the one Lettice Davenport had written? Or had Libby McKinley, their latest writer – who just happened also to be Lettice's granddaughter – twisted the ending to fit her own story?

Posy picked up the script in front of her to find out – just as several others did the same.

'Like I said: Moira.' Bennett snapped his script closed. 'She must have faked her death.' Posy frowned. That couldn't be right.

'Mine says it's the uncle's second wife,' Tristan corrected him. 'That's Keira.'

'And mine says it's you, Bennett. The uncle's friend from India.' Kit shrugged and dropped his script back onto the table. 'How about yours, Posy?'

'I've got cousin Bertie and his wife,' she replied. 'Gabriel and Scarlett.'

'And mine claims Charles did it,' Rosalind said. 'Which I suspect means we're being played with. Correct, Anton?'

Posy looked up to find the director standing in the doorway, amusement twisting his lips into a smile. 'Not *played* with, Rosalind. I wouldn't dream of such a thing.' Rosalind raised that eyebrow again. 'It's simply that we cannot risk our chosen ending leaking to the public before the movie is released. A large part of our publicity campaign is going to hang on the idea that we're recreating Dahlia Lively for the twenty-first century, and that means anything can happen. After all, why would people want to come see a murder mystery where they already know for certain who the murderer is? So we'll be filming five possible endings, so that no one can be sure which is the real one!'

A murmur raced around the room at that, although whether it was in appreciation for the tactic, or because of the extra work and time involved, Posy wasn't sure. Knowing Anton, she wasn't surprised at the publicity gimmick. Something to make a big deal about in the press – and something else for people to talk about that wasn't the curse that seemed to have haunted the movie last summer.

'Now, if we're all here, why don't we get started?' Anton made his way to his chair, in the centre of one of the long sides of the oval table, then stopped. 'Where did Brigette go? She was with us in the hallway, before that Rhian woman side-tracked me with more of her bloody questions.'

Dominic laughed. 'Story of my marriage to the woman, Anton. Whenever I thought we were ready to leave to get somewhere on time, there was always something else she needed to do first.' Posy waited for the 'and that's why I divorced her' punchline, but it never came. She remembered the last interview she'd read with Dominic, maybe six months ago now, where he talked about their power couple heyday in the nineties and noughties, and how Brigette would always be the love of his life.

Obviously, she'd felt differently, Posy concluded.

'She ducked into the room over there to take a phone call.' Keira waved towards the still closed door. 'We were having the *loveliest* catch up when her phone buzzed, so of course I left her to it and came in here.' She smiled around her. Posy got the strangest feeling they were supposed to be grateful for her presence.

'Well, Brigette said she wanted to be here for the read through, but if she's too busy sulking—'Anton started, but Keira jumped to her feet and interrupted him.

'I'll go and find her.' Keira flashed that too-sweet smile back at the director, and darted for the door. 'Won't be a moment.'

They all sat there in the strange stillness of the falling snow, waiting for her to return. Over the table, the candle bulbs in the ornate chandelier flickered for a moment.

'That's strange.' Keira reappeared in the doorway. 'The door won't open.'

Anton stalked out into the hallway and glared at Rhian, who hovered just outside. 'Is it stuck? Or do these doors just lock themselves, now?'

One by one, the rest of the cast also migrated into the hallway.

'I'd imagine Brigette might have locked herself in there to keep people like Keira out while she had a private conversation,' Rosalind, who'd come up beside her, murmured in Posy's ear. 'I know I would.'

Posy attempted a smile, but the knot that had suddenly formed in her chest wouldn't allow for it.

Something about this didn't feel right.

Rhian knocked on the door, then, when no response was forthcoming, tried the handle.

'You see? Locked,' Keira said, triumphantly, as Rhian reached for the heavy keyring that hung at her waist.

'I'll see if I can open it.' Rhian slipped the key into the lock and turned it. Posy held her breath as the door swung open and—

Silence.

The room, they could all plainly see, was empty. No sign that Brigette had ever been there at all.

'She must have left already, and the door locked itself.' Rhian bent to pick something up off the floor just inside the room, then pushed the door fully open. 'Sometimes they do that. Would you like me to look for her?'

Anton shook his head, sharply. 'No need. If she wanted to be here, she would be. Now, let's get started. If we could all get *back* into the dining room and take our seats?'

Posy did as she was told, a frown furrowing her brow. She'd been sure that Brigette had gone into that room, too. She'd had a view of it the whole time, and hadn't seen the door open again, or Brigette walk out. But how was that possible?

Perhaps she was mistaken. But from the way Keira kept glancing across the hallway to the study door, she wasn't the only one confused by Brigette's sudden disappearance.

Beside her, Rosalind stared down at her script. Posy leaned close, intending to whisper her thoughts about the mystery to the older Dahlia – but then she saw exactly what Rosalind was staring at.

A postcard, tucked into the pages of her script. One that hadn't been there before.

One that read:

Watch out.

I'm coming for you.